THE IMMORTAL SHUDDER

Lisa Borne Graves

Authors 4 Authors Publishing
Marysville, WA, USA

This is a work of fiction. Names, characters, incidents, and dialogues are products of the author's imagination and are not to be construed as real. Any resemblance to actual events or persons, living or dead, is entirely coincidental.

©2023 Lisa Borne Graves

All rights reserved. No part of this publication may be reproduced in any form without prior written permission from the publisher, except for use in brief quotations as permitted by United States copyright law.

Published by Authors 4 Authors Publishing
1214 6th St
Marysville, WA 98270
www.authors4authorspublishing.com

Library of Congress Control Number: 2023930615

E-book ISBN: 978-1-64477-169-3
Paperback ISBN: 978-1-64477-170-9
Audiobook ISBN: 978-1-64477-171-6

Edited by Rebecca Mikkelson and Brandi Spencer

Cover design ©2023 Practically Perfect Covers. All rights reserved.
Statue from cover image:
Athena the Defender by Drosis
Academy of Athens
Athens, Greece

Interior design and layout by Brandi Spencer.

Authors 4 Authors Publishing branding is set in Bavire. Titles and headings are set in Goudy Trajan and Mr Darcy. Text messages are set in Source Sans Pro Semibold. Handwriting is set in Reey for Lucien, Architect's Daughter for Callie, Allura for Archer, and Tall Abbey Sans for Athena. All other text is set in Garamond.

THE IMMORTAL TRANSCRIPTS III
SHUDDER

LISA BORNE GRAVES

Authors 4 Authors Content Rating

This title has been rated 17+, appropriate for older teens and adults, and contains:

- Frequent implied sex
- Graphic violence
- Strong language
- Death of a child
- Death of a parent

Please, keep the following in mind when using our rating system:

1. A content rating is not a measure of quality.

Great stories can be found for every audience. One book with many content warnings and another with none at all may be of equal depth and sophistication. Our ratings can work both ways: to avoid content or to find it.

2. Ratings are merely a tool.

For our young adult (YA) and children's titles, age ratings are generalized suggestions. For parents, our descriptive ratings can help you make informed decisions, but at the end of the day, only you know what kinds of content are appropriate for your individual child. This is why we provide details in addition to the general age rating.

For more information on our rating system, please, visit our Content Guide at: www.authors4authorspublishing.com/books/ratings

DEDICATION

For Diane and Robert Graves, who are better in-laws than Aphrodite and Ares themselves—despite a vast ocean between us.

WORKS BY LISA BORNE GRAVES

Celestial Spheres

Fyr
Draca
Bladesung

Wundor (June 2023)

The Immortal Transcripts

Quiver
Fever
Shudder
Glimmer (February 2024)

Stand-alone Titles

Apidae
"Dare"

TABLE OF CONTENTS

Note to Reader	1
Chapter 1: Lucien	3
Chapter 2: Callie	6
Chapter 3: Athena	12
Chapter 4: Archer	17
Chapter 5: Callie	24
Chapter 6: Archer	33
Chapter 7: Lucien	39
Chapter 8: Athena	49
Chapter 9: Callie	58
Chapter 10: Archer	66
Chapter 11: Callie	72
Chapter 12: Lucien	79
Chapter 13: Athena	87
Chapter 14: Lucien	99
Chapter 15: Callie	108
Chapter 16: Archer	117
Chapter 17: Athena	127
Chapter 18: Lucien	135
Chapter 19: Athena	146
Chapter 20: Archer	158
Chapter 21: Callie	166
Chapter 22: Lucien	175
Chapter 23: Athena	184
Chapter 24: Archer	191
Chapter 25: Lucien	198
Chapter 26: Athena	204
Chapter 27: Lucien	211
Chapter 28: Callie	217
Chapter 29: Archer	231
Chapter 30: Lucien	236
Chapter 31: Athena	243
Chapter 32: Callie	250
A Message from the Gods	257
Olympian Family Tree	258
Olympian Pantheon Aliases	260
Acknowledgments	263
About the Author	265

NOTE TO READER

The following is a faithful transcript for the use of the newly formed International Republic of Immortality (IRI) in its inquiry behind the altercations involved in the Olympian sector. As far as the signed witnesses state, everything was recorded with complete honesty, arranged chronologically, and written separately so as to not influence one another's accounts. ~~The IRI reserves the rights to this manuscript, and it is by no means to be reproduced nor shown to any creature mortal. Mortals who read may be subject to permanent silence.~~

In case we are executed for our "crimes," I pass this on to you, mortal, in hopes to continue our memories into the future. Welcome to our world.

CHAPTER 1

Lucien

Ancient Greek expletives left my lips, which meant I was beyond mad to the point I reverted to my native tongue from over three thousand years ago. Why wouldn't I, Apollo—aka Lucien to the mortal world—be irate? I had lost my best friend, Archer, over Callie—a girl I loved, whom *he* got to marry. To top off that heartbreak, I'd lost my family since I refused to allow my father—the overbearing "almighty" Zeus—to kill said girl. Oh, and my dad tried to kill my kid, his own grandson, Hymenaios. Just another day in the Olympian family. All of this was enough to make me curse, but I was more pissed off about where I was.

In one of my abominable dreams.

Fog, gilded gates, walls of stone, and fields of barley. Themis had summoned me yet again to Elysium for a prophecy. I was through with these because I always got shafted in them. What would happen if I refused to enter?

I felt the tell-tale pull, tugging me toward the gates. I had never fought it before. Beautiful Themis was always inside, a prize to win, her pomegranate-tasting lips and curvy bronze body beckoning me. My feet move forward without me telling them to. I never could resist a woman, even one who was about to tell me ill tidings, but the way my feet moved on their own volition, I would be forced to meet her.

The gate soundlessly swung open for me, and I walked forward into the fields, running my hands along the tall barley. Such a strange and beautiful place. I took a deep breath, feeling the warm, pleasant breeze on my skin. The babbling brook in the distance, the sun peeking out from a light smattering of clouds in a blue sky, the scent of flowers permeating my senses—it made me wish to stay forever. There would be no fights, no angry friends or family members to face, no broken hearts—

"I would not make wishes like that, or they might come true, Apollo." Her voice made me jump.

I beheld Themis in all her beauty. Her comment had been teasing, but there was no mirth upon her face. Her eyes were sad, her expression tight. This would be worse than the former prophecy of Love changing our world forever, worse than Callie and Archer's reunion splitting the family in two, leaving me an outcast. It was going to be downright catastrophic.

"Can you show me something positive for once?"

The wispy clouds drifted back over the sun. It had peeked out merely for my benefit.

She shook her head. "You already know what I will tell you."

"War?"

"I think you know by now that it's inevitable."

"Show me." I crossed to her, impatient to wait for a prophetic vision I didn't want to see. I dreaded the future, yet if I could learn something from this seer, maybe I could prevent a war.

"I cannot."

I was stunned. Never had an oracle denied me a prophecy. My living one spoke in the ancient riddles. Themis visited me in dreams bringing me to Elysium, where only the blessed dead resided, despite me being very much alive.

"What?" I could say no more but stared at her, lost. Thousands of years of prophecies, and now she was shutting me out? "Then why am I here?"

"I cannot show you, or it may change everything. One wrong move means the end of the Olympians—all of you."

I swallowed hard. "Help me stop it, then. Show me."

"I foresaw nothing good if you knew the future, but listen carefully." She paused, surveying the fields to ensure we were alone and no threats were heading our way. I could do without running for my life from the shadow dogs which frequently happened when I outstayed my welcome. "A great sacrifice must be made to save Callista of Olympus. If she dies, war will continue until the last Olympian falls. The one who betrays them must pay the price." I flinched at hearing Callie's married name as it would've been in ancient times, as it would've been too if she married me instead; we didn't have surnames back then. I shook some sense into my addled brain. I was fixated on my shattered heart when Themis was informing me of an Olympian war which could kill us all. Saving Callie and my loved ones was now paramount.

"I betrayed them. What do I need to do?"

"No. You made a difficult decision. Your intent was to save your child, not to betray your friends. A greater one looms in the future."

"Who betrays them?"

"Again, knowing will steer you off course. You cannot know."

I had to go into this blindly. Why? Because I would pulverize this person or prevent them from doing it? I would think steering in that direction would be best. Did I not want to know who the betrayer was? Would their identity hurt me? It had to be someone I knew and cared for in the past. Vindictive exes came to mind, especially the forbidden-fruit goddess. No, she would not mess with the Olympians; it was not her nature to start a war. Or was I reading too far into this and simply stopping the betrayal would spin events into a worse direction? My mind was aching, reaching for logical answers without enough clues.

"I need more to go on than this."

Themis said nothing.

I was the god of prophecies. It was mine for the taking, and she should be sharing it with me. I grabbed her wrist, touching her; contact allowed me to see images. Usually she filtered them into me, and now I was trying to pull them out. I only got a few flickering images as she struggled to get away from me: *My mother, Leto hugging me. The statue of Liberty. Glass raining down upon the streets of New York City. Artemis firing arrows. Callie lying on the ground, unconscious. Lightning clashed against lightning.*

That was it. Themis had turned to smoke in my hands and drifted away. Her disappearance couldn't be good. She'd never done something that strange before.

Wanting to get out of Elysium, I rushed out through the gates and fell into the fog, getting disorientated before I suddenly shot awake in bed with a shudder.

"Lucien!" My current oracle was knocking on my door. I had moved her to New York to protect her, posing to the mortals as my grandmother, and it was nice to not be alone. My son was still healing at Dionysus's place, but I think things were a bit too frictional between us for him to move in with me.

I sat up, trying to process what I saw. There would be a war in New York? Callie looked dead due to some betrayal, and there needed to be a sacrifice. We gods left behind the barbarism of sacrifices ages ago, so this didn't add up. Neither did lightning striking lightning, unless—

"Lucien! Phone call. It's urgent."

I hopped out of bed, pushed prophecies to the back of my mind, and focused on now. I was sure it must be news about Callie and Archer. I hoped they were all right. I hadn't heard anything from anyone since the lovebirds got married and left New York. It had been five days.

CHAPTER 2

Callie

I couldn't move a muscle. Everything hurt (literally). I lay in the sand, the tide coming in, lapping at my feet. We needed to move, but I couldn't. Archer, Himerus, and Anteros lay there huffing out breaths, exhausted from traversing more than a thousand miles over the ocean with their godly abilities to manipulate gravity. This tiring trip was after fighting Zeus and Hermes, where Archer was struck by lightning and somehow the "lovely" sensation was funneled to me. Next, Poseidon sank the ship I had been briefly imprisoned on with a massive tidal wave. Safe to say, it wasn't a good time (starting to forget what that was).

I finally broke the silence. "We need to move."

"Not yet," Himerus childishly whined. He was by far the most tired; he had swum and run the entire way at his freakishly fast pace—even faster than other immortals. His wet black hair clung to his forehead, half covering his eyes.

Archer moaned. He had his eyes closed, his pale lashes damp with salt water. He was probably the most injured, but I was too distracted by his relaxed posture to be concerned. Like Psyche sneaking a peek at Cupid, I inspected the smooth angles of my husband's face. His normally golden-blond hair was a waterlogged dull brown, making him seem more mature, a tad closer in appearance to his three thousand plus years (still mind-boggling), Despite his age, those angelic features were frozen at eighteen, as they were for most gods. "She's right. We should find shelter before Zeus looks for us."

Then I remembered something. "Can he really turn into a swan?" (I felt so stupid asking, but I knew what I saw.)

Archer's beautiful blue eyes opened, meeting mine. "Yeah, but it takes him a lot of energy to transform to it and back. Did you see a swan?"

"Yeah. I thought it weird, swan in an ocean, and Poseidon yelled at him—"

"Poseidon?" Archer shot to sitting at immortal speed, his mouth agape and eyes wide.

"It couldn't have been Poseidon," Anteros told me in that know-it-all tone parents use on kids.

"It was." I explained to them how he spoke in my mind somehow, sank Zeus's boat, gave me air, and pulled me to the surface.

"It must've been Proteus." Himerus shook his head.

(Ugh!) Why didn't they believe me? To them, I was the dumb mortal tagalong. "I met Proteus, and you know he was badly wounded in Belize. This man was almost identical to Zeus, but his eyes were a bit different, and his beard was tinged green, probably from phytoplankton. It was him. When I said his name, he looked right at me. Then he was gone."

Anteros and Himerus argued with me, but I refused to give in (while wondering—being family now—if smacking them upside the head was allowed).

Finally, Archer cut us off. "Enough!"

They shut up right away.

Archer stood up, stretching his limbs out gingerly. "If Zeus is a swan, he can cover a lot of ground and possibly find us and come back later to finish us off. They're arguing with you because Poseidon cannot come to the surface. He's locked underwater, the same as Hades being stuck in the Underworld." He offered me his hands and pulled me to my feet.

My sore muscles protested. "I know what I saw."

"I believe you." Archer draped his arm around my shoulder as we started to walk inland.

I leaned into Archer so we could support each other's exhausted bodies. "It explains why he was so freaked out." (Understatement, more like horror-struck.)

"Poseidon breaching the barrier?" Anteros asked in disbelief.

Himerus whistled in astonishment.

"What does it mean?" I hedged.

Archer supplied, "It has never happened before—I don't think—so I dunno. But I know he's on our side."

"Because he saved me?"

Archer gave me a weak smile. "That, of course, but also think about it. Who would you side with? The brother who suppressed you in an underwater domain for thousands of years or...anyone else?"

"Good point." I tried to process everything, but before I could, we were on higher ground, and I had to take in my surroundings.

This place was no normal island. The sand under my feet and clinging to my clothes wasn't quite sand but dirt. Stretched out before us was a land that appeared to be liquid but was actually solid; it was as if someone had frozen a river of mud. Buildings were under it; roofs or higher-story buildings stubbornly remained half sunken into whatever this was. In the distance, a volcano quietly smoked, which meant it was active. Soufriere Hills. This must be Plymouth, the city on Montserrat buried under volcanic ash a few decades back. It looked more like the setting of a sci-fi movie. I half expected aliens to pop out (gods exist, so you never know).

Anteros and Himerus were in just as much awe as I was, but Archer's face hardened, his eyes inadvertently darting over to the volcano. Not long ago, he'd foolishly almost jumped into it until I stopped him. I didn't understand my sight or how I had prevented it, but I was thankful for the power to save him. What did they all think about me saving a god?

I took Archer's hand in mine. He stoically turned his head away from his past and met my gaze. "Those buildings over there. They look like apartments or hotels." Archer pointed them out to us.

"Oh, here, Callie." Himerus dug into the pocket of his jeans and pulled out my necklace, careful to clasp both ends so the charms wouldn't fall off.

"My necklace!" I had completely forgotten it in all the chaos. Had I remembered, I would've given it up as lost. I took it and smiled at Himerus, but he didn't seem too cheery. Perhaps he was inwardly blaming me for the attack because I stopped for a charm.

Archer helped me clasp it back on, and then we trudged atop the dried volcanic mud toward a cluster of taller buildings. None of the boys complained about walking my sluggish mortal speed, so they were definitely exhausted.

Archer stopped at the first building. "This one looks good."

The boys shrugged. None of us cared. If it had a roof to hide and protect us and it wasn't going to cave in, it was fine with me.

Most of the windows were broken or missing, so Himerus approached the first opening. The window opening was half-hidden under the volcanic mud-ash, leaving enough room for him to peek in. When he backed out, he shook his head to tell us it was uninhabitable. I guess gods could deal with many environments but turned their noses up at the idea of sleeping on ash and dirt.

Anteros jumped high, grabbing the ledge of the next window. "Ow," he whined. "Hold on." He flung himself into the room.

We heard a little tinkling sound, and tiny glass fragments rained upon us. I closed my eyes and ducked my head down (a warning would've been nice).

"Watch it!" Archer shouted. "A mortal's down here, remember?"

Anteros's head popped out. "My bad!"

Archer gave me a once-over. "Are you—"

"I'm fine." It came out a little harsher than I'd wanted. Archer was being uber overprotective, but I shouldn't blame him because we'd almost died. My anger was directed at myself too. There were things I should tell him, but how can you explain something you don't understand yourself? I needed time to figure it out. Dad would know, but when would I be able to call him?

Archer frowned, sensing something (my secrets?), so I kissed him quickly to wipe the suspicion off his face.

"Come on, lovebirds." Himerus offered his hands over the window frame. He had also climbed in through the window during the exchange between Archer and me.

Archer put his hands on my waist, creating butterflies in my belly as he lifted me. Himerus pulled me up and in the window as if I were as light as a feather. Archer floated in right behind me, similar to an astronaut floating through space. Still weird to see his powers in action (flying cherubs in paintings came to mind).

The place appeared to be a former hotel. There was a bed, a nightstand, a TV on a dresser, and three doors—most likely a closet, bathroom, and the obvious front door. Everything was old and warped. The wallpaper was curling down the walls and was faded, but it had been some kind of tacky vines, flowers, and fruit pattern. The carpet was a vibrant green—how vibrant before it was covered in dusty ash? I didn't want to know. The TV was a massive box, crowding the entire dresser.

"That TV is ancient," I blurted out. No one was speaking, but surveying the room, and I had to stop the uncomfortable silence.

"Is it?" Archer mused, glancing at it, as if he'd never paid attention to the fact TVs nowadays were thin flat screens.

"It's like from the nineties or something," I said. "And the wallpaper. Ugh, look at the bedspread!" I hadn't seen the bed monstrosity upon entering. It almost identically matched the wallpaper.

Anteros rolled his eyes at me. "The nineties were days ago to us, *sweetheart*." He went to pry open one of the doors.

"Yeah, sorry it isn't the honeymoon suite in a five-star resort." Himerus's snide tone made me feel judged as the worst snob ever.

THE IMMORTAL TRANSCRIPTS: SHUDDER

It was not what I had meant, and I was not making a good impression. "I was just trying to make small talk, guys. It's like walking into a time capsule for me. I wasn't alive in the nineties, remember?"

They didn't respond (great).

"You're right about the nineties, Callie," Archer said. "Soufriere Hills became active again then and wreaked all this damage."

"Yeah, well, it's still freaking active, so we gotta come up with a plan." Himerus was definitely in a mood.

Anteros managed to open the heat-warped door to the bathroom. "Got it."

It probably wouldn't flush without running water, and who knew the state of the pipes, but at least there was somewhere to go (oh, gross). Could things get worse?

Anteros moved to the front door, but it was stuck too. Impatient, Himerus yanked it open, ripping the handle off, but it did open.

"We'll look for provisions," Anteros said.

"They won't be good enough to consume." Archer busied himself by taking off the comforter. Underneath did not appear as dusty.

Anteros rolled his eyes. "Yeah, for your mortal."

Archer took the fancy covering off the pillows and tossed them into a pile atop the comforter. "Suit yourself. You won't die, but you can vomit just like a mortal."

"Whatever." Anteros stormed out the door in a bad mood too, Himerus following.

"Stay in this building!" Archer called after them. He plopped onto the bed, tucking his arms under his head and sighed. "Don't mind them. Come, it's not too dusty. We need rest."

I sat on the bed and lay back, my head resting on his folded arm. "They hate me."

"No, they don't."

"Then they hate what they're going through because of me."

We were both staring at the ceiling. It felt like heaven—or the Elysium—to lie down, but my stomach rumbled in hunger. We had missed breakfast and probably lunch by now and were miles away from civilization and food. This wasn't good. I wanted to rest, but we couldn't stay here long.

"No. My brothers are just moody because they're hungry and because of where we are. They're afraid."

"Of?"

"Heph lives on the other side of the island. We'll have to go to him for help. It's why my dad sent us here instead of a closer island."

According to the myths Dad had instilled in me, Hephaestus, or Heph as they called him, was the god of fire and forging metal and stuff. Heph was Aroha's ex—and I'd mentally donned him with the pet name "Beast" when we'd met (I'd never tell Archer that). "They're scared?"

"Yes. Heph won't hurt us, but he's not a fan of Anteros or me since it reminds him of how unfaithful my mom was. He will have a hard time tolerating Himerus—"

"Because of your dad, right?"

"Yes, and it didn't help Heph thought I was his kid for my first five or six years."

"Man, your family is twisted."

"You can say that again." Archer laughed. "Oh, the stories we have, Callie. It would take forever to tell you."

I was too tired to ask for more stories, and my eyes kept closing. I must've fallen asleep because it felt like seconds later when the boys were back with "provisions." They were all expired foods and beverages. I didn't dare to try anything, and neither did Archer. We'd snag a mere couple hours rest, and after, we planned to head toward a town and get our hands on some real food. Archer would then take us to Heph's shop.

Despite my hunger, exhaustion overtook me. I fell asleep again in Archer's warm, comforting arms, feeling safe, despite the likelihood I was not.

CHAPTER 3

Athena

After three days of living with Ares, I was ready to wage war. With him. He was sloppy and expected me to cook, clean up after him, and constantly converse about inane topics. He wasn't coming from a patriarchal or chauvinistic frame of mind—although, in the past, he had been prone to it. His behavior seemed completely ignorant of the fact that, being a grown man and a guest in my house, he should take care of himself and be polite. The gods were spoiled by Zeus's wealth, which is one of the many reasons I avoided staying long at Olympus, only going to Fiji when summoned for business.

I had been going to Oxford again, this time seeking a degree in biochemistry—which I had a fascination with since it made warfare more interesting—when Zeus uprooted me to oversee Archer's trial for the murder of Thanatos. Being the god of death had made Thanatos a bit of a scoundrel, but he was merely trying to do his job and follow my father's orders. I had persuaded my father to let the girl live, but being the swindler he is, Zeus tested Archer. I have no idea how Hermes got the trickster moniker, because our father outshined him in deception. I had held my breath, hoping Archer's selfishness would not choose instant gratification over her life. Initially, Love chose love, as is right with the world. Justice served.

Zeus had been furious. He destroyed his office after Archer left and ordered Callie's death anyway. Again, my cool logic calmed him. He could not kill her but had to wait for Archer to fail or lose interest in the girl. I knew it would've been the former. The kid falls in love hard, and when his heart breaks—I can't even stand to be near him. As logical and level-headed as I seem to be on the outside, I feel so much inside, it becomes unbearable. When Archer lost his daughter and Psyche, his pain became mine, and I'm barely related to him. It's that way with all immortals—even the *others*; I empathize with their sadness and anger so deeply, it overwhelms me. I have to get away from them, so I run and hide. This time, I chose to escape to Iceland. As a result, they called me formidable. I can be tough in the name of justice, wisdom, and war, but people, socializing, expressing my emotions—not so much.

"Thena?" Ares—Chase, I should get used to calling him—drew my attention. Great, he had asked me something. I had been lost in my own world for a moment.

"Was thinking, sorry."

He was standing in the kitchen in front of me, and I was on my laptop at the table.

"What's new?" He smirked. Yes, he was well versed in my attention difficulties. For a second, I thought he was insulting me. No, the twinkle in his eyes and the wry little grin told me he was teasing. "Coffee?"

I nodded, looking back at my laptop. I had typed two words while lost in my thoughts: **She is**. I closed the laptop quickly, not trying to shut it down but to silence my subconscious. I was growing confident I knew who Callie Syches—or now Ambrose or Olympus—was. I never paid much attention to what gods did about names when they married, since I'd never change my own in that outdated practice. Callie's ancestry was becoming clear, but I didn't want to admit it to anyone if I were wrong. Part of me wanted to be wrong. The only way to be sure would be to find Prometheus and demand answers, which would be highly difficult.

Of course, she was from Psyche's lineage, and I was the lone Olympian who was privy to Psyche's controversial beginnings. I was the goddess who had brought her to Athens and settled her with a nice mortal royal family, hoping she'd stay well hidden. Of course, Eros had found her through what hindsight now told me could not have been dumb luck, as I had formerly supposed; luck wasn't a credible explanation for how he found Psyche's descendant thousands of years later too.

Ares—ugh, I meant, Chase—placed two coffees down, then sat. His face studied mine, which was unnerving. "You're the smartest person I know—"

I shook my head. "I'm not a person."

He gave me a loaded stare with those intense amber eyes, where it seemed like fire burned behind them. Unable to deal with the depth of the pool of emotions in his incandescent eyes, my gaze darted away. They literally lit up during war as he worked himself into a state of raw wrath. He wasn't truly angry now, merely annoyed. I had interrupted him, which was probably rude, but it was an impulse I never mastered curtailing over millennia. Our godly natures never altered much over time. "Anyway, I know you know way more about Callie than you've told me. You're too smart not to have cracked this puzzle."

"I need more information." Thank goodness Apollo wasn't here to see through my omissions.

"I've told you everything I know and some theories of mine."

"And I have told you mine." I gave him my best poker face; it felt similar to playing that game, only lives were the ante.

"All of them, Thena?"

Hades! He was onto me. I could trick anyone or talk them into or out of something when I could apply logic, but Chase was very good at seeing through me. I would have to give him some kind of truth. "In a sense, I have. I didn't tell you details because they are all suspicion and conjecture. It's nothing more than what I told you when we spoke about her last. All hypotheses do need test—"

Chase rolled his eyes and huffed. "We are past the point of worrying about writing up a scientific lab, Athena."

"I have to see her first, find the missing piece of info, and then I'll tell you everything. Once I find proof of who she is, who she belongs to, I will swear on the Styx that I'll be on whatever side protects this girl."

I could see the gears churning in his head. "Who she belongs to?"

"Even you, Chase—no offense—know she's much too powerful to be only Psyche's."

"Of course, but then whose?"

Right, I shut the conversation down. The implications of what I suspected her identity could be chilled me to the bone, despite the ichor regulating my actual temperature. So many conflicting emotions began to rise. "I have to go...to uh, find out. You can stay here, a safe house. Beware the Norse, and stay put until I return. I will smooth things over via Freya."

"Freya?" His wife and Freya never got along too well. Love goddesses get competitive, but Freya was so much more than Aphrodite-in powers and personality.

"She lives a few doors down. She can inform Odin why you're relocating to his territory."

"Is that wise?"

"How would you feel if a war god secretly strolled into Greece?"

Chase gave in instantly. "Good point. I'd kill him."

"Exactly."

"We have to gain some allies, just in case."

"I've got a few, but people respect you more."

"Let's make a list, draw up some plans." I preferred planning mode. I get in the zone and do it for hours.

Chase's phone rang.

I tried to use it as an excuse to leave the room and stood.

Chase's anxious tone stopped me in my tracks. "What?"

My pulse quickened, absorbing Chase's anxiety acutely as if it were my own. My breaths grew quick and shallow. My chest constricted. Curse my empathy. I was all too much.

"Dite, slow down. What happened?" He paused.

My immortal ears could hear Dite or Aroha—these aliases were too much to keep up with. I waited, with bated breath, to hear what had occurred. Her voice grew too shrill to make sense of it from across the room via phone.

"I'm sure they are fine. Please...darling...I can't even understand you." So, Chase couldn't either. She must be hysterical. Why did I even use that word? Its etymology was utterly sexist. I shook my head, hoping it would dispel the distracting thoughts, but in times of stress, my attention issues increased. Not a good thing in a war, let me add.

Chase was quiet for a moment, his face stoic and devoid of emotion, but he was anxious, shown by how one hand curled into a fist, his knuckles turning white. I hoped he wouldn't break my things in one of his raging fits.

"I sent Iris with a message. They know where to go. Call Heph, and tell him to look out for them in the meantime, but I'll find them myself if I have to." He ended the call and met my gaze, his eyes exposing his anxiety and fright. It was not an expression I had seen on his face before. I glanced away, not due to his high emotions but because beholding someone's gaze was tantamount to touching his soul, too intimate and horrifically jarring. Years of Hera forcing me to make eye contact since it was "a necessary civility" was mind-warping torture. She was my wicked stepmother, after all. It was to be expected.

In the quick moment I had registered his emotions, Chase only held it together for Dite's sake.

Now he was reacting. "I should've gone with them, but—"

"Zeus would've followed you. He *did* have his people follow you. What happened?" Why wouldn't he get right to the point? If the girl was dead...

THE IMMORTAL TRANSCRIPTS: SHUDDER

"Zeus attacked them."

"That's against the contract. Archer has a year." My mind went quickly to law and justice. My brain would not let me wonder about the result of the attack for more than a millisecond, but I scrolled through my database of immortal laws, cross-referencing those from different godly tribes.

"You think Zeus will bow down to his own laws?"

I didn't respond because we both knew the answer. No one was above the deals, pacts, and documents gods agreed on together.

"If he killed her..." Chase could not finish.

My stomach dropped. "No. No. Don't assume anything yet. Is there no word from them?"

He shook his head. "I have to go."

"Give me two minutes to throw some things in a bag. I need to go too, to find someone."

"Who?"

"Prometheus."

He cocked his head in confusion. "Good luck?" It was well-known among the immortal community that Prometheus was impossible to find. He had gone into hiding long ago, but the truth was he was hiding from Zeus. Prometheus knew more than Zeus himself, being able to see the future better than any Olympian god. He was a Titan and would know what would happen to Callie and Archer in the future. Prometheus had the missing piece of the puzzle. I was sure of it.

"I'll find him."

"I'm sure you will," he said as I left the room. He didn't believe me, and he was right not to. I'd never find Prometheus, but if my logic served me well, he would foresee me coming and find me instead. That was my hope.

I hadn't even taken a sip of my coffee. I went to pack, knowing this journey might be futile, but I had to try. I could not stay in hiding while my fellow family struggled against my father's tyranny. Justice would not permit it.

CHAPTER 4

Archer

A gentle hand on my shoulder woke me, and I thought it was Ma until I realized she was in New York and I was in a volcano-devastated hotel. Callie was fast asleep in my arms. It was dark, pitch black due to the lack of electricity on this part of the island.

My groggy, exhausted mind came into focus. Who in Hades was touching me? I grasped the hand tightly.

"Ow," a female voice gasped.

Callie mumbled. I drew her closer to protect her at all costs. No one was allowed in the exclusion zone, except for planned tours only when the volcanic activity was low. This had to be a goddess.

"What's wrong?" Callie asked, waking up.

"Who's there?" Himerus's deep voice demanded.

I heard a strange sound, and the female's hand yanked out of mine. Definitely a goddess to break free of my immortal grip.

A light came on, weak at first until the winding sound continued. My brothers must've found a hand-crank emergency flashlight. It was now shining in my and Callie's faces before it moved away toward the intruder. Belle these days, formerly Aglaea, one of the charities, stood before us.

"Belle?" I asked since no one spoke.

She turned away, blocking the light from her eyes with an outstretched hand. "Point that thing somewhere else," Belle scolded. The flashlight went down, dimmed, and the crank was heard again. Another flashlight clicked on in Belle's hand. "I'm here to take you to civilization."

Thank the gods—excluding Zeus. Callie needed water and food badly, and I had worried about how far we would have to trek on foot to get to it. Montserrat was not widely populated, being a small island with a lot of uninhabited land.

But could we trust Belle? Where had she gone after her visit to New York? Back to Zeus and Olympus? Why was she here? Visiting Heph? Otherwise, no god would come to inhabit an island next to an active volcano. Heph was on our side, or at least I hoped. I couldn't trust anyone just because they were family. My own grandfather was the one trying to kill my wife and me.

I was out of options. I had to get Callie somewhere habitable. We got up, but Callie was still dragging. I touched her head. Feverish, great. We climbed out the window back into the ruins of where a city had been. The barely visible "hills" in the distance smoked, creating a chilling sensation of doom in the dark night. I could not look at them and think of what I had almost done the last time I had been here.

Belle led us a quarter mile to her jeep while explaining how Ma had called Heph, and he and Belle had split up and searched the whole south and west coast, figuring we were coming from the direction of Belize. The volcanic activity interfering with the godly ability to locate other Olympians, she had been searching for hours until she'd found fresh footprints. We climbed in her jeep—my brothers in the back and Belle at the wheel. I sat in the front passenger seat and pulled Callie onto my lap. I wrapped the seatbelt around both of us and clipped it while Belle texted Heph. The seatbelt was too tight, but Callie was too mortal and breakable to rely on just my grip holding us inside the jeep on such rough terrain.

The way Belle drove terrified me. My brothers laughed and cheered over every rock and bump as if it were a thrilling roller coaster. Callie dug her nails into my arms, and more than once, I had to put my hand out so her head wouldn't hit the dashboard. "Belle, you think you could slow down, damn it? Callie is mortal." As if inadvertently supporting my suggestion, my brothers' heads made a resounding crack as they were thrown together; they simultaneously said, "ow."

Belle scoffed at us, but the speedometer needle dipped down a bit, and the bumps were less jarring. I thanked her.

We drove for about fifteen minutes until we found smooth roads, then entered neighborhoods with houses. Belle turned a few times onto a main street with shops and pointed at a building. "That's Heph's place."

We all turned to see the jewelry store. I tried not to think about the day I visited there, asking him to kill me. Those melancholy days were behind me. I was happy now—worried and anxious as all Hades too, but blissfully in love with my wife.

I thought we would turn the corner to stop there because maybe Heph had rooms connected to his business, but she kept driving. Soon we were leaving town, and our view became houses, which grew larger as we moved on. I sensed our direction was leading back to the ocean. Belle turned suddenly, revealing gates. She put in a passcode, and they swung inward. We traveled a long inclined drive and stopped in front of a villa, or more so a mansion. It was quite large for one guy; as far as I knew, he never was with anyone after my mother—mortal or godly. Then again, we were only in contact when he was trying to win my mother back, which had been on and off about every two centuries or so.

Belle turned off the car and climbed out. Before she closed the door, she glanced over at me, her mouth drawing into a perplexed frown. "You coming, or what?"

"I'm guessing this is Heph's place? Is he going to be okay with us being here...*all* of us?" I darted my eyes, but in the dimly lit drive, I wasn't sure if she saw my gaze pinpointing Himerus.

"I'd worry more about your mortal wife's life than his."

"That doesn't make me feel any better, Belle."

She scoffed. "Heph won't hurt anyone. He's a big old softy, a teddy bear, really."

I raised my brows at her. A teddy bear?

"I agree with the term bear," Anteros said, "but he's one that can light us on fire."

"Aww, will the itty-bitty cupids feel better if I promise to protect them?" Belle mocked in a baby voice before she stuck her tongue out at them.

They did it back.

"Seriously?" I gave each of them side-eyes. How embarrassing could they be? "Are we back in childhood again here?"

"Nope, not at all. You were waaaaaay more fun then," Anteros teased. He was smiling, and Himerus laughed. At least they were relaxed now.

I undid the seatbelt to realize Callie was asleep again. She must've dozed off when the roads smoothed out. I awkwardly climbed out of the jeep with her in my arms.

Anteros headed toward the door. "Well, technically, Archer was the most mature one out of us. Hey Belle, where's Thalia and Ada?"

"It's, uh, just me here. And Heph." As she unlocked the door with her key, I wondered how long she had been here.

"Weird," Himerus said.

"You're weird," Belle shot back.

"Seriously?" I think she knew what I was asking, but she ignored me. Belle directed us toward a living room. "This way."

19

THE IMMORTAL TRANSCRIPTS: SHUDDER

As I tried to place Callie gently onto the sofa, she woke up again. Her eyes were glazed. I needed to get her medicine. "You wouldn't happen to have any fever reducer, would you?"

Belle gave me an odd look. "What humor is out of balance?"

Of course, why would we gods have it when ichor killed every germ, virus, or bacteria? It was my turn to match her mind-boggled expression. "Her humors? What are you like still in 400 BC?" She was talking Medieval, literally, about the belief of mortal humors—blood, phlegm, and bile—being out of whack causing them illnesses. They sort of were onto something in the past, because lifestyle balance and moderation—our Greek mantra—did create a healthy mortal. However, the solutions back then to balance "humors" were absolutely dimwitted. There was no way I would let Belle dabble in bloodletting or suggest cold vegetables would miraculously cure Callie.

Belle rolled her eyes at me. "Well then, dittany. Herbs are timeless. I'll make tea with some of Heph's supply." She raced from the room at immortal speed. She was definitely a bit comfortable here, but it made sense Heph would keep the stuff. He didn't burn, not really, but his craft left him with cuts, and something in his makeup made him heal a tad slower than us. It was a pretty fair trade-off: can't die by fire but still can heal faster than a mortal.

Himerus fidgeted, his gaze darting around. "Where is the man of the house?" He didn't sit, but Anteros did.

"Probably still out searching for us. Guess we were closer?" I pointed out to what they already could surmise since Belle already told us. They were nervous, needing reassurance.

As if speaking his name conjured him, Heph lumbered inside. He met my gaze, his eyes softening. "You made it, I see." He made a weird grunting noise at my brothers, barely glancing at them. It was a better greeting than we could've expected. Then his gaze took in Callie.

He was over by her side in a second, kneeling, with genuine concern etched upon his face. "What is it? What happened?"

Anteros huffed out a breath. "What didn't?"

Heph shot him a glare, and Anteros was off the couch, now as uncomfortable as Himerus, who was biting his nails half off and watching Heph's every move.

I had to be the one to speak for all of us. "He's not being rude, Heph. A lot happened, and it's a long story. Short version—Callie was attacked, kidnapped, and zapped by Zeus's bolt via me. Then she had to undergo a thousand or more miles of our island hopping; plus, she's half-starved and feverish."

"He tried to kill her?" Heph blew out a breath, his confusion shifting to shock. "What was Zeus thinking?"

"He was trying to kill me too."

He stared at me, his mouth agape.

I nodded. "He struck me. His bolt. Several times."

"Boys," Heph directed, staring at their feet rather than their faces. "Go down the hall, third door on your left, the wine cellar. Get a bottle of nectar."

They looked at me, utterly lost as to why both of them had to go, but I nodded, and they trudged off. Heph wanted to talk to me alone. Would he kick them out?

"He struck you, and it affected her? You didn't do what I think you did, did you? With a mortal?"

Callie roused. "What?" She was groggy, but she'd be coherent enough to remember.

"Nothing." I gave Heph a warning look to keep his trap shut.

He stood up, yanking my collar to make me follow, and said softly, for immortal ears only, "How does she live?"

"Please don't say anything. Don't make a big deal. You saw me. You know I wouldn't live without Callie. It was to protect her." We vaguely spoke of my immortal marriage to her. Callie and I were soul-bound now, our souls linked in every way possible. My stronger immortal one would protect hers. "Swear on the Styx you won't tell anyone about it. I already made my brothers do the same. I don't want Ma and my dad to find out."

Heph rubbed his hands down his face in frustration. "I swear on the Styx I won't tell anyone you were dumb enough to immortally marry a mortal. You two better live. There's one reason I never murdered your father. Dite immortally married him. To hurt him would hurt her, and I'm not talking about your heart. Now Zeus knows this? Great! He'll kill you, kid, and then your father will end the entire world."

I was going to protest, but knowing how close my father and I had grown these past months, he might very well do that. "Well, help me stop all that."

"What do you think I'm doing?"

My brothers were back, saving me any more awkward confessions. Belle brought in the tea. My brother handed the nectar bottle to me, and I took a few swigs, feeling my energy return, the aches from Zeus's bolt fade, and the dread and anxiety lift. I passed it around to my siblings, then sat with Callie as she drank the tea.

Heph took the bottle out of Himerus's hand and tipped some into Callie's teacup.

Worry edged into Anteros's voice. "What are you doing?"

"Demigods can handle it. She's had it before." The day we were attacked and she learned who I was—before they wiped her memory clean—she had handled it. Ma gave her some often to improve her health when we were apart. These memories brought down my mood. When would I be free of regrets and be able to only focus on her happiness?

Poor Callie. She needed the nectar badly. Between the dittany lowering her fever and the nectar giving her strength and good health, she was back to herself in minutes. Belle decided we should have a midnight feast—although I was sure it was far past that hour.

In no time, she called us into the kitchen. There was a spread of bread, meats, cheese, dips, and veggies, an authentic mezze platter. We ate heartily. The conversation was limited. Heph didn't really like us, and my brothers were terrified of him. Belle tried, but we were all exhausted.

We were shown two rooms upstairs—unfortunately, next to each other—my brothers getting a room with twin beds and Callie and I a luxurious king-sized bed. I was surprised but knew with Heph's clubbed foot, he rarely would come upstairs. The primary suite had to be downstairs. Belle handed clothes to each of us and informed us there was a bathroom next to my room. She said goodnight and entered a guest room a couple of doors down the hall.

I flopped onto the bed.

"Archer, at least change. Our clothes are so gross. I need a shower."

"Ladies first," I told her. When she went to go, Himerus was trying to snag the bathroom before I stopped him. "No. Go change. I'll get all our clothes washed. I doubt we'll want to walk around in Heph's large clothes drooping on us in the morning."

Himerus sighed, annoyed I gave Callie the first shower, and went back to his room.

Once I had all our clothes in the washer, I snagged the second slot for a shower and then crashed into the bed next to Callie. I pulled her into my arms. She was half-asleep, and I watched her groggy state, wanting to memorize every facial feature and expression of my wife. She had this adorable line between her brows that scrunched when I disrupted her, unconsciously annoyed with me in her sleep. I'd never seen that expression, never sleeping by her side until recently. I couldn't wait for the years to come when I'd learn to anticipate every expression. I tried to fasten her unruly dark curls behind her ear, but they would not stay put—as stubborn as her. After tracing her now calm features for a moment, I closed my eyes. The curtain tried to block the light out, but the sun was rising. Despite the room brightening, I easily fell asleep, my breathing pattern adopting Callie's. We were one.

CHAPTER 5

Callie

When I woke up, I was refreshed but still feverish. The fevers definitely appeared stress-induced (I mean, like almost getting killed), and if that were true, my entire life would be lived through this feverish haze. The stress wouldn't stop until I was dead or Zeus gave up. I didn't think he was the kind of god to ever give up. If only I knew why he hated me. If only I didn't care that he did. It was the same bitter sting of rejection I'd felt back in middle school when I realized the popular girls didn't like me because I was smart. New York had been different because of Archer.

Archer had me trapped in his arms, in a warm cocoon I'd happily stay in all day. I had to pee, though, so it started feeling like a prison. I turned in his arms, and he sighed in his sleep. I stared at his breathtakingly beautiful face. How did I end up with the god of love? More importantly, what was really going on with me? I didn't want to think about what happened the night before the wedding. Thankfully, Aroha unknowingly covered for me by giving me nectar, which would've healed my wound anyway. I should tell Archer, but he was so stressed out, and how could I explain it anyway? I didn't understand the *how* or *why* these things were happening to me. How could I tell him that in the time it took Raphael to take the glass out of my arm and clean the wound, it had somehow healed itself? Raphael had been only slightly shocked, which meant Dad had predicted this. Which meant he knew something and hadn't told me. I was too afraid of a possible truth to ask him, and then I was whisked away. It had to do with my mother. When he gave me Mom's necklace, Dad had said he would tell me something later, which meant he believed I couldn't handle whatever info he wanted to impart (at the time, so true).

Archer's eyes opened, and he smiled at me, completely content. "How long have you been awake?"

"A few minutes. You sleep like the dead, you've held me prisoner, and I have to pee...really bad."

"Sorry." He let go of me, and I dashed down the hall to the bathroom.

When I returned, Archer was slipping a T-shirt over his finely-sculpted abs, making my stomach flop. Then it growled, insisting food was more important than spending the morning in bed with my new husband. (My stomach's priorities were annoying.)

At breakfast, I realized we had spent most of the day in bed sleeping. It was dinnertime. The others were around the table eating. Himerus looked at us and whispered something quickly and quietly in Anteros's ear. Anteros laughed, almost choking on his food.

Archer pulled a chair out for me as he directed to Himerus, "I heard that."

I sat down, and Archer sat next to me. "What did he say?"

"You don't want to know."

"Oh, never mind, I can imagine." Himerus probably made some bawdy joke about us being in bed all day. Let them think whatever they wanted.

Heph sat at the head of the table, his mouth full, staring at me as if trying to puzzle me out (me too, Beast, me too). Belle sat next to him and patted his arm as she told him something about her sisters. I swear there seemed to be a reserved intimacy between them, the kind seen between an elderly couple, comfortable and content in each other's company.

"How long have you been here, Belle? I mean, Aglaea." Gods and aliases were hard. How did they keep track? (Note to self, make a chart so I'd never forget.)

"Oh." She appeared surprised by my question. Her gaze swept over to Heph, making his dart away, and both of them blushed. (Ooooo) I take it back. Not like an old couple, but a very new one. Maybe they were best friends who felt something for each other, but no one had fessed up their feelings yet. (Great, now my fevers were writing romance novels.)

"I came here right after I left New York last fall." Belle was more interested in what was on her plate (fabulous steak) than the conversation.

I didn't think much of her eyes being awkwardly glued to her plate, but Archer's brow wrinkled in thought. His brothers exchanged a weirded-out, surprised expression. I wondered why they thought it strange.

"Oh, really?" Archer's tone and expression had changed to amusement. He noticed the relationship too.

Belle glared at Archer.

Heph cleared his throat. "You went back to Olympus for a little while, Belle, so you weren't here when Eros...I mean, Archer...was here the first time he was...uh...here."

Archer shifted uncomfortably and was interested in his dinner as well. His weakest hours had been on this island, twice. I clasped Archer's hand in mine. He squeezed it and smiled at me, the sadness seeping away, replaced by love and strength.

"Interesting you're here without your sisters," Anteros dared to pry.

Himerus went wide-eyed and shook his head at Anteros, obviously terrified of Heph and not wanting to poke the beast.

Belle turned her angry attention onto Anteros. "I don't need a chaperone. I am older than you, you know."

What was going on? I wanted to try again—with this fever—to read their minds to see what they thought of each other. I had read Aroha's and Lucien's minds before.

I tried Belle first, pushing my mind away from me, being careful to keep my face neutral, and focused my eyes on my plate. There was resistance before I broke through. *This is mortifying. How does the doofus duo know I have feelings for him when Heph can't even tell?* (Interesting)

Heph's mind was hard to break into. Archer was trying to change the subject to help them out, but I tuned out his words to focus. I pushed my mind harder. *I'm going to strangle those brats. How dare they insinuate that? Wish it were true. Someone like me doesn't get another chance at winning the heart of a beautiful goddess.*

Archer nudged me, which booted my mind back into myself. "You okay?" His brow was wrinkled in concern.

"Fever. I'm fine. Did one of you guys shoot them with arrows?"

Archer was lost in my random shift in topics, and we all got distracted by Heph's fork loudly clattering to his plate. He had a melted fragment in his hand, and the bottom and top pieces had disconnected and fallen off. Smoke rose off him in little tendrils (uh-oh).

"What?" Heph growled.

"Heph, calm down," Belle warned.

Heph glared daggers at me. "What did you say?"

I swallowed hard to find my voice. I repeated my question, wondering what trouble I'd just gotten us in. I had to get Heph to calm down, but I didn't know how.

"No," Archer said firmly.

Heph intermittently glared at Archer, Himerus, and Anteros.

I had to get his attention off them. "I'm sorry I asked. It's these fevers."

Archer grew concerned, touching my head. He withdrew his hand immediately, wide-eyed, terrified about how ill I was but also pleading for me to stop talking. "She's burning up."

I didn't think I could back down now.

After Archer's denial, Heph's attention went to Himerus. "It obviously wasn't me!" Himerus threw his hands up in exasperation. Then he smirked. "Wait. Why? Do you feel lustful or something?" Himerus dared to make a joke when the fire god was pissed? (Death wish.) Realizing his mistake, he rushed on, "Maybe it's unrequited? That damn pointless power."

Poor Anteros was now the object of Heph's glowers. "I'm necessary because not everyone can love everyone, okay? Sometimes heartbreakers need to be punished. To do it to gods, though? No way!"

Himerus crossed his arms. "Nemesis. You've shot her."

Anteros was wide-eyed at his buddy's betrayal. "That was different. I did it for...my mom."

"Who abandoned you."

"Your dad abandoned you too."

"I didn't try to buy his love by keeping a goddess thwarted in love."

"I'm not buying her love. I was helping *your* dad out, too, you know. He doesn't love Nemesis, and I didn't need to shoot him to make him indifferent to her. And you're not trying to buy your dad's love? What about—"

"Stop!" Heph punctuated his command with his fist on the table, making everything on the table vibrate.

I had to do something. "If you two would just talk, you'd realize you're practically in love with each other and too chicken to do anything about it." That hadn't come out right. (Why did I open my mouth? They'd kill me now, for sure.)

Archer rushed to interject, "She sees things with fevers." He was trying to save me from Heph's wrath, although I'd tried to do the same for him. "She can read minds. Our minds." He left out the future dreams, but I was freaked out by how I could do that, too, and maybe he only trusted them so far. Like Belle's visit to Olympus could be a red flag for all I knew.

"Reads gods' minds?" Disbelief laced Belle's tone.

No gods ever believed me. Maybe I should take it further so they'd trust me and stop hiding their feelings.

I pushed my mind forcefully out and pointed at Heph. "He's thinking right now about how he hadn't even thought about Aphrodite in months, not until her kids showed up." Then I pointed to Belle. "She's thinking I'm full of...no, wait, now she's pleased with what I just said about Heph.

THE IMMORTAL TRANSCRIPTS: SHUDDER

Himerus, don't think about meddling. Anteros, this is not that funny, and dear husband," —I turned to Archer— "I am majorly freaked out too."

Everyone was stunned for a moment, including me. I had just easily and quickly jumped minds, with the ease and feeling of changing a TV channel.

Archer recovered first, clearing his throat. "Well, that's that. I think Callie needs some fever reducer and to go back to bed."

Himerus smirked and looked at Archer and me with a creepy leer. "I thought headaches meant women were avoiding—"

Belle went all maternal on them, "That's it. Get out! Go into town, and don't come back until midnight, you two," chiding their behavior as if she were my Ma commanding the love entourage back in Rome.

Anteros punched Himerus in the shoulder. "Good going." They got up, sulking frowns on their faces. "I didn't get to finish my steak."

Himerus rolled his eyes, grabbed the thin strip of steak off the plate, and slapped it into Anteros's hand. They bickered like children as they left.

Belle sighed in relief.

"They're a handful," Heph muttered.

Belle scoffed. "You didn't have to grow up with them."

"They're loyal," Archer defended them the only way he could, given their immature antics.

Heph and Belle didn't hear him. They were timidly meeting each other's gaze, small smiles spreading across their faces.

I slipped off and headed back to our room. Archer came in moments later with some medicinal tea and some pills someone must've gotten me while I slept. I felt so out of it; I was drowsy again. It seemed to be all I did—live in a haze and sleep. I heard Archer slip out of the room.

The next morning, I woke up in my welcomed Archer cocoon, feeling so much better. I woke my husband (I couldn't think or say that word enough) with a shower of kisses that quickly escalated. When we went down to breakfast, Archer's brothers were groggy and quiet, so no lewd jokes today. Good, because I would not be able to contain my telltale blush.

Belle entered with Heph, holding hands, abundantly pleased with themselves.

Archer said quietly in my ear, "And they call me the matchmaker," before he kissed my jawline right below it, that spot that made chills shoot down the side of my body.

After Belle sat, she looked at Archer and said, "It's all clear, but stick to Brades Road and go north to the beach. The...uh..." Belle stumbled over her words. "Cabeiri will watch over you," she finished awkwardly.

Cabeiri. I wasn't sure what that was or where we were headed.

"I understand." At least Archer did.

There were some quiet words between the new couple, and Archer talked over them to give them privacy.

Archer glanced at his brothers. "You guys coming with?"

"Are we invited? Or is this a honeymoon thing?" Anteros sneered, his childish attitude showing he was grumpy.

My guess was the god of unrequited love felt quite left out when there were only two couples and a brother for company—well, not blood-related, but a brother nonetheless.

Archer rolled his eyes. "Safety in numbers, and you told me Chase said never to leave our sides."

"Glad I signed up to be a babysitter," Himerus muttered.

Belle snapped, losing the happy demeanor Heph had instilled in her. "Do you see a baby? Would you rather be in Fiji?" For a goddess of beauty, her face screwed up into an intimidating grimace of fury when mad, not that I'd ever mistakenly equate beauty to goodness after Aroha's past proclivities.

"I just meant—" Himerus tried.

Eager to end the spat, Archer cut in, "We'll stay in the same vicinity. You guys do your thing, and we'll do ours."

Heph appeared to be having a hard time with the boys. It had to be difficult or awkward to deal with your ex-wife's past indiscretions, and her current husband's, while trying to forge a new relationship of peace.

Archer changed the subject, and everyone relaxed (somewhat) over a quick breakfast. Soon after, we were out the door into the blazing sun. It was definitely hot, but bearable; the humidity was high, but I wasn't overheated or too sweaty, despite us walking a half mile to the main road. The wind increased in strength as we got closer to the beach.

On the way, I had to ask, "What or who is protecting us?"

"The Cabeiri? Heph and Ma never had kids, but when it came to sea nymphs after the first divorce, he had kids—many, many kids. Sea nymphs are very...um...fertile. There is pretty much a small army watching over us." Archer leaned into me as we walked, his hand trailing down my back before it anchored on my hip.

"Above water?"

"Yep. Proteus's grandkids. I wouldn't mention it in front of Belle. She seems the jealous type."

Yes, the stuttering when she mentioned his kids was proof of that. A beauty goddess with some self-confidence issues? This explained a lot about my mother-in-law. Aroha lashed out at anyone who stole the attention she thought she deserved. Not that she ever lacked admirers: tall and thin, with all the right curves—not to mention her blue eyes—and perfectly coiffed blonde locks framing a gorgeous face. I thought she was the prettiest being on Earth, but I was a bit biased because Archer's face was simply a chiseled manly form of hers.

Thinking of parentage, it struck me how the charities were supposedly his cousins? "Wait, so whose kid is Belle, or I mean Aglaea? How can she be your cousin, or is it like a half or distant cousin?"

Anteros frowned. "Cousins?"

Himerus nudged him, and they exchanged a coded look.

Archer was hiding something—obvious, from how uncomfortable he suddenly was, his hand slipping off my hip to his side and curling into a frustrated fist. "It's complicated. The Charities' mother, Eurynome, is a Titan. Before Zeus banned interbreeding—"

"Inter-what?"

"Breeding."

"This sounds so backwards. Are you animals or gods?" I was uncomfortable with the conversation.

Anteros laughed. "Callie, you married into a majorly twisted family, girl."

Himerus began, "Well, mythology is really gross—"

"A lot of myths have fabricated details, lies." Archer shot him a furtive look. He was the one lying.

I stopped, crossing my arms, and gave Archer a look that could kill—if he were mortal. "Like them being your cousins?"

"Burn!" Himerus shouted as he high-fived Anteros.

"Yeah, good luck, bruv," Anteros slapped Archer on the back.

Himerus winked. "See you at the beach later, dead meat." The two of them walked away, laughing.

I did not enjoy being part of their joke.

"I didn't want to lie. The myths say Zeus was the Charities' father and Eurynome, a Titan, was their mother."

"That would make them your aunts?" It was boggling my mind.

"Not exactly. Uh...their birth father is mortal. Back in the Iron age, Zeus expanded our ranks by making a lot of demigods immortal. To legitimize them, Zeus claimed them as his offspring. Nowadays, yeah, it's kind of weird, but they didn't worry about those things back then."

"So, you're not related at all?"

"*That's* what you fixate on out of everything I just said?"

"You lied to me?"

"How could I tell you the truth? 'Callie, by the way, I'm the god of love, and this is my entourage? I promise I don't like them more than friends.' Would you have believed me?"

It sounded ridiculous, and he had been trying to protect me from Zeus—which he was right to worry about. Still, he had lied. "Of course not, but you could've said they were your friends."

"You were extremely jealous already, so 'friends,' I doubt you would've been okay with."

"I was not!"

He gave me the side-eye, and his lips upturned into a know-it-all smirk, calling me out on my own lying. (I had been insecure—still was, sadly.) "You had no reason to be. I never felt anything for any of them. Plus, it doesn't matter now. It's you and me, always."

He had a point, but so did I. "You're not off the hook yet."

"How about I make it up to you? Spend a ridiculous amount of Heph's money on you."

"Shopping is your solution?"

"It makes my Ma forget she's mad at me." He shrugged and pulled me in for a kiss. "Plus, we each have one set of clothes to our names."

He was right. We had to replace what was lost in Belize. Thankfully, the only things Aroha packed for me were materialistic items and a ton of terrible lingerie I'd never wear. I'd miss that red bathing suit, though.

"You're frowning." He took my hands in his, kissing them.

"My red bikini."

"Oh, we are so ordering the same exact one online as soon as we are settled. For now, we'll see the island's selection and make do." He kissed me passionately.

A man on a scooter cat-called us, which broke us apart, making me giggle.

THE IMMORTAL TRANSCRIPTS: SHUDDER

We bought enough clothes for Archer, his brothers, and me to make it through a few days, as well as bathing suits. I wore my new yellow and green madras plaid bathing suit—Montserrat's signature color of clothing—under my clothes, and we left the bags with the owners to grab them on the way back. We made our way toward the beach to see more authentic boutiques, and I had to check out every one.

Right before the beach, I noticed a sandy path that led a bit off the road, not quite wide enough for a car to fit down. At the end of it, hidden behind more impressive buildings, was a shanty-type dwelling with a wooden sign fastened to the wall. Painted on it was **The Asphodel Meadow**.

I stopped. Despite the heat, a chill swept over me. Impulsively, I was drawn to the store. I had to go in. I sensed I'd find something vital there. My knowledge of mythology solidified my conviction, and I walked forward down the sandy path.

"Callie? Where are you..." He must've read the sign. Archer would know this store was named after the place in the Underworld where most mortal souls ended up.

"Archer, I found Death."

CHAPTER 6

Archer

My wife was scaring the crap out of me. I should have been impressed with her abilities, but the fact they were so powerful and inexplicable worried me. She seriously just said she found Death. I mean, the store's name was an obvious allusion to Greek deathly myths, but I've seen an array of the occult: real oracles becoming possessed by prophetic visions out of their control, mortal frauds pretending, and then demigods, like Callie, who were legitimate in-betweens.

"What? How?" I had so many questions that I didn't know where to begin, but those two were a good start.

She shrugged. "I don't know. I feel it, like a beacon." What she described was similar to how we gods recognized other gods; it was an inkling, an eerie connection, like when I'd almost thought Callie had been one of us when we'd first met by that elevator. But a demigod finding a supposed demigod? Unheard of—if Callie was right. Part of me wanted her to be wrong so things could return to normal. I only wanted her safe. If she could find demigods, Zeus would never stop. Not only because of all of the children he had with mortals who he didn't want my grandmother to find out about, but he would also irrationally fear us making an army of them or something similar.

With trepidation, I followed my wife into the little store. Inside was a tiny room. From floor to ceiling—which was only about a foot from my head—were shelves lined with all types of occult merchandise: tarot cards, herbs, voodoo dolls, and other hodgepodge items spanning many cultures and eras. The room was much smaller than it appeared from the outside. It had a glass case, which also served as a counter, with jewelry inside it. Callie headed straight for it, perusing. There was a door in the back next to the counter I only noticed because it opened. An elderly woman came out, wiping her eyes. Another woman followed her and noticed us as the older woman thanked her profusely.

I joined Callie at the counter. She pointed at the painted sign and prices on the wall: **Contact with the dead $50**. With the exchange rate from US to Eastern Caribbean dollars, it was around twenty bucks. For that price, it was likely she was a fraud, but if this woman was legit, Callie had found a death demigod. I was so confused and more anxious than ever.

After the proprietor ushered the woman out the door, she turned toward us, her face beaming, genuinely happy to see tourists in her shop.

Her eyes rested on Callie. "How are you doing, most beautiful lady?" she asked in her welcoming, thick island accent. Her eyes were a warm brown, full of kindness. Her skin tone matched her eyes, making them vibrant, and her figure was slightly curvy—maternal was the word that came to mind since she looked in her thirties. Her black hair was pulled atop her head. Any anxiety slipped away. She would never hurt us. The vibe I got from her was much like Hestia, goddess of the hearth and home, my great-aunt, Hera's sister. "You eying my jewelry? I handcraft them myself. Whatever you need when it comes to the occult, Maizie's got it. If not, and you are in town for a few days, I can make it."

"Could I communicate with someone, please?" Callie asked.

"What?" Maizie and I asked simultaneously. Her shock was more than mine, her maternal face slipping into a confused frown. She recovered and smiled again, but it was tight, dare I say, frightened. Of what? Callie?

"Fifty dollars is the price to pay."

Who in Hades did Callie want to contact? My wife handed over the cash, and they headed to the back. I followed.

Maizie stopped and gave me a chiding motherly look. "You stay out here, lover man. I need someone to watch the shop. The spirits get skittish with a crowd." She allowed Callie into a small room and, when she entered, shut the door behind her.

I didn't want to part from Callie, even for a moment, but I also didn't want to be rude. I tried to keep my cool, but recalling how she'd addressed us unnerved me. "Most beautiful" was the meaning of the name Callista, and she'd called me "lover man." Did she have a sense of who we were, actually some kind of demigod psychic? I tried eavesdropping, but she had some sort of soundproofing or occult magic keeping my immortal ears out. I decided I'd mentally project myself to make sure Callie was safe, but before I made it into the room, the door opened, and they came out, making my mind return to its rightful place. Maizie bustled out, obviously distressed, repeating *no* many times.

Maizie shook her head. "Oh no, lady. No reading for you. I'll refund your money."

"Please, just listen to me. I know what you crave most, and we can give that to you."

Maizie's hand hesitated on the register, frozen. I had no clue what was going on either. "What are you?" She trembled.

Callie ignored her question but created distance, allowing the woman to feel safe on the other side of the glass counter. "We met your father once. He was unkind toward me, but nevertheless, he has passed away."

"I don't care about my father. He was worthless. He gave me nothing and only gave my mother me." Maizie tried to hand the money back over, but Callie made no move to take it.

I couldn't move or speak, grappling over the conversation to figure out what was going on and trying to figure out how my wife knew all this.

Callie continued. "He gave you your gift."

"My mother was talented—"

"Not as talented as you are." I had caught up to what Callie must've read off the woman's mind. Thanatos, god of death, had taken souls as far and wide as he could for sport. It would make sense for him to be attracted to women who could speak to the dead; I hate to imagine, but when you dabble in the world of spirits, meeting Thanatos must've been like meeting your own personal god. Guilt enveloped me. He hadn't been that bad of a guy back in Greece. He simply retrieved the mayhem my father created. Rome was when he broke. Death became sport. He wanted to compete with other death gods. He became sadistic and cruel. His bloodlust never left after that. I had done justice, although I was loath to admit it. If Callie was right and Maizie was Thanatos's daughter, she would make a wonderful Death; dying wouldn't be something to fear, but more like eternally coming home to your mother.

"My mother said my father was talented, but he couldn't have been your kind," Maizie said.

To fish out what she knew, I challenged, "So, what am I?"

My gaze was on Maizie, so I hadn't noticed Callie move, but a stinging sensation on my arm, followed by throbbing pain, drew my attention. Peering down, I saw Callie with a knife in her hand, which sizzled from my blood. She must've taken it down from one of the shelves to cut me.

"Ow," I retorted, curious why she was slicing me up.

"Proof." Callie shrugged as if slashing your husband's arm was commonplace.

Maizie watched me heal in awe, but in her eyes, a fire burned. She wanted immortality.

Great. I hope Zeus wouldn't try to murder some demigod because of this. "Callie."

THE IMMORTAL TRANSCRIPTS: SHUDDER

"I've read her mind, Archer. She knows who you are and is thinking many thoughts about me, but most of all, she remembers her father coming here when she was ten to collect the nineteen souls who passed away during the eruption of 1997. She was fascinated, envious he could help those spirits who were stuck to move on."

Her lips quivering, Maizie spoke. "I only bring solace to the living through communicating with the dead. It is unfair the dead suffer here on the Earth when their bodies give up. They deserve peace. I envied his ability to take them home." Tears formed in her eyes, caring more for trapped spirits than her father had cared for anything.

Callie sympathetically tilted her head. "What if you could become immortal and usher the souls to the Underworld?"

"Wait. Hold on one second." I took Callie by the elbow and steered her outside.

She crossed her arms and gave me a pert little glare that I found adorable and distracting. "What? She's perfect."

"Callie, you realize when we create Death, the person near the top of the list—"

"Is my dad, yes." Her face fell, and her eyes dropped to her feet.

"And you still want to do this?"

She sighed and peered back up at me with such resilience in her eyes that I wondered how such a young woman could face so much strife and not let it break her. "My dad is tired of fighting. I had this epiphany while you were gone. I realized I no longer needed him. I have grown up. If I lose this opportunity, what will happen to him when his body is done? Will he be trapped? What if Zeus chooses Death? What if his Death is as horrible as Thanatos was? I have to put all personal feelings aside and do what is right for the world, for my dad, even if it means he dies."

She had definitely grown up. She'd been mature for a mortal teenager when we met, but now she was a force to be reckoned with, strong and brave. Then, her eyes glistened, her tears breaking my heart. I cradled her chin. So strong and yet so feeling.

With a torn conviction we'd actually found Death, I took Callie's hand in mine and led her back inside, intertwining my fingers in hers.

"Yes," Maizie said.

Since I hadn't been too kind to Lena when she had been made immortal, I asked Maizie, "Do you need some time to be sure or to say goodbye to friends and family?"

LISA BORNE GRAVES

"I just need a day to sign over the business to my friend. Most of my family and friends are already dead." She said it with a smile; it gave me the chills yet made me realize she was perfect for this role. She would be reunited with them if they hadn't passed into Elysium.

Callie perused the jewelry area, most likely searching for a charm for her necklace. This would be a honeymoon to remember; that was for damn sure.

I spoke about my fears to Maizie. "You need to know that you cannot tell your friends or anyone what you'll become. We only stay in places for ten years, although some of your time will be spent in the Underworld anyway. If mortals expose you, Zeus will kill them. It is how our secret has been kept for thousands of years. Oh, and something else you should know: Zeus wants Callie—and me, if needs be—dead—"

"Why would I ever take the lives of the beings who offer me the gift of immortality? The people who fulfilled my dream to help the trapped souls I yearn to pass on?" She looked at me as if I had lost my mind, maybe even offended her.

"It had to be said. You'll be taken to Fiji to become immortal and then sent on to—"

"So, Hades will be my boss?" She was grasping this quite quickly and with zero trepidation and knew basic mythology.

"Yes. There may be some trouble and a great divide among us gods."

"I'll be on your side."

I lowered my voice. "I do ask one favor. My wife's father is at the top of the list. Please delay it a bit until she gets her goodbye."

She patted my cheek much like Ma often did. "I will, lover man."

"How much is this book charm?" Callie's voice took Maizie's attention off me.

"You paid me in a forever, so it is free for you, pretty lady. Anything you want."

Callie picked the charm and a book on the history of Montserrat.

We left the book to pick up on the way back and headed to the beach. Two out of three immortals set. One more left in my sentence.

Callie looked at me. "What now?"

"After I arrange for Zeph to take Maizie to Fiji, we head for New York." Zeph would be discreet when taking her to Zeus, who'd give her the ambrosia to make her immortal, but it would be madness to stay here in case Zeus tortured our location out of him or Maizie.

THE IMMORTAL TRANSCRIPTS: SHUDDER

"Is it safe?"

"Does it matter? Here will no longer be safe."

She pondered for a moment.

"Callie, trust someone who knows. A real goodbye is a much better closure than never having that conversation." My stomach felt sour thinking of my daughter Hedone and the goodbye I could never muster to give her.

Callie sighed and leaned into me. "I know. I saw this coming."

"Yes, when we left, your father had not been doing so well."

"No, I mean, yes. Obviously, he's barely holding on, but I dreamed I went back to see him, to say goodbye."

"This isn't one of your scary premonition dreams, is it?" If she saw her father dying in her dream, she'd go to New York. She deserved a real goodbye, but I was scared after all we had been through. Zeus would never stop hunting for my wife. He would kill her.

"I think so." Her lack of confidence in her response should give me a loophole to believe it was untrue. I could convince myself we wouldn't go to New York and instead head to the safehouse Dad was setting up, but my wife had a gift. We would go, no matter what, because she deserved—her father needed—to say goodbye.

I draped my arm around her, pulling her in more. My words were honest, but I knew they also made me a hypocrite. I had to go to the Underworld one day soon and let Hedone go. Maizie's emotional description of trapped souls hit me in the core of my heart. A love god could not afford such a burden.

CHAPTER 7

Lucien

The phone trembled in my hand. Five days had passed since Callie and Archer left for Belize and Zeus had tried to slaughter my son. I was positive the news would tell me Zeus had found them. No matter what they would tell me, it had to be terrible. Archer was alive, of course, or Chaos would've momentarily lashed out in our minds as she had when Thanatos died, but Callie might not be. I didn't know what we'd all do, how we'd all come back from her death.

"Lucien?" Chase's casual tone confused me, but the tension seeped out of my shoulders.

"News?" I demanded, not having time for simple civilities.

"They're alive. Everyone is okay."

I sighed, relieved. Some of the guilt left me.

"We're coming back to New York."

"Are you insane?" It came out before I could arrange my thoughts more logically and kindly. I wasn't scared of Chase; I merely wanted to avoid that nasty annoying temper of his. "It's not safe."

"I know that," Chase said firmly. Oh yeah, he was all "peaceful" now. We'd see how long it'd last. "But they're insistent. To be honest, I don't know if, in all good conscience, I can stop them. They found Death. Callie chose to go forward for Zeus to make this demigod immortal, and the woman is in Fiji now. Callie needs to say her goodbyes."

I needed to tell him the prophecy, but it would probably get the god of war all excited. He might incite a war. On the other hand, if I didn't tell him, Callie and Archer could die.

"I understand." Only, I didn't really. Surely, her father and all of us should veto Callie's wishes and keep her safe. Mortals die every day, and she had plenty of time to prepare herself, knowing her father was dying. Then again, I hated my father, my sister who'd sided with him, and the minute I was deemed a man and moved out, my mother had no time for me. She had time only to raise orphaned kids, a couple of mine too, and was busy ensuring mortals had lots of babies. She was the Titan goddess of fertility, so of course, she loved kids. She only had Artemis and me, twins. Some twin-bond *that* ended up being; I wanted to tear my sister to pieces for watching her nephew burn.

"Obviously, travel is a delicate situation. Please go scope out Aroha's apartment and text me when it is secure."

I had thought Aroha was home and resentfully ignoring me. "Where is she?"

"Not important. She's not in New York right now." He was being vague and shutting me out of plans. Probably a good idea if I was honest with myself.

"When should I expect you guys?"

"About a minute after your all-is-clear text."

"See you then."

Chase ended the call. They'd travel by a wind god who could teleport.

I went into my desk and grabbed the spare key Aroha had given me, as she was known to lock herself out, expecting Archer always to be there as if he didn't have a life of his own to live.

I wanted to take time to get to their apartment, so I walked down Park Ave. Traffic was so congested that my brisk mortal pace was almost faster than the cars. I needed a few minutes. I had to prepare myself for many things. Archer and Callie would be furious with me, and I dreaded seeing their blissful happiness rubbed in my face. Once people are married in every sense, they never notice their comfortable body language speaks volumes of intimacy. I pushed my jealousy and longing down. They needed me. I was being selfish, but in all of Hades, when would it be my turn? I'm the "god unlucky in love," a mocking motto they gave me in Rome. I wondered if it were true; more than three thousand years and never truly being able to hold onto love? I had a couple exes I truly loved, but something always got in between us: mortals died, my libido led to infidelity, or our unions were forbidden. Aroha would still tell me it was my fault, but there had to be someone out there for me if it wasn't Callie. I tried to focus on my friends instead of maudlin thoughts of my love life; only, I doubted they would see me as a friend anymore.

When I entered their building, I saw Dr. Syches's servant, Raphael, rushing through the lobby toward the entrance. He slowed when he saw me. His brow wrinkled in confusion. So even the mortal knew Aroha was away before I did; otherwise, he might expect me in the building visiting her. I was an outsider now, kicked out of my own family on all fronts.

"They're coming back. There's a new Death, so..." I tried to quickly explain because he seemed hurried.

"That explains it." The man cryptically returned.

"What?"

"Oh, Dr. Syches made a bad turn and had to check into the hospital today. I came for some of his things. They say he won't leave." If that were true, I wondered why they didn't send hospice and let him die in his home. Maybe the hospital visit was to prolong his life long enough to see Callie.

"I'll let them know when they get here." *Fabulous*, I'd be the harbinger of bad news to boot. Yeah, they didn't hate me enough already.

Raphael nodded, then hurried out the door, the doorman holding it open for him.

I took the elevator to the apartment, not worried at all if there'd be someone there waiting to ambush me. This would be the last place Zeus would expect Callie to be. He was probably still scouring the Caribbean. Zeus underestimated mortal emotions, having few of his own to reference, so he wouldn't think Callie would risk her life to see her father. Second, he wouldn't think we'd be dumb and ballsy enough to bring her here—and it *was* stupid and brash. If they didn't stay too long, they might get away with it. Or they might not.

The apartment was clear, not even one planted bug to monitor it. The god of truth can see these things. I texted Chase and waited. A minute later, Zephyrus appeared with Callie and Chase. Interesting pairing. Callie was the primary target and Chase the best protector, so it was a logical move. I just didn't think Archer would part from her for a moment. Zephyrus could only relocate about two people successfully. How he discovered his cargo limit is a terrible tale involving some poor mortals who were not whole after his little experiments, but that is a tale of little importance.

Callie was thin, but the tan she gained in the islands made her look healthier than she had been, glowing actually. Not seeing her for days made my longing for her more acute. How could she be so beautiful? Dark wavy hair as wild as her personality, tan skin that begged the Sun to touch it, adorably pouty lips, I wanted to—I had to stop thinking about her that way. When those mahogany eyes met mine with resentment and censure, my heart broke all over again. Oh yeah, she hated me.

Zephyrus disappeared and reappeared two more times. Next was Athena and Archer, followed by Archer's brothers. The silence was deafening. Archer glared at me, Callie too, while everyone else looked around awkwardly. Archer was haggard, as if Zeus had fileted him. Maybe he had. It was clear the guy needed some nectar badly.

THE IMMORTAL TRANSCRIPTS: SHUDDER

Himerus—technically my nephew in this dysfunctional family—whistled annoyingly, which merely amplified the tension. The anxious mood was upped by the negative mood-enhancing war god and his spawn.

Finally, Athena spoke up. "I'll be on my way now." She abruptly left the apartment.

What was going on? She was as antisocial as they come, but not even a "hello" or briefing? I understood her, and we were friends, but maybe she wanted to boot me out too.

"First thing's first. I broke my lease, but Aroha still rents this place. I can camp out here with Archer and Callie, but where can these two stay?" Chase forked his thumb toward Anteros and Himerus as if they were the baggage he and Aroha often discarded, and yet, he didn't even seem to notice or care he was in company with his wife's bastard child.

What a big happy little family. I wanted to puke. "With me," I offered unwillingly. "Once my son heals, they'd be glad—"

"He's alive?" Anteros and Himerus asked in unison. You'd swear they were related—although technically, they weren't at all by blood.

"Yes, and mending with Dionysus."

The two of them grinned and went on and on how they knew he had to be alive and how tough he was. I wasn't in the mood for the immature love entourage at the moment.

Thankfully, Chase shushed them as a proper father would. *Wow.*

"Zeus thinks he's dead. He had said so," Callie said in a clipped tone, not even looking at me.

"He'll have to come with us when we decide to leave. Zeus thinking he's dead will keep him alive, safe. We continue that lie." Chase decided.

I cracked my neck. I hated lies. This one was about my kid. I hoped I could keep up this new lying business.

"Where?" I asked.

No one answered. Of course, they didn't trust me.

"I have a right to know where my offspring will be taken."

Himerus, looking so much like his father with that cocky stance and clenched jaw, dared to challenge me: "You never cared, man, and now you do?"

I shouldn't have to explain myself, how I often mentally checked on my sons, how I never had the disposition to be a good father in person. "Chase, tell your child to heel."

Both of them ground their teeth trying to reign in the infamous Ares's temper.

Callie scoffed. "Seriously?"

I met her cutting glower. Powerful, sensual, and unavailable—not mine. I tried to hold her gaze, but she had found herself as of late. Ever since their engagement night, she got her airs and became more domineering rather than the sweet, innocent girl I'd met who had borne the weight of the world on her shoulders; she had been an Atlas but still tried to smile. Hardened, strong.

"After everything you've done, you are trying to put down the very people trying to protect me, protect your son, and for what? The *truth*?" That one was a sucker punch to my emotional gut. "And if you tell Archer to tell me to heel like some misogynistic god, I'll punch you in the face right now."

It was tempting. My anger at Callie clashed with other feelings about her. I loved a strong woman, but with Callie, I wanted to heal her, mold her back to life when she was down. This girl was different. I'd be a liar if I said it didn't turn me on. A woman with power was hot, one equal to me in power, the sexiest thing in the world. Only, Callie was no goddess, not quite my equal.

I put my hands up in mock surrender. I wasn't stupid enough to set Archer off when I had betrayed his trust already.

"These guys can stay here with you, Chase. Archer and I will stay in my room down the hall. I want to see my Dad."

Oh. Gods above and below. There was no saving me from this. "Um, the sleeping arrangements will work, but your dad isn't there. He's in the hospital."

Callie gasped. "What?"

Archer held her shoulders to bolster her, glaring at me. "Why didn't you tell us this when my dad texted you?"

"I just found out in the lobby when I ran into Raphael. Don't get mad at me!"

"Don't get mad at you?" Callie stepped forward. "Don't get mad at you? Lucien, you are the blindest, most self-centered person I know. You tried to destroy—"

"I had no choice!" I lashed out. "I didn't betray you because I didn't know if you were really there! It was my son's life on the line." My voice cracked. I took a deep breath. "It was my son or where I thought you were. What would you choose? I didn't know Zeus would still—"

"Lucien," Archer's gaze wasn't as angry as his wife's—*his* wife. It burned a hole in my heart.

THE IMMORTAL TRANSCRIPTS: SHUDDER

Did I detect a smirk on Anteros's face? Was he enjoying my unrequited love? I never understood him or love. He enjoyed it when some lovers were spurned but took revenge on some others. It was utterly messed up how we could pick and choose whom we helped. Anteros would not ease my pain.

Archer rubbed his neck uncomfortably. "We're not mad that you told Zeus where we were." All thoughts of my spurned love left me. "You had to do it. He's your son, and he almost died. We thought he had."

Because of them. No, why could I not be fair? Where was my truth? It was Zeus, his fault, all of it. At the same time, it was Archer and Callie who got my son into this. Zeus hinted Hymenaios had been involved. There is only one reason Archer would ask my son to marry them as well as having the human ceremony. He must've wanted a mock immortal marriage. So romantically idiotic.

"We're mad for how you withheld the truth, tried to break us up, and weren't supportive of us. We don't trust you anymore." What Archer said hurt because he was right.

I wanted to lash out and blame them, but I had been in the wrong too. "I understand." I let myself out. An apology was too much for me to bear. I hadn't been wrong to tell him about Callie's lineage. Archer had to have been told the truth about marrying Psyche's descendant. Hiding that kernel of knowledge from him was monumentally erroneous; my own interests in the breakup didn't matter. I trudged back to my apartment, bitter and resentful. It didn't help Chase asked me not to tell anyone they were in New York. They didn't trust me. How could I redeem myself? More importantly, did I want to?

The next morning, I was awakened by a text from Chase: **Safety in numbers, Lucien. We all need each other. I trust you.**

Groggy still, I read it over twice. I had to respond. I wanted to tell him he shouldn't trust me. I was hardly trusting myself about anything related to Callie, yet I wanted her alive more than any other fantasy in my head. I wanted my friends, my family back. The loneliness was overwhelming. I typed, **They don't. They don't even want me around.** It sounded so bratty and childish, but I sent it nonetheless.

They're at the hospital but should be home around noon. Go make peace, Phoebus.

The war god promoting peace was laughable, and he was being a jerk calling me by the name I loathed. He trusted me, but he was also asserting he was in charge. What did he really want? Immortal world domination? The thought instantly left me; he was different now. I hated how I couldn't quite glean the truth from texts and words. I needed the tone and body language as well. The digital world put me at a disadvantage.

I got out of bed and went for a jog. When I returned, my oracle had bagels and coffee for us. She gave me that quintessential maternal chiding look. Great. She was getting ready for a lecture. I didn't want to hear it but sat and spread some cream cheese across a bagel.

"Lucien." She sighed. "You are so unhappy."

"And?" I avoided her sympathetic eyes that were clouded with old age but could see more than other mortals, so much more.

"It won't be long until I pass on and your new oracle latches onto my spirit." This was worse than her lecturing me. I didn't know what to say. This oracle, I hadn't been very close to. In my youth, I had been close to them—too close—but falling out of love and then losing them every so many decades made me become accustomed, distanced, and desensitized to their deaths.

"Thank you for choosing to be of service to the gods," I told her.

She laughed and shook her head. "I'm not asking for a pat on the back. I want you to be okay."

"Why wouldn't I?"

She pressed her lips together, disappointed I didn't see something she must. I didn't want to ask. I had enough crappy things on my table. Some oracle's concern about a vision of hers was the last thing I needed. She would tell me if it were vital.

We ate in silence, and I went into my closet to see what things I had about. When making peace, you must bring a gift. When a god married, there were particular gifts we traditionally bestowed upon each other.

I nipped over to Dionysus and paid him back for the nectar whiskey that had saved my son's life, and my own, and picked up a few things. I spent a few hours with Hymenaios, who was much improved, sitting up, with a light fuzz of hair regrowing on his head. His anger at me had abated, and things were as they had been prior. I guess when you have a second chance at life after almost dying, you have to be thankful your father chose to save you—even if he had been duped.

Ten minutes after noon, I stood in front of Callie's apartment, my hands shaking as I knocked. I was inexplicably nervous, but it mattered greatly to have Archer and Callie forgive me. It took a minute for Archer to get to the door, and my angry thoughts turned to why. Did I catch them in the middle of newlywed bliss? A moment later, Archer opened the door, his expression wary. I'm sure mine was too.

"Who is it?" Callie asked, walking to the door. She stopped, her expression full of surprise. She crossed her arms with a tenacious but adorable scowl on her face.

Archer noted my gift, motioned me in, and closed and locked the door behind me. He joined in our silent standoff, his gaze darting back and forth between Callie and me, not quite sure what to do.

"I came to apologize and to drop this off." I lifted the basket.

Callie scoffed.

Archer took it from my hands and said, "Thank you."

"Really?" Her eyes rested on Archer, brows raised in challenge. My gods, Aroha's attitude was rubbing off on her.

"I can't stay mad forever, Callie."

"That's the thing, you actually could."

This would be harder than I thought. Callie was more obstinate than I'd bargained for. It was easy to see who would control their relationship if things continued in this fashion. I followed them farther into the apartment. Boxes were everywhere.

"Packing already?" It seemed premature to me.

"Callie's father won't leave the hospital. We don't know when we can come back. Aroha and Raphael will get things into storage for us later, but I wanted Callie to have some of the things she likes most with her." Archer placed the basket on the breakfast bar and sifted through the contents.

As he was inventorying them, I said, "Traditional fare but lots of extra nectar and some of my herbal remedies for Callie's fevers."

"Thank you." Things were stifled between us, way off. Archer was no longer my best friend, but he was trying to be civil.

It was time to face it head-on. Him being mad would be better than this weird pseudofriendship. "Look, I'm sorry for what I did, on your wedding day of all days. I should've told you after I visited Nice."

Archer didn't look at me when he spoke. "You should have. Nothing would've stopped our wedding, so I'm not mad about that. But you, of all people, lied to me—your best friend." The truth hurts; the mortal expression had validity.

"I've explained that. Something is changing our natures or what restricts us; Zeus's hold on us is weakening. I think it's her." I pointed at

Callie, who turned to me, her brow contracting in confusion. She had been pretending to ignore us and packed more, but she had been listening intently.

Archer met my gaze. The pain in his eyes made my stomach sour. "You said it felt like you had a choice and didn't have to blurt out the truth when she showed up in New York. A *choice*, Lucien."

Archer was right. I had chosen not to tell him, even when he asked. "I can't explain why because I can't understand it myself. First, I was shocked about the lying, and I didn't want to hurt you, thought I was protecting you. Someone had told me, via Iris, that I needed to withhold the truth. I have no clue who. Then Callie begged me not to tell you."

Archer's head whipped around to her.

Her anger turned to sheepishness. "I...I was afraid I'd lose you because of it. I know now I wouldn't have."

Archer didn't look pleased. "All of you were hiding things from me. I'm not some weak, sad fool. You keep forgetting: love makes me stronger." He alternated his gaze between us as he continued, "Neither of you will hide anything else from me, hear me?"

Callie nodded and turned away, quickly going back to the boxes. By Poseidon's trident, she was hiding something from him right now. Calling her out had its perks of making them fight, but they were married. She was his now. There was no point in stirring the pot when I was trying to garner her forgiveness, but I would root out her lie sooner or later.

"Understood," I said. The tinge of guilt was tiresome. I was pretending not to know Callie was lying, yet again. "For what it is worth, I'm on your side, the save-Callie-from-psycho-Zeus side."

Archer gave me the quick mortal bro-hug, with the handshake and back tap, and I knew I was forgiven. His trust, though, would take longer to regain.

Callie came over. "Protect me for how long? Until you turn on us?" Hades's helm, she was difficult!

"Callie." Archer's tone warned and groaned at the same time. He wanted her to stop but figured it was pointless.

"What? he *will*."

"You don't know that. Plus, you changed these visions of what happened to me," Archer pointed out. "Who's to say they won't alter again?"

A chill shot down my spine. She was seeing things again, but I didn't want to acknowledge there would be a future betrayal. I pushed the prophecy from my mind. It and her vision could not be related, surely. She must be referring to what I had done already. "I did betray you already to save Hymenaios."

"That wasn't a betrayal, Lucien. It was making a hard decision between people you care about that you should have never had to do. I'm glad your son survived; believing for a moment—days—someone died because of me was horrible." She sighed. "A betrayal is uncoerced, an action not prompted by someone else's life on the line."

"Have you seen it?" I demanded.

Archer and Callie exchanged a coded expression. "In a vision, someone said you had done it."

Archer's eyes commanded her to say no more. "Hey, Callie, look." He pointed to the items I had given them as a gift. Her eyes alighted on the jewelry, and she smiled.

"You're partially forgiven...for now," Callie said before she asked Archer to clasp on the necklace. I knew I wasn't. It was her pretending jewelry had swayed us into peace. She would watch me like a hawk, which was good. I didn't want to betray them nor pay some steep price for it. The prophecy weighed upon me more than ever.

CHAPTER 8
Athena

I didn't stay in New York after Zephyrus dropped us off. I didn't want to chat, be slowed down, and I had people to see. Family reunions were tedious and often ended in a fight, not that I would fight with the crew inside the New York penthouse apartment since they were my allies. I took a cursory glance at the girl, who did seem fatigued and ill. Maybe my wild hypothesis was wrong if she were sickly. When our eyes met, mine involuntarily darted away, and my hair stood on end. I withheld a shudder. Her face inexplicably unnerved me. I didn't have time to even take in her features, so I wasn't sure how that was possible.

I was out the door before I had to say anything more than announcing I was leaving. Chase would explain.

I sought out the closest bus station and bought a one-way ticket to Knoxville, Tennessee. It was a pitstop, but I was hoping my instincts and intuition would guide me where to go next. I was a go-by-the-gut goddess, an impulse rider, and it usually led me toward the path most suitable—but who knew what the right path was at the moment?

No intuitive hunches came during my ride, unfortunately; grasping at straws, I randomly chose the next leg of my journey. I sent a prayer of luck to Caerus for a favorable outcome, hoping he was on our side. Maybe Prometheus would've foreseen my travels and placed himself in my path. If this didn't work, I'd go to Proteus, the only god good at finding Prometheus—if Proteus still wanted to be involved in this family feud after being injured at what was now being called the Battle of Belize City.

Buses were a tedious mortal way of travel, wasting lots of time, but I no longer trusted my father or the skies he controlled, and I had no clue where to go. This would be safer, although by far circuitous. It would take time for my intuition to guide me. I spent my time researching on my stealth phone, thankful I took the precaution to cover my tracks best I could. I gave up, finding nothing new on Callie's mother or her accident. It seemed so limiting, making me wonder if someone tampered with the records. Inexplicably, her mother's car had gone off the road into a reservoir. The autopsy revealed a broken neck, the cause of death being drowning. The newspaper didn't bother to publish a picture; the husband was unable to comment and left the country shortly later. Strange, but not really. Mortals died all the time in random ways, and distancing oneself from trauma was something that extended to us gods as well.

I tried to read a book instead, but even then, I found myself easily distracted. Next, I slept.

I arrived in Knoxville about eighteen hours after we left New York. I was an hour from my destination, Gatlinburg, so I called an Uber. I put in earbuds and listened to music to avoid talking to the persistent driver, who seemed to hate silence. I know it was her job and was just small talk, but I was too exhausted to focus on social pleasantries that I had to actively think about so I wouldn't say something wrong. When I arrived, I got a room at a motel and paid with cash. Next, I hiked the many trails until I was far removed from mortals and halfway up the base of the Smoky Mountains' wilderness when I took out my phone. I opened my compass app and changed my course a couple of times until I came across a tiny cabin in a small meadow full of beautiful spring flowers. The fact they were still alive in the heat of the dwindling summer told me I was at the right place.

I knew I'd find them here. Every summer, Demeter and Persephone spent August in the Appalachian Mountains, a retreat of sorts, and time together before she would have to return to the Underworld. Persephone sat on the porch steps, not seeing me yet. Her head was bent low, appearing forlorn. The myths would say she lamented leaving her mother. I knew better. She missed her husband. The poets always portrayed Hades as the villain, stealing away Demeter's daughter—and Demeter herself is responsible for this particular rumor.

The truth? Persephone had met Hades when he had found a way around Zeus's barrier that had imprisoned him in the Underworld. It had been the helm of darkness. Invisibility allowed him to slip through, and secretly Hades wooed her. Zeus destroyed the helm, of course. Somehow, Hades found another way to see her—I'm still perplexed about it to this day, which is annoying for someone who prides herself on knowing more than most others. Back in the Olympian days, Persephone agreed to go with him into the Underworld. She chose to eat those pomegranate seeds but could not be forever parted from seeing the sun, from bringing spring—not even for true love. It was a win I had over Aphrodite: logic beat love. Because she kept her wits about her, Persephone came and went as she pleased since there are always springs and summer between the hemispheres. Not only her love for Hades made her return to the Underworld, but also there was a price to pay after eating food while there. If she stayed away too long, the pomegranate seeds poisoned her, making her ill. She needed Hades to keep her well during those times. Ridiculous romantics and their immortal marriages.

Demeter only saw her daughter every August. To this day, for one month, Persephone gave in to her helicopter parent.

Persephone looked up, her doe eyes taking me in for a moment until she broke into a smile. Always beautiful but never vain about it, she was a goddess everyone loved. "Athena." She stood and bounded toward me. She slammed right into me and gave me a bear hug.

Never reading people right, my arms hung limp at my side before I awkwardly patted her until she let me go. I was absolutely uncomfortable with her squishing her body against mine.

In her hand was a bouquet of flowers, wilted. I stared at them, wondering what was amiss. "Killing flowers?"

She shrugged. "He loves me; he loves me not." It was a game she had played as a child, blooming flowers, then wilting them. Persephone had the power to create and foster life or take it away—for plants, that is. Mortals, immortal—and I believed animal life—eluded her. Over thousands of years, she could not bear a child. My educated guess was that full-term pregnancy was an impossibility in the Underworld, a place she never could leave long enough.

Her smile sank as if she understood my thoughts. "Zeus sent you?" It was accusatory.

"No." I left it simple. I wasn't sure what she knew and whose side she was on, but given the opportunity, I could easily surmise which one she'd choose. I had to test the waters carefully, though, and I needed to get straight to the point while Demeter was off somewhere becoming one with nature. "What gossip has your mother told you?"

"You're here about the Eros situation? Mother told me all, painting him in the worst light, but I find it utterly romantic. Like Hades and me, forbidden love triumphing." She sighed dreamily, thinking loving thoughts about her husband. "There was a time I fancied Eros, but that was long ago."

THE IMMORTAL TRANSCRIPTS: SHUDDER

I laughed, remembering those days. Eros and Persephone were around the same age, and she would trail after him like a lovesick puppy. I don't think he ever even noticed. "Eros is thick in it," I told her.

"It isn't only him. Mother said the Oceanids are playing up, breaking the surface more than ever, flashing their little "tails" at mortals. Mnemosyne is working overtime to wipe their minds of it. Death is—well, she took on a job when it was utterly backed up... It'll take ages for her and Hades to catch up. It doesn't help the death they chose is graceful and caring in the process, so it takes way more time than Thanatos's cutthroat method."

"Isn't that good?"

"Of course. Thanatos..." she shivered and pinched her eyes shut momentarily. "He is not missed. Hypnos might miss his brother somewhat. Hard to tell with him as he's always half asleep. Oh, and we got Lena out of the deal. I kind of hate her, to be honest—a bit of a nasty streak in her—but at least she's company, I guess. It's just, all she does is mope, whine, and curse Eros. She swears revenge one day. She chose eternity over a mortal life; I don't get it. I insisted she let it lie, and she kept being a miserable bore, so I punished her by leaving her behind when I surfaced to meet Mother. Lena acts like she's in prison, but like me, she is not bound to the Underworld by Zeus's power. She has Proteus's blood, Titan, not Olympian. It's like she wants to stay there and suffer so she can complain. Anyway, we got off topic."

That tends to happen frequently to me, but she was kind enough not to blame me for it. "I have a feeling Zeus will not stop until Eros's wife is dead."

Persephone gave me a pointed look. "So, you came to make sure my husband doesn't order her soul taken?"

"More than that. I think things will get worse. There already are sides forming. I thought—"

"The god of death would choose your side?" Persephone snapped. "What if he wants to simply stay out of it?"

"I understand, Kore." I used her childhood nickname. It softened her expression. "If I were married, I would want to keep my husband safe. That is all Eros is trying to do. What is more important is Zeus's overreach of power. He cannot dictate whom one can love!"

"Thena, calm down."

As the rational goddess, it was strange for me to lose hold of my emotions. I noted my fists were balled up, and I had raised my voice at her. Very odd of me. I took a deep calming breath.

Her probing eyes bore into mine, making me look away. "Did Zeus do this to you as well or something?" Her question felt like she'd stabbed my heart; the pain was equally acute. I'd know. It happened once to me during the Crusades.

I took another deep breath. "I'm just angry at his abuse of power in many situations. I am the goddess of justice." I deflected. There was no way I was going to dredge up those distant, buried memories. Still, some things leaked through: *stolen kisses in the shadowy corridors in Mount Olympus, his tan hand in mine, fingers woven together, those dark eyes full of love and desire*—I shut it down, unable to focus on what we were talking about a moment ago.

Persephone guided me back. "Athena, what is it you want from me?" She was always one of those immortals who read others well, and she knew my attention span was always in a million directions, a computer with too many browser tabs open.

"I want to talk to your husband. There will be a war, and I know your husband would jump at the chance to be free from Zeus's binds. What if he could break through the barrier, stay up here?"

Persephone's face shifted quickly through too many emotions to read. "Don't give me false hope, Thena!"

"You might be able to have a—"

"Stop!" she thundered. She turned away, about to storm inside. "I will not give my husband hope when time has already proven it is hopeless."

"I'm not trying to give false hope, merely a shred of it and some motivation. Without Zeus, would there be the barriers he imposed?"

"War?" Persephone repeated, now calmer but shocked. "Against Zeus? We have never attempted it because it is impossible. The Titans, a prime example."

"I think Zeus is losing power and more than those little blips there had been before. It is lasting and getting much worse."

"It's like Helen and Paris, the face that launched a thousand ships." At least she was back to her foolish romantic notions and no longer angry—nor was she listening to what I was saying though.

How was Helen similar to Callie? "Helen cheated on her husband," I returned.

"Whom she was forced to marry against her will. You just don't get it, and you never will, being the maiden goddess. When you love someone so much that you give yourself over—mind, body, and soul—it's worth a war to preserve your connection."

I wasn't going to correct her about my sex life now that I had her almost on my side. "Precisely, Helen and Paris then, Eros and Callie, the same. Let us hope for a much better ending, though."

Persephone nodded, took my hand in hers, and closed her eyes. The wind whipped, and clouds came in. All around us went dark, only around our close vicinity. The sun shined, but we were in some little bubble of darkness, so dark I could hardly make out Persephone right next to me. I had never seen anything like it. It did not scare me, but I was full of excited wonderment of something new after years of inactivity.

"Don't move," Persephone said, her voice strained. "I've spent thousands of years trying to perfect this. Once he connects, he can take over since he is much better at it."

"At what?" I whispered.

"Shadow linking."

Hades. She was trying to link to the Underworld. I never thought it possible, but the darkness was encroaching, and he was coined the "god of darkness."

"Darling? Are you all right?" Hades's voice was everywhere as if every particle of the shadow enveloping us spoke. His voice was rough and rumbled, but I recognized its cadence despite the distortion.

"I'm fine." Her hand relaxed in mine. "Athena needed to speak to you."

"Athena! How are you?" He sounded so excited. My poor uncle was starved for living company, visitors, or seeing his family.

"I will try to visit soon to catch up, Uncle, but this is important. I think we might be headed to war... against Zeus."

The shadow was silent.

"Hades?" I prompted.

A shaky laugh replied. "I've waited my entire life for this moment. I'm on your side. Whatever you need. Consider all my people in." I wondered if Hypnos would obey that command. I also wondered how much he could do from his prison if we couldn't spring him.

"Thank you. I have some alliances to take care of, and then I'll visit with particulars."

"Deal." He turned his attention to his wife. "Persephone, how much longer must you stay up there?"

I was uncomfortable being in the middle of a private moment, but she had told me not to move. I wasn't sure what would happen if I did.

"Just another week, my darling. I'll be back for a few weeks before I head off to the southern hemisphere."

He sighed. "I'm counting the days."

"Me too."

The shadow dissipated, leaving us in the blinding light of day. I blinked, my eyes taking a second to adjust. Persephone was forlorn. "Please don't mention the shadow linking to Mother. She doesn't know and would be furious." Demeter wouldn't be angry but jealous, for she coveted the time with her daughter and hated Hades.

"Don't tell her anything about this war either. We don't know what side she would choose."

Persephone opened her mouth but then shut it. She nodded. Her mother's inclination would be to side with Zeus, because he was her brother, but would she go against her daughter?

"Shadow linking?" I raised my brows. I had been too shocked and focused on business to ask questions, also afraid of disrupting what was going on.

"It was how he courted me after Zeus destroyed his helm of darkness. Hades realized he could travel—spiritually—through darkness. Every night he would visit me to talk..." She paused and blushed, making me wonder whether he could do more than talk in shadow form. "Anyway, it wasn't enough, so I agreed to marry him. He broke the barrier and swept me off my feet."

"How did he break it?"

Persephone shrugged. "One of those blips in power you talked about. The first time we ever noticed one, remember?"

My stomach churned. I did remember. It made no sense, and yet the timing did. When Persephone left, I was away from Olympus suffering my own problems... I needed to find Prometheus. He had to make sense of all this for me.

As if speaking of her mother made her appear, Demeter—overbearing and proud, goddess of harvest and agriculture—came cresting over the hill with a companion. When they were closer, I saw her friend's playful gait and his dark unruly hair. It was Aristaeus, one of Apollo's sons.

He noticed me and came running up. "Athena!" he cried out, hugging me, and then peered down at the flower in his hand. He looked at me expectantly, his innocent green eyes filled with unaffected joy.

THE IMMORTAL TRANSCRIPTS: SHUDDER

I kindly slipped out of his arms, hiding my discomfort. "Is that for me?"

He nodded, flopping his hair about, and I took the flower. On it, a bee was collecting pollen before it flew off. "Bye, friend," he called after it, waving.

Aristaeus, the beekeeping god, was raised by Leto and then Demeter after his mother died. Demeter wanted to make the demigod immortal, but the transitional fever affected Aristaeus's brain. Not even Dionysus could fully repair the damage, nor could Apollo fully heal his own child. Aristaeus was eternally childlike. Some called him ill-fated, but part of me wondered how nice it would be to live in such innocent bliss. Nothing upset him but dying bees, and due to these times, the god had his work cut out for him with their endangerment.

"Ari, wait for me," Demeter chided in a maternal tone as she caught up. Demeter—I had to give her credit—protected him from the evils of the world, mainly mortals who had no room for those with differences.

"Sorry, but look! It's Athena."

"I see her, dear." Demeter tried to smooth his cowlick down, but it popped right back up. She scrutinized me next. She had these cold dark eyes that bore through you, and her hair was the color of wheat. Daughter and mother shared no similar features except the dark eyes. "What are you doing here?"

"She's heading to the Underworld soon and wanted to know if I had any messages for Hades." I was glad Persephone was so practiced in lying to her mother.

Demeter scoffed at his name. "Are you staying for dinner?" Her tone told me I was not wanted, so I was unsure why she'd bothered to ask. Demeter had a love for nature alone and only a few gods. I was not one. War hurt nature, even if inadvertently, so I was disliked by proxy.

"No. I was in the area and stopped by before I headed to Hades."

She scoffed again.

"Will you see my dad?" Aristaeus asked.

I was not following his logic because Apollo was in New York. "Uh, eventually."

"Tell him I said hi, and I love him. I named my latest hives after him. Apollo one, and two...all the way to thirteen now."

"Will do." I sure hoped his latest hive didn't suffer the same stressful fate of the space shuttle of the same name. Apollo loved to brag about his spaceships as if they were really his. The Titan goddess Asteria had helped mortals with the whole space travel thing, while Apollo did nothing but relish in having shuttles named after him, as he would these hives.

Demeter's angry face blamed me for a son's love for his absentee father. Jealousy was definitely her godly fault. She had raised Aristaeus, only to be usurped in his heart by his deadbeat father. It was kind of fair since her jealousy was out of hand, yet not at all just for Aristaeus, an innocent soul who deserved to be loved and cared for by his father.

I left, waving to them all. As I walked downhill through the fields, I texted Apollo his son's message. I didn't get a response. Not that I expected one. Apollo never wished to talk about his faults or his inability to create lasting relationships with others or his offspring. So, I fired off another text telling him what I thought about him not getting over his inability to be a real parent. He'd see it as hypocritical since I had no children. What he didn't know, what most gods never knew, was how I desperately wanted to be a mother, precisely as much as Persephone. It angered me when those who could, abused the position. I never would if I were blessed with a child one day...again.

I headed southeast, hoping to find Prometheus before I hit the tip of Florida. If I didn't, what would I do next? Continue to Belize?

Come on, Theus, see me.

CHAPTER 9

Callie

So far, I'd have to say, my marriage wasn't going so well, not that it was Archer's fault at all (as he was divine). The many forces around us—the gods who wielded such powers—made our new life together difficult. There was a looming cloud over us (Zeus). Then there was the elephant in the room: death. My father was to die, and so might I, if Zeus had his way. I really had to ask Archer about this immortal marriage thing. It was obviously more than what he had told me about being soul mates, but pressing him might be a bad idea because questions were reciprocal. I was hiding things too. Not being open to each other was obviously a bad thing. Once we were safe and settled, we'd hash it out (when our stress levels weren't so epic).

When we got to New York, it was too late to visit my father before morning. It was a restless night, so I rose early, showered, and changed before Archer had gotten up. Then, as soon as visiting hours were open, we visited Dad at the hospital. He looked so frail and thin, I wanted to break down and cry. That would do him no good. He needed to see me strong, happy, and unafraid. We didn't stay long, because he was sleeping most of his days away, so we spent the rest of the day packing. Keeping me busy distracted my maudlin thoughts away (likely Archer's ulterior motive).

The next day, as soon as we entered the hospital, I could sense her. Death. I knew yesterday Dad wouldn't make it more than a few days. Now, I was worried I might be too late. I hurried, trying desperately not to run, and the way Archer tugged my arm to slow me down with a puzzled look on his face told me he found something off with me. I did not want to talk about that. I needed to see my dad.

We entered the room to see Raphael reading a magazine. Dad was asleep. Raphael went to wake him.

"Let him sleep," I said.

"He asked me to wake him as soon as you arrived." Raphael gently touched my father's shoulder and whispered in his ear.

Dad opened his eyes and blinked several times until his eyes focused on me. He turned his head slowly. I hated seeing him like this: a man with a brilliant mind whose body gave up on him. He pulled off his oxygen mask. His face was sallow with blotchy red patches. Worse than yesterday (a million times worse).

Raphael put the cannula in dad's nose so he'd still get some oxygen to breathe. The way his chest rose and fell in short breaths showed his struggle. "Callista." He smiled, eyes full of joy, excited to see me just as he had been yesterday.

Raphael exited so Archer would be able to join me, since visitors were limited to two.

"Hey, Dad." I sat next to his bed and took his hand in mine.

"You are glowing."

"You say that every day." I rolled my eyes at him.

"Because it's true." It took effort for him to speak. "You're happy. It makes me comfortable, knowing that as I leave this world."

"Dad, don't..."

Archer entered and stood behind me, resting his hand on my shoulder, and gave me a reassuring squeeze.

"Ignoring the fact I'm dying is not going to stop it. I know..." He struggled for breath, and his lips were turning blue.

Archer was on the other side of the bed suddenly, putting the oxygen mask on my father's face. Dad took in a couple of breaths, and then Archer tentatively removed it.

"...I won't make it through the night."

"Dad..." I wanted to protest but couldn't. He was right, and any words I could express got choked up in my throat. My eyes stung. Death was here. This would be the last time I'd ever see him.

"Let me speak before I can't. There are things I needed to tell you—not just legal or financial things, because Raphael will help you through all that—but it's about your mother."

Now, this piqued my interest. He never talked about Mom. Archer put the oxygen back on him. Dad was smiling, so happy, even though he was suffering. It was probably all the oxygen he was inhaling, but it was nice to know his last moments would be happy, and I would be with him.

When Archer removed it, Dad continued. "I knew, in the end, it would be difficult to speak. I can't do the story justice, but I wrote you a letter. It is in *the* box in my closet. The key is in my safe. The code is your birthday." He struggled for breath. Archer helped him again with the mask.

"But..." I needed to know about my mother. I didn't want to wait.

"I don't have the energy." His voice was muffled by the mask.

"Dad," I whimpered. I could feel it too. Death was closer. He neither had energy nor time.

"Off," my dad said.

Archer obeyed, taking the mask off. He backed away from the bed, leaning against the wall, his eyes not meeting mine, his hands pressed behind his back to stop the urge to help my father.

Dad was asking to die. "What is Death like?"

I couldn't form words but started choking on sobs.

"Everything you could ask for," Archer said quietly. "Warm, welcoming, caring."

Dad closed his eyes, smiling. "Good."

"Dad," I cried. "I don't want to lose you!" I was grasping his hand tight as if I could tether him to my world, so he would not be some place out of my reach.

He opened his eyes and met my gaze, but his image blurred through my tears. "Callista. I am so tired. I saw you grow up, get married. I had a wonderful life. I completed my lifelong goal to find the gods."

He struggled to breathe, his lips now purple. My fingers longed to put the oxygen mask back on him, but that was selfish of me.

"You will be fine. I brought you home." He was staring off. I'm not sure what he was saying, but I think he was beginning to hallucinate or his mind was shutting down. "Ellen..." he breathed out my mother's name.

"Dad, I love you," I said quickly, hoping he could still hear me.

Without needing to turn around, I knew she was there. Death (the one I had chosen). She came into my peripheral view, her face solemn, her eyes reflecting my own pain. "It is time. Let go. Let me ease his suffering."

"I can't."

"Callie," Archer begged, coming forward to pry my hands off my father's. I refused, and he seemed confused for a moment. "His body is done, and now he is trapped, unless you let go."

I forced myself to look at my father. His chest did not rise and fall, his eyes were closed. "He's just sleeping." I knew it was a desperate lie. "He'll wake up now. You'll see."

The flatlines on the monitor's screen mocked me.

"Callie," Archer's voice cracked.

I met his gaze. His eyes were swimming. Immortal marriage. I could feel how torn he was watching my pain, just as my agony was shared with him. I let go of Dad, and Archer pulled me in tightly. I buried my face into his chest and let go. I didn't want to watch Death take my father.

I whispered, "Get me out of here."

A split second later, we were in the hallway.

"She's burning up. We have to get her out of here now," Archer said to someone.

My face was still buried against Archer's chest, and I didn't want to come out. There was more talking. Chase's voice, but I couldn't register his words. Archer led me out of the hospital and to a car. I closed my eyes, wishing Death had taken me too.

When I awoke, I was in a dark room. Archer was sitting in a chair by the bed I was lying in—my bed in my room. He sighed.

"Why am I in bed?"

"You were out for two days."

"What?" I sat up quickly.

"Take it easy, Callie. Your fever kept you out of it. Lucien had to sleep on the couch out there so he could bring your temperature down every couple of hours."

"My Dad. The memorial?"

"Raphael has taken care of it all. Your father had left Raphael in charge of it, legally speaking, so I couldn't stop it."

"Stop what?"

Archer's face was lined with sorrow; he met my gaze, bracing himself for my upcoming reaction. "He's been cremated."

I swallowed hard, unable to process the fact Dad was gone. I would never see his face again.

"Did Raphael explain my father's financial things and his business and all that?"

"Ye-es." Archer wondered where I was headed. "I can explain it to you later, but you have a lawyer carrying out your father's wishes until you decide what you want to do."

"Good. Fire Raphael. Give him a good severance package."

"Let's just get through the next few days first. Now is not the time to make big decisions."

"He cremated my father without my permission!"

"Did you really want to see him again like that? It was your father's wish."

THE IMMORTAL TRANSCRIPTS: SHUDDER

"I don't care!" I was being irrational, but I had to lash out to rid myself of this rage against the world, against Zeus, and against my dad for leaving me.

"Callie, Raphael is a mortal who knows about us. He is leverage Zeus could use against you. You told me once he was like part of your family."

I nodded. (Ugh, why did Archer have to be right?)

"Hello?" Aroha popped her head in. "You're awake. Archer, your dad needs to talk to you about the travel plans."

"You're back?" I asked her.

Archer left, and Aroha came and sat on the bed. "Yes. I'm sorry for your loss. I wish I had been here for you. Still, enough of this going unconscious and fever business. Archer was a mess. Never left your bedside."

In typical Aroha fashion, the moment she said something sweet, she moved to scolding.

"Sorry."

She surprised me by putting an arm around me and leaning her head on mine in a maternal gesture. "Did Archer ever tell you about his other siblings?"

I nodded. Would she tell me more about Archer's deceased ones?

"Chase and I had four children together, Archer being the eldest. After him, we had two identical twin boys—Deimos and Phobos—followed by my long-desired daughter, Harmonia." The way she said her daughter's name was mixed with pride and sorrow. She took a moment to collect her thoughts, and it made me realize that over her extensive life, she rarely talked about this to anyone. "They died in the Battle of Thermopylae."

Archer had only told me a little about them.

"The twins were favorites of Chase's, being instillers of horror and fear, and Harmonia was my everything—you see, Archer was already grown up and out of the house when they were born. Harmonia was a peace bringer. She was killed trying to force peace and save her brothers. The mortals were onto gods back then and burned them."

I had no idea what to say to her. I had seen the result of a god die from fire, one of the only ways they could die.

"I tell you this, Callie, so you know that even we immortals are susceptible to death. We know the pain of losing someone dear. It will take you time to be able to talk about it, but when you are, I'm here to listen."

I asked her the question burning inside of me: "Will it ever go away, the pain?"

Aroha pulled her head away and met my gaze. Her lips were firmly set, and she squeezed my shoulder. "It lessens from an acute pain to a dull ache, but it never goes away." She sighed. "Anyway, if you are blessed to live as long as I have, people sometimes replace the hole left in your heart—if only momentarily. You'll have to be my daughter now, if you'll have me as a mother."

I was rendered speechless by her honest and kind words. I had lost my mother long ago and now my father; she wanted to ease both our grief by being a mother to me. I nodded, and she hugged me.

Archer opened the door, interrupting the moment, but it was all too much to handle, so I was thankful for that. Aroha left quickly, giving us space with that annoying mom-knowing look. I wasn't used to this, but it was comforting all the same.

"We brought you here, but now I'm thinking you might be more comfortable at my place."

"No, I have to face it. I have to pack all this up. For all my dad's things to be taken or destroyed..." I took a deep breath. "I'm not ready, but I have to be." More importantly, I had to see what was inside the locked box, my mother's things and the letter about her my father had promised.

"I will be by your side, always."

"I know." I stole a few kisses, then felt guilty for feeling happy in his arms and pulled away.

Archer didn't meet my gaze, so something was up.

"What?" I asked with trepidation.

"Raphael tentatively scheduled the memorial service tomorrow, but the invites did say it would be postponed if you were not well."

I took a deep breath, "Yes. I have to do this so we can leave. My dad wanted my safety foremost." Past tense. He was gone. I knew all of this pain was worth nothing if Zeus killed me. I had to survive.

"You are so strong, so brave." He kissed me. That's when I noticed he held something in his hand.

"What's that?"

Archer stared at his hand as if he'd forgotten about it. He opened his hand to reveal Persephone's box. "Oh, I wanted to know what to do with your father's artifacts. I'm putting them in storage, as you asked, but wasn't sure if you wanted to even keep this."

"Why wouldn't I?" It was the one thing that brought Archer back to me (morbid, yes, since it put me into a comma, but still).

THE IMMORTAL TRANSCRIPTS: SHUDDER

"Yeah, it is dangerous, but I see you are as sentimental as I am about it. I resented this thing for so long, but now..."

"It brought us back together."

"Yes." His eyes locked on mine, and so many emotions flickered in their blue luminescence. "We'll need to keep it safe. Locked up."

I pulled him to me and kissed him, not wanting to talk practical. I let myself get lost in those kisses and the comfort of his touch because I needed to feel something other than loss or pain.

The next morning, all the blissful emotions of last night were gone. I was numb, almost catatonic. Archer got me up, walked me into the bathroom, and helped me into the shower. After I got out, Aroha dressed me and did my hair and makeup. It was odd—similar to my wedding day prep, without the happy, nervous jitters.

As we all congregated in the living room—dressed in black—Archer whispered, "We have a visitor, but if you're not up to seeing her..."

My mind tried to process. I surveyed the room and saw no one outside of our family. It was Archer's family, Lucien, and Raphael. How had I blamed him for following my dad's wishes? His dark eyes met mine and darted away. I nodded at Archer to let the guest in and rushed over to Raphael to hug him. When we parted, his eyes were glistening. He loved me as a daughter, and he'd loved my father as a brother. He *was* family.

I wiped my tears away and momentarily worried I'd smudged the makeup Aroha had plastered on me but realized it was waterproof. When I turned around, I came face-to-face with Linda. Her eyes swam with tears, and before I knew it, she threw her arms around me in a crushing hug.

"I'm so sorry!" She rubbed my back, which was comforting, but her apology after our distance shocked me. She pulled away and looked around at our company. Linda blushed but pushed on, "I'm sorry for more than that. I'm sorry for my jealousy. When I found out from Dan that Archer was alive, I came here to apologize, but you were already married and on your honeymoon. I'm so happy for you. Seeing how bad you were doing without him—this was the best thing I ever could've hoped for you."

I thought she might swoon and almost wanted to tell her how bad the honeymoon went toward the end of it to knock her giddiness down a notch (I refrained). As much as I liked Linda, and she had been my only real friend in New York outside my Olympian family, she was still an outsider who could never know these godly secrets.

"I've, uh...dunno what do you call it? 'Broke up' with Emily? Ditched her? The way she reacted to the news of Archer being alive and you two marrying? Well, maybe I was slow on realizing what she was truly like—since she was always nice to me—but she was...just horrific."

I didn't know what to say, so I said, "Thank you. We are heading to the memorial service soon if you want to come. If not..." I didn't know the plan.

Raphael led Linda away and told her the place and time for the wake luncheon. Archer bolstered me, kissing my forehead. It gave me strength. Linda left, promising to come to the luncheon. Too bad I had to leave town and go off the grid. I really had valued her friendship before Lucien ruined it with his unrequited feelings for me while he'd dated her.

I braced myself for the hardest day of my life. Surely, with literal gods behind me, I could do this. I took a deep breath and prayed to Oizys, goddess of grief, to spare me from all those horrid feelings that accompany a loved one's death. (Thank you, Dad, for this knowledge of gods, which will forever help me).

CHAPTER 10

Archer

After I got dressed and tamed my hair, I inventoried the piles of boxes Callie and I had packed. As soon as we had arrived, when I mentioned putting things into storage to keep her busy, she had gone on a packing frenzy. It had kept her mind off her grief. I had packed all her father's things for her, except a small chest she had wanted set aside, and there was a huge pile headed to storage until she decided what to do with them. We had a modest pile to ship with us, breaking my father's cardinal one-box rule. There was also a massive pile Callie wasn't sure about. Part of her wanted to keep everything so, one day, when we settled down, we would have a home ready; the other part of her wanted to toss it and never look back. I texted Raphael to get a bigger storage unit. These were decisions she shouldn't have to make right now, so we'd keep everything and figure it out later.

I couldn't delay any longer, numbly staring at boxes. It was time. I went to Callie's bedroom and tapped lightly on the door. The door swung open slightly. She was sitting on the bed, wearing an elegant black dress and light blue cardigan, her hair atop her head. One hand was squeezing the pendants on her necklace, and the other was holding an opened letter. Her eyes were round in shock.

"What are you reading?" I asked. The chest she'd wanted to come with us was on her bed.

Startled, she quickly folded it up. "Just a letter...from my dad."

I expected her to tell me what it said, but she put the letter back in the envelope instead, her hands shaking. It was *the* letter Dr. Syches had left her.

I could not press her to confide in me while she was so distraught. Instead, I said, "It's time."

She nodded.

I pulled her into my arms. "I won't leave your side." I kissed her. It was the only way I knew how to soothe her, because there was nothing I could do or say to make her feel better. After Linda left, Callie had retreated to her room. The lighter mood she had from Linda's apology was gone, likely due to whatever was in that letter.

I led her through the motions of the memorial service. She stayed strong, only crying when Raphael struggled through a speech her father had written ahead of time. After the service, we went to a late luncheon at the Greek restaurant where Callie and I had our first date. It had been a favorite of her father's too.

As we walked in, I whispered. "This is where I found out you were the girl who found Olympus and stole a god's heart."

She smiled. "More like I fell into it and your life."

"Never letting you go." I could not help but kiss her.

"Come on, Cupid, let's get this over with," she teased.

She could call me any name she'd wanted if it lessened her pain.

We sat down. Chase and Aroha followed. As soon as they were seated, a voice cleared. "I'm sorry, this table is reserved for family." A middle-aged, thin-lipped woman with frizzy red hair and pale skin gave Aroha, Chase, and me a haughty glare.

"Oh, hi, Aunt Judith," Callie said. "Didn't Dad tell you? I got married."

When the only response Callie received was a gaping mouth, she showed her aunt the rings on her finger as proof.

"Married?" Her high-pitched volume turned some heads.

Great. She was one of those attention-seeking mortals who turned everything about someone else into her own drama.

"I thought he was joking. You're only eighteen!"

I was irked by anyone questioning love, particularly my own brand of it. Part of me wanted to lash out at her.

"And now alone in this world, except for him. Archer *is* my family."

My anger slipped away into pride—and a lot of lust, to be honest—at my wife's power and wit. Why was it so hot to see a beautiful woman put a self-righteous ignoramus in her place?

"There's plenty of room for all family at this table, don't you think?" There went my dad, being all creepily peace-hungry—if that was a thing.

The aunt's two sons were hitting each other; one was screaming and tugging the back of her dress, but she didn't seem to notice. Instead, she carefully inspected Chase, Aroha, and me, searching for faults. On gods, you don't find them outwardly. Our flaws are on the inside.

The aunt challenged Chase, "You are related to Callie how?"

Damn it. We were too busy dealing with Dr. Syches's death to think about a cover for nosy aunts.

THE IMMORTAL TRANSCRIPTS: SHUDDER

"Well, Aroha is Archer's sister, and I'm Aroha's fiancé, Chase Gideon. Pleased to meet you." Dad flashed her a dimpled grin, making her blink rapidly.

"I see the resemblance," she said about Ma and me, although she still stared at my dad. Then she shook her head as if dissipating his spell and asked, "So, Archer, what family are you from?"

Great, a snob as well. Without parents in the influential Upper East Side social circles, the Ambroses were no one. "The Ambroses. My parents are abroad too often to solidify connections in New York."

The screams of the boys started to gain attention. She barked at them to go to the kids' table, although we never assigned any seating as this woman was trying to instill. In fact, there was only one other kid present who belonged to some business associate of Dr. Syches's, the man who ran the antique furniture part of the company. He had offered to buy Callie out of that part of the business, but it wasn't something she could face yet.

The boys ran off, and Callie's aunt chased after them. We thought we had gotten rid of her, but after reprimanding and depositing two sullen boys at the "kids" table, she returned with her husband. He was a tall, broad man but could no longer pretend his tubby frame was muscle, nor could he pretend he had hair, although he tried with a greasy combover. They sat directly across from us. Callie introduced him as "Uncle Tony," only after her aunt prompted and scolded her for lack of manners.

As the server got drink orders, the uncle inspected each of us. His eyes moved to my watch, Callie's ring, Aroha's earrings, Chase's cufflinks. Money. That was this man's deal. He wanted to see how wealthy we were, solely judging off appearance. I inspected back. The cut of his suit was not tailor-made, and he had no adornments such as a watch or cufflinks. I understood him without needing to enter his mind: he obsessed over money because he wanted more of it or felt he didn't have enough.

The man's eyes moved over to Callie. "So, Callie, whatcha gonna do now?"

I suppressed the urge to punch him. Who'd ask a question like that directly after a memorial service?

"NYU or somethin'?"

"Oh, uh...I haven't really thought about it." She spoke softly, staring down at the table.

I took her hand in mine, squeezing it reassuringly. "Callie and I are going abroad for a while, an extended honeymoon of sorts."

"You don't say." Her uncle's brows rose, and his eyes went wide.

The aunt frowned. "I don't think that's a good idea. The school year starts soon. It's not too late to enroll. You should go to college. It was what your father had wanted."

"Nah, have your fun, seeing other cultures if you can afford it. College is a waste of time and money. You should put your money to good use, invest it. Say, Callie, you ever think about buying into a business? Mine is doing well, and I could use a partner to—you know—expand it. With more dough, I could open another store or—"

I was up so fast, the chair fell to the floor behind me, making the man jump. I clenched my fists to stop myself from tearing her uncouth uncle to pieces. "This isn't the time and place to speak of Callie's inheritance. In fact, I can't think of any time it would be appropriate."

"Oho, I'm sorry." The man laughed, hands up in mocking surrender.

Callie's eyes narrowed as they met her uncle's.

"Got yourself a little boss man here, Callie, don't you?" He made a scoffing noise before directing his attention to me. "What are you, kid, eighteen?"

I bit down my retort about exactly how old I was and tried to douse my temper. Aroha halfheartedly told me to sit down. Chase busied himself righting my chair and remained standing as well; he had my back on this. Callie was digging her nails into my sleeve; a suppressed smile was fighting to come out. Good. She was more amused than upset about me arguing with him.

"He's right, dear," the aunt finally broke the awkward silence. "Discussing money at a wake luncheon is tactless." She smiled at me as if she did me some huge favor. "Callie's future is what is important here. School, *then* family."

"She can do both if she wants to," Ma finally piped up. I was surprised she had enough restraint to wait.

Callie tugged my arm, so I sat back down. Chase did as well.

The aunt shook her head. "No, she can't. Everyone thinks they can, but they end up dropping out and never going back."

"Callie can do whatever she likes," I ground out.

Ma stared the woman down. "And she'll have our help."

"And burn through her daddy's money?" the heartless prick interjected, again fixated on trying to get ahold of Callie's money.

I glared at the insensitive peon. His gaze oscillated between Chase and me, and his expression shifted from cynicism to nervousness. Dad was sporting his horrifying I-want-to-tear-you-to-pieces face, and I inherited his intensity. The guy was getting scared, perfect.

"I come from money—if you must know—and I will support her." Only after it was out did I realize it wasn't quite true. We were now cut off from Zeus's purse strings. We had saved a ton of money over the years, but our stash would eventually run dry supporting my brothers and whoever else left my grandfather's side. We'd have to work, which would devastate Ma, but, at least, the petty fights she and Dad would have over her spending habits would be entertaining.

"Raphael?" Callie finally entered the conversation. The servant had been idly watching a few feet away. "Will you please find my aunt and uncle their own table? I'd feel more comfortable if this table only had my friends at it. Then, Raphael? Join us."

"Very well, Mrs. Ambrose." Raphael used her married name, and the sound of it dispelled my anger and warmth washed over me. "Mr. and Mrs. Harper, right this way."

In a huff of anger, the uncle took off ahead of Raphael, and the aunt gave us a scathing glower before hurrying to catch up.

"Oh, my gods," Aroha breathed out.

Callie started laughing. Although it was wonderful to see her light up with happiness on such a day, I was confused.

"You two." Callie pointed at Chase and me, still giggling. "You were ready to start a war in my honor. Honestly, my father and I never saw them much because they were always like this. Since we came to New York, they came over once, and that was to ask for money Dad refused to give them. I never let them get to me. Dad usually just made them look stupid by cracking jokes over their head, but this was entertaining too."

Dad shrugged. Then we all laughed it off.

"Raphael said to head over here?" Lucien hedged, interrupting our laughter. Linda and Hymenaios were with him. Linda and Lucien being friends again was weird and new. A warning would've been nice so we'd know what to say about Hymenaios in front of the mortals, but Lucien immediately launched into a greeting after he gave Callie his condolences. "You guys remember my little brother, Aios."

What alias was Aios supposed to be short for? Hymenaios's—or Aios now—hair had grown back to a very short buzz cut, and aside from being a tad paler, he appeared unscathed by his near-death experience. He pulled Linda's chair out for her, and she seemed to have stars in her eyes for him.

Another interesting development. Was it wrong of me to relish in how awkward this was for Lucien?

Ma stared at Aios and Linda, picking up on exactly what I had. "When did you two meet?" There was something there, but the way he blushed told me it was too soon. Feelings weren't out in the open yet.

Linda smiled. "I went over Lucien's to make sure it was okay to visit Callie, see how she was doing, and Andraios was there."

Ah, Linda revealed to us the hasty-sounding alias.

"Please, sit," Callie told the hesitant Lucien. "But you're not fully forgiven yet."

"Forgiven for what?" Linda's gaze flickered between them.

"Nothing of consequence, right, Callie?" Lucien teased her, well-knowing she couldn't say anything in front of Linda. He flashed her a mocking smile. "Does it even matter now?"

Normally, I would cut in with an insult, not liking him picking on my wife, but it was friendly banter, the way he teased me—friendship rather than flirting.

She scowled at him, rolled her eyes, and said, "No, I guess it doesn't." She gave me a look that spoke a thousand words, most of them being of love. I could not resist her power to entice me and kissed her.

CHAPTER 11

Callie

After the memorial service and late luncheon, Archer and I returned to my apartment. Only, it wouldn't be mine much longer. The lease was up next month, and I decided not to renew it and not to buy it. I couldn't live there without Dad. I think those were his wishes, which would've been why he paid the steep rent instead of buying outright. As I took in all the boxes, I realized how uncertain my future was. Would I ever get to go to college? How long would we live out of boxes? Could I even have the family I longed for one day? The way Aroha described how some people can help fill the hole in my heart made me think of having children. Zeus trying to kill me quickly dashed the idea.

Archer's arms wrapped around me, pulling me into a backward hug, his chin resting on my head. I felt whole again, complete in his arms. "What did you decide about Raphael?"

(Ugh, decisions, so many to be made.) "He knows. Like you said, we have to protect him. Do you think he'll be safer left behind here than with me?"

Archer let out a heavy breath, stirring my hair. "I'll talk to Dionysus. Maybe he'll look after him until things are safe. I know Raphael really wants to work for you still."

"For us, for all of us." I stared at the glass case of artifacts that I still needed to pack. They meant so much more now. I had to keep them.

Archer's mind was also on them. "Crazy how your dad was right all along. And how he found us."

"First, I thought they were just harebrained ideas, and then when I found out the truth, I knew he was a genius. Now, I know he had help."

Archer turned me around, his eyes puzzled, searching mine. I really wanted to show him Dad's letter, but I couldn't (so wrong of me). I couldn't even digest some of the things written in it. At least one part I could tell him about. "In my dad's letter, he explained how he met a god and how this god would pop into his life randomly and tell him what to do."

"Who?"

72

"He never knew, nor did he hazard a guess in his letter. I'm sure he figured it out but took the info with him. This god was there during my mom's accident..." Memories, faint and only images, flickered in the back of my mind: *Dark eyes, tan skin, dark wet hair, the star pendant on a chain.* "I remember little bits of that day." I told him what I could of the god.

"That describes quite a few gods, but if he was able to control your dad's life, then he had to be some type of "seeing" god; he'd have to know the future, which limits it down to Proteus or Prometheus, if we're sticking to gods I know personally. The former can appear as anything or anyone he wants, but you described the latter. Yet, there are the others, too, so..." He sighed, letting go of me, a worry line forming on his brow. *That* was why I hid things. He would just worry himself sick about me (well, if he could get sick).

"Where can we find Prometheus? If it is him, he's the only one who can answer these questions for me."

"He can only be found when he wants to be. The only beings who ever found him before were Proteus and Athena. In fact, she's searching for him now because we need his foresight to win a war against Zeus."

I cringed at his name. Dad would've scolded me for the action and lectured me to fight, not flinch, to never show fear.

Archer pulled me in and kissed me. "Let's speak of better things."

(Yes, please.)

"How about we treat this hiding trip as a real extended honeymoon?"

I had zero problems with that, but he kissed me before I could agree. I became lost in his mind-erasing lips for a minute, forgetting whatever I had just been worrying about. One kiss led to another, and before I knew it, I was tearing open his shirt and shucking the sleeves off him. He backed me into the table, the bedroom being too far away. (Literally, it was right there, but...) I pulled away as he unzipped my dress. I stared into those eyes that literally lit up with love and desire for me. I couldn't imagine a better turn-on than having Love's love directed at me.

I yanked him back in as we fell back onto the cool table. It was urgent. I needed him, the distraction, the heady sensation of physical love to wipe away my mental anguish and worries of inexplicable things my father told me in his letter.

There was a knock at the door. Archer groaned on my shoulder. "Ignore them."

"It's my aunt. She won't go away."

THE IMMORTAL TRANSCRIPTS: SHUDDER

He came out of hiding and gazed upon me, his adorable brow wrinkling in wonder. "How do you know?"

I tapped my temple. "My sixth sense."

I tried to push Archer up, but he gripped the sides of the table with a grin, leaning into me, trying to trap me in a pleasurable prison. Maybe I would simply ignore her.

"Forget her then." I smiled as Archer kissed me roughly, resuming where we had left off.

There was more knocking we ignored, followed by a muffled "I know you're in there, Callie. The man at the desk said you were home."

Archer kept kissing me, but logic was starting to override the passion in my mind. We should just get rid of her and enjoy ourselves later. I shoved the unsuspecting Archer away from me and slipped out. I got my dress righted and zipped it as far as I could as I made my way to the door.

"You little water nymph," Archer said playfully. Bam! He was right in front of me, blocking my path to the door.

I bumped right into him. "No fair." I ducked under his arm, but he turned and snaked his fast immortal arms around me, pulled my back flush against his body, and kissed me in that magic spot where my jaw met my ear that rendered me senseless. He kissed down my neck, leaving a trail of goosebumps, as his hands roved over my curves. When I opened my eyes, ready to turn around and attack him with kisses, my Aunt Judith was standing in front of us, arms crossed and eyebrows raised. Her presence doused my desire as if someone threw a cold bucket of water over me. "Archer, stop."

Archer stopped and noticed my aunt. He let me go and zipped my dress to the top for me. He scooped up his shirt, slipped his arms in, and tried to button it, but couldn't because I had popped off some of the buttons when I literally tore it off his body. (Don't know my own strength, I guess.)

"I came to talk to you, Callie, but I can see you're rather *busy*." It was pretty accusatory, as if she were a mom walking in on her teen being naughty. I was married, though, and a legal adult. She had no right to pretend to be my family now.

"We're newlyweds, so get over it, Aunt Judith," I retorted (I so should've thrown in a curse word).

She glared at Archer as if he were the one who spoke. "I crave a word a-*lone*." Even the way she spoke was annoyingly grating on my already frazzled nerves.

LISA BORNE GRAVES

Archer gave me a questioning glance. I nodded that I'd be okay. "I'll be at my sister's packing my things." Archer walked around Aunt Judith to leave but childishly stuck his tongue out at the back of my aunt's head first.

I tried not to laugh.

As the door closed, the tension between my aunt and me grew.

"I'm honestly worried about you, Callie. You shouldn't go traipsing all over the world with that boy. There's something odd about him. How long have you even known him, a year? The marriage seems rushed. Did you even make him sign a prenup? What would your father say about—"

My anger was overflowing. "Don't pretend to know what my dad would say. My father gave us his blessing, and your rude assumptions are not about some boy; they are about my *husband*." She didn't even know Dad. She was my maternal aunt, but even then, not blood related since my mother and aunt were adopted. Calling Archer a "boy" too? She didn't know who she was insulting. I wish he'd show her, but immediately regretted it (kind of).

"I just think you should be with family. Why don't you stay with us for a while? Or even better, we could stay here with you. What does this place have, three bedrooms? The boys could share a room. You need to be with family right now. You and...what's-his-name...Archer could treat this as an engagement to make sure it works out before you move in together. You could buy your own food, pay the rent, you know, so you don't feel like a burden to us." She was unbelievable.

"Do you need money or something?" I was testing her to see what she'd say. I wasn't about to give her any.

"What?" Her over-the-top reaction, mouth gaping and her hand-on-hip posture, told me I was right. They were still after Dad's money, only my aunt was more deviously discreet than my uncle in her attempts. "Of course, I don't. How could you—"

I couldn't take it anymore. "We'll never agree on this, so I'll have to ask you to leave. I'll also need that key Dad gave you for emergencies. The lease is up."

"You can't give up this place!"

"Before you try to worm your way into 'watching' my apartment for me, let me be clear: I'm not renewing the lease. Give me the key."

She took out her keys and slipped it off the ring while muttering, "Turning on your own family over a boy of all things."

THE IMMORTAL TRANSCRIPTS: SHUDDER

"You're not really family anymore, and you know it. I have seen you maybe five times in my life, and each time, you tried to get loans off Dad. You never 'cared' about me until now, and the only reason you pretend to is to get my money."

"Well, if that is what you think..." She turned her snobby nose up in the air. "I guess I will see you someday when you return after you and this boy don't work out."

"Don't pretend you forgot the reading of Dad's will is tomorrow."

Her hand hesitated on the doorknob. "See you tomorrow." Finally, she dropped her act. How could people be so... (Grrrr!) There were so many ways to describe her that my enraged mind couldn't settle on one.

I shut the door behind her and turned, almost having a heart attack when I registered Archer was standing in front of me. He must've done his rooftop climb, slipping onto my balcony just like the night I had found out who he truly was. He hugged me. "Soon, we'll be free of her."

"I'll survive."

He placed his hand on my forehead. "But she got you worked up, and stress brings on these fevers. You're already warm."

"Maybe someone got me all warmed up before we were interrupted," I teased Archer, running my hand down his chest.

***

The next morning, Archer was already awake, making tea, when I came into the kitchen. He handed me a little vial. I gave him a quizzical look.

"Herbal concoction Lucien gifted you with."

"His last ones didn't do a thing."

"This one might. It can't hurt. They were made by his son, Asclepius, who far surpasses Lucien in the medical field, but don't let him hear you say that."

I drank it down—anything to feel slightly better.

Raphael drove us to the firm's building, where the will would be read by Dad's lawyer, and came in with us. Dad had left him something. We were shown to a conference room. My aunt and uncle were already there, as well as Dad's business associate, Mr. Kaminski, and Dad's lawyer.

I sat between Archer and Raphael. The lawyer got started promptly at nine and read the will. As soon as he read the words my father had written with him, pain shot through my heart. Archer squeezed my hand to show he was there for me. He picked up on my pain just as I sensed his empathy. I took a deep breath. I only had to listen.

Dad left his stock shares of the antique business to Mr. Kaminski, which was good because I didn't want the responsibility with my limited knowledge of old furniture's worth—although Archer probably could date a lot of items. Dad left money to a couple of charities, Raphael his Rolls Royce, which I knew was still worth a couple hundred thousand, despite being used and a few years old. It was enough for him to live comfortably one day in retirement. Next, my aunt was given any of my mother's belongings that I didn't want to keep for her to remember "the few good times" she and my mother had (oh, Dad, you're hilarious), and then left my uncle "the antique coat rack" he had "so admired." Dad had known he had been trying to butter him up for a loan when he said he liked the old piece of junk. Here was my dad, making one of my worst days become better through his eternal humor. He was having a joke with me from beyond the grave. If he could somehow see what was going on here from the Underworld, he would be laughing.

Archer squeezed my hand, whispering, "What's funny?"

"My dad and I are sharing a joke right now."

The lawyer continued, "Last, I bequeath both Judith and Tony Harper a $100,000 donation to the American Heart Association in their names to show their generous and giving natures."

I bit my lip not to laugh as they reacted: Aunt Judith's face drained of color, and Uncle Tony's turned a splotchy red and purple as if his head would explode.

"Ah, I see," Archer whispered.

Uncle Tony stood, fuming. "You dragged me down here for a coat rack?"

"And my sister's junk?" Aunt Judith gawped. "That's it?"

The lawyer they had interrupted stared at them. "And a massive donation in your name to the charity of his choice."

"They'll be harassing us every year for a follow-up donation. We know how it works," my aunt spat out. Funny, I didn't peg them as the charitable type; then again, that "harassment" was their excuse never to donate.

"Get out," I said quietly.

"You can't—" Uncle Tony began.

"Callista Ambrose is of age, so legally is the executor of the will," the lawyer said.

Judith stood and glared at me. She was no family of mine.

"I have every right to keep my inheritance unknown to you. I would like you to leave. Your items will be delivered to your house tonight."

THE IMMORTAL TRANSCRIPTS: SHUDDER

They stormed out of the conference room, bickering.

The lawyer proceeded. "To Archer Ambrose..."

Archer and I looked at each other, shocked. Dad had to have changed his will recently. "I bequeath my artifacts to do what he wishes with them or perhaps return them to the ancient homes I have robbed them from." A wish Archer could easily perform. Realizing the artifacts belong to living gods, who he knew personally, must've made Dad feel more like a thief than an archeologist.

"Last, to my beloved Callista, I leave all of my remaining estate in hopes to give her a brighter and much longer life than the Fates permitted me." At the last words I'd ever hear that he had written, I started to cry.

A few signatures were needed before I rushed out of there, letting Archer and Raphael lead me through the rest of my day. I couldn't wait to get out of New York, plagued by the memories of the one person who was no longer in it.

CHAPTER 12

Lucien

I hated the amount of time my son, Aios, was spending with Linda. It wasn't jealousy, because I no longer had feelings for Linda. I was more concerned about having another Callie situation on my hands and having Zeus try to kill Aios again if Linda found out what we were. My, how things had changed. Before, Zeus had simply warned Archer away from Callie, and now Zeus was ready to kill his own family over her existence. I couldn't imagine this Olympian family could ever be repaired or go back to the way things had been.

Plus, I thought the entire Linda-Aios situation was weird. Despite our dating history, she was still interested in Aios. It didn't seem to matter to her he was my younger brother—not like we could explain he was actually my kid. I was also worried because Aios was no serial dater. In fact, he spent very little time away from Olympus and his overbearing mother—who chased girls away, I'm sure. I wouldn't put it past my ex, Euterpe, to prevent our son becoming anything like me. Aios and I still hadn't heard from her. Even though our new cells were Ares-approved stealth phones, we never changed our emails. Euterpe was silent about the abduction and attempted murder of her son. I hoped she was well and feared she was trapped.

Chase invited me to Iceland, finally trusting me enough to disclose their safe house location. Well, he made me swear on the Styx, so that's about how much they trusted me. I'd die if I told anyone Archer and Callie were hiding out in Iceland. They also wanted to take Aios for his safety, and my son would only go with me. At least that would separate him from Linda. Aios didn't want anything to happen to her, which meant he was already in too deep. Using mortals is one thing, but falling for them? Just look where it got us.

Archer's brothers arrived in New York only hours before it was time to leave. The eight of us boarded a cruise ship to Reykjavik, which Aroha had arranged safe passage through her *fishy* ancestry. Poseidon would follow us underwater, and he and the Titan Oceanus's offspring, the Oceanids, would protect us if Zeus attacked. I was less worried about a sinking ship than I was about Callie's fevers. They were relentless, due to the amount of stress she was undergoing after her father's death and then being forced into hiding. I was utterly surprised Zeus hadn't attacked here in New York. It didn't seem like him to give someone time to say goodbye to a loved one. Something was up. Perhaps he was biding his time. After his last screwup, he would have to plan better.

On the cruise, I gave the couple space, not wanting to see their happiness, but we all had dinner together each evening. The first day was smooth sailing, and we docked in Halifax. Chase wanted us to stay on the boat, but Himerus, Anteros, and Hymenaios whined enough to get their way. Being cooped up with Zeus for centuries had not afforded them the massive world travel we had experienced. The "core five," as Chase coined us, stayed behind because we could not be seen in case Zeus had spies. It was highly doubtful, but I was happy playing it safe.

On the third day, we hit the open waters of the northern Atlantic, known to be choppy, but as the day wore on and massive storms unyieldingly bombarded us, even us gods started feeling a tad seasick—except Aroha. It made dinner almost impossible to stomach, but we were there, trying.

Waves rocked the boat. "I'm going to say it because no one else will," Anteros addressed us in a quiet tone. "Zeus doing that?" Anteros matched Archer in looks, but simply seemed to lack Archer's golden boy visage—the hair was bland dirty-blond, poker-straight, and his eyes a muddy hazel.

I think Aroha condescendingly called him a "sullied Archer." I mean, I was a terrible parent, but Aroha and Chase weren't winning the parents-of-a-millennium award or anything.

"Poseidon will protect us if he is." Aroha shrugged it off as if an almighty sky god trying to sink our ship were no big deal.

Chase closed his eyes and then opened them. "Not my dad. I only sense Poseidon."

I scanned as well, seeing blips of mortals seeking truth around me, but no other gods nearby, aside from Poseidon and his oceanid crew. Zeus was not causing the cruiseliner's problem.

The ship tipped precariously, so much so that, for a moment, out the side windows, I only saw ocean before it righted, and our view was again of the horizon. A few mortals gasped. The ship dipped yet again, and Callie's hand clasped mine momentarily. Strange, she grabbed onto me instead of Archer, but then I felt a tiny slip of paper in my hand. She gave me a significant glance and turned her attention to Archer.

"I don't feel well enough to eat. I think I'm going to lie down," she said.

"I'll come with you," Archer said.

"No, stay and eat. I'm going to rest. I'll take some Dramamine and have a nap. I'll meet you guys at the club."

"Dancing mmm-hmm," the always bawdy Himerus cut into their conversation.

All of us ignored him, except Anteros, who laughed.

"Will you be up for dancing?" Archer asked dubiously.

"With some rest, I'll be refreshed enough to watch these two make fools of themselves." She nodded at his brothers.

Anteros laughed again, and Himerus scowled.

Callie kissed Archer, lingering just a second too long to call it innocent, and left as the main course came out. During the conversation between Callie and Archer, I had covertly unfolded the paper and left it in my lap. Chase was an extremely perceptive person, and I was worried he had seen Callie touch my hand. I didn't dare read it until I went to place my napkin back on my lap: Tiki bar top deck. Alone.

I dug into my main course because leaving right after her would be highly suspicious, but as I worked my way through my delicious steak, the rain whipped against the dining room windows. She would be out there, in a storm. Either Callie was crazy, or this was some serious private conversation she wanted to have.

Worried about her, I stood before I thought of an excuse to leave. "I gotta go to the bathroom." I rushed out, hearing Aroha worrying about food poisoning. That kind of thing could affect us but not badly. As embarrassing as her assumption was, it would give me a one-on-one with Callie. I hurried at a measly mortal pace to the top deck, and not espying a single person, I dashed through the rain in immortal speed, taking refuge under the closed tiki bar's overhang. She was drenched. I wanted to fold her into my arms and warm her up, kiss her.

"Don't you dare," she scolded.

"Don't what?" I froze, standing under the overhang, keeping a foot between us.

"Don't do what you're thinking about. I knew you might get the wrong idea about meeting me, but I had to talk to you alone, which never happens."

Because Archer was a jealous and possessive husband and never allowed it.

"I'm reading your mind, you know. Archer trusts me, not you. I can read minds unconsciously. Lucien, you've got to help me."

"Why me? You hate me. Thought you didn't even forgive me."

"You'll betray me, Lucien, but for now, I need you. That's why you're here."

"I won't betray—" I tried to step closer to her, but she stepped back.

"You will—don't argue—I've seen it. It was only a dream, but my dreams—"

"Come true," I finished for her in a whisper. I still loved her. Why would I ever put her in harm's way?

Large waves battered against the boat, spraying so far into the air that droplets reached us. It was really dumb of her to risk coming up here.

"I can't be mad at you when I saw what happens after that."

"What happens? Something to me?" An icy chill shot down my spine as Themis's prophecy came back to me. Someone who betrays them would pay the price. Callie believed it was me.

"You're the god of prophecies! Why are you asking me?"

Why did no one understand prophecies? They were far from an exact science.

"Look, I'm really sick. I've been downplaying to Archer and Aroha because they—"

"Are overbearing?"

"Worry too much." She gave me a glare for my criticism. "The supplements and medicines aren't working. Not even the nectar Aroha keeps trying."

Half my mind wanted to return to what could possibly happen to me, but the other half wanted to solve this illness. How could I not stop this? I hated fevers. They unnerved me. I was also distracted by the massive waves making the boat dip and rise at horrific rates. What in Hades was Poseidon doing?

She gestured wildly with annoyance at her head. "Can you get rid of this fever for now? I don't want Archer to know."

I sighed. She was putting me in an impossible position, but I learned the hard way that neither of them wanted truth from me. "Why are you hiding things from your husband?"

She refused to answer.

I touched her temples, registering 104 degrees. "Holy Hades, Callie. You have a high fever." I poured in my power, cooling her. I decided to let my fingers linger longer than needed and gave her my version of a CT scan. I detected no illness, but her heart was beating fast. Too fast.

"Are you having a panic attack?"

"No." She batted my hands away. "I asked for fever relief, not a scan of my vitals."

I removed my fingers from her temples. "What else are you hiding?" Anger started to bubble up inside me.

A blur of movement caught my attention, and Archer was in front of us, his face troubled. "What's this? What's going on?" His tone was guarded as if he was holding back his full-blown jealousy. More movement, and now our entire crew was huddled close together under the tiki bar's roof.

"Isn't it obvious? The fevers. Nothing is working, is it?" Aroha cut in to spare us any resentful lover drama.

"Or maybe she's pretending she's sick for Lucien's attention?" Anteros said. We all glared at him. "What? Sorry. God who takes revenge for unrequited love over here. It's what I always see."

"Callie?" Archer stared her down.

"I'm sicker. I didn't want you to worry more."

He looked to me for answers. "She was 104 degrees, and her heart—"

"Is fine." She gave me a reprimanding stare. She was hiding something big, a health issue?

"Your heart?" Archer grasped her hand. She still didn't explain.

"Beats irregularly fast," I said.

The boat swayed so much, we almost lost our footing.

Callie elbowed me in the stomach with her free arm. It kind of hurt. "It's just stress."

Archer's face was concerned. "Lucien?"

I didn't know what to say. I didn't know what was wrong with her. "Could be. I have no idea what this is, Archer. I think we should summon my son when we get there. If Athena and I cannot figure this out, Asclepius would be our last hope."

"Please, stop worrying. I know what's going on with me. Give me a minute!" The last comment was not directed at us. Was she hallucinating?

Archer's tone was terrified, "Callie?"

"Please. Be quiet. He's not going to give me time to explain. He knows about me, and he's impatient. I don't blame him. I'm not just sick. There's more to it, and I don't understand it. Archer, my father's letter...the things he said confused and upset me. Damn it! Give me a minute!" Callie shouted, pointing her fist at the sea.

THE IMMORTAL TRANSCRIPTS: SHUDDER

"Callie." Archer gripped her shoulders, much as my instinct had been to do. We were stumbling across the deck into the whipping rain.

Callie was perplexed. "You guys can't hear his voice?"

I exchanged a quick glance with Archer, the rain getting into my eyes. We were lost.

"Poseidon," Callie said.

A bunch of us looked to Dite. She threw up her hands in exasperation. "I told you so many times that I'm not directly related to him. He told me as much." When she finished speaking, she cursed under her breath.

I turned to see what made her uncharacteristically swear: a tidal wave coming down upon us. Poseidon had turned on us. Or he lost control of something far worse from the depths of the ocean. The wave crashed upon us.

I was slammed against the deck, my jaw and an arm breaking on contact. Pain radiated through me. I healed them, trying not to think about the water pressing upon me, trying to invade my lungs. We couldn't drown, but I wasn't keen on feeling like I was. The water lessened, then moved away as the cruise ship righted itself—or Poseidon stabilized it.

I heard coughing and groaning. I wiped my eyes, ignoring the salty sting, and took in the scene. My brethren all were in my state, except Dite, who was somehow still standing and ready for a fight, war-crazy as Ares himself. She was probably angry about her ruined dress and hair.

"Cal-lie!" Archer's voice screamed with such raw emotion my stomach did a somersault. All the gods in Olympia, she wasn't aboard anymore. My heart dropped to my feet.

Dite ran off sprinting and leaped over the deck, diving into the rough waters, making a splash.

"Dite!" Chase shouted, leaping to his feet before I even sat up, and ran to the railing, scanning the dark ocean.

Archer was up next and trying to jump overboard, but Chase held him back with a lot of effort, slipping on the wet deck before he could get a good hold of his son. I joined them to see what could be done, but it was all darkness below, only little reflections of the full moon casting limited light on the water in the middle of the northern Atlantic Ocean. Oddly, the waves had majorly calmed down.

"What would Poseidon want with Callie?" I turned to the bewildered group.

Archer's vibrant eyes were staring at the water, his breaths coming quick. He seemed as if he were underwater, drowning. A thought occurred to me, but surely, he wasn't that stupid. He seemed connected, *truly* connected to Callie, which meant...

Someone popped up and took a breath, and I leaned over trying to see, but it was completely dark below, even with godly hypersenses.

"I can't find them!" Aroha's voice rang out as she swam to keep up with the ship's speed.

I had to do something. There was only one thing I could think of. I placed my hands on the railing for support and took a deep breath. I channeled all my energy into the sky. This far north, mid-August, surely, I could get a grip on it. I surmised the time. Nine pm. My sun was still there, making its descent toward the horizon. I held her there, like lassoing the hottest and strongest power in the world. It hurt, but I also had to disperse the clouds. She needed to come through. My frame shook uncontrollably. I only recognized the scream of agony was my own after someone said, "enough."

I fell to the ground, immobile, using my only strength to hold the sun there. As it shined through the clouds, a bit of strength returned. Hymenaios stood over me and offered me a hand, his face proud. He yanked me up. "Look, Dad."

I peered over the side of the boat and saw someone swimming toward us at an insanely rapid pace, keeping up with the ship's speed, Callie holding onto his back as if she were riding on the back of an orca in those tragic now-banned aquarium shows. As they neared the boat, Aroha—who clung to a rope someone must've thrown down while I was busy—tried to hoist Callie up, but the man clamped onto her wrist. I squinted. *Who was...?* Poseidon? Callie slipped her hand into his while Aroha hoisted them out of the water and onto the rope. They climbed onto the deck.

No one spoke. I let the sun go and groaned. What could we say? Poseidon had risen from his watery prison of thousands of years, and it had everything to do with this inexplicable girl Zeus wanted to kill. What in Mother Gaia was Callie?

Poseidon stood there, trembling, the expression on his face a cross between horror and glee. He took everything in as we all stood there staring at him, unable to believe what we were seeing.

Callie was the first one to move. She let go of Poseidon's wrist, and he grabbed her arm, afraid to lose contact with her, probably afraid he'd somehow be propelled into the ocean and imprisoned again. His grip on Callie wiped away Archer's shock, and he reacted. He was across the deck in a split second and had Poseidon pinned against the opposite railing. We hurried over to try to stop him.

"Archer, stop." Callie tried to pry his hands off Poseidon's throat.

"Great-nephew, let me explain." Poseidon's voice was gravelly from disuse. Underwater, he'd make a telepathic projection into our heads if we needed to communicate. Callie had been talking to him that way somehow above water.

"It's okay. I'm fine," Callie said.

"No, it's not. We… I mean, you could've died." Archer's slip up was telling.

Chase and I simultaneously looked at Aios. He stared at the ground. Aios actually had immortally married them. How in Hades had I missed that lie? I was hurt. My own kid had lied to me. He was the only god who could link souls together via soul-sharing, in friendship, family, charity, or desire. Immortal marriage? That was linking all four in a permanent bind, only for souls perfectly suited for each other. *That* was the reason Zeus tried to kill my son, not simply officiating an innocuous wedding. Aios had lied about it, and being distracted, I hadn't noticed. More importantly, why in Tartarus would Archer do something so stupid?

Archer let go of Poseidon but then punched him in the jaw. Poseidon spit out blood, and his split lip healed instantly. "'Kay, I probably deserved that, but I was desperate and had to get her overboard."

"Because you knew she could break you through Zeus's barrier. Because it happened in Belize." Archer deduced.

Poseidon nodded. "I couldn't do it again on my own. I didn't know how."

"How did you do it?" Archer demanded of Callie.

"I don't know." She shivered, and Archer took Callie into his arms, his anger fading as quickly as it had come.

"But…but…how are you on the surface?" Aroha demanded.

Poseidon shrugged. "There's something about this girl." We all turned our attention onto Callie.

"Don't look at me! I don't know," Callie ground out. "I need to get warm and dry." She closed the subject, but I could tell she knew something and was hiding it. Being the god of truth, I would find out what.

CHAPTER 13
Athena

Someone prodded me awake. The bus driver stood over me. I had fallen asleep. "Hey lady, this is the end of the line."
"Where am I?"
"Myrtle Beach, you know, South Carolina. Was this not your stop?"
"No, yes. I need to get to Miami, but I knew this bus didn't run that far south."

He whistled. "Well, from here, you can catch a bus in the morning and check with the station, but I think it'll still take you a couple of bus changes and days."

"That's fine." I stood and grabbed my bag. It was not fine, but that's what you have to tell people so they wouldn't feel at fault. Mortals. Always blaming themselves for trite things and others' mistakes. It was my fault entirely. I should've gotten my connection a couple of stops back, which would've been a more direct route. I contemplated renting a car instead. It would only take me about ten hours to drive. Despite my bus nap, I was too tired and doubted I could rent a car at this hour. It was dark. The Greyhound station was tiny and on a side street not far from a highway. It was also closed. The few people who had been on the bus were walking away or getting into cars. All that remained was one seedy-looking guy who had been on the bus. I walked quickly toward the highway, noting the tangy scent of the sea and the weight of the humid air. Warm and comforting, but for mortals, I was sure it must be oppressive.

I crossed the highway and saw a few hotels but kept going. The best would be on the beach. And "best" in a place you've never been would mean the more expensive ones. This part of town wasn't bad, but it also didn't seem quite safe either. As a god, I didn't fear for my life, but my focus. I was easily distracted, and when injustices or evil deeds were around me, it sent me into hyperfocus where I had to right things—everything—merely to function. I'd lose track of my mission to find Prometheus if I let myself get sidetracked.

A couple of blocks later, I found a great place. They were busy and only had a small room, overlooking the busy street since no ocean views had been left. Only wanting to sleep one night to figure out my next move, I couldn't care less about room size and view. I checked in, went to my room, and plopped onto the bed. I fell asleep instantly, able to ignore the injustices brewing among mortals around me.

I arose early, got dressed, and decided to go to the beach to watch the sunrise and think of what to do next. Despite the hour, people were running and walking on the beach.

I was wasting my time. How does one find the most hidden being on the planet, particularly when he can see you coming and evade you? I thought he would've guided me, helped me. He had to foresee my need to find him. I was disappointed. I thought he'd care.

Families started showing up, and the heat increased, warming my skin, improving my mood. You'd think I were Apollo with my love for the sun, but it was merely a preference.

I noticed a little boy by himself sitting not far from me who glared at a group of children. They were poking a dead moon jellyfish with a stick, taking turns. One boy stabbed the jellyfish, lifted it off the ground, and launched the clear blob at a girl, who screamed in horror and jumped out of the way. The jellyfish landed in the sand, was forgotten, and the children moved on.

The boy stared after them with scorn until he noticed my shadow and suddenly peered up. He had wise, oceanic blue-green eyes, which betrayed his identity to me immediately; they were too old, too intelligent, too full of suffering and experience.

"Proteus," I greeted, sitting next to him. "Your eyes give you away. That and your love for the invertebrates."

"As do your eyes, always, Athena. Few humans have that hue of gray." He sighed. An odd thing to say since I had my very-human mother's eyes. "Savages, the poor creature wasn't quite dead when they began to torture it. Mortals. Makes me wonder why I come to the surface at all."

"Yes," I soothed, patting his back. "They know not what they do."

"What brings you here?"

"Don't you know?"

"I see the future. I can't read your motivation." His gaze scrutinized me, making me ill-at-ease. "Knew you'd be here but didn't know why."

"I need your help."

"Ah... A lot of people do lately." He stared at the sea.

"Please, Proteus, where is he?"

His bemused expression told me he had expected me to beg questions of the future. "Who?"

"The most elusive god ever known."

"Prometheus? How would I know where he is?" He was lying, but getting the truth out of Proteus was not easy. He was not one to be bullied or outsmarted. At any moment, he could run out into the sea, turn into a shark, and vanish into the deep waters. He relished in his dramatic escapes to avoid gods' questions. More often, he shapeshifted to avoid detection like this boy persona he used now.

"Because you've helped me find him before." I ignored the break in my voice and avoided his gaze by staring at the horizon.

His voice was soft. "That was different. You really needed him then, and he foresaw it. I only found him because he wanted to be found."

"We need him now." I insisted, trying not to think about the last time. The situation I had been in was precarious, and only Proteus, Prometheus, and one of the Norse who had owed me a favor knew about it.

"Wouldn't he come to you if you truly needed him?" His impish smile told me he was enjoying my struggle.

"Proteus. This is imperative."

"Don't worry, Athena. You're the wise one. You'll find him." He patted my hand gently, an awkwardly adult gesture for the little boy he appeared to be.

"How?"

"Think about it. What made you come here to this town?"

I shrugged. "I fell asleep on the bus."

"Well," —he stood up, brushing the sand off his bathing suit— "I wouldn't stray too far. The Fates have a way of putting you where you need to be." Proteus winked at me.

"He's here?"

His playful tone and hints about the Fates clicked. How had I—the wisest Olympian—missed that? Prometheus was in Myrtle Beach.

"He's been here for a couple of years. Good town for a god to lie low in."

"Will he be mad you told me?"

"No." The visage of the boy smiled mischievously. "He knew when you would get here. He told me to tell you he was here."

"You... Oh, I could smack you." I growled at Proteus for toying with me. How dare he meddle with me when he knew Prometheus was here from the beginning? I hopped up and threatened to give him a good backhand.

"You can't hit me. Child abuse." He stuck out his tongue.

Mortals were watching us. I dropped my hands down and grabbed his shoulders instead, making my squeezing gesture look more like a comforting one. "Seriously, Proteus, things are so complicated and unnerving—and dangerous. How can you joke at a time like this?"

"Grow a sense of humor, Athena. Whatever happens, happens. Knowing what will happen doesn't change the fact it will still occur. You can't change the future, so you just gotta laugh it off and go with the flow."

I glared at him. He turned his head, squinting up the strand toward a section of looming hotels. I doubted he had that same mentality in the Battle of Belize City, but his positive attitude hopefully alluded to some calmer times ahead.

"Well, time for my exit. The elusive one comes," Proteus said quietly.

I let him go and ruffled his hair, gaining another scowl from him.

"Hey, Zeph." Proteus whistled for Zephyrus.

A swirl of wind whipped around, stirring sand everywhere, and Proteus was gone. No one batted an eye. It was such a quick action that I doubted the mortal eyes could discern it or maybe they did but second-guessed what they had seen, brushing it off as a figment of the imagination.

I peered down the beach and instantly recognized the familiar know-it-all-before-it-happens swagger of Prometheus. My pulse sped up. I hadn't seen him in years; it was bound to be awkward. I ridiculously wondered how I looked and regretted not putting on any makeup. Why on Mother Gaia did I care? I hadn't spoken to him since 1959, and long stretches of time had gone by without any contact before that. I felt self-conscious and anxious. Finally, I walked toward him, unable to stand the awkward tension of waiting for him to get to me, those social cues of greeting someone as they got closer. I'd rather he'd randomly pop out, and I could gasp a "Hi!" to get it over with.

Closing the distance gave me something to do, to focus on. I mentally subtracted the yardage in portions each step we took. As I neared him close enough to see him squinting, a great smile formed upon his lips. I stared at the ground to avoid his gaze. People stared irregularly long in others' eyes, but for me it could be too much, too overwhelming—even with loved ones. In his eyes, would I see the pain of his long and excruciating punishment? Would I see all of his strain knowing the future of the entire world? Would I see things I never wanted to face again?

I stopped when I saw his feet. I forced myself to behold him. His dark eyes were as old as his years, much older than me, even older than Zeus, and one of the first immortal beings to grace the earth. To be so old and see the entire future, how tired he must be of what was and will be. His brown hair was sun-bleached at the tips—a thousand years being chained to that gods-forsaken rock tanned him permanently, darker than his original skin tone. He was beyond the Mediterranean bronze of his youth. It finally clicked he was only wearing a bathing suit, which made my stomach flop uncomfortably when I saw his "six-pack" as the mortals were oft to say. I focused on his face to ignore his body.

Prometheus was inspecting me as well. I don't think he ever forgave me; in fact, I believe he blamed me for his punishment of being bound to the rock, the eagle plucking out his liver every day. I often blamed myself, but it was his fault. He had known what would happen and still let it take course. Perhaps Proteus was right: we were helpless to alter our futures.

"Athena," Prometheus said, his voice guarded.

"Prometheus," I said back, my voice sounding meek for a warrior goddess.

"It has been a while." He ran his hand through his hair, a nervous tick of his, which meant he was just as uncomfortable as me.

"I need your help," I began, waiting for him to further the conversation. He'd know exactly why I was here.

"For?" he prompted.

"You mean...you don't know?" Or maybe not so much. I was astounded. How did he not know?

"My vision gets...clouded at times." He appeared self-conscious, his normally self-assured, strong confidence about the future gone—he seemed suddenly so vulnerable and weak.

"Eros is in trouble—" I began.

"Oh, yes. Archer and Callie. They're safe now?" He began to walk, and I fell in step beside him. Moving was thinking. It let me focus better on our words and not his face with its map of emotions etched upon it. He knew Eros's alias and about Callie, so his statement about not seeing had been a lie. What was going on with him?

"I hope so, but she's really sick, and I thought—"

"That I'd know? You mean you and Apollo can't figure it out?"

"You see the future." I shrugged.

"But you are the smartest creature on earth." A small smile crept upon his face. "We made a good team, didn't we?"

THE IMMORTAL TRANSCRIPTS: SHUDDER

My cheeks burned, and I looked away, unable to focus when I saw those lips turn into a grin. Many images came forward of moments seeing that smile, making my stomach flop with nerves.

"Still blush at compliments after all these years," he teased.

"We did solve problems well together." I desperately tried to steer him away from flirting.

"I wasn't referring to that, Thena," he said softly, using an old nickname I hadn't heard from him in years. Others said it, but when he did, it was a whole different level of intimacy.

I changed the subject quickly. "I need you to come to Iceland, to help me find answers, to help me save this girl. There's something about her, Theus." I stopped, suddenly aware he was staring at me with an odd expression on his face.

"What?" I asked. I had missed something. Sometimes complex expressions eluded my heightened intellectual powers of deduction. I had no idea how to label his face—maybe entreating? But was it more eager or anxious?

"Nothing," he shrugged it off. "When do we leave?"

"You'll come?" I was surprised, thinking he'd need a lot of persuasion—but not the kind of convincing he likely had in mind.

"Of course, Thena. Why wouldn't I?" He was a bit crestfallen, with those wounded puppy-dog eyes that filled me with guilt.

What social faux pas had I made now? Or was he in one of his moods? Anyone would be moody if they had dreams and awake visions of the future. At times, he seemed completely in a different world, unaware of those around him. I did that too, but he wasn't retreating into his mind palace as I did during those episodes. He'd see the future, but he would never tell anyone about these visions. It was his burden to carry like all Titans—Atlas with the world on his shoulders, and Sisyphus with his boulder he eternally rolled up the hill only for it to fall down again—Theus foreseeing everything but being powerless to stop it. In the past, when we had been closer, he would tell me things, little details to warn me about impending events. Proteus was right, though; I could not prevent anything from happening, no matter how hard I'd tried. The Moirai, the Fates, ruled over us.

"You knew I'd end up here, didn't you?" I asked, changing the subject.

"Of course. At first, I saw you heading to the mountains, but another dream told me you'd head for the coast and fall asleep. I've been here waiting for you. Three years now."

"Three? You used to be so...precise."

He tapped his temple gently. "Vision's cloudy, as I said. I'm going off memories of prior visions these days."

"Frustrating." We could use his all-seeing eye on our futures right now.

"No, *liberating*." He smiled widely, dimples exposed. "I feel so...normal."

"I guess that's...er...good, I suppose."

"It unnerves you, doesn't it?" The smile wouldn't leave his lips.

"Of course. It doesn't make any sense, and it doesn't help me at all."

"You don't need me, Thena. You have all the answers in that brilliant head of yours, but you're not thinking in the right direction. My brother would be a better help to you."

His brother, Epimetheus, was the god of afterthought, which meant Theus was pointing me toward the past. "What in the past would help me?"

"You'll figure it out. You always do." Prometheus said quietly. His hand grasped mine.

Unprepared for the gesture, I instinctively withdrew my hand from his. Then I blushed at my instant rejection of him and crossed my arms, tucking my hands under my elbows.

"Just like one day soon, you'll hold my hand again." He stared off at the ocean. "Thena, you need time to process the issue, as you must with all things. You are always forward-thinking, and I know you don't like revisiting the past. It'll take you time. I'm a patient and biding god, knowing there would always be a day when I get everything I have always wanted."

"Revenge?"

He hesitated before saying, "Among other more important things."

I was growing uncomfortable with his hints. "We'll leave as soon as I can book the flights."

"We're going to fly in Zeus's sky?" The terror on Prometheus's face was priceless. I couldn't help but giggle.

We couldn't get a flight, or more properly flights, for almost a week. Prometheus insisted we stay somewhere nice; despite being immortal, he did worry about my well-being. However, being the end of summer, the town was packed and bustling, making rooms difficult to find. Prometheus finally found a room in a very expensive hotel. At least that was what he claimed. I wondered if he was trying to impress me and booked it in advance. Then again, he had been waiting for three years, so how would he really know when?

THE IMMORTAL TRANSCRIPTS: SHUDDER

We entered the room, and I checked it out. As extravagant as it was, I only noticed the one king-sized bed. I looked at Prometheus.

"It's all they had." He shrugged with a smirk. "I'll sleep on the floor."

"No, you slept on a rock for Zeus knows how long. *I'll* sleep on the floor."

"No, Athena," he said in such a commanding tone I did not dare to argue further. It was as if I insulted him somehow.

I could not sleep. Prometheus snored softly from the floor, able to sleep anywhere. My mind reeled, trying to fathom these fevers of Callie's. He'd said I knew the answers. It had to do with the past, the issue Prometheus and I were dancing around, trying to ignore the elephant in the room. Or more like he was trying to impart something, and I was distractedly running away from it and the floodwaters of emotion that would come with it. I would not figure this out until I allowed myself to remember things I had long since buried, things I wasn't strong enough to face. I was not ready to reopen memories that would trigger flashbacks, anxiety, and depression.

I gave up on sleep in the early morning, listened to every voicemail, and read every text. Callie not only had a few terrible fevers, but they were struggling to keep her conscious, maybe even alive, on the crossing.

Lost in my reveries of how to solve Callie's problem without enough information, a hand touched my shoulder, making me jump. I turned to see a groggy Prometheus yawning.

"My guess is you didn't sleep at all. Athena, when will you learn a simple problem is not worth all the effort? 'Truth will out.'"

"Simple problem?" I raised my voice at him. "This girl is on the verge of death!"

His gaze hardened, making me feel chastised, for I know not what. He sighed, now more disappointed than mad. "C'mon. I want pancakes. We'll talk it out."

At the diner, I told him the specifics of Callie: age, a descendant of Psyche, the spouse of Eros, and how Zeus wanted her dead...

"There's only one reason Zeus wants anyone dead. They threaten his power. I am surprised he's never killed me. I know the key to his downfall, but perhaps that's why he keeps me alive, hoping one day he'll be able to get it out of me. Or he's scared of my sisters." Prometheus mischievously peered at me over his cup of coffee as he took a sip.

I ignored his reference to his siblings, the Fates, latching onto the mystery of Zeus's downfall. "What is it? His downfall?" I asked. Hope suddenly sprang as if there was a chance to bring Zeus down, to have ultimate justice, a balance: a democracy instead of a dictatorship.

"I can't tell you, Thena," he said playfully. "And for you to ask me to reveal a secret when withholding it keeps me alive, well, that's just downright cruel. Do you want me dead? No, scratch that. I'm afraid of your answer."

I shot him an unamused glare and then took a few bites of my pancakes. When I looked back at him, his face was studying my own in a painful expression. I realized I should have assured him I wanted him alive. By now he should know my social inequities, but he was such a sensitive soul, letting his emotions override all logic. So opposite, and yet we were kindred spirits in some way.

Finally, I formulated a response. "It should be you wishing for my death. If it hadn't been for me...that rock." I shook off the thought of the suffering he once endured, not for giving man fire, as the myths proclaim, because he did that long before Zeus found immortality, but for loving me. His punishment was what motivated me to help and endeared Callie and Archer's plight to me—no lovers should be forced apart. It was not the romantic ideal that Persephone had pointed out but a logical one.

"Thena, that was not your fault." The hard planes of his face cut into a serious expression.

"Wasn't it?" I felt foolish, tears building, so I stared at my food.

"Thena, look at me." I forced my gaze to meet his. His dark eyes were intense but open and honest. "I was punished for one reason alone: I would not reveal the name of the person who would usurp Zeus's throne."

His hand rested upon mine, and this time, I did not take it away.

"Why wouldn't you tell?" I asked him to distract myself from how comfortable it was to have him touch me again, even if it was merely my hand.

"I honestly couldn't condemn someone to die. Could you?"

I shook my head. I could not utter someone's name, knowing Zeus would smite them, even if they were my enemy. All this time, I'd thought Zeus punished him and me for wanting to be together. Something was missing from Prometheus's explanation, but I could not bring it up. There were things we had promised to never speak of again, and I don't break my oaths.

"So, this unsolvable problem with Callie, how do you know it won't solve itself? Maybe she'll get over it?" Prometheus changed topics.

THE IMMORTAL TRANSCRIPTS: SHUDDER

"Prometheus of the Titans, god of fire, foresight, and the ultimate trickster, if you know something, stop toying with me, and tell me what is going on." I tried to sound intimidating, but it merely made him smile. I withdrew my hand from under his to punish him.

His smile faded. He waved his hand dismissively. "She'll be fine. Don't worry about her."

There was something, so many things, he was hiding from me. I swallowed my fears and insecurities, which seemed to crop up in his presence, and held his gaze. It was an unnerving feeling, seeing into someone's soul—and highly distracting—but he had to know I was serious. "Tell me everything."

"I will, and don't take offense to this, but you need time. Just know that I have seen Callie before in visions where she is alive and well in the future." He explained.

"How far in the future?"

He shrugged. "I'm not some fact-spitting computer, Thena. This is the best I can give you."

He was mocking my encyclopedic brain. We sat in silence for a moment. After a few minutes, he sighed. "Athena is not satisfied. Fine. Let's play Socrates." He referred to a game he had always used to get me thinking; only, he had often turned it into flirting. In the end, it was a great way to get through to me when social aspects such as small talk and flirting didn't come easy. He found a way, and my heart warmed at the thought of him wanting to find our connection again. "Who are Callie's parents?"

"Mortals. Both dead. Father was a demigod, a distant descendent of Psyche." Repeating myself was a bit tedious.

"Mother?"

"Mortal."

"Humph," Prometheus looked out the window, his face strained by aggravation. "Never mind."

"What?"

"Nothing. You know, when I was chained to that rock, I had time to think about things, about everything. I could see the future better than I ever had before. It let me see what actions I needed to perform in order to have everything I desired come true. And, Athena, I want to tell you things. You can't understand how hard it was or is to hide things from the one you..." he stopped, realizing he was about to say "love" or "loved."

I wasn't sure which tense I'd prefer. I'd be scared to fall for him again, but it was equally taxing to know he used to love me and no longer did.

He snatched my hand from under the table. "If I told you some things, Thena, it could ruin everything."

"What is everything?"

"The future. What bothers me is you know everything, in a sense. You know who the usurper was, but you just refuse to see it."

"Was, past tense," I noted.

He squeezed my hand. "Yes."

"I don't want to talk about the past."

"If you forget the past, you'll never reach the future. Thena, what are you so afraid of?"

I wanted to tell him I was afraid of him, of the future, of the past when Zeus destroyed our happiness, and afraid of failing Callie and Archer—I wanted to spare them the pain Theus and I had suffered.

"Everything," I whispered.

"I will protect you."

"You can't protect me from myself, and you can't protect me from you." I tore my hand out of his again and stormed out of the diner, desperately trying to behave like a mortal. My twenty-five demigod years of life were so long ago that mortalling no longer came naturally. I took quick panicky breaths. It was all too much, these feelings. The sound of traffic, the waves of the beach a block away, the bright sun. Too much. I was going into anxiety mode. I was heading for a meltdown. I walked. If I got far away from him, the noise...

I hadn't gotten two blocks away when he stepped out of an alleyway, blocking my path.

His face expressed too much, and I squeezed my eyes shut. Guilt, regret, my pain reflected in his soulful eyes. "Too much."

"I know." His arms wrapped around me from behind, and I almost started to smack him off, but soon it turned into a big crushing bear hug and everything dissipated. The crushing sensation focused my attention and allowed me to regroup my emotions and thoughts. I took one more deep breath to make sure I was calmer.

Embarrassed and not wanting to discuss my outburst, I feigned a light tone, "You paid, didn't you?"

"I work in a restaurant right now. Of course, I paid."

"Good," was all I could say.

"Right, Thena. Let us just speak of simple matters until we get to Iceland. Then we'll hash it out."

THE IMMORTAL TRANSCRIPTS: SHUDDER

"Good idea." I concurred. "Simple things, hmmm..." I tried to fathom what simple things happen in a deity's life. Nothing came to mind.

"What have you been up to for the last fifty or so years?" He politely asked as we walked on.

Still, the simple comment brought back the fateful day I had last seen him. I pushed away and buried the melancholy memories and focused on logic. I simply would tell him what I had done. It was merely a conversation, sentences made of words, strung together.

I could do this.

CHAPTER 14

Lucien

Poseidon, now a stowaway, hid in my room. It wasn't like he could check into a cruise in the middle of the Atlantic. He was afraid if he entered the water again, he'd need Callie's help to resurface, and we weren't about to let his theory be retested in the middle of the Atlantic. He slept on the sofa bed, not affording us much room and zero personal space, but the guy had served a three-thousand-year-plus underwater prison sentence. He deserved a massive suite...and a barber. His hair was a long, tangled mess of white-blond locks stained a green hue by the sea. His beard matched his hair. He looked so much like Zeus that the phytoplankton-dyed hair and the sun-tanned skin were the only determining factors to tell them apart.

Wait—and those eyes.

Poseidon's eyes were more of a blue-green rather than Zeus's gray-blue, but there was more to it than that. Poseidon had humanity in his eyes, which contrasted my father's cold, unresponsive ones.

The fifth morning on the boat, a knock on my door woke us. Poseidon sat straight up, choking on air, most likely the same feeling we gods have when waking up underwater. Atlantis, deep inside The Great Blue Hole, had a fortified palace with air in it, but it couldn't be this fresh. Poseidon and Hades had all kinds of contraptions or methods to ensnare fresh air and bring it to their imprisoned worlds, merely as a nostalgic extravagance, not because they needed it to survive.

I got out of bed and answered the door to see an exhausted Aroha, and when I mean she looked tired—she was makeup free with tangled hair. Aroha disregarding her appearance? I was on high alert.

"Callie is sick, and Archer isn't doing well either."

Great. The last thing we needed was another emergency in the middle of the Atlantic. I took a deep breath and snapped into medic mode. I threw on some clothes, splashed my face to wash away the remnants of my grogginess, and followed her to Archer and Callie's room. The lovebirds were camped out across from me and five doors down. Chase let me in; the formidable war god was scared. His dark brown mane of hair was loose, not in his trademark ponytail, and the stubble he sported wasn't tidy, hair creeping down his neck. Him being frazzled enough that he didn't care about his appearance, and Aroha allowing him to let it slip, was telling.

I peered beyond him into the room. Callie was worse than I'd thought. Her svelte form thrashed around in the bed, and sweat beaded on her face, which was pale and not her Mediterranean bronze that matched mine. Her hair was damp and sticking to her neck, although the thermostat had a cool reading.

"Temperature?" I asked.

"Down to 105," Aroha said.

"Down to?"

"It hit 107, and we doused her in ice."

Okay, not all sweat, some water, but the high temperature unnerved me, and I started checking her vitals. "How long ago?"

"An hour." Chase supplied. The ice had all melted within an hour? My heart hammered in my chest at how familiar this felt. Flashbacks from thousands of years ago hit me, watching Aristaeus—whom the nymph Queen Cyrene had birthed for me—almost die from a high fever during his transition into immortality. Wait, it might not be *like* my son's situation, maybe it *was* the same. Had someone slipped her ambrosia? How? Poseidon? No, he had no access.

Callie's body was now still. She was pale, and her chest rose and fell erratically. She was close to seizure territory. I knelt next to the bed and touched her temples, channeling in my healing powers. That's when I noticed an asleep Archer snuggled against her in the bed, looking more than terrible.

"Is he *sick*?" I asked in disbelief. Gods didn't get sick. Never. Only a little during our teenage years when the powers kicked in—well, for Archer at birth, but he was an anomaly similar to his father. Ares was older than me, but the stories said he was the same; I think it was because Zeus had obsessively pushed and abused him into using his powers early. The negatives of being the firstborn, I suppose.

"I don't understand it." Aroha fretted.

I moved from Callie to him, and he was burning up as well. "Go get Hymenaios, now," I ordered.

Chase was out the door.

"What can he do?" Aroha asked.

"I need affirmation. I think they immortally married. Wouldn't it make sense? He goes through what she does, and Zeus tried to kill my son out of retaliation. He said my son married them. I foolishly misjudged Aios's claim that Archer wanted to marry her as Eros to mean it was only a mortal ceremony."

"And you didn't think to tell us?" Aroha's eyes bulged, and then she shook her head in admonishment.

Of course, it was all my fault, not her precious boy's for being so reckless. "Because I thought it was impossible he'd be so stupid. I think he did it, though."

"No, Archer wouldn't link his soul to a mortal."

"He almost died without her. Is it too far-fetched that he'd sacrifice himself to keep her alive? You and your brood of romantic fools!"

For once, Aroha didn't chide me about my disdain for the irrationalism of love.

"Call my son." I dipped the washcloth in the water and bathed Callie's forehead with it to cool her. She shivered.

"Chase is getting him."

I leaned over and placed the washcloth on Archer's forehead. He shivered as well. This was not good. I placed the washcloth down and started channeling my healing powers into both of them.

"No, my other son. This is beyond him or me. We both must work on them together. I'm going to need to lie out in the sun in a bit. I'm already draining."

"You call him."

"Aroha, you called him a twerp once. I apparently ruined his life, so…"

She huffed at me and dialed her phone.

I wasn't sure about this. I hadn't spoken with Asclepius in hundreds of years. Not quite true about me ruining his life. Myths aren't always the truth. Yes, Asclepius's mother did cheat on me while carrying my son, and I forsook her for it, but my bloodthirsty sister—who loved to kill women in childbirth like some fascist chastity enforcer—tried to kill them both. I performed the first C-section ever to save his life and failed to heal her; well, I failed to stop my sister's lethal arrows as I brought him into the world. He blamed me more than his aunt, goddess of childbirth, whose hatred of libidinous men caused some biased decisions during delivery.

Artemis and I had a rocky relationship after that, but it was completely severed after the Hymenaios incident. Maybe before that. The number of people I seduced during Greek and Roman days angered her, but her real issue was rejecting her own sexuality then; now, embracing it, she surrounded herself with her girls. Her "purity" status was a joke when you included women.

Aios entered the room, groggy as well. His hair was askew, having finally grown out a bit.

"Look what you did." I scolded.

Aios was shocked for a moment, taking in Archer's poor health, but then understanding crossed his features. But instead of his normally calm demeanor, or the apology I expected, he glared at me. "He asked for this! I tried to stop him, but I can't deny the request when they're soulmates, can I?" In a calmer tone he continued, "Dad, all of them combined—*philia, storge, eros, agape*—make a perfect match: best friends, married so their family, obviously the desire part's there, and selflessness. I mean, he's willing to die for her." He threw up his hands in defeat. "I don't think she even knows. I can't imagine she'd ever use him to survive."

"She wouldn't," Aroha said. "Can you stop this fever or not?"

"I said to call my son!" I lashed out. Deep down, I was mad about Archer making such a grand gesture and not even telling Callie about it. The things the two hid from each other would destroy their marriage.

"You need to do that, Dad. He won't come anywhere near you unless you call."

"You have to, Lucien. For Archer." Aroha sighed, holding up her phone. "He's not answering me."

I cursed in ancient Greek. "I shouldn't leave them like this."

"Stop with the excuses. I can control it for a little bit." My son was scolding me now.

"No offense, but you're no healer."

"I can control the link of souls and can momentarily untwine them so that Archer will be okay. It will make her sicker, so hurry up. He's taking half her fever for her right now. Tell my brother I said this is not about him or me or you but about saving Eros. He will come if you apologize."

"For what?" I meant it as the many crimes he could accuse me of, but Aios took it the wrong way if his glare was any indicator.

"For being a deadbeat."

Yep, I deserved that one, and it smarted.

I hurried outside and called my son, the healer, who only reconciled with me briefly to steal my knowledge of the art of healing and took it beyond any of my abilities. We had doctors and modern science in the world because of him.

I dialed and was greeted with "What the—"

I jumped in before he could throw expletives at me or hang up. "Eros has a problem. This is more important than you and me. Have Zeph bring you. Now."

"I...I...fine." He hung up. He so wanted to deny me, but he and Archer had grown up together, and everyone loved Archer. He had been the darling of Olympus, the first grandchild of Zeus, but now the wayward outcast.

I went back in, and Archer was awake, arguing with Aios. I went to Callie's side and touched her temples. She was burning up. "I have Asclepius coming to help. We can't deal with two of you like this. Aios had to separate you two. Immortal marriage? What were you thinking?"

"Link us back!" Archer demanded. "If my suffering keeps her alive, join our souls again."

"You're not separated. You know I can never undo it, Archer." Aios told him. "It's momentary. No matter who tries to part you, you'll be forever drawn back together."

"Why did you?" I pleaded, staring deep into Archer's intense eyes, alight with emotion. He was my best friend, despite everything. I loved him and needed him; I could not lose him. The missing part of me, which sucked in normal relationships and familial ones, connected with Archer. For the first time, I realized he was more important than my shattered and disappointed heart, my loneliness, my self-preservation, everything. "You're my best friend."

Archer was taken aback by the power of emotion in my voice. As the god of love, he understood all the forms of love. He was like my brother, my friend-soulmate, *philia*, part of my existence. This action he had done proved how far his love for Callie went. I wanted her, but he would die for her. Again—in so many ways—I was the lesser man and did not deserve her.

"Give us a minute," Archer told the others.

In a huff, Aroha left. Aios patted me on the shoulder as if to wish me luck.

Once they all left, Archer immediately spoke: "She has to live."

"I think it's the stupidest and most ingenious thing you've ever done."

Archer cocked his head. "I expected the first, but 'ingenious'?"

"It's the best protection she could hope for. Do you think Zeus will risk killing her if you die too?"

"He already tried."

"Fair point, but if he succeeds, there will be a war beyond what we have seen in years." There. I finally was letting the prophecy out, although

THE IMMORTAL TRANSCRIPTS: SHUDDER

Archer wouldn't know it was one. I could not add to his worries by telling him war was inevitable.

He swallowed hard, and his gaze met mine, a look of apology on his face. "Look, I'm sorry, Lucien. I didn't think about you, my parents, anyone, except her. I didn't question it. I couldn't live without her. She could not live without me. It was simple. I needed to protect her."

I completely understood his rationalism, but not the guts to actually do it. I nodded in acceptance of his admittance, an apology.

"Let's say she dies..." Archer's frame shuddered at the thought. "Is there a way to gain a connection for her from someone else? I need to see her for part of my life if the worst should happen."

I sighed. The situation was hopeless, irreversible, but I couldn't tell him what he already knew. I had to say something, though. "Like Castor and Pollux? They only had a soul-share, *storge*." I reminded Archer that his case was different. By immortally marrying Callie, he had a four-way soul-share, a bind. Castor and Pollux were twins, spawns of Zeus and the famous Leda mortal—well, Pollux was Zeus's son, while Castor wasn't; it was as complicated as all Olympian life was. The important bit was Zeus intervened, making Pollux immortal, who in turn saved his dying brother Castor by having Hymenaios share his soul through their deep familial love. Of course, the myths praise Zeus as the hero, saving the day, and my son isn't mentioned at all. As mortals and immortals well know, history is written by those in power.

Archer shook his head. "Not like them. Half a soul, so half a life up here and half a life in Hades but never together? That's not what I want. That would be worse than death."

That was the drawback of Pollux saving his brother. Sharing his immortal soul to a mortal resulted in them taking turns with that immortal soul, never seeing each other again.

Archer's eyes pleaded with me to find a solution. "I know it's selfish and insane, but I need her, Lucien."

He was sounding insane. Asking someone to give up half a life for a longshot of Callie surviving for a partial life? "Look, you won't even get a Castor-Pollux situation. You are bound to her, not simply borrowing a piece of a soul. This is completely uncharted territory. No one has tried to soul-share with people who are immortally married. No one is crazy enough to. There is soul-sharing to keep someone alive, but you two are immortally married. What happens to that particular connection? Let's say someone soul-shares via *storge*, like Pollux had." I purposely mentioned family, so he wouldn't get any more ideas. That would limit candidates of this ridiculousness because she had few gods who truly loved her in a familial way. "I don't know if it would work, and if your familial bond to her is weakened, we have no idea what might happen."

"I'd never ask anyone anyway." Archer sighed and brushed Callie's hair out of her face. "But, by all the gods, I will die with her."

"It won't come to that," I lied. I was worried the prophecy was forewarning me that it would be true.

The door opened, and everyone entered. Asclepius squatted next to me, placing down an old-fashioned physician's bag. He met my gaze, those green eyes meeting my own. Other than the unruly black hair and matching eyes, he looked like his mother—a constant reminder of her for eternity. "I came for Eros, not you."

"I know." I removed my hands from Callie's temples so he could properly assess her. "I'm glad you are a better being than your hatred."

"No thanks to you."

"I'm so glad to see you, regardless." I touched his shoulder. My son. Why was I so bad at being a parent?

"A case you can't solve intrigued me. Showing your incapability is highly motivating."

Ouch. Still, I would not risk a negative rebuttal. Archer and Callie needed him here. "Still trying to outshine the old man, huh?"

"Not trying. I always do." He bumped my shoulder, which was tantamount to a hug from him.

My heart pitter-pattered with pride.

Asclepius's face screwed up in confusion, and his eyes darted to me. "Has she been given anything?"

"Just your elixirs, some nectar—she seems to handle it well."

"That's it?"

"Yes," Archer affirmed.

"Apollo, is he lying?"

I was irritated that Asclepius refused to use a fatherly moniker, but let it go. I surveyed my friends' blank expressions and concluded with a shake of my head. "None of them are lying." They were as puzzled as I was. Asclepius was insinuating she had been given ambrosia. Was Callie becoming immortal?

"Stop everything. You've been treating her wrong. Her fever needs to pitch and break. I don't understand how this happened, but I know this is how to heal her," Asclepius said.

THE IMMORTAL TRANSCRIPTS: SHUDDER

"No. You can't pitch it. She went as high as 107 degrees. Any higher..." I didn't need to finish.

Asclepius's eyes met mine. Instead of hatred, sympathy was in them. "She's not Aristaeus. She'll be fine." He stood up. "All our remedies have prolonged her illness. Serves me right for sending elixirs without seeing the patient first. You all meant well but were too close to the situation to realize what was actually going on."

Aroha threw her arms up in vexation. "What *is* going on?"

My son glanced at each of us in turn, his gaze resting on me last. He was hiding something. The omission was growing, nudging me to figure out how this happened. Callie was becoming immortal. I gave him a slight shake of my head. We could not tell Archer this. If we were wrong and gave him false hope...

"I don't want to even guess. Her body is fighting the fever, and you guys are helping her fight, but if you ease up, it'll pass. Don't let the fever go past 107; otherwise, do nothing but give her this." Asclepius pulled out a small bottle. It was D's Godhoney Nectar Rum 151. It would knock Dionysus himself into inebriation; it was that strong.

Aroha gasped. "Don't! It'll kill her."

"No," Asclepius said. "Just one spoonful. It will knock her out, but her fever will break. It can heal all beings."

Aroha looked at my son dubiously. Aios remained quietly pensive, as did Chase.

I wondered if their minds were concluding the same thing as mine. "Yes," I added. "She can handle it. Didn't she drink some of D's whiskey he had used to heal you after Zelus's attack?" I directed at Archer.

He nodded, staring at her. He was desperate for a cure but so worried. No wonder. It wasn't only her life on the line.

Asclepius wished us good luck and was out the door. I followed him as he headed down the hall to meet Zeph and head home. He rounded on me. "I'm not going to tell Zeus where you are, and neither will Zeph. In fact, I'd like to pretend we never saw you guys. I wish you didn't pull me into your problems, though."

"My problems? These are Archer's problems."

"I highly doubt they are only his. How did you miss her illness?"

"Because it's impossible. No one gave her ambrosia. I would know if they were lying."

"You were the one who showed me how to spike fevers to ease

immortal powers. I remember the stories of you saving Archer's life when he was a baby. You spiked it."

"He was im..." I stopped the pretense. He knew and so did I. Or I was finally admitting what had been right in front of me—even though unbelievable.

"Why won't you tell them?" Asclepius asked. He was frustrated with me.

"If she doesn't make it through the night or isn't immortal after the fever? Do you know how Archer will react? He's unstable. Once she makes it through this, we can celebrate it."

He stared at me. "Who is she?"

"Psyche's, but there is more to it we don't understand. She's important."

"More important than the lives of your sons?"

It was a big stab at me, and it hurt like a real knife. "Hymenaios makes his own choices, as do you. This girl—Asclepius, I can't tell you details without endangering you—is capable of profound and inexplicable things."

"A freaky immortal whom my grandfather wants dead? Yeah, I don't want to know."

Hearing it outloud was too much. Callie, immortal. I changed the subject. "You saved Archer's life today too. I'm proud of you."

"Don't be." He glowered at me. Then, at immortal speed, he was gone. I sighed. I hoped his resentment of me wouldn't tempt him to betray us.

I stayed in Archer and Callie's cabin, checking her temperature and vitals every half hour. Only once did her fever hit 107, and I had to funnel a smidgen of healing power into her to maintain that temperature. She was sweaty, thrashing around, and mumbling. I fed her the nectar rum, which instantly put her at ease, and she slept deeply. Guilt and regret filled me. She had to live through this. It was my fault. I should've known spiking it would be the right course. My mistake might cost Callie her life. Some healer I was.

At some point, I managed to drift off to sleep.

"Oh-my-gods!" Archer's frantic voice woke me.

Oh, no.

Dread filled my heart as I opened my eyes.

CHAPTER 15

Callie

When I opened my eyes, I felt well rested and fantastic, as if rejuvenated after my excitement in and out of the sea. Who knew Poseidon would be able to come out of the water? I mean, I somehow saw him do it before, but now everyone had to believe me. The daunting thought was overwhelming: I was the only one who could free him (things were getting weirder with me by the minute).

I turned to see my beautiful husband sleeping next to me. He was on top of the covers, looking so peaceful. I had to shake him awake since Archer always had me trapped in his arms. It took several attempts before his eyes shot open. "Oh-my-gods!" he shouted (give me a heart attack, Archer).

Then, in a blur of movements due to his immortal powers, he was out of bed and had scooped me up in his arms, kissing me, and murmuring things too fast for me to keep up.

"I see you're better," a bleary-eyed, rumpled Lucien muttered from the sofa.

Archer let me down, my feet touching the floor.

"I was sick?" I asked them, meaning more sick than I had been.

"Two days you were out." Archer's voice cracked, his eyes gazing to the floor. He was hiding the pain I caused him, but I could still feel it.

"I've gotta stop going out so much, then." My joke did not amuse either god in the room.

Archer ran his hand down my hair, which must be a frightful tangle of frizz. "The fever was relentless and high. I thought I was going to lose you."

"I'm fine. In fact, I feel great." I showed him by twirling around the room.

Lucien harrumphed, then turned on his doctor-mode mood. After treating me like a science experiment, where Lucien concluded I was healthier than ever, Archer relaxed a bit. When Lucien's eyes met mine, I saw the truth in them. He knew, just as I knew, beyond a doubt now, *it must be true*. I still couldn't face it and tell Archer without a full understanding of *how* it was possible. The way Archer was acting told me Lucien was keeping my secret. Uncomfortable for many reasons, Lucien jetted out of there.

The next day, we docked in Iceland. We hardly got to sightsee, Chase only giving us an hour, eager to move on for my safety. He and Aroha left us immediately to get rental cars, while the rest of us went off to shop, being told where to rendezvous. Then we traveled north from Reykjavík, all the way to Ólafsfjörður, in two vans. Aside from lovely scenery, it was an uneventful five hours. I was happy for things to be boringly normal, for once.

When we entered Athena's ski cabin by a lake, the place was warmed and heated with a fire burning. It wasn't cold out (as the country's name makes you think), but a cool fifty-one degrees. It was definitely different from the stifling nineties we had in NYC before we left, but the temperature dip had been gradual as we traveled across the Atlantic (the parts I was awake for). The sun was still shining bright since we were so far north. I wondered whether it ever got dark this time of year? Aroha poked around cautiously since we had been told Athena wasn't home.

A woman stepped out with a tray of tea in her hands. She was gorgeous, her skin so pale white, it almost matched snow, her eyes like glistening emeralds, and her hair a shockingly vibrant red.

"Greetings." She bowed her head with a smile. "I am Freya."

"Norse goddess of love," Archer whispered in my ear (great, more mythology to study).

"I welcome you since Athena is away. If there is anything you need, please, I am just three doors down." She pointed to the left to show us the direction she lived. "The kitchen is fully stocked and beds made up." She stared at me for a moment, inspecting me (creepy).

I hugged Archer to me as if to protect myself from her probing gaze.

"Thank you for that. Please stay for dinner then." Aroha stepped forward and shook her hand.

All the gods around me seemed a little ill at ease. I got the vibe that gods of other countries weren't exactly buddies with one another. I found it strange that these gods had been alive for thousands of years and yet never took the time to get to know other cultures' gods. (Why?)

"Thank you." Freya smiled awkwardly.

THE IMMORTAL TRANSCRIPTS: SHUDDER

Archer gripped my hand tightly after Aroha announced dinner would be in an hour. "Let's pick out our room." There was a flirty mischief in Archer's voice. He led me up the stairs and found a master suite. "Will this do?"

"It's huge and gorgeous. Won't your parents want it?" I asked. Even stranger, why hadn't Athena taken it?

"It's our honeymoon." Archer pulled me in and gave me one of the commanding kisses, ordering me to stop thinking and to give in to my desire.

"They found their room." Himerus snickered at us, which broke Archer and my lip-lock.

I shot a glare at him and Anteros.

"There are only four bedrooms. Where will we all stay?" Anteros asked.

"Not in here," Archer hinted for them to go away.

They didn't.

"That means leave us alone," I said sweetly, closing the door in their faces.

Archer laughed and took me into his arms, kissing me. "My cleverly cruel Callie."

I kissed him back, making the most of it...

At dinner, the two little brats kept whispering, laughing, and gawping at Archer and me. I tried to ignore them, but it got irritating. Sometimes, they were like the two protective big brothers you needed, but then again, most of the time, they were the little brothers you wish you never had. I scowled at them. "Oh, grow up."

"That's it." Aroha dropped her fork. "She's right. I don't know how much more silliness I can handle from you two. Find your own lodgings tomorrow."

Himerus groaned. "Aww, man."

"There's no room for all of you, here, anyway. You can stay with me." Freya turned to Poseidon. "I always will help any love god, but I'm also curious to hear the many tales from Poseidon about the sea."

"Is everyone covered then? We have four bedrooms, but the downstairs one belongs to Athena. You two took the master, so Dite and I will take the one in the middle..." Chase said.

I was really glad we had snagged the master now. There was a bathroom between the master and other bedrooms, but the last two bedrooms shared a wall. No way was I sharing a wall with my in-laws (Ew).

Chase directed his attention elsewhere. "That leaves one more room. Lucien?"

"I don't want to part with my son," he said.

Aios stared at his plate, but a small smile tugged at his lips.

Chase had a gleam in his eyes. "Perfect. They're bunk beds."

Lucien snorted, annoyed, but said nothing else.

Exhausted from the traveling, Archer and I went upstairs, ignoring more crude comments from his lusty brother. I fell asleep as soon as I hit the mattress.

The next morning, I awoke to Archer's arms wrapped tightly around me, trapping me like an inchworm in a snug cocoon. I peered over my shoulder to see his angelic face peacefully sleeping. I needed him to break this habit of holding me prisoner in his sleep, his strength too intense against my own to break free, but he was unconsciously afraid for my safety (with good reason, obviously). He had his reasons to be clingy, but this had to stop soon. I had to tell him what I thought, what I knew now must be true. Without knowing how it had happened, would he worry more? Would he get more overbearing and overprotective?

This morning I didn't want to wake him, but his iron-clad arms were always unbreakable. I turned slowly around to face him, and as I had learned about my new husband, a Poseidon-level earthquake wouldn't wake him. I traced the contours of his face, his bowed lips, dimpled chin, angular jaw, his cheeks—manly but with just enough boyish smoothness to them. His short hair was tousled about in funny patterns as though he had been tossing. In reality, he slept like a lump, a statue, frozen.

I tried to slip from those arms, which bound me in a captivity of covers, but couldn't (as suspected). I struggled to get my arms out and slipped the comforter down; then, I tried to pull his rock-hard grip of one hand from around his other wrist, and to my astonishment, they pulled apart. Had I used all my strength? Had he inadvertently loosened his grip? He hadn't since our wedding night. Perhaps he finally relaxed, being safely hidden in Iceland, where his family affirmed we'd be safe. His peace of mind was comforting.

I slipped out of the room and downstairs, almost tripping at the bottom as if the ground moved awkwardly under me. I wasn't a clumsy person, and ever since I woke up on the cruise, I felt great. It was probably stress and nerves—the unknown was an itch that could never be scratched. My life would never be the same. I was fever-free and physically better than I had been in a long time.

THE IMMORTAL TRANSCRIPTS: SHUDDER

I was alive, and I had Archer. Today, I'd surprise my husband with breakfast. However, before I had an egg cracked into the frying pan, I heard Archer frantically calling my name.

"I'm down here!" I called.

Instantly, with his incredible speed, he was in front of me, scaring me half to death. I dropped an egg, and it broke on the floor.

"Archer," I scolded.

"Don't do that to me." His eyes were a bit wild, as he inspected me all over as if I had been attacked in his absence. My thoughts of him being laid-back, feeling safe in Iceland, went right out the window.

"Don't you move like *that* around me," I snapped.

"Sorry, but, Callie, seriously, how did you get out of bed without waking me?" His features softened. He wiped up the egg in one quick motion and threw it in the trash can, then slowed to a speed I could follow as he paced.

"How? Well, you sleep like the dead, Archer." (Duh.)

"No, my grip."

"So, you purposely held me tight so I couldn't get out of bed?" I thwacked him in the shoulder. "Archer." (If he did it anymore, I'd sleep on the couch for spite.)

"To keep you safe, love of my eternal life." He batted his eyes and smirked before trying to kiss me.

I was angry. I turned my face away from his. He could use all his cherub charm; it wouldn't faze me.

"Callie," he begged, taking my face in his hands.

I broke away from his grasp. Archer grabbed my arm roughly in his steadfast, godly grip, his face confused.

"Archer, stop it!" I pulled away, turning my back on him. I went to the fridge to get out some bacon and sausage, deciding to start them first since eggs would be casualties at the moment; plus, I hadn't thought about how they'd get cold. Dad only ate an egg, maybe some bacon (how I missed him). These were gods, and there were five of them and me (if the others didn't come back from Freya's early). How much would they each eat?

"Callie." Archer's voice cracked.

I turned to see him staring at me oddly, wide-eyed, like I'd grown another head.

"What?" I was still angry. I hated when he used his powers against me.

"You...you...how..." he stuttered.

"Archer?" Now I was worried about him.

"You're too strong."

Now, I wasn't a hardcore feminist, but maybe I needed to be. What was that supposed to mean? "What?"

"Yes, I was trapping you in bed, and now I held your arm as tight as I could, and you broke free. Callie, how can you ..." he stopped talking, his face pallid (crap, crap, crappity crap). Was he going to faint? Not at all like him, but he was putting two-and-two together. I didn't have the words to explain myself either.

"Archer, sit down." I forced him into a chair.

"Callie, it's like I'm rubbing off on you or something—my powers."

"Is that even possible?" I was terrible for not telling him the truth, but he was so anxiety-ridden, and I had unfounded information without backing. Saying something would make him lose it completely. I should've said something ages ago. Now my omittance of what I suspected had grown into something so insurmountable, he'd never understand why I'd hidden it.

"No. Where's Athena?" He stood and started pacing.

"Still traveling, remember? Relax. I'm fine." I tried to force him to sit again, but he stood immobile (liar, liar, Callie).

"Hmmm." He inspected me again. "Perhaps it's only when you're angry."

"Testing me?" I scoffed at him. "I'm not a science experiment, Mr. Ambrose." I dumped the sausages into the pan, and they sizzled, matching my mood.

A moment later, two warm hands gently gripped my waist, and a face faintly brushed against my neck, the stubble prickling my skin and lips pressing gently against my jaw. All anger washed from me with his touch.

"Callie?" Archer's voice was a rough whisper.

"Hmmm?"

"I'm sorry. I'm just scared and confused. Are you hiding something from me? Tell me everything. I need to know how you're feeling."

"Feeling?" I asked, a little lost. How could I explain how I felt? I was a turmoil of mixed emotions: depressed about Dad, ecstatic to be married to this amazing being, scared of getting killed, annoyed at everyone's overprotective concerns in me, and terrified about what Dad had told me in his letter.

"No more secrets, Callie." He turned me around (super-duper crap). He placed his palm on my forehead, and on finding me at a normal temperature, he sighed.

"You have secrets," I protested (cough, cough—immortal marriage).

He gave me a soft smile. "I've told you everything you've wanted to know. You're very persistent."

"You didn't tell me *everything*." I tried to bargain. If he explained what it was, maybe I could explain what was wrong (or right?) with me.

"The important things."

I gave him a leveled glare. "Your—what?—three thousand years was so simple that you have nothing more to tell?"

"Pretty much." He shrugged.

I was not letting him off the hook, and I needed time to figure out how to drop a bombshell without upsetting him (probably a pointless endeavor).

Archer breathed deeply out as if he was dreading how far I would go with this. "Fine, I'll tell you everything."

"Okay." I tended the sausages.

"How do you feel?"

"Physically or mentally?" I shot back.

"I know what you're mentally going through. I've been there, and I'm there now." He moved his hand flippantly as if to dismiss the issue. He slipped himself up in one fluid motion to sit on the counter next to the stove.

"Strange," I told him, but he awaited more. I told him about the clumsiness, the surreal dreams, the out-of-body experiences during my fevers, the ability to use my intuition further than I had before, and now how I felt completely well. The truth nagged in the back of my mind.

Archer didn't respond after I finished, but his brow wrinkled deep in thought. If he could figure it out, I wouldn't have to say the words. "I don't understand it, Callie. I wish I knew, but we'll figure this out. Even without Athena, we'll get to the bottom of it. I just want you better."

I didn't want to point out that I already was.

The questions ended when Chase and Lucien's rumbling tummies brought them down the steps for food, and I kept cooking until Aroha insisted on taking over. "You'd be surprised how much these monsters can eat, and stoves do not cook in immortal speed." She gave me a wink. Ever since the wedding, Aroha had acted as a true family member. I was so happy the Aroha I had met with her icy exterior had melted into this warm being.

I sat next to Archer, who slid his plate to me, letting me eat the rest of his breakfast rather than let me wait for a plate. I loved my new family, but

I was still in the honeymoon mindset, wanting Archer to myself. He distracted me from everything plaguing my mind.

Despite both our efforts, we didn't get alone time until after supper. Lucien and Aios were at Freya's, while Aroha and Chase claimed the back porch for a date. She glared at us as if to say we better stay inside with the curtains closed. Maybe I read her mind a little and closed the curtains myself (mind-reading was quite gross at times).

Once alone on the sofa, watching TV, Archer pulled me onto his lap, and I leaned against the snug, soft corner of the couch and draped my legs comfortably across the couch cushion. I wanted Archer's side of the bargain. He let me off easy this morning, so I was wary of asking difficult questions. The more info he gave me, the more likely he'd press me for more answers to these growing powers, strength, and dream visions, but I needed to know more about him. I could never have enough of him.

I took a deep breath and directed my attention away from the TV onto that adorable face. I could spend immortality with him (focus, Callie!). "Your turn."

"My turn?" he asked me, seemingly stumped.

"This morning?"

He sighed. "And here I foolishly thought we were going to enjoy our time alone."

"We can. I just want your side of the deal paid up."

He laughed softly and pulled me closer. "What do you want to know?"

Now or never, I dove in. "Everything about immortal marriage."

He stiffened, his easy demeanor fading away. His gaze averted from mine. "I told you. Our souls joined, making us soul mates."

When he looked at me, I rolled my wrist gesturing for him to keep going.

"You've probably figured it out by now, but we are joined in many ways. I felt what you did when your dad passed away. I inadvertently took on some of the grief for you."

If what he said was true, I never wanted to know the full force of grief all at once.

"When Zeus attacked me, you inadvertently took some of that on too. We're lucky I was strong enough for us to live. Callie," —he grew serious and leaned in closer— "soul mates mean our souls are bound. We cannot be parted. You die, I die." He kissed me, his lips trembling. "I will not live without you," was whispered on my lips.

THE IMMORTAL TRANSCRIPTS: SHUDDER

I kissed him back, my lusty thoughts overpowering the rational anger in my head about him doing something so drastic without asking me first, without telling me what binding souls really meant. He would have sacrificed himself, thinking he was saving his weak mortal wife when really—I wasn't quite sure what I was anymore (identity crisis here). His kiss and touch wiped those thoughts away as well as the anger from him hiding something so monumental from me. I would not live without him either. Never. It was Archer and me together forever.

He pulled away. "Let's go to bed." The connotation of his phrase was not lost on me.

"It's early, isn't it?"

"No, it's past midnight. The sun set not long ago."

It was so weird to have only so many hours of darkness.

"It'll rise again in a few hours." Archer got to his feet and offered me his hands.

"How will we sleep then?"

"You didn't notice it yesterday? There are blackout curtains." He pulled me up so hard that I landed in his arms. His smirk said it had been on purpose.

"I was tired."

"Rightfully, after a rough cruise trip, but you're not too tired now?" He kissed me.

I kissed him back to show him I was far from tired. Hours with him behind blackout curtains was all that was on my mind, the worries drifting away. There was always tomorrow to admit secrets.

Now, I was too distracted to talk.

CHAPTER 16

Archer

For the first time since I reunited with Callie, I felt as if we were safe—safer, at least. Athena was right in claiming Iceland was off Zeus's radar. I couldn't sense his presence overshadowing us any longer, and when I closed my eyes and scanned the area for him, he thankfully wasn't nearby. Weeks had passed, and nothing had happened. Athena was also right about the Norse immortals. They kept to themselves and tolerated our presence. One, in particular, had been interested in helping us. Freya was the equivalent of my mother as a goddess of love and beauty. She was equally beautiful as my mother but in a different way—pale, clear-skinned, with fiery red hair and emerald green eyes. Callie seemed to befriend Freya instantly, but something in me was oddly on edge around the goddess. I didn't trust her, and her presence was consumingly irritating. She didn't do or say anything wrong, so I had no idea where my hesitation came from.

Athena's cabin was nestled in the mountains, with the sea to the north and an inlet to the south in the little town of Ólafsfjörður. We kept to ourselves and ventured out little, Freya gathering our groceries, or sometimes someone else would go out heavily disguised. Poseidon took daily dips in the cold sea with no issues resurfacing, and my brothers ventured out for some extreme sports. After a mere three weeks, we were already on each other's nerves. Ma yelled at my brothers daily; my dad went for runs and swims and still was full of pent-up energy. The worst was Lucien, who moped, rolled his eyes, and had a snide comment any time Callie and I were romantic, intimate, or sweet. I realized it pained him to see us happy when he was brokenhearted, but I wasn't about to suppress my feelings as the god of love. He'd have to deal with it. I mean, Callie and I were newlyweds, entering a new and important part of our relationship that would set the foundation for the rest of her life, our life. Part of the immortal marriage was done because I would go when she did. Mortals cannot live forever. I had a long life, and I could not start afresh when she was gone.

This morning, Callie and I were in the kitchen, awake earlier than everyone else, per usual. Her hair was twisted up in a messy bun, showing the nape of her neck, the part I loved most to kiss. We were cooking breakfast again—well, she was, and I was trying desperately to coax her back to bed. Habitually, these breakfasts woke the others, and I wanted more alone time with her.

"C'mon." I put my arms around her, kissing that sweet spot on her neck, which I knew drove her crazy.

"Archer, the food will burn." She turned to kiss me.

I made the most of the kiss, trying to get her back to bed. I felt as if nothing could break us apart, every fiber of my body being electrified by her contact.

A loud scrape of a chair against the ground and someone clearing their throat interrupted our perfect moment. I broke away from Callie to see Lucien, his face poorly masking his annoyance at finding us in an intimate embrace; his jaw clenched. Awkward. Callie went back to cooking. I poured myself some coffee, thankful the Icelanders were as crazy about it as we Greeks were.

"You have a room," Lucien muttered, toying with the saltshaker. His dark hair was a mess and hadn't been trimmed in a while. Neither was he shaving. I wondered if he was trying to bring back the nineties grunge look.

"So do you," Callie shot back, not turning to face him.

"Callie," I scolded softly. She couldn't see his pain as I did. Being the god of thwarted love, Anteros suffered from it the most, but he couldn't avenge Lucien without messing with Callie or me. Lucien had to get over Callie the old-fashioned way: time.

Callie turned, pointing the spatula at me, "Don't you defend him, Archer." She pointed her spatula at Lucien. "You will *not* make me feel guilty. If you can't handle it, then you're welcome to leave whenever you want." Callie turned back to the stove.

Lucien didn't say a word but stared at me, awaiting some kind of support. I shrugged, suppressing a grin at my wife's tenacity. Lucien moodily left the kitchen. He should've gone to stay with Freya too. Part of me wanted him to leave; he was a shadow of guilt looming over me for my natural feelings for Callie. He was this lurking presence always catching us.

Sure enough, the smell of breakfast brought the others. It became an endless cycle of us taking turns cooking. We were stuck with them until someone put on a history program, and Callie and I snuck away to our room. I doubt they'd notice our disappearance. History programs are more like comedies to us as the mortals tried to fetter out the events we had seen firsthand; they often got things wrong or a bit off.

As soon as the door closed, I pulled her in and kissed her wildly. She kissed me back eagerly, her nimble fingers unbuttoning my shirt. I stopped, realizing she had it undone in a split second—way too fast. I knew how cagey she was about the newfound level of her powers and had let it go for weeks, waiting for Athena to bring us answers, but this was vastly beyond anything normal.

I took her hands up, "How..." I stopped, my mind whirling. The fevers were gone, and she had been completely better. The strengthening powers were unusual, and I put her secretive and dismissive behavior down to stress, but this was inexplicable. An illness couldn't cause excessive speed, and it was not a demigod trait—that took ichor in one's blood, *pure* ichor.

Our eyes met. She was definitely hiding something. Callie tried to kiss me, mainly to distract me.

"Stop," I told her. I couldn't believe she wouldn't be open and honest with me. I'd answered every question she had wanted to know about me.

"What's wrong?"

I buttoned up my shirt. "Unbutton this as fast as you can."

"Archer." She giggled. "Is this some kind of game?"

A chill went down my spine. She didn't even realize she was doing it.

"Just try as fast as you can."

Callie rolled her eyes and unbuttoned my shirt again in record speed. This time, she realized what she had done, how she moved too fast. She examined her hands, shocked, then me, her mouth agape.

Before she could ask questions I couldn't possibly answer, I took her hand in mine and raced back downstairs, interrupting Aroha and Freya, who were having a private conversation. Both were caked in the current paint-your face-on style of makeup, like Hollywood actresses on set, which I found ludicrous since Ma didn't leave the cabin often. Love goddesses competing over beauty, as always. Lucien, probably hearing the racket of our hurried footsteps, stood in the living room and gave me a quizzical glance.

Reading my terrified face, Aroha asked, "What is it?"

"Show them," I told Callie. I squeezed her hand.

"Your shirt," she said quietly. I glanced down to realize it was still unbuttoned. I rebuttoned it, in case her doing it in reverse wouldn't be as fast.

Callie reached to perform the task, but Lucien interrupted, "Oh, come on."

"Just watch!" I ordered him. "Seriously, watch."

THE IMMORTAL TRANSCRIPTS: SHUDDER

Callie unbuttoned it again in a flash of blurred hands—too fast to be mortal. They all stared in awe. Ma sunk into a chair, her hands over her mouth.

Neither Freya or Lucien seemed surprised.

"How?" I asked them.

Neither met my gaze. They already knew.

"She's pregnant?" Ma questioned. "I've heard of some rare cases where mortals experience powers when carrying an immortal's child."

"I don't think..." Callie said, meeting my gaze, blushing.

I pulled her into my arms, comforting her. I hadn't thought about that. The idea made me nervous but way more excited about the prospect. We weren't taking precautions to avoid children, not that many worked against gods, but the fevers were something altogether different or unrelated—or were they? Damn it! We needed Athena. No contact from her. Where was she?

"Surely, she wouldn't show signs already if she were." I stared at Freya, surmising she'd know the most. My hands instinctively touched Callie's belly, trying to see if I could somehow tell.

Lucien sighed, frustrated. It was too much for him to handle. Or something else? I wanted to press him. He knew something too.

"We need Athena," Ma muttered.

Yeah, my thoughts exactly.

Freya said nothing but stared at Callie thoughtfully. Athena and Freya were close-knit friends, despite coming from different godly tribes. She knew something we didn't and, for some reason, wouldn't tell us.

"What do you know?" I demanded from her. "And you, Lucien?"

"Me?" His tone was offended. His gaze flickered over to Callie and back to me. "Don't pull me into this."

"I'm not the god of truth, but I can tell everyone else in this room is hiding something from Ma and me."

"Maybe you'd make a decent god of truth then," he muttered.

Distracted by his admittance, I hadn't realized Freya had moved, but she was by the sink now. "It's not at all what I actually *know*, Eros. It's what is obvious. Even your little wife knows." Freya said, drying a paring knife off on a dish towel.

Did Callie shake her head at Freya?

Freya crossed to Callie, placed her hand on her shoulder. "I don't know *how*, but the guilt in your eyes tells me it's true. Tell him, tell us. How did you become immortal?"

Callie searched our faces for assistance. "What?"

My mind was spinning. Had Freya lost her mind? Or could this be true? Was this what my wife had been hiding from me?

Lucien rolled his eyes and huffed at Callie. "Don't look at me for help. This is all you."

What did he mean?

"Fine." Freya sighed. "We'll show them."

In one swift motion, Freya lunged at Callie. A crimson stain spread across Callie's abdomen. Freya held up the knife, gleaming red blood running down it.

My instincts took over. I dove upon Freya, restraining her knife-wielding hand. I slammed her into the floor, hearing a bone crunch.

"What's wrong with you?" I demanded through clenched teeth. I was struggling to restrain myself. I wanted her dead.

Oddly, Freya smiled at me as if I were pathetically ignorant.

"Archer." Callie's worried voice forced me to tear my angry gaze away from Freya. With trembling hands, Callie lifted her shirt showing me she wasn't injured.

I stood up, releasing Freya, and instantly examined Callie's stomach. All evidence of the cut had vanished, except for a faint white scar and the charred hole in her shirt. I couldn't believe my own eyes.

"Ichor," I affirmed, reminding myself of the night Callie had found out I was a god, the night I knew things would never be the same again.

"How? Ambrosia?" Ma asked.

Callie stared at her feet. She was avoiding my gaze on purpose. How long had she known?

It was time for me to force answers from her. No more playing it safe due to her grief, illness, and to prolong a blissful honeymoon. I had to know now. "Who gave you ambrosia?"

Her eyes darted up to meet mine, and in them were pain and disappointment. I must be as angry on the outside as I was beginning to feel on the inside: betrayed, lied to, and excluded—by my soulmate, whom I'd trusted enough to bind my soul to hers.

Soon everyone was cluttered in the kitchen, wanting to know what was going on, due to our raised voices. Immortals can hear from a bit of a distance, but getting here so quick, they must've been right outside. Now everyone was talking over each other.

"Everyone, shut up!" Ma shouted. "She's immortal, okay? Everyone, go sit down in the living room, and let's discuss this as rational beings."

THE IMMORTAL TRANSCRIPTS: SHUDDER

We all followed her orders, and with limited seating, I pulled Callie into my lap. I was mad at her, but it didn't change how I felt about her.

"Archer has the strongest motive out of anyone here. We can't ignore that." Lucien stared at me, trying to see lies that didn't exist.

"Yeah, thanks buddy," I said with thick sarcasm. He was my best friend, but he was allowing Callie to be a wedge between us when she shouldn't be. "I can't lie and say I wouldn't ever do something like this to save Callie, but I had no access to ambrosia."

"That we know of," Aios added, ganging up on me. Always seeking his father's attention, he'd pick his dad over a friend in a heartbeat.

Ma came to my defense. "What would be the point of lying now? It's already done. If Archer had done it, there's nothing to fear by telling the truth."

"I never had ambrosia," Callie said faintly.

No one acknowledged they heard her but me. "Someone could have given it to you without knowing. One of those fevers could have been your 'transition,' so to speak."

"What about you?" Freya pointed at Chase.

He laughed. "Me?"

"Your sister has direct access to it."

Ma dismissed the notion with a wave of her hand. "Chase isn't clever enough for that."

Dad gave her a hurt glare. "Gee, thanks."

"I meant off the battlefield, dear. You're a genius out there."

"What about the dufus twins?" Lucien pointed at my half brothers with his thumb.

They protested simultaneously, "Hey!"

"Oh, they wouldn't," Ma defended.

"Don't they want to be in good graces with the mommy and daddy who abandoned them? Don't they worship and idolize their big brother?" Lucien pressed on. I had the sense he had thought this through for a while and was still lost, throwing blame around anywhere.

Himerus frowned. "That's a bit uncalled for. I don't worship anyone."

"Except women." Anteros nudged him, and then they laughed, not taking any of this seriously.

"What about you two?" Poseidon mused about Lucien and his son.

I didn't even notice he was there, such a quiet and reserved being, due to his underwater life making him use telepathy for the most part.

"Huh? What motivation would I have?" Lucien laughed it off. "No offense, Callie, but why would I make such a risky move for her to live forever?"

"Because if she lives forever, in your twisted mind, you think you'll have a chance with her," Ma, in rare form, said. Bit harsh, but he kind of deserved it.

"He had access to her in the last year," Chase added. "He's in love with her."

Lucien glared at Aroha, who steadily held his gaze, unwilling to back down. I could see him grow tenser with every word Ma and Dad had said. She finally broke her bitter glare.

Lucien growled. "I didn't do it, despite what lies you all think of me."

"He didn't. No one did," Callie tried again to deaf ears.

Lucien paced. "What about the rest of you? Poseidon was able to leave his domain. Wouldn't he want that opportunity to live forever? And Aroha, how far would you go to keep your son alive? Maternal instinct can drive one to desperate measures. And Freya," he rambled and gave her a measured look. "You are full of secrets and lie constantly. It makes me wonder why. How did you know she was immortal?"

All of us glanced at each other in turns, wondering if any of Lucien's accusations were valid.

"Don't lie, truth god." Freya sneered. "You knew too."

Lucien was silent.

I couldn't believe him. "You knew and didn't tell me?"

"For a little bit, yes, after Asclepius's visit on the cruise. I don't know who gave it to her though."

"I can't believe you hid this from us!" I shouted.

"They all suspected it, and Callie is hiding a ton. I can sense it," Lucien fired back.

"Stop it!" Too quickly, Callie was out of my arms, standing in front of us all. "No one gave me ambrosia, okay? Stop fighting amongst yourselves."

I guiltily stared at the floor. "C'mere, Callie. I'm sorry." I pulled her back into my lap and touched her beautiful, immortal cheek. "How rude of us all to forget your views. What do you think happened? Mortals just don't turn immortal overnight. I've let it go because you were grieving and ill, and then when you were well, you were happy, but you've hidden something from me. It's time for answers."

She looked at me, her eyes frightened, trapped. My stomach dropped. Here it was. She was about to hit us with something profound, this secret I

THE IMMORTAL TRANSCRIPTS: SHUDDER

had not pressed her about. "I didn't tell you everything. I couldn't tell you..." She froze, her eyes welling up. "It hurt so bad."

"What?" I begged.

Callie took a deep breath. "My dad, his letter, it said some things, Archer, including I was one of you. I guessed it before that, though."

"How long have you've known?" I raised my voice at her. "You knew, and you didn't tell me?" I didn't mean to be so accusatory, but she had hidden something huge from me. "I immortally married you! I've feared for my life daily on top of yours, thinking that just any little thing could kill you and me, when all along, you were immortal?"

Aios gave a here-we-go whistle and bolted. Everyone else also dispersed, giving us space, murmuring things to each other. They, sure as Hades, would be listening in though, desperate to hear how she became immortal.

"I didn't understand what was happening to me. I didn't know for sure until my father's letter. And then..." She shrugged. "How can I explain what I don't understand?" Her eyes were filling with tears. She was scared. There would be time to celebrate the joy of eternity together later, but the shock and feelings of betrayal needed to fade first.

I clasped her hand. "Start from the beginning." She needed to collect her thoughts; although I wanted to shake the information out of her, I patiently waited.

"I was never really sick as a child, and I don't remember any major injuries. I never consciously thought about it, but in retrospect, it was more than luck. And with the fevers, my innate sixth sense went crazy. The night you proposed, when you and Lucien argued and broke the cases, well, Raphael cleaned my arm up. The bandage was for show. I healed instantaneously, exactly like Freya demonstrated earlier."

"You're a god." I huffed out a breath. "I don't get how. Most gods come into our powers and get fevers in our teenage years, and some get them earlier, as I did. I can't believe we missed the possibility, but your parents were mortal, so I still don't understand."

"There's more. Remember I told you my dad's letter said he met a god?"

I nodded, still trying to reign in my anger. She had told me that part, so why not trust me with it all, let me read it?

"There's a whole story about my mom. She went to the grocery store, and on the way home, there was an accident. I always thought she was hit by some reckless driver, but it was lightning. The car was struck, and she lost control, and it went into a reservoir." Callie paused to take a shaky breath.

My hands tightened on hers at the thought of her pain. Zeus must've killed her mother. Why?

"I've been told her neck was broken, and she drowned." This didn't answer anything. If her mother and father were mortal, how in Hades did Callie become immortal? That key missing piece was burning a hole in my mind, damn it.

"Archer, my dad wrote something in that letter that I had never known: I was in the car with her." She paused, meeting my gaze as I pieced it together. She was immortal even then, as a child. How? "Dad said a god—the one I described to you before—had tried to prevent it but got there too late. He saved me, took me home to my Dad, and told my dad his ideas were right and to leave the country. This star pendant was my mother's and from that god, given to me the day it happened." She lifted the pendant on her necklace.

I examined the pendant which rested between the arrow and book. A star? The titan Astraeus was the star god and Zeph's dad, but he was still imprisoned in the Underworld. I had suspected Prometheus as this failed savior, but he was not related to any star symbol. Nothing was making sense. We gods were overly symbolic. The pendant meant something.

"My dad didn't know how this happened to me, but he knew I was immortal and purposely brought me to New York, to you, guided by this god, probably for protection. But, Archer, where is this god now? He could explain everything, I'm sure of it. If we could go—"

"No. We are staying put. We are safe here. Athena will return soon, hopefully with answers and with Prometheus. I think he's the god who saved you. It's just the star symbol...things aren't lining up."

"I know you're mad, but you hid things from me."

"To protect you."

She gave me a loaded look as if her omissions weren't as bad.

"Really? Not the same, Callie. Keeping you ignorant of my identity was saving your life."

She continued to give me an accusatory stare, one which told me I was a hypocrite. Yes, ever since the verdict Zeus had given, banishment from her, I had been a bit unstable. Love can drive you crazy, and losing it could potentially kill me. It wasn't the same, but I could see how she was trying to protect me—although wrongfully. She was young. She hadn't known this news would make me happy and relax—a tad. She was immortal. I marveled over the fact she would not age and die.

"I'm upset you hid this from me," I admitted because the thought of her living forever eclipsed my anger. "But now, we have forever."

I kissed her. One kiss led to another. In one swift motion, she had me pinned on the couch. I still wasn't used to her being so powerful. It made my mind spin off into fantasies of new possibilities. "Callie, I've been holding out on you, but now that I know you're immortal..." I trailed off and flipped around to pin her down playfully.

"Hmmm..."

I kissed her lips faster and faster until she kissed me back at an immortal pace. I pulled myself away and helped her up. Then we raced up the steps, hand in hand, in immortal speed.

It was our true wedding night, an eternal one.

CHAPTER 17
Athena

"You sure you want to do this?" Prometheus brought me out of my own world.

I had been nervous about this, not because I dreaded seeing his family. Since we were related to some of them, their family tree was as twisted as our Olympian one. I was anxious because I knew the intimidating Titans would judge me, but Prometheus insisted on a detour before heading to Iceland. I was actually going into their territory, into Thessaly, via Iris—well, no, she wouldn't step foot there, but she delivered us as close as she would dare. I didn't question her loyalty after Zeus had tried to kill her in Belize, but when we returned to Iceland, I would not ask another god to risk taking us places.

"Huh?"

Prometheus chuckled at my lack of focus and delayed response, but the way he did always resonated with tenderness, loving everything about me that made me unique. I completely understood why he'd find it endearing without ever needing to talk about it: different was not predictable, even to a god who saw visions of the future. My need for logic and certainty matched his need for unpredictability and uncertainty.

No, no, no.

I could not afford to think about these things. This was not the time to ponder on compatibility and the nonsense of how opposites attract—strongly, magnetic pulls. *Stop, brain!*

The notion of compatibility was wiped from my mind as we approached the iron gate of the "free" Titans, meaning Zeus hadn't given them eternal punishments on the Earth or in Tartarus. It was a compound, a magnificent prison, guarded by Roman-born Janus. This parentless god—*cough, cough,* like me—was Zeus's child with a mortal, a lie created to save his marriage. Janus was my two-faced half brother, loath as I was to admit that. He didn't actually have two faces, but had two distinct personalities, where one was always awake, making him the perfect guard. Having two people in one body made Janus hypocritical and the worst decision maker possible.

127

THE IMMORTAL TRANSCRIPTS: SHUDDER

I groaned, answering his question, which had now registered, "I don't have a choice, so let's get it over with."

Prometheus had been eager to delay our return, likely to spend time with just me, but his excuse was that the others needed the time to figure things out on their own, that my interference could be bad. One does not argue with the foresight god—about the future at least.

"I got this," Prometheus whispered, gently touching the small of my back.

"Prometheus. It is nice to see you!" Janus said in a kindly tone. "But you, what schemes do you have?" Per usual, he became waspish and challenged me. He had been given two jobs: to keep the Titans in and Olympians and demigod heroes out.

"I'd like entry to see my mother," Prometheus said.

Janus flinched. He could not deny a Titan entry, and he could not deny a son from seeing his mother's statue, a memorial of her. But Janus, being of two minds, knew Prometheus gained his foresight abilities from his mother and would wonder if he were up to something.

"Your mother is dead."

Prometheus rolled his eyes. "Her temple."

"Why is *she* with you then?" He pointed a finger right up in my face, making me back up.

"Why can't she be?" He laced his fingers through mine, which unnerved me, but he was making a statement, and if I cringed, I'd ruin it, so I suppressed the urge.

Realization dawned on me: I was only surprised by the motion, not upset by his touch. It was too much and yet not at all enough.

Janus thought upon his response. "What, are you 'together?' Or is there a plan to spring everyone out of here? Because you can't."

"We know we can't, so why is that an option in your logic?" I countered.

"Don't listen to him," the other side of Janus now responded about his other self.

I preferred this side and had learned long ago when I pointed out illogical things, the annoying one shut down instantly, much like a retreat in battle.

Fun Janus unlocked the gate and said, "He adores rumors, and those in there are all about false news. They speak of some demigod who will liberate them. Same thing every few hundred years. They never learn."

We were allowed in. I had never seen inside the compound, called Othrys, which sadly was named after their mountain abode they could see every day, yet not live in again. I never understood why Zeus didn't allow them to live within the mountain, but it was part of his bitter resentment against their betrayal, which now increasingly seemed like his betrayal after further study. He and his father-in-law Cronus had a fallout, and Zeus took advantage, brainwashed us into his cause, painting them as the enemy. Here, I was in enemy territory—no, I should say the prison of the victimized enemy.

Theus squeezed my hand, drawing my attention. "You okay?"

"Being too empathetic," I admitted.

"Nothing wrong with that."

The gate closed behind us with a resounding click, and the lock turned. I squeezed his hand back. He would not bring me here to die. I was safe, despite his fuzzy vision. It was illogical to believe that, but I had to convince myself to get through this. "What's the plan?"

"I'm going to meet with my mother, and you will talk to my brethren."

"Wait. What? She is dead—no offense—and they won't talk to me or tolerate my presence. I can't do this."

"You can. You need to. For me."

When he put it that way, it seemed an important task. As we neared a cluster of them, I gazed at the mountains in the distance, thinking of Prometheus's brother Atlas, who bore the figurative weight of the sky there—not the world as the mortals falsely replicated in their artwork. I wondered if he would ever be free of that cruel punishment Zeus had bestowed.

"Atlas has many regrets," a voice broke my stare. I peered into Epimetheus's face, Prometheus's brother who looked the most like him but with darker and sharper features. Many mortal myths had it wrong, because their mother Themis went by a few different names, so they had half siblings as well. "As do you, Athena."

"Give her a break," Prometheus scolded. "I have to see Mom."

His brother snorted as if to wish him luck, stood, and hugged Prometheus in greeting.

"Small talk, Brother. Keep it light, please?" Prometheus laughed and waved quickly to his other family members. He hurried to the temple, leaving me with his mopey brother and a bunch of women I hardly knew

THE IMMORTAL TRANSCRIPTS: SHUDDER

and who hated me. I had helped my father put them here, although I learned to regret it.

"How is my grandson?" Phoebe asked.

"Fine. Err...good." She waited eagerly for more about Apollo. Her smile was starting to fall.

What to say? What to do? I hated small talk. What was the point of it? "He lives in New York." I had to stick to what was and not where he was hiding.

"Yes, yes, I know that. He sent his sweet oracle to me for safe keeping." She swept her arm to point out an elderly woman at the end of the table playing cards with three others.

Mnemosyne, who was seated next to the oracle, glared at me. Honestly, I hated how Mnemosyne had her airs because Zeus gave her day passes out of prison when mortals needed their minds wiped clean.

Phoebe continued, "I see a great war coming. Imagine our intellects entwined. We would not lose."

"Will you help us?"

Her smile fell as fast as if I slapped her. "No. You know what happened last time." She touched her necklace, probably given to her by her husband—in Tartarus where most Titans ended up.

What else could I say? "Sorry, you're right."

"You might want to make sure you don't end up here either," the bejeweled Theia commented as she moved ever so slightly, glimmering with her eternal and external light. Her voice was so beautifully catty.

Helios, one of the few men who remained out of Hades, sat next to her, making up the crew. Some of their children, whom Zeus saw as a possible annoyance, lived there too, but they were likely inside the buildings right now. Some other Titans roamed free, such as Apollo's mother, Leto, but only because my father used them for pleasure.

"I won't," I answered Theia after a beat. "How do you know what is going on while being stuck in here?" I doubted they received many visitors.

Theia pointed, her hand adorned by what must've been ten rings and double that in bracelets. It took me a second to yank my gaze away from the gaudy display of jewelry to see a massive spring.

"Oceanus and Tethys. One of them comes by to chat every few months, gives us news of the world and spoils of the sea," Phoebe said. The water couple were Titan-blooded and not bound by Zeus's barrier.

Theia smirked. "We know all about Eros and his mortal wife."

I could not read her face well. Perhaps she thought the information was some tidbit to give me. "And?"

"Quite adorable, but hopeless. *You* know what that's like." Ah, she was trying to attack me. The Titans knew about my past.

"That's enough," Epimetheus said in his slow draw. "My brother said 'civil,' and Athena regrets many things strongly enough. She needs no rebuke from you. Athena, had you done things differently, the outcome would've always been the same...or worse." This he always said to "cheer up" others as the god of afterthought. He thought it a pointless power, but I always saw the importance of afterthought. He could see our mistakes, and we can learn so much from that.

But I wish he'd stay out of my head.

Theia made a face and acted bored, picking at her cuticles. She'd be chatting about our visit for ages as soon as we left. A long uncomfortable silence formed.

When it became unbearable, I finally said, "How have you been?" It seemed the right thing to ask someone you haven't seen in a thousand years or so. The last time I was there was on business for Zeus.

Theia giggled. "Nothing ever happens here. What do you think?" The rest of the table laughed, except the oracle. Epimetheus held back a grin out of kindness.

My face flushed. This was exactly why I hated these situations. I never knew what to say, and when I said it, it was always wrong or awkward or simply not "normal," whatever that was supposed to be. "Normal" eluded me for thousands of years as the one facet of knowledge I could never acquire. It changed every now and then as well.

"Well, then," I said. "Don't see why you wouldn't want to take a joyride into war then, if it comes to it. It's better than sitting here, moping over eternity in a compound." I turned my back on them and headed over to the temple built in Themis's honor. I stood outside waiting, not daring to interrupt Theus in there.

I could sense the glares from the small group while I pretended to be busy on my phone, but soon their eyes left me. Thankfully, moments later, Theus came out. His face was etched with worry and his shoulders tense. He jumped when he noticed me standing there. It was difficult to surprise the god of foresight, so he was heavily preoccupied by what he had heard from his mother. I had been skeptical about how he communicated with her, but the pallid hue of his normally tan flesh proved he could speak to ghosts.

THE IMMORTAL TRANSCRIPTS: SHUDDER

"Thena." His shaky hand took mine in his, and he kissed my fingertips. Instinctively, I pulled my hand away, instantly regretting it, despite him not even reacting. He had expected rejection, not from foresight but from knowing me.

"I'm sorry. I'm sorry." I tried to suppress the tumultuous emotions building inside me. "What was it? You look shaken."

"I am. I don't...I don't like to see her, my mother. It's why I use oracles and Apollo, or I rely on Phoebe when I can. I...have a hard time seeing her. It's not what she said but seeing *her* say it."

Literally, he saw her then. Heavy. I didn't know what to say to that. How could I comfort someone who must communicate with his dead mother, despite it paining him every time to do so? Out of the all the words in all the languages I could speak, no combination came to mind that could ease this type of pain.

I grabbed his hand and tugged him around the corner of the temple where the little group of Titan gossips couldn't see us. He stared at me, lost, the god who always knew the way, now so vulnerable yet still so gloriously handsome. I could not give. Emotions were a weakness, but he needed me.

I pulled him into a hug. He froze for a second—again, not expecting it of me—but then his arms wound around me, squeezing so tightly, I thought he might break me. If I were mortal, I might not be able to breathe. His head fell into the hollow of my neck. He did not cry. Prometheus had once told me he cried the tears of a lifetime each day when he was hidden and chained in the Caucasus Mountains, getting his liver pecked out. I believed him. Each time I saw him in anguish after those fateful years, he would shake with fury and sadness, but no tears would come. This was the same. I held him as he took the pieces of his wrecked self and mended them back together. Only when he was whole did his face leave its hiding place. Those dark eyes drank me up, and I knew this was not the right time to give in to him because of his vulnerability.

Before I could push him away, he tore himself away from me, mumbled something that could've been "thank you," and turned away. He paused, his back to me, with his hand outstretched away from his body at an odd angle. It was an offer or—because of his emotional outburst and my comforting him—an ultimatum. I came to his side and took up his hand. He squeezed it as if it was a pact, friends for eternity more than anything else, best friends. There was nothing more rational and stronger than the love of a best friend. It mattered more than any other kind of love. Sure, add in sex and lust and devotion, but friendship was the core of every strong relationship. This was a step toward a relationship, but asking for hand-holding rather than attempting to act out the passion I had seen momentarily in his eyes was a small request. It was something I could give.

"You tried recruiting them, didn't you?" His voice was raspy with emotion. "I knew you would."

"It didn't work."

"Oh, don't underestimate your ability to shake the Titan tree."

"Meaning?"

He gave me a stern look. "Come on, clever one."

"This conversation will make them think, and they'll change their minds in the future?"

"My brethren are scared and comfortable in their powerlessness form due to conditioning, but there will come a time when we show them Zeus is lesser than all of us combined. Learn from me, though. Thena, have patience."

I glared at him. He let go of my hand and wrapped his arm around me, pulling me against his side as we walked. I didn't mind it or his chuckling at my expense. It was good to see him back to himself after seeing him unravel for a moment. When he pressed his lips against my forehead, I let it slide too. It seemed friendly, a loving gesture rather than a sensual one. How long could I keep him at bay? More importantly, how long till I no longer wanted to? As a rational creature, I was well aware there were things I had to face head-on and get over before I allowed myself to love again.

"Let's get to Iceland." Even though it would lead to the answers I both longed for and feared, I was more worried about the others than my own comfort.

"You're ready for that?"

"What's going to happen?" I asked dreadfully.

"What do you think?"

"Truth will out."

"Don't you think it should, goddess of justice?"

"Except, I don't know the truth, even though you insist I do."

"Oh, you'll know." His tone was suggestive in nature, but more of the mind, that this puzzle would be fun for me to crack and would bring us together.

I could never resist a puzzle begging to be solved. Now, I was even more eager to get back. I needed to see Callie was safe and figure her out. It was this imperative drive, more than seeking justice or answers. It was tinged with emotion, which was unlike me.

THE IMMORTAL TRANSCRIPTS: SHUDDER

I glanced at Theus, who was too close in his arm-draped posture. His face was telling: I'd unravel it and more. Those dark eyes, which held so many secrets, glimmered with promises of many things.

Dread of the past faded. If I had to face it to help Callie and mend things with Theus, then it must be done.

Truth would out.

CHAPTER 18

Lucien

Callie was immortal. I was loath to admit I had mixed feelings about it. I was glad, of course, because she would be safe, but I was left uneasy. The group of my so-called friends and family had called me out, saying I would have my own motivation to make her immortal. The accusation didn't bother me since everyone was blaming each other, but what frustrated me was how they were right. If she did live forever, one day, she could love me. These thoughts made me weak, pathetic, and hopeless, but as always, when it came to Callie, I didn't care. I loved her, and I wanted to stop because she would likely never love me back.

Callie was a wedge between Archer and me, one that would never go away. This realization made me all too aware: the basest part of myself wanted Callie gone because then the problem wouldn't exist. Thankfully, my abundant truth-seeking IQ knew that this vile concept of her death would make everything worse. The Fates did not cut the cords of love or friendship when death came. It made us long for what we can no longer have more acutely than ever.

My melancholy thoughts were cut short. This afternoon—a month after their hasty wedding—the couple were at the kitchen table, arguing. They were quiet about it, trying to keep the volume low, but there was no hiding from immortal ears, nor were they kidding anyone listening that there weren't heated words being exchanged. I went into the kitchen, ignoring them. They momentarily stopped speaking when I passed by. Sadly, I wanted them fighting and unhappy, which was my jealousy manifesting and projecting into an outward loathing and a desire for them to feel as I did. I knew these were terrible thoughts, but I couldn't stop the wheels of my mind.

"Let's talk about this later," Archer said firmly.

"Everyone can hear us anyway. Privacy is impossible when everyone has supersonic hearing."

"You will, too, once you tap into the powers. I'll teach you." He was trying to placate her, turn her mood around because she was super snappy as of late.

THE IMMORTAL TRANSCRIPTS: SHUDDER

I poured some juice.

"You're changing the subject. I want to tell them. They have a right to know. What if they can prevent it all?" Callie said.

I pretended to mind my own business and went into the living room, but Callie's comment piqued my interest.

"We talked about this. You can't challenge them. You cannot beat them. Don't you think we gods would have by now? Thousands of years of trying to escape prophecies. Do you think we'd let our family members die if we could somehow stop it?" Archer's voice was strained. He was thinking of his siblings and his daughter. Prometheus and Zephyrus had tried to help Archer prevent Hedone's death, but they arrived too late.

This was getting heavy. This wasn't a lovers' tiff, as I had suspected, but some deeper philosophical debate about escaping the future.

"My dreams though—"

"Could just be dreams, manifestations of the imagination."

"Or prophetic. I dreamed about the volcano, Archer. I stopped you. If that was not prophetic, what was it?"

"Call Raphael then," Archer urged.

"And say what? My dad died, Archer. This was his life's work."

"No, Callie. You are his life's work. You getting killed over a book would be the opposite of what he would've wanted." Archer was speaking from the perspective of a grieving father, but he was right.

"I know I can't let Raphael publish the book, but I don't think he'll listen to me over Dad's will. Legally, he could be bound to execute Dad's wishes. Just like his cremation."

Death and exposure through a mortal's book? Great. Another piece of crap to add to an Olympian mountain of shit called life, or more properly, immortality. I was over this. I was exhausted of this everlasting existence, or spending it forever alone. I must be cursed by the Fates for abusing so many hearts in my youth. A couple came to mind. Euterpe, particularly, but then another blue-eyed goddess came to mind. Callie wasn't the only one I had wasted my heart on. My gods, I never seemed to be able to hold onto love of any kind. I'd always muck up a situation and lose a loved one's favor. Even with my kids. I was wondering how long I could hang onto Aios.

The lovers' conversation turned to softer whispers. Soon they would maneuver back to something stupid and romanticize it as they had the volcano business. They'd discuss how they were so lucky to escape death, a preventable situation had they both not been so pathetically asinine to think death was the answer to a breakup. They'd then get all lovey-dovey and gushy. Gag me.

I slipped out onto the back deck that overlooked a massive downhill slope into a forest, closing the glass door behind me. Ah, no more human noise—or godly, I should wrap my head around—now alone with nature. The tree leaves were turning those beautiful fall colors of vibrant yellow, orange, and red, with bits of green dotting the mountains. The sky was still light, although summer was long gone here. I had only been in an area to see the Northern Lights once before, so if we spent winter here, I'd see them again. It's amazing how many things I got to see in my existence, but even more troubling there were probably things I had unknowingly never seen.

As if she knew I was futilely trying not to think of her, Callie came out on the porch a few minutes later sans Archer. She leaned on the railing next to me, gazing at the picturesque mountain range. The peaks of the mountains were covered with snow, and each day it seemed to slowly creep down. Soon we'd be stuck inside for the winter, avoiding snowstorms and missing sunlight. Winter here would be Tartarus for me. With things as magnificent as the Northern Lights came long nights and less sunshine.

"This is all a lot to grasp," Callie said solemnly. "My father always knew. I didn't until recently." Yes, we all had heard the conversation. She had hidden things from all of us for weeks, and just like that—snap!—Archer forgave her.

"Your father was an extremely clever man," I commented, not wanting to upset her in any way. I sure was not bringing up what I overheard about the man's book.

"There's so much to digest."

There was so much I wanted to say to her, but I refrained. "At least you have forever to do it in." I risked a glance at her long neck, her messy ponytail being an advantage for that view. Her cheek was smooth and round, full of youth, yet those pouty lips and almond-shaped dark eyes spoke sensuality.

"Ah, there's the joking Apollo I'd met." She flashed her smile at me, her eyes meeting mine. The brightness of her features dimmed all too soon, like a sun setting. "I thought you resented my immortality?"

I had not given Callie's sight enough credit because it scared me to think she could read our minds and possibly foresee the future. "Resentment and confusion are not the same. It troubles me, but if Athena can find Prometheus, we will get most of the answers. The two of them can decipher any puzzle. I need them too. I need help with a prophecy."

"Hmm, I need help with my dreams as well."

I took the bait, too curious and with a need to feel useful. I was not doing well cooped up with everyone with no purpose but to raise the sun and set it daily, which I had learned to do unconsciously as a young man in my first century. "What kind of dreams?"

"About the future. Exactly as it was before, when I saw Archer jump into a volcano, but I stopped it. Are there ways to change the future?" she asked. "If I did it before, I can do it again, right?"

Whoa. I was now understanding her conversation earlier, and this was not a good path for a "new" immortal to go down. If she thought she could outsmart the Fates, the Moirae, she was either overconfident as Icarus or unhinged.

"Callie, the future is set and unchangeable. The Fates do not allow it to alter off course, so no matter what you do to stop something, it will occur anyway. My speculation is you didn't see the future when you saved Archer but saw Archer's thoughts. What you altered were his plans. You gave him a reason to live, so the suicide plan didn't occur."

"None of it makes sense. We barely stopped him in time. That would have to mean the Fates always wanted me to stop Archer?"

"Precisely. This is all conjecture, of course."

"And what if one wanted to change something they see occurring in the future?"

"Well, you have to change the person's mind, the one who makes a decision that steers a specific course of action, but it's virtually impossible. I've never been able to prevent a prophecy in all my years. I've never outsmarted the Fates, even with knowledge of the future in my hands. No seer has, not even Prometheus, and he knows them best. They are his sisters."

"There's another way. There has to be." She was perturbed about something, very animatedly so. Her features scrunched up, so cute in her anger, like an innocuous cat...until realizing the impact of its claws.

"Well..." I hesitated. "If one could convince the Fates to change their mind? It's never been done successfully."

"What if one um...destroyed the Fates?" Callie asked.

My heart hammered in my chest. I looked around as if the Fates would swoop down and cut our lifelines for just discussing it. "Holy Hades, Callie! Don't ever suggest such things."

"What would happen, though?"

"First off, Chaos would be freed, and who knows what Titans would emerge from Tartarus. The entire world would lose all order. It would probably be a free-for-all, a giant mess forever and ever. That's if you could even surprise a Fate. They'll cut your life string before you could blink. Look, what is it you want to prevent? Does something happen to Archer?"

She turned away, a bit miffed at my reaction. "No."

"What is it?" I leaned over the railing more to ascertain the expression on her face. She was mentally exhausted and quite sad, which didn't fit in with the great news of her immortality. Zeus couldn't easily kill her, and she would never age again—a girl's dream come true, right?

"You will betray me, Lucien. I don't know how. Don't interrupt. Just listen." She put her hand up to prevent the outbursts of denial on my lips. "You will do this, but I forgive you, okay? Don't do anything reckless or ridiculous because you feel guilty. Promise me that."

My mind replayed the most recent prophecy. I was the betrayer, the one who would pay the price because of guilt, according to Callie. There's only one thing that would make a selfish creature like me volunteer to pay a steep price.

"You die?" The blood drained from my face as my terrified eyes met her defeated ones. "I do something to cause you to die?"

"Promise me you won't do something stupid, Lucien, or you'll be the one who dies."

Her making me promise to let her die, and Archer by default, must mean... "You've seen my death?" I was dizzy. I could see it plainly. I would do something rash in hopes to save her and die for my efforts. There were worse ways to die than being a hero, so why deny me that path?

"I need Prometheus to figure out the *when*," she said quietly.

Confirmation. Shit. Panic welled in me. Hero status of my heritage drifted away to fear.

"I die," I said in disbelief. Being immortal, one never thinks of it. Suddenly, despite longing to end my suffering heartache, I felt the nagging desire to live. I suddenly saw everything I would miss. There were things I still needed to do—repair the relationships with my sons and impart my knowledge to Hymenaios. In the event of my demise—being my eldest child—he would take on all my powers and responsibilities until other beings of truth, sun, and prophecies were born. I also needed to fix everything between Archer and me, and gain forgiveness from Euterpe. I played with many mortal hearts, but the immortal ones were my next concern after my ex wife. I had to allow them closure if there was time. Suddenly, the *when* of my death was extremely important.

I realized I had been quietly contemplating for quite some time when Callie's voice brought me back to reality: "Was it wrong to tell you?"

I met her gaze, truth in my features. "No, I just realized I have a lot to do before—"

"You're giving in?" Incredulity laced her tone.

"You can't change fate, Callie. I've been alive for over three thousand years. I'm tired. If it's my time, it's my time. I really need to set everything right...in case."

She sighed, not at all satisfied. "Don't tell Archer. He'll jump to conclusions of why you'd feel so guilty." Before I could respond, she was gone in immortal speed.

It took a moment to click. Her comment answered my questions earlier: Callie was going to die too. Not only would she die, but it would be all my fault. Callie and I would be together in the underworld. That was not at all comforting. Archer would join us, and then Ares would lose his mind and bring on the end of the world. Perhaps this was how the end of days would happen. Not that we Olympians believed in monotheistic apocalyptical events, but we did believe in the end of ages and starting afresh. The way the mortals were these days, I wouldn't be surprised if man was doomed soon to fall into dark ages and need to cycle around again to a rebirth as old Vico had professed. Some honest mortals always left an impression upon me. To think of old Vico at a time like this. Maybe it was for a reason. Maybe my death would somehow lead to a rebirth for the others?

When the sun started setting, I realized time had gone by with me alone in my thoughts. I went back inside, avoiding Archer because I couldn't hide what Callie had told me. I sought refuge in my room but was interrupted after a moment by someone tapping at the door.

"Dad?" Hymenaios inquired.

"Come in."

Now was not the time to impart all my wisdom to him. He was such a caring softy. I could not imagine how he would cope with my death.

"You okay?" he asked, reading my mood.

"Yeah, restless is all."

"I was thinking it was getting a little crowded in this town. You wanna travel? Poseidon says he's heading back soon. He's landsick or something."

"Yeah, okay."

Hymenaios stood there motionless, merely staring at me, unsure what to say or do. "Dad?"

"I'm fine, Hymenaios. We've never been much for talking, have we?" As I said the words, guilt swept over me; I wouldn't have much more time with him. "I'm sorry. We should talk more."

Hymenaios shut the door. "I think we should leave. I hate to see what this all does to you. I can tell you love Callie, and it's destroying you. She's safe here with her family and the Norse masking her presence. Why don't we just...go." His face was an embarrassed blush during his speech. He was such an interesting creature—Euterpe and I combined forever. He was my kid, but I didn't quite know what went through his head at times.

I nodded. "I agree, but we must wait for Athena to come with news. Then, if we still think it best, we'll set off. Think about where we should go."

"I want to contact my mom when we leave. She needs to leave Fiji. I mean, there will be a war, won't there?"

"I hope not," I told him. "I thought she'd break away after Zeus tried to kill you."

"Does she even know? Do we know if she's still there?"

His well-grounded questions sparked energy into me. "We will go. Keep traveling. Sitting here waiting is pointless when we could be ascertaining allies and feeding that info back here."

He smiled mischievously. "Spies?"

"Nothing dangerous. I'm not letting you step foot in Fiji or near my father again. Just put out feelers."

"Sounds like a plan."

The next day, Poseidon, Aios, and I went out in the early morning when it was still dark, making it easier to not be seen. Poseidon was leaving us momentarily, swimming his way back to The Great Blue Hole. It was a long trip, but he'd return when needed. As we walked to the fjord, he was quiet and reflective. My guess was the world atop was too much for him to handle after being away from it so long. He probably should take it in doses.

We stopped by the fjord's edge to say goodbyes, hoping we would see each other in better circumstances than war in the future. Things were eerily calm and quiet. The silence made me uneasy, and the hairs prickled on my neck in the chilling breeze. Something felt off.

THE IMMORTAL TRANSCRIPTS: SHUDDER

I heard the whistling sound before I saw the spear flying straight at us as if coming from nowhere. It impaled Poseidon through his stomach. I grabbed my son and shoved him out of the way as another spear struck the ground where he had been standing.

I surveyed the area as Poseidon pulled the spear out of himself, trying not to scream out from the pain. I sought the sun, urging her to rise a bit earlier than usual, but still, I couldn't see the enemy. I scanned in my mind to find the enemy was not Olympian. I surveyed the area next while pushing my son to the ground and crouching to diminish possible target trajectory. Not far from the rocky cliff where we stood was a large cluster of trees. I forced the sun to rise higher to increase my sight and strength.

We were sitting ducks, so I had to negotiate. "Hello?" I called out, holding my hands up in universal unarmed gesture. "We come in peace."

"Who goes there?" a gruff voice bellowed from the trees. It echoed off the rocky chasm below.

"The Greeks?" Another voice asked, this one sounding rough as gravel being brushed against the pavement.

"Yes," I answered hesitantly.

They came out of the woods: four men clad in ancient pelts, with beards and hair long and scraggly.

Confused by their attire, my gaze was probably unkind; it felt as if I was back in 900 AD, stepping onto English soil for the first time to see the Vikings suddenly in power.

"Ah, Apollo." The scruffy creature with auburn hair and a ruddy face smiled. It was Thor, Norse god of lightning and war. "Sorry, thought you were the Celts."

"The Celts?" I asked, confused.

Odin, Loki, and Týr were with him, all dressed in the ceremonial garbs.

I laughed. "What's with the outfits?" They were examining Poseidon, and I was suddenly protective of my uncle, hoping he'd have the sense to dive into the fjord if they attacked again.

"We kind of have a mock battle with the Celts. An ode to the old days." Thor sounded embarrassed.

So, mortals weren't the only ones who liked reenactments. "Interesting."

Thor offered me his hand to shake. I took it, and he zapped me with a high current of electricity. Instinctively, I withdrew my hand, shaking it, as he laughed with his friends.

I gave him a sinister look and then let go, out of my mortal form, allowing all the light and energy I had bottled up to rise to the surface and shine.

"Oh no, men, close your eyes, here he goes," Thor mocked.

As my skin got hotter, the Norse gods began to whine and complain, covering their eyes with their hands to block the intense light I was blinding them with. I reversed it and drew all the energy back in.

"Ha ha," Thor laughed. "I told you the Greeks were fine."

Odin's one eye studied us. "Still want to know what *he's* doing here."

Thor studied Poseidon. "That's not Zeus, Odin. Zeus has mean, cold little eyes, and this guy is broader, stronger."

"Meet my uncle, Poseidon. We...uh...sprang him." There was no point in me hiding it.

Odin and Thor hated Zeus and, by association, most of us. Once, Zeus had unsuccessfully tried to suppress and rule the Norse. It didn't help that Tyr was also a god of the skies too; it got "complicated" at times.

"How'd you do that?" Odin pressed, still seemingly wary for a supposed all-seeing one-eyed-god.

Poseidon shrugged. "Dunno." He was nervous, his eyes darting to me. He would be protective of Callie who had been his savior, but it also tipped me off. Odin—like Zeus—could no longer see as well as he could. Was this caused by Callie too?

"You better tell us how, fishman." Thor pointed his hammer, named Mjölnir, at Poseidon. Electricity and water was not a good combo.

"Hey guys, what's with the hostility?" I tried to make peace. "Give the guy a break. He hasn't felt the sun and wind on his skin for millennia."

"I'm not my brother." Poseidon put his hands up in surrender. "In fact, I hate his guts. I have half a mind to lock him up and half a mind to kill him."

I got whiplash for how fast I turned around in surprise. I knew he resented Zeus, obviously, but did not know it'd made the easygoing god such a zealous ally.

"Is Ares planning a war?" Thor asked.

I didn't like the eagerness in his eyes—too ready to jump at the chance to join. "He's 'Chase' now and all about peace and defense." I knew mocking him would make the war gods happy.

The Norse were quiet as they looked at one another. Then they all burst out with a pleasant uproar of laughter and came over and shook our hands, being sure to give us a crushing grip. Gods measured a lot by a handshake, cross-culturally.

"Sorry 'bout the spear," Odin told Poseidon quietly. "You're identical to your god-for-nothing brother."

"Yeah," Poseidon said awkwardly.

My brow wrinkled in thought; they had said they thought we were the Celts when they confronted us. Had they been lying, thinking my uncle was Zeus?

"The false bravado's not there," Tyr said. "Definitely not Zeus."

"Come, come, get some grog. Brewed it like the old days. The Celts are here and all. We'll find them and end our little reenactment skirmish. Come." Odin motioned us to follow. "We'll confuse them by making allies we didn't have the first time."

Poseidon hesitated, so close to the water's edge. I hesitated as well. Was this an alliance for reenactment's sake or was Odin suggesting this could be a real-life one if I were daring enough to suggest it?

"Fishman, you may only get to be on the surface until that god-for-nothing brother of yours discovers you. You should live it up," Thor pressed.

"What about Ares?" I asked.

Poseidon smiled, finally relaxing. "He'd love this."

"Nah. I've got a better idea. After we get good and drunk, let's stake him out and attack him," Thor said.

"Way-hey!" The Norse cheered. They had a type of distaste but respect for Chase, so I had to let them have their fun at his expense. Only then could we negotiate a true ally.

The three of us went into the woods with three Norse gods. If I had not known nor trusted Thor, I wouldn't have ventured. Most of the others stay clear of one another. This was an odd alliance forming, but we were all linked together in our mutual hatred of Zeus. We needed allies—or my family did—I would not live to see Callie safe. I would do what was right while I still could.

Poseidon left that night. Aios and my plans to leave were put at a halt. Negotiating with others to help Callie was more important than my impending doom. Even if Athena returned tomorrow, I wouldn't leave until necessary. It was all about finding compensation for my betrayal. Unlike Callie, I knew Fate controlled me. No matter what, I would betray Callie and she might die. I would make sure the Norse would be there to stop that, even if it meant I would pay the price.

Even Chase would be proud of me if he knew. We Greeks came back with our shields or on them. I would be the latter, dying for my people in a way that would save Callie and Archer. There was no better way to go but in honor.

CHAPTER 19

Athena

As soon as I entered my warm cabin in Iceland, I was bombarded with questions, concerns, and greetings. It was clear I'd missed a lot, but it was overwhelming to say the least. They were all talking over each other, and I couldn't focus on one voice until Prometheus silenced them.

"Wait, I know you." Callie pointed at Prometheus. Wonderment and recognition were in her dark eyes. I finally took the time to scrutinize her. Callie was to the shorter side, with loose curly dark hair, a thin figure, and an adorable cuteness—softly rounded cheeks and pouty lips.

Archer wrapped a protective arm around her. "That's not possible. Is it?" He was wary, his eyes betraying he had been busy worrying the entire time I was gone.

"Does it matter?" Aroha scoffed. "Athena, Callie is exhibiting traits—okay, no, that's sugarcoating it—she's immortal."

"What?" I managed to squeak out.

"Freya decided to double-check that," Archer said, glaring at her. "With a knife."

I looked to Freya, who shrugged as if it had been nothing. I directed my gaze next to the supposedly immortal Callie, who blushed as if she was committing some social faux pas for existing. I could relate to that.

Chase crossed his arms. "No one admits to giving her ambrosia."

My mind whirled. Before I left, Freya and I had been attempting to figure Callie out. We knew about Psyche, but how on Mother Gaia could a demigod *become* one of our kind without ambrosia?

"She didn't need ambrosia," Prometheus said matter-of-factly. "She was born a goddess, but her powers took time to develop, as they often do."

No one said a word. It was a bombshell none of them could fathom, including me. Instead of rationalizing the *how*, my mind, bubbling with emotions, went to the *why*. Why had Prometheus hidden this from me?

There was an outburst of disbelief, some laughed as if it were a joke, and some confusion arose among the group. I pushed away the feelings of betrayal and fixated on facts. My mind went into overdrive—hypothesizing, calculating, digging for truths of what I knew and what possibly could be. Whose was she? One possibility struck my mind like a sledgehammer.

I gasped. "Theus?" I faltered and held onto the kitchen counter to steady myself as my head spun. Was I going to faint? Weakness was strange to me, but I had suppressed the past and buried all the emotions tied to it in the Tartarus of my subconscious. If I opened it, much like Pandora's box, the ills of my world would burst forth into the forefront of my mind, and there would be no putting them back.

Prometheus's rich brown eyes probed into mine. "Yes." He was answering my silent question, one he knew I could not voice.

Now there were so many thoughts reverberating through my brain that I had no clue what to think or what to say. Theus needed to explain, for I couldn't. I had no clue how it was possible, and my mind was even struggling to do the simple math of subtracting years to determine if it were possible.

"My dad was a demigod, and my mom was mortal." Callie was distressed. She needed answers, and I needed to pull it together to give them to her.

"Whose is she?" Lucien asked Prometheus, pointing at Callie, his patience thin.

Prometheus walked up to Callie and touched the chain hanging on her on her neck. He pulled, bringing it out from under her collar, holding it in his palm. It had pendants on it, one being a star.

Callie's eyes danced across his face, calculating, remembering something. "The accident. I saw you when my mother died. You saved me, and you gave me this?" Callie rambled out.

Prometheus smiled tightly and nodded. "I was too late for your mother. Zeus acted suddenly without premeditation. I didn't have enough time. The vision came minutes before he took action."

"Zeus killed my mother. I knew it." Her dark eyes narrowed, akin to Prometheus's glare. The resemblance was faint, but I saw it in their eyes.

My heart raced wildly, and my stomach churned. My eyes stung. All this time, I'd believed she had died without descendants, but she lived on in Callie. "Eleutheria," I whispered, blinking tears away, taking in Callie's features. There was something familiar about her nose.

"Freedom," Chase whispered in awe.

I could see the gears working in his mind as he translated her name. She was the liberty goddess, and for that, she had been slain, more than once.

THE IMMORTAL TRANSCRIPTS: SHUDDER

Lucien cut his hand through the air, being firm that I was wrong. "She was a rumor, a myth, a simple demigod in my sister's gaggle of girls." I couldn't yet speak against his assumptions, still stuck on the *how*.

Callie's dark eyes met mine. "Tell me who I am." She was crying now too. A hand gently touched the small of my back, and the fact I didn't cringe at all, I knew it was Prometheus trying to give me strength through reassurance.

"She's partly mine," Freya interjected, shooting me a wink.

She was saving me, giving me a moment. I had to pull it together. Athena was rationality, wisdom, not a blubbering emotional mess. I focused on the steadying hand on my back, grounding me, helping me stay focused.

Freya continued, "I had an affair long ago with a mortal. Athena, who was here at the time, took my child away to protect her from my husband. I found out later about his many infidelities, so it was pointless, but I could not seek my daughter out because by then, she was married to you." She pointed at Archer, whose face scrunched up, not following. "You all knew my child as Psyche." Archer's expression slipped into wide-eyed shock.

There was a collective gasp in the room. My, I forgot how theatrical Freya could be.

"Thena, let us all sit down." Prometheus led me into the living room, sitting me down.

I sensed their eyes on me in wonder. I, the wisest, with the strongest constitution, was crying like a baby, and they had no clue why.

After most of us were seated, an annoyed Lucien said, "That still doesn't explain anything."

"Hush," Aroha censured him. "I think Athena might have something to say if we give her a moment." The catty goddess whom I'd butted heads with for millennia, arguing about love versus rationality, was there giving me encouraging looks. Either I had misjudged her, or part of Zeus's control had made her ten times vainer prior.

So many expectant pairs of eyes were fixated on me, and my frame shook as I attempted to re-establish my autonomy.

"I've been suspecting this for a while, but it took Prometheus to affirm it just now. I...I hardly know where to start." My mouth was incapable of expressing my jumbled thoughts. Surely, Prometheus would know this and jump in to help.

Prometheus perched on the arm of my recliner. "From the beginning." His hand grasped mine with firmness and warmth, and his fingers intimately weaved in between mine. The gesture spoke the words he could not: he would stand by me through it all. Nothing—this time—would force him away from my side. Not Zeus, especially.

I didn't need his foresight to know this, nor did I need honey-sweet promises from his lips sealed with kisses. I felt it in the rhythm of his heartbeat, which echoed louder in my ears than any other sound in the room, in sync with mine. I was stronger, more in control.

I took a deep breath and then blurted out, "Prometheus and I were married a long time ago." I ignored the gasps of astonishment, focusing on delivering the facts. "Secretly, because we could tell Zeus despised our relationship. He truly hated Prometheus. We all know the only Titans he truly tolerated were Hera and the ones who let him into their beds."

Lucien frowned, most likely not liking my candid reference to his mother, Leto.

"Zeus, of course, found out when I became pregnant."

"Maiden goddess? Told you she wasn't." Himerus whispered to Anteros.

"Shut up, dude," Anteros said back, likely empathizing with the thwarted-lovers' situation, as was his nature.

Aroha smacked the back of Himerus's head.

I ignored them. "Our child, Eleutheria, was born about three years before you, Archer—in fact, because she existed, I think that is how you two," —I pointed to Aroha and Chase— "were able to conceive him in the first place. She was the freedom goddess."

Chase nodded. "Freedom from Zeus's control, from his suppression, from whom he told us to marry. It all makes sense. Except how are we free now? Even Poseidon is out of his prison—"

"What?" I blurted out. Poseidon had surfaced?

"Catch them up with the past before we delve into the present, shall we?" Prometheus— always ready for me to go down a tangent and another and another, never finding my way back—directed my focus to task.

He was right. I needed to get all this out, but I could not continue. I could not explain the memories, long buried and willfully cemented behind walls to protect me.

He knew me. Prometheus took over the story. "Ares—er, Chase—is right. She was the goddess of free will. Obviously, Zeus wanted her out of the picture. Her existence threatened his control over us. Eleutheria made it to her fifth birthday before Zeus killed her."

THE IMMORTAL TRANSCRIPTS: SHUDDER

His words forced the memories through my mental fortress, blindsiding me: *Zeus tearing my daughter from my arms as she reached out, crying for me, "Mána! Mána!" I struggled against the hands that bound me and transported me away from her, but not before I heard her piercing shriek cut off suddenly. Hermes's conflicted face and weeping apologies before he vanished, leaving me alone in the middle of nowhere, distraught, horrified, and broken.*

"Why haven't we heard of this?" Chase's voice broke the spell.

I was back in the present, pushing those horrible images behind my mental wall.

"Shush," Aroha reproached him.

"After..." I cleared my throat awkwardly. "Afterward, Zeus forced our divorce, and when he realized we wouldn't stay apart, he chained Theus to that gods-forsaken rock."

"Well, it was more than just *us*, Thena," Prometheus added. He had vaguely mentioned a usurper.

"The myths say you were chained there for giving man fire, though," Callie said self-consciously.

"Zeus's cover story. Man discovered fire long before I existed. Even you all knew that was a lie."

Chase nodded. "I thought you had been plotting to overthrow him."

"Not quite. I was mainly punished because I would not tell him *who* would overthrow him." Theus continued.

"You could have told him and not suffered for a thousand years?" Aroha piped in, astonished.

"I couldn't. I knew the usurper would be from my line. I knew it would be Eleutheria one day, a version of her at least. How could I condemn one of my own children?" The passion in Prometheus's voice reminded me of his strength, tenacity, and that unshakable patience so opposite mine—the traits I adored in him.

Lucien paced. "Hold up. Everything you are saying is pointing to Callie doing the same, yet Freya confirmed she's Psyche, so explain this and quit the storytelling."

"Patience, sun god," Prometheus teased. "We are old, so stories are long. Without the *why* you will never understand the *how*." A man who knew me through and through, who tuned into my thought process. It emboldened me.

Trying to finish the tale quickly, I skipped through time. "In Rome, you knew our next daughter as Libertas."

"But she was an orphan," Lucien said.

I narrowed my eyes on him. He better not have meddled with my daughter. In those days, Lucien chased anything with two legs.

"Orchestrated. Remember Athena went off to conquer other lands?" Prometheus supplied.

"And you left warfront with me to spy for almost a year," Chase filled in, realizing I had taken an espionage maternity leave.

"Yes, as you pointed out, Lucien, the 'rumor' was a real girl. She did join your sister's—whatever those girls are to her—and I had hoped she could live because she'd taken the maiden vow to never have children as your sister demands. But Zeus killed her anyway."

Lucien made a scoffing noise.

"You don't believe me?" I demanded.

"No, I do." He was shocked. "I'm scoffing at the fact I don't know who in Hades my twin sister has become. Letting Zeus kill one of her own 'sisters' and recently attempting to kill her nephew."

Hymenaios stared at the ground, his fist clenching. The young, sheltered god had been shaken to see that family sometimes betrays us, but he would hopefully learn it could be your pillar of strength as well.

"Libertas had been born during Julius Caesar's reign, and she didn't live to see the empire come to be," Theus said quietly.

"Some might say that was a blessing for what it had become," Freya scoffed.

I glared daggers at her.

Prometheus was up, his hand out of mine. "Freya." His voice wavered. "I'm not smashing you to bits because you have done the biggest favor for us to bring us to this point. You have convinced the Norse to shelter us. I thank you, but say one joke or snide comment about my deceased daughter, and I will breach the peace!"

I stood, blocking Prometheus from doing anything. Her comment was tasteless and cutting, in more ways than just losing my daughter. It had been the greatest triumph of Chase and mine before it turned into a disaster. We underestimated mortal brutality and Dionysus's obsession with foiling us by making important mortals go insane. In my grief over my daughter, I left Chase, Nemesis, and others to run it all to ruin. I hated Rome in retrospection; it took everything from me, including Prometheus.

Prometheus continued, "It became clear that Zeus could somehow discover our children. Even hidden, masked as a 'demigod' orphan, no child of ours was safe. I had foreseen it all though, obviously, but time is hard to tell with visions."

THE IMMORTAL TRANSCRIPTS: SHUDDER

"Thank you!" Lucien interjected.

I took over before Lucien dared to make this moment about him: "We didn't resume our affair—"

"Marriage," Prometheus corrected, which silenced me. I still was the maiden goddess by godly standards. He was my one and only. If he thought we were still married...

I started pacing. Moving helped me focus. "Until the 1950s..." I ignored his comment, storing it away for later, and going back to the story. "That's when I was forced to ask Freya to return the Psyche favor. I came to Norway, where the Norse then resided, and gave birth to another Eleutheria."

Prometheus took over because I didn't know what had happened after that. I had refused to hold her; losing my other daughters killed a part of me. Having a child physically torn from you and witness her death was beyond anything any being should endure. Seeing one from afar grow up to be cut down young in godly terms, another blow. I had been afraid to let myself get attached to this third child or know anything about her. Prometheus had told me she'd die if we kept her. I had disconnected myself from thoughts of the child as I carried and birthed her.

"When the most recent Eleutheria was born, I agreed the only chance she'd have for survival would be far away from us. I gave her to Theus, asking never to know where she was or anything about her. I abandoned my child so she could survive." I looked up and should not have. All eyes were on me and were full of pity, sorrow, and sadness. The emotions were too overwhelming, so I stared at my hands again.

The silence stretched out, and the others were impatient but too kind to push me to speak.

Prometheus did instead. "It was something I insisted upon. We had to have no contact. I thought, perhaps, Zeus had traced Athena and I, but it wasn't only about trying to save my child. It was to free us all from Zeus. We had needed a free will goddess for so long. I took her to America. Placed her in an orphanage, followed by a boarding school, paying through a lawyer so no one could trace it back to me. I didn't see her again until she was expelled at seventeen for getting pregnant. The father was a mortal uninterested in becoming a father."

Theus continued filling the gaps of time I wasn't aware of. "I took the child from Eleutheria and placed her daughter in an orphanage. She was angry with me, not understanding why she must make such sacrifices. I made the fatal mistake of telling her what she was. She had known she was different. Her powers had been unbelievably strong, and she'd used them too often. Eleutheria had some of my foresight, Athena's brains, but she also disrupted Zeus's control. Not only that, I had no control over her. My blood did not demand her obedience, so no elder would be able to check her if I couldn't."

A movement stole my attention. Aroha and Archer had exchanged a knowing glance. He had defied her, which meant it'd been going on longer than I'd thought. I wanted to ask questions, but knew Prometheus wanted to stick to chronological order. I squelched my impulse to interrupt—difficult feat, actually—because I needed the end of this story. I extended my pointer finger, pressing it against my leg to physically ground my question; it always helped me remember if I had to wait and my mind wandered elsewhere.

"I had other suspicions, but..." Prometheus sighed.

Here it was, I held my breath and stood still.

"...she did not live long enough for me to see the full range of her powers. Zeus found her in no time after that, and she was killed at the tender age of twenty. That demigod baby I had placed in the orphanage was your mother, Callie. You're our great-granddaughter." Prometheus concluded, touching my shoulders.

I tensed, balling my fists. "Why didn't you save her?" My daughter was dead. "You said we had to give her up for her to *live*." He had lied to me. After the words came out, I realized I had no expectations my daughter was alive, but confirmation made me finally grasp the truth: he made me miss my daughter's life for an empty promise.

Everyone shifted uncomfortably, sensing a fight coming on. With so many gods around, the tension was palpable. Prometheus sighed, walked up to me, squared my shoulders to face him, and then forced my gaze to meet his by tilting my chin up. Although I hated eye contact, his eyes were like ebony pools of knowledge and acceptance, sucking me down a hole I longed to go; I could not look away. I blinked a few times to not fall into the abyss behind those eyes to note his expression was pained. "Those were not my exact words, Thena."

I ignored the others whispering about never knowing we were together, and they asked a million questions of each other, but I pushed their voices away into the periphery, not letting myself get distracted. "You said—"

"That she would die if she stayed with us. I've told you many times how forethought works. I altered the path, but the path realigns and tends to happen anyway. She would've made it a couple years with us, and if we separated, I could've kept her by my side for maybe five. You? This time, you would've died defending her. Maybe that was selfish of me to not let you be with her for a couple years of bliss, but I couldn't let you go, Thena. I knew for a fact I could keep her hidden long enough to bear a demigod, one Zeus *wouldn't* find, and one who would give birth to Callista. From the moment I was chained on that rock, my life's work for us—you and me, for all gods—was to ensure a path that led to *her*." He pointed at Callie.

All this time, particularly during his punishment, he had plotted this out. The patience invested in such a long plan was mind-boggling to me.

"But Zeus did find my mother, and wait—why me?" Callie appeared worse for wear, shocked and conflicted. Archer had his arm around her, rubbing her shoulder in comfort, love shining in his eyes.

I wanted to soothe her somehow, like he was. Words were not aligning in my scattered mind.

Prometheus went on. "I think Zeus found *you*, Callie, but mistook your power as your mother's. He wasn't threatened by the child but by the adult in the car. He guessed wrong, and that is what ensured your survival—and my intervention. He lost track of you after I made your father flee New York. He thought his work was done."

"Still, how is she fully immortal?" Lucien asked impatiently.

"Athena understands genetics better than I, but recessive genes can become dominant..." Theus began.

"Yes," I said, suddenly excited. Facts, science, so much better than the difficult past and all these emotions. I could picture how—all the answers—Callie became immortal. I scanned the room for something to demonstrate to them what happened in terms they could understand. I saw the canister of sugar sitting on the table with the tea someone had abandoned making when we'd barged in.

I dumped the sugar out onto the table and drew in it with my finger as I spoke. "The short of it is a demigod has a mortal dominant gene and a recessive immortal gene, so this is Callie's mother's genetic make-up." I drew a large square and cut it into four boxes making a window. Next, I drew an *M* and *i* on the left side outside of the box. "Now, Callie's dad was also a demigod descended from Psyche, with a mortal and immortal gene as well." I drew the same initials above the box. I was drawing the basic Punnett square diagram they'd all understand, which predicts genotypes of offspring. Or I hoped they'd grasp it since they took high school and college biology gods knew how many times. I kept drawing. "Therefore, when Callie's parents had children, they had a 50% chance of having another demigod, a 25% chance of having a completely mortal child, and a 25% chance of—"

"Having a fully immortal child." Lucien cut in. He was frustrated and pacing.

Callie stared at my diagram:

	M	i
M	MM	M$_i$
i	M$_i$	ii

Callie's finger circled the *ii* representing her two recessive genes that gave her immortality.

Chase was the first one to recover from the shock. "Has this ever happened before?"

I told him, "No, not that I know of. Zeus keeps track of these things. All gods do. Remember the insistence on forbidding relationships with any *others*? Despite Hera, Leto, and few rare others, Zeus seemed to want the Olympians to stick together. Demigods have never married demigods before. He didn't allow it, and if it happened, he would've squashed it without us knowing."

Freya smirked. "But he can't trace Norse demigods."

"Nor Titan," Prometheus added. "Just Olympian. That's why he overthrew us. We were something he could not control, and it was why he watched us so carefully."

"Then he only could've figured her out from the traces of my blood," I concluded. Why did I feel guilty when none of it was under my control?

Chase whistled. "Callie has three god lines. Explains why your Norse lot will protect her. I would assume the remaining Titans would help us?"

"Stop it," Aphrodite scoffed. "This is no time to talk of war. It's a time to let Callie, Athena, and others digest this information."

I nodded. There was no way my mind could turn to war at this moment, and I did not want to disappoint him about the lack of support the Titans had given me. Instead, I cleared my mind and stared at my

THE IMMORTAL TRANSCRIPTS: SHUDDER

descendant. Emotions swept over me as if I was seeing a piece of my daughter again, echoed down the line—a sliver of her, but enough.

"I...I have a real family, who are alive?" Callie asked. Her wide-eyed stare and the longing in it prickled my cold heart. She was so alone and longing for family.

Archer frowned, being his overly sensitive self.

Without even needing to see his face, she said, "You're my family, of course, Archer, but this is something in addition to that." People to help fill the void her father's death had left.

Callie met Theus's gaze, then mine, and it was too much. Every difficult and complicated feeling flowed through me. Hopefully, we'd have centuries or more together for me to figure all of them out.

The room was silent, uncomfortably long. It made my skin crawl.

"I guess we should probably give you guys some space," Chase said. It was a declaration to disperse, and we'd all reconvene later.

I managed to tell Callie we'd have a private chat later. I needed to process, to think of what to say in a situation like this. Prometheus—always knowing—led me out onto the back deck. The late September air was crisp, but the sunlight was still warming, not that temperatures mattered much to us. He pulled me to him, touching my cheek as if he would kiss me. I looked down, struggling to formulate my feelings into words. He propped my chin up, his warm, dark eyes meeting mine.

"Why didn't you tell me she lived, that we had descendants?"

"You told me never to tell you. You said the only thing that would keep Eleutheria safe was everyone's ignorance. Did you want me to spend another millennium bound to a mountainside—alone, tortured?" He lifted his shirt to show me the unfading white scar where the eagles had repeatedly plucked out his liver.

I traced my fingers along it, shaking my head. He was right not to tell me. Callie was our surrogate daughter and the most important goddess to grace this Earth. She could let us live free lives, the one thing I always envied of mortals.

"I've missed you," I struggled to say.

Prometheus's hand closed on mine, holding it against his abdomen, right under his ribcage. I felt how his pulse was raised, his hands clammy, his breaths short. I dared to meet his gaze, our faces only inches apart; his eyes dancing wildly before locking on mine. He wanted me in all the ways a man wants a woman. The knowledge of the power I held over him, and he over me, was staggering.

I pushed away from him and turned. "Are we really going to begin this all again?" I asked.

"Thena," he coaxed softly.

"Really, Theus, can you deal with all the pain again? A love like ours is not meant to last. It's too intense, too evanescent..."

"Stop rationalizing, Thena. Love isn't rational, nor is it measurable."

"Just...not now," I begged, unable to hold myself together. The horrific history of our secret marriage, how we were torn apart, our daughters murdered, now put out in front of our family and friends made it all come rushing back.

I was suddenly alone. He had given me space, but knowing Prometheus and his level of passion, it wouldn't be long until he would be trying me again.

I had enough emotional turmoil for the day and blamed my false fatigue on traveling. I didn't sleep. Having the downstairs bedroom, I heard them talking and moving about. It grew late, but they kept on with my favorite board games to distract themselves: Trivial Pursuit and Risk. Without me there, Lucien won the first, Chase the latter. No one spoke of serious matters, enjoying their very mortal-feeling night.

When the house went quiet and the door opened, I feigned sleep. Prometheus. I sensed him. How could I not? He moved around in the dark, making a little noise—cell phone and wallet down on the table, shoes off. Then he had the audacity to climb into bed behind me.

I was not ready for this. I tried not to react.

"I'm not going anywhere, and I'm not trying anything," he whispered. God of Foresight much? He should be called the god of mindreading instead.

I didn't say a word, although we both knew I was awake.

He draped his arm over me, pulling me a tad closer. "Deal with it, Thena. I sacrificed so many mortal lifetimes just to get back to you."

How could I counter that? My cold, rational heart thumped frantically in my chest, betraying the effect he had on me. I closed my eyes, hoping I'd stop thinking about him, the past, and the possible future.

At some point, I fell asleep.

CHAPTER 20

Archer

It was a massive relief to have answers to Callie's ancestry and how she became immortal. I was able to let go of at least one worry and better enjoy our time together. I became carefree and happy. Although Zeus wanted her dead, it felt peripheral, a bothersome gnat we could ignore. Strange, but when one goes from thinking one's wife is a feeble and sickly mortal to finding out she is a goddess of three bloodlines and no easy target, it makes one feel like a new god. We had the Norse in pocket too, and Athena and Dad were forging allies to be on standby. The only concern was whether any of the other godly tribes would tolerate a Greek-Titan-Norse freedom goddess usurping their control, well, if she could. How far did Callie's freeing power go? The entire god-world, just Olympian, or the three lines in her blood?

The next day, after things calmed down, my beautiful freedom fighter—she hated my moniker when I said it earlier—was sprawled out on the living room floor by my feet, and I was sitting on the couch, halfheartedly watching TV, some history program my dad had put on. Callie was poring over mythology books, trying to learn the history of her other ancestors, the sun pouring through the windows onto her. Beautiful.

"Archer?"

"Hmm."

"Do you realize we are related?" Callie got up, kneeling, and shoved a book of Greek mythology into my lap. Had I not quickly closed my legs, the book's spine would've nailed me in the balls. I didn't need to glance at the family tree on the page to guess the issue; I knew it would crop up as soon as we found out Athena was her relative. Right, so now I had more than one concern, damn it. She was about to freak out about something so minuscule to us gods but taboo to contemporary mortals.

"Oh, this will be good," Himerus said, the anticipation of drama in the air thrilling him. Not much in the way of any entertainment had been going on, but I'd rather not provide a reality show for him. He threw his leg over a chair, straddling it, and leaned his arms across the back, staring intently at us. Holy Hades, we had an attentive audience.

Anteros copied him. Not blood-related, and yet they were behavioral twins. Athena glared at them, pointing the paring knife in her hands at them from inside the kitchen. Prometheus, who was helping prepare food with her, chuckled.

I groaned. "Related? Barely. Like three thousand years of distance."

"But not generations of diluted DNA," Callie pointed out. "Athena is my great-grandmother and also your aunt."

"Half aunt," I tried.

Callie gave me her censorious side-eye, telling me it didn't change a thing.

"Is there a name for what you two are?" Anteros asked. "Not being funny, but seriously?"

"Maybe first half cousins twice removed?" Dad unhelpfully said.

Great. Dad was making it worse by giving it a name. "How would you know that?" He sounded unsure, and I wanted to yell at him, but a question had popped out of my mouth instead.

"Because I realized I'm her great-great-uncle—by half—but, then again, maybe not?"

"Welcome to the most twisted family ever." Himerus punctuated his statement with that annoyingly leery sounding laughter of his. I wanted to throttle him. My family was the worst.

"So, Zeus is my great-great-grandfather, but he wants to kill me?" Callie ventured.

"Like I said—" Himerus started.

"She heard you the first time," I snapped.

His smile fell.

"By mortal standards, first cousins twice removed only share 6.25% DNA, and on top of that, introduce the fact of half siblings, it's even less. I'd say about 3% of shared DNA." Athena started getting technical, which was not much better because numbers were facts. "However, godly DNA isn't quite the same, Callie," Athena finally saved me. "Our DNA doesn't become flawed in any way from blending or overlapping. Ichor heals everything, including birth defects. Although myths say we are all related, we are not as close as texts profess. But yes, distantly, we are mostly all related. Zeus's line of born gods or demigod half siblings, both often married Poseidon's children."

THE IMMORTAL TRANSCRIPTS: SHUDDER

"Okay," Callie let go of the book and sat back on her heels—away from me. She wrapped her arms around herself. She was not at all okay.

What could I say? I had no clue Athena had been her ancestor, so it was no fault or omission of my own, but I feared she would resent me or be repulsed by me.

"Callie, relax. You're a Titan." Prometheus said it with pride.

"Yeah. Nice way to try to cover it up." Himerus was enjoying this way too much.

Prometheus walked out of the kitchen, wiping his hands on a towel. "I'm not making allowances. Think how DNA works, the godly kind, I mean. The defect in Ares with the emotion and eyes connection is in his blood, his DNA. It passed down two generations. Now, this eye defect—"

Dad interjected, "Can we stop calling it a 'defect'? And it's 'Chase,' as you well know." He was still half absorbed by the TV but listening well enough to take a mild offense.

Prometheus rolled his eyes. "Fine. 'Chase's genetic blessing' then."

"When did you study godly DNA?" Athena asked.

"I've been alive longer than you, sweetheart. Can I finish?"

Athena gave him a fake glare. "What? Hundreds of years was all."

"I can do science too, Thena." Prometheus teased.

She threw a handful of flour at him. It was so weird to see them flirt.

"Can we let him finish?" Anteros seemed put out, wanting to hear about the eye thing.

"Anyway, Chase's eye 'blessing' is a dominant trait when it came to Eros but no other child of his. Like human DNA, mom and dad pass things down, but when one godly parent is stronger and more potent than the other, the more powerful DNA will win. Athena is a demigod-birthed goddess, so she is—no offense, Thena—not as powerful as me. Our child had my powers passed down to her demigod child, which was passed to Callie. Freya's Psyche, again, only a demigod made immortal. My bloodline is the strongest—ergo, she is a Titan."

"Let's do a DNA test." Athena seemed excited at the prospect.

I was wary. What if Prometheus was wrong and the results put Callie off? What if she wanted a divorce? I could not lose her. We were bound forever, and there was no way I could not love and desire her.

"Thena, when it shows your DNA is hardly there?" Prometheus asked her softly. "This is a bad idea."

"It has to be there. What? You really think your DNA wiped mine out? Am I just some vessel for Titan spawn?"

"No. Of course not. I'm trying to assure Callie that she's less related to Archer than she believes. It proves something more important than any of this: Zeus is no match in power if his bloodline bowed down to Freya's or my own."

"So, we're all as powerful as Zeus then?" Dad took his eyes away from the TV.

Callie had her back to me now, but she crisscrossed her legs and leaned against mine. I played with an errant curl that refused to stay fastened in her ponytail. She didn't bat my hand away, at least.

"He's saying you god-born are. Us 'hybreeds' aren't. I'm weak and useless, only intended to carry children to get us to this point." Athena's teasing and flirty tone was completely gone. "I feel so necessary."

"Was that sarcasm?" Anteros asked.

"I think it was," Himerus said, shocked.

By Poseidon's Trident, they were an annoying pair, but they really knew how to ease the tension by changing the subject.

"So what?" Athena shouted, and the paring knife ended up in the wall right between Anteros's and Himerus's heads. They gawped at the embedded knife, then each other, and turned to her. "I'm not serious 100% of the time."

A bunch of us stared at her because she usually was serious, often missed our jokes, and sarcasm was not her thing.

"Thena, you carried the child who led to a descendant who can forever free us from a tyrant's reign. Without your military expertise and logic, we can't win a war against Olympus. And who do you think we'll look to for leadership if we carve our own futures without Zeus?" Prometheus made an attempt to mollify her.

"You, I assume, the all-seeing eye. Next, you'll want all the Titans freed from Tartarus!" Athena was pissed off all right because that was a touchy subject.

Prometheus flinched at her words and went rigid.

"Chase! Outside!" Athena glared at him.

"What did I do?"

We all were as dumbfounded as he was at her sudden shift of anger.

"I want to spar."

I was still lost, unable to follow her eccentric line of thinking.

"I'm in." Dad yanked himself away from the TV as if he hadn't been sucked into it for over an hour.

"Can I come?" Himerus asked.

THE IMMORTAL TRANSCRIPTS: SHUDDER

Dad was surprised. He stared at Himerus, hesitant for a second, before he gave a wry grin and said, "Yeah, kid."

I wonder if he realized how much it meant to my brother to be accepted and included by him. Anteros, on the other hand, seemed a bit left out. I'd talk to Ma later about being more inclusive, but I had the Callie identity crisis situation at hand right now.

Callie stood and plopped next to me on the couch, putting her head on my shoulder. Or maybe the situation was over?

I ventured, "Still weirded out?"

"Not as much, but I didn't want Athena upset just so I felt better." She stared off, pensive, her eyes vibrant. A smile broke upon her face. "Callista of the Titans. Badass."

"Actually, Callista of Othrys before you married me." Good. She was calmer about it. I couldn't imagine what I would do if she didn't love me.

She hit me playfully with a pillow. "Titan sounds so much cooler."

"My Titan freedom fighter." I leaned in to kiss her.

She backed away. "No, not yours if you dare call me that." She smiled, though, so I kissed her. All was well again.

Then it wasn't. Two hours of sparring, a shower, an argument with Prometheus, and after what appeared to be an armistice, Athena took DNA samples and went into the cellar that we had no clue had been there. Apparently, there was an underground laboratory for the mad scientist beneath a trap door in her bedroom. It really didn't surprise me, if I were honest.

By dinner time, Athena rushed into the room in a huff, fire in her eyes, and her jaw set. She threw a piece of paper onto one of Callie's books. Prometheus was right behind her, his face taut and his eyes full of concern, but she shut and locked her bedroom door before he could enter—right in front of his face. I had thought Callie was tenacious, but Athena proved to have a massive temper.

Prometheus didn't attempt to knock or get into her room. He paced, waiting.

I didn't need to read the paper to know Athena had cracked Callie's DNA and Prometheus had been right. Callie picked it up and read aloud: "Matching 24.1% Prometheus, 12.5% Freya, and 0.9% Athena."

Callie was by far a Titan. So much of Prometheus's DNA carrying down—the missing pieces being mortal DNA mixed over generations—meant he was her closest relative.

"Archer?"

I glanced at the last number on the paper: Eros 0.025. I pulled her into my lap, thankful for godly DNA's power. We were pretty much as related as strangers would be on the street.

Athena came back out, pacing. "This doesn't change anything. I'm still her great-grandmother."

"Of course, you are." Callie stood and walked over to her. "I'm sorry I freaked out about it. I'm sorry that me knowing the truth hurts you."

Athena stared at my wife, trying to see something in Callie—herself maybe—but failing. Callie threw her arms around Athena, hugging her. Athena went stiff. One does not hug the goddess without her instigating it, which was rare. Surprising us all, Athena embraced her back in a tight hug with a shuddering but pleased sigh. Callie was actually the one to instigate pulling away.

"So, now this little crisis is over with, Callie, let's talk powers. What can you do?" Prometheus asked. It was a diversion tactic, blaming the drama on Callie alone, but we were all glad Athena was calm and the genetic project over.

"Wait, so could Callie be like both Prometheus and Psyche?" Ma had that irritatingly wild and giddy look in her eyes, excited at the prospect. You'd think she heard there was a half-off sale on shoes or something, the way she was getting riled up.

Athena shrugged, "Perhaps." She did not take offense at being left out, but I'm sure my mother's tactlessness cut deep.

"I can read minds, immortal ones if I try hard, but mortals are easier. I foresaw some kind of future. I still don't understand it," Callie said.

"She foresaw what I was doing or maybe planning, but it was more than that. Callie, you saw where I was in the present, and you were able to reach me telepathically *before* the fever spikes," I added.

"Don't forget she is free will, as you said. Don't you all feel it? I prefer war, but I'm no longer imprisoned by it. She cures us of the natures imposed on us by Zeus," Dad said.

Lucien ticked the powers off on his fingers. "So mindreading, foresight, and justice. Sounds like she's a trifecta."

Athena smiled at this. Good for Lucien, slipping in the free will as justice to make her see herself in Callie, regardless of genetics.

Dad confirmed what we all had been thinking all along: "She's the usurper of Zeus's power, position, of everything. That's why he wants her dead."

THE IMMORTAL TRANSCRIPTS: SHUDDER

"It's why we were all drawn to her," Aroha added. "We had this innate sense to protect her because she can free us or, as Lucien put it, give us justice."

Lucien turned to Aroha, stunned.

Good, maybe he'd realize his love for my wife was misplaced. Maybe his passion was born of the need to protect, and he was drawn to liberty as much as he was to truth. He and Athena had a platonic relationship, which reminded me of something: how did Ma and I—and my brothers—miss the whole Athena and Prometheus relationship? One of us should've picked up on it, but then again, Athena was great at withholding emotions and Prometheus at disappearing for centuries.

"I don't want to do that. Usurp him. I just want a normal life as possible with Archer." Callie leaned over me, pulling my head back, giving me a sweet smile. She gave me an upside-down peck on the lips. I pressed back in agreement. It was all I wanted likewise.

"You don't have a choice." Prometheus dispelled my fantasies of endless futures of houses and careers and children with my wife. "Her very existence usurps his power. All she has to do is live to do so. Unfortunately, she has the same effect on me as all of you. I'm not foreseeing so well these past few decades, but I think I gleaned enough knowledge prior to this 'blindness'—for lack of a better word—to forge a way to protect her."

"You *think*? Oh, that sounds helpful," Lucien scoffed.

Prometheus countered, "Where are your prophecies, Apollo?" I saw the tension in the Titan's shoulders. He was ready for a fight. I think he was prepared to get his anger out about his Athena troubles on someone else.

However, Lucien's stunned face distracted me. He knew one.

"Out with it!" I demanded. "Lucien, you are always hiding things and holding back. Just because you don't have to tell the truth all the time because of Callie, it doesn't mean you should hide things. Look at his face. He knows a prophecy."

He was so taken aback by my change in tone, Lucien almost fell off the arm of the recliner Ma was sitting in. Lucien and Callie exchanged a coded-glance, and he stormed out of the front door. Hymenaios ran after him, calling for him to wait. What in Hades was that about?

Everyone stared at Callie. She knew, and she quickly caved into all the immortal gazes upon her. "He'll somehow betray us, and he will die because of it. I don't know how or why. I only see Death coming for him. He told me he had a prophecy which told him of a betrayer paying a price. He knows his death is coming."

No one knew what to say to that. It was an intense two days of discoveries, both great and terrible. The worst discovery to me was knowing my wife withheld the truth from me, again. She breached my trust and couldn't confide in me. The acknowledgment stung.

CHAPTER 21

Callie

"Concentrate." Archer's face was stern after the tenth time he asked me to focus. He wasn't truly angry with me anymore, but we did have our first real fight after he found out I had hidden a few things from him. I couldn't deny it, but he wouldn't acknowledge he had been overprotective and that telling him things would've made him more unbearable (truth!).

I refused to promise I'd tell him all my visions because of what Lucien had told me about the futility of fighting fate. My dear Archer would lose his mind if he couldn't prevent my death. There was no way I could tell him what I had dreamed. Over the past month, the dreams would not stop, and unfortunately, they varied. When I admitted the dreams kept changing, Archer compromised when I said I'd tell him about the consistent ones.

I smirked at him. "You're a lousy teacher."

"Lousy teacher, lousy student. I don't know which one of us is worse." He was speaking about more than his helping me with my powers at the moment. We both had to grow into this relationship. I had to learn how to deal with these visions and learn to open up to Archer, trust him, but he had to relax, trust me, and stop trying to be some hero defending me.

"Maybe I just don't have controllable powers." I shrugged it off. Perhaps I only existed to threaten Zeus as Prometheus said, and my visions would be as random as Lucien's prophecies (boring and useless). The whole freeing thing was great and all, but what point were the visions if I couldn't control them to stop them? I saved Archer once before thanks to them; betrayer or not, I wanted Lucien to live. I didn't want to die either, and Archer could be involved too. The same dream kept coming back in variation: one, two, or three deaths (the exact reason I kept them mostly to myself).

"We need to sharpen your skills and get them under control." It was the same thing Archer said daily.

The same routine for a month now of this practicing, trying to control the visions, and tune into the immortal senses. At least those were sharpening. I wasn't as clumsy and could hear things farther away. Nothing as cool as flying, but I had to let Archer feel special since I—Titan blooded—was supposedly stronger than him. Images of kicking Zeus's butt by myself came to mind (too bad it wasn't a vision).

Archer was right. Zeus wanted me dead not only for stealing his power but also because, like my grandmother, I'd be a huge liability if I couldn't be controlled. I would be a threat to Zeus, my family, my friends, and other gods. It made me wrongly afraid of myself and what I was capable of. Of everything I had gone through, lack of control was worse than the feeling of being displaced. I was abroad, with the new role as a wife, my discovered immortality, compounded by the loss of my father—not controlling these powers outweighed that. Three daughters and a granddaughter murdered? Could Prometheus and Athena keep me alive?

My husband's lips brushed mine. Perhaps Athena was wrong in assuming I was different from her because of my DNA. Here I was rationalizing everything, lost in my own world for a moment. The fact I enjoyed the thought of being like her was paramount. She was unusual, anxious, and antisocial, some might say, but that frenetic uniqueness about her warmed my heart. We were family. Dad had brought me home as he'd promised.

What had Archer just said? Sharpen my skills (I think). "I know that, Archer, but I'm not as powerful as I was when I had the fevers."

"It wasn't the fevers, Callie. You should be able to control your powers unconsciously now, as easy as breathing once you're used to it. Imagine if Lucien had to consciously raise the sun every morning and time it right across his territories." He sighed, and the tension fell out of his shoulders.

I was kind of interested to know how the sun gods—since it was clear there were many cultures of gods—controlled the sun in shifts around the world, and if they ever messed up.

"C'mere." His tone softened. He was reclining on the sofa, and I stood over him, still irritated by my "lessons" as he coined them.

The student-teacher mentality made me feel inferior, and finding out the truth confirmed I wasn't, yet all his years of knowledge and experience blighted mine. I had to learn from someone, and I'd rather it be him—a kind teacher—than someone who would be severe. Athena already proved to lack patience; Chase was only interested in teaching me combat, which I agreed to for my protection, but he was as brutal as what I imagined a drill sergeant would be. Aroha was very disorganized and flitted about from topic to topic, so it was impossible to cohesively learn from her. Lucien was brooding over his problems, and Prometheus was helpful but busy negotiating with the Norse or trying to get back into Athena's good graces. Archer was the only teacher I had. He was good but, at times...distracting (okay, admittedly both our faults).

Archer's hands sought my own, and he pulled me, with immortal strength, into his lap, turning me so my back was toward him. "I love not having to be careful with you anymore." His voice was husky, insinuating more. He kissed my neck softly, then began to massage my shoulders (like now, yeah; he was distracting).

"Clear your mind."

Now that was easier said than done. I tried to think of nothingness—a big dark open abyss—but things kept popping into my mind. I was easily sidetracked with his body pressing against mine, our hearts beating quickly in tandem, and our matching breaths. I squeezed my eyes closed, willing my mind to stay blank. I relaxed into a deeper calm as Archer's fingers dug the tension out of my neck and shoulders.

Suddenly—on this calm, blank, black canvas in my mind—vibrant yet distorted images appeared. I concentrated, trying to focus while keeping my deep breathing steady, matching his. One image, in particular, was blurry but familiar. Archer? I homed in, trying to relax even more, allowing the vision to sharpen itself. Some noises came into play, not ones around me, but low, quiet murmurs, which echoed as if in a tunnel at first until they steadily became clearer.

"I'm going after him," Archer growled, *his voice still a little muddled. The image sharpened. He was on his knees, crouched over something, his head bent down as if mourning a loss.*

"No, you're too weak." Aroha placed her hand on his shoulder. Her other hand was occupied holding whatever they were leaning over. "He'll destroy you."

Their voices were crisp now. Everything was as if I were there. Where? I didn't know.

"Ma, I'm dead without her. We are dead already. I can risk myself to free you, Dad—everyone. Zeus must be stopped," Archer said, *his voice breaking.*

I was the person lying by them. As I made this realization, I willed the scene to move, and it spun around until I saw their distraught faces staring at me. I was lying on a gray tiled floor, looking lifeless and pale.

"Archer..." Aroha stopped, realizing there was no comfort she could give him.

Aios was there suddenly, or perhaps his image had been unclear until that moment. *"We're keeping her alive via Archer, but..."*

"*The Norse can't get it here in time,*" Himerus said softly.

Aroha's face was frozen with shock as she stared at Archer, his hand cradling my head. Archer paid her no attention but smoothed the hair off my forehead and kissed it. There was no regret upon his face, just pure love.

"Archer, immortal marriage. You can't risk yourself out there. You'll hasten her death," Aroha pleaded.

"Yes, it's more of a reason for you to stay so both of you don't die," Aios implored. "Maybe we can think of something to save you."

"I want his head," Archer spat, his voice venomous, features distorted in fury, the power emanating from him matching Ares's. Then he softened, leaned in, and kissed my immobile lips. He stood quickly.

Himerus gripped his shoulder. "If you get killed, she'll die instantly."

"It doesn't matter anymore. I'll meet her in Hades."

The scene went blank. Something interrupted it. I opened my eyes and scanned the room. Himerus and Anteros were snickering at Archer and me.

Anteros mocked, "Aww, look at the lovebirds."

"Look at them? I *heard* them last night. Entire town heard them." Himerus guffawed, giving me a lascivious smile (gross).

I chucked a pillow, and to my astonishment, with perfect accuracy, I hit Himerus square in the face.

They retreated, muttering about wishing I were a mortal again.

Two warm lips pressed upon my neck, and Archer whispered, "Ignore them."

I spun around and kissed Archer. He responded by kissing me back. I needed to dispel the horrible vision from my mind. I knew I'd die and foresaw Lucien being at fault, but now it was likely Archer might do something rash to cause us to die too. I needed to figure out what would kill us so I could try to stop it. Lucien wasn't even in the vision. Had he already died? I knew enough of Lucien that he would never purposely physically hurt me (mentally, the guy would try any barb). Now more than ever, I was determined I'd fight the Fates. I needed lessons from Prometheus, but spending time with Archer was paramount.

We had recently married, and I had discovered new family members. I had to divide my time carefully, not to upset him or them. Of course, Prometheus and Athena had demanded every detail of my life story and got it, trying to compensate for missing their own daughter's and granddaughter's lives, and then their great-granddaughter's childhood. Archer should understand that, but I could tell he wanted more of my time. Now, this vision made our remaining time together even more vital.

THE IMMORTAL TRANSCRIPTS: SHUDDER

Archer pushed me away gently, his eyes scanning my face in confusion. My kisses gave my fear away.

"You saw something." His voice was proud, but his face sank in the realization it probably wasn't a good vision or I would've told him. "What was it?" He frowned adorably (Why did he have to be so distractingly cute?)

"Nothing." I tried to feign a smile. "It was a bunch of blurry noise."

"Callie." His voice brooked no denial, knowing I was lying.

Hiding things had upset him greatly. I could handle his wrath but not his disappointment. I had to tell him. "So immortal marriage. If one of us dies, could we have half lives?"

"So, in your vision, who dies? You or me? That's what you've seen?" Archer's expression was grim, but he was hiding emotion. He was terrified (didn't have to read his mind for that one either).

"Huh?" I stalled.

"Immortal marriage means our souls are forever linked. I told you this. You know about Castor and Pollux?"

"Of course. Twin brothers—please don't tell me Zeus was a swan really when he and their mother—"

"No." Archer laughed. "I mean, he did sneak past her husband, the king of Sparta, to get to her as a swan, but no, nothing gross like that." He shuddered.

"When one of them was dying, he asked Zeus to save his brother so they both could live."

"That's the short of it, yes. It's much more complicated than that. They were the first heteropaternal superfecundation we gods had ever seen."

(Um, superfund-what?)

He read my expression, which demanded an explanation. "It's when a mother gives birth to fraternal twins fathered by two different men. Castor was a mortal, Pollux was Zeus's, so a demigod. In the end, Zeus intervened and saved his son by offering him immortality, but Pollux wanted to give it to his brother. The myth stops there, but the truth was more complex. No mortal prior had been given a fast-track full dose of ambrosia until Castor. Zeus did it for his son, but probably as an experiment too. In the end, Castor wasn't going to survive, and Pollux forced Hymenaios to link his soul to his brother's. It had never been done prior. It's not like immortal marriage, which is a deeper connection, two souls merged. A soul-share is allowing two different bodies a turn with one soul, one lifeforce." He sighed, and I sensed his nervousness about what he would reveal next.

"They were brothers and used that family connection to share souls, and maybe a bit of selflessness. It's complicated."

I narrowed my eyes. (How dare he insult my intelligence.)

"There are four ways to share a soul, according to Aios, but all take an intense amount of love for someone: familial, friendship, romantic, or charitable. In Pollux's case, the act of charity was how he was willing to give up his immortality for his brother. But the moment I decided to marry you and bind my life to yours, we have all four links. That is something irreversible. Our souls are entwined."

Marriage, friendship, love, and...sacrifice. "What happens if one of us..." I swallowed hard, thinking of my vision of Archer running out to fight whom I assumed to be Zeus. "I can't deal with that. You can't ever put yourself in harm's way again."

"I won't be in a world without you in it," he said simply as if I'd missed an easy point.

"Don't say that."

His brow crinkled in concern. "Why? What happens? What did you see?"

I bit my lip. I couldn't lie to my husband while we were banishing the ones between us, but how could I tell him what I saw? I was beginning to understand Prometheus's predicament. If one tells someone the future and fate is apparently inescapable, then what good does it do? No matter what, I would be cold on the ground, and Archer would run to fight Zeus. I had to somehow stop that, for both our sakes.

I ignored his question. "How could you do this without asking me?" (oh, guilt) I was deflecting. If he hadn't done the immortal marriage, could I be dead from Zeus's lightning? I felt better after the fevers stopped on the cruise. If that never occurred, would I have transitioned into immortality? I was an accidental goddess, a genetic anomaly. I would never know these answers.

Archer kissed my forehead. "We both know we would never live without each other. The immortal marriage is what we both would've chosen, right? The volcano, Persephone's box."

I wanted to disagree but couldn't. I willingly entered eternal sleep rather than let him die, and he almost threw himself in a volcano when he thought of a life without me in it. So, our souls were intertwined. I loved him, and he loved me. It was a commitment more than he had ever had with anyone else. Still, these visions made it look dire, like a huge mistake.

I nodded, agreeing with him despite my reservation.

"What did you see?" he pressed.

"Callie?" a voice interrupted. It was Prometheus to my rescue. His eyes met mine in understanding. He probably had been eavesdropping.

It was strange how close I felt to Prometheus, for lack of a better word, as if he were family—an uncle almost—even though a month was not much time to get to know a relative. I was beginning to realize how tight the bond of blood was among the immortal kind, this familial bond. It was as if Freya and Prometheus were my tight-knit family. Their blood was in my veins, and it called out to them in comfort and understanding. Athena's pull and connection to me was lesser, but it was still there.

"Could we have a minute, Prometheus?" Archer asked politely.

Prometheus shrugged. "I would if I could, but I can't."

"What?" Archer glared at him, a bit put out (my grumpy little Cupid).

"Callie can't be sure of what she sees. In the beginning, it is hard to discern between what will be and what is in someone's mind." He hesitated and said diplomatically, "Do you mind if I try to help?"

"No," Archer said, his voice a little sullen. I didn't understand why he'd be upset at someone helping me. "Your descendant, your abilities. I mean, if anyone could help with foresight, it'd be you." This concession seemed to hurt Archer's pride (men or male gods—all the same).

I squeezed Archer's hand, and he gave me a small smile before kissing the back of my hand.

"Callie." Prometheus sat across from us. "What I say now is the most important information you will get. There are visions you will have. True visions of the future, meaning things the Fates have set in stone, almost always unchangeable—"

That wasn't what I had been told. "Wait." I thought they were *always* unchangeable. "Lucien said—"

"You asked Lucien?" Archer frowned.

"No, it came up, that's all, but he said fate could not be changed."

Prometheus sighed. "It should not be malleable, yet I've been alive longer than most gods, and at the same time, I can see the world end. I've had time to test the Fates, to act opposite of what is supposed to happen. I have altered it once or twice, successfully. It took a lot of trial and error, but you are here, are you not?"

Did Prometheus truly mean I was not supposed to exist? That his errors were his inability to save his daughters?

"You were supposed to die with your mother, Callie. If I had not sent your father away from New York, funded his expedition to Greece, commanded him back to the US, then directed your father to New York again, we might not be having this conversation. I did it all to hide you and your powers; in New York, you were masked by Aroha and Archer—Lucien and Dionysus as well—all to evade Zeus,"

"So, you manipulated fate repeatedly?"

"Yes, but I failed twice before. Do not falsely believe it is easy to bypass the Fates. What you need to know most is you might see inside people's minds—their intentions, motivations, hopes, fears—more than the rest of us. Psyche could see into the souls of others without effort."

"Okay, I get that part. I read Archer's mind before. I'm still not sure if I saw the future and changed it or I saw his intentions and changed it with the whole volcano situation. How can I distinguish between the two?"

"That's my exact point." Prometheus shook his head. "It's hard. It takes time, but what I can say is if you have visions that strike you down, overwhelm you, and hit you like a blunt force object to the head, then it is real. Otherwise, you must wait to see if the vision changes or occurs constantly."

"I came way too close to acting on it. Callie saw the future and stopped me," Archer said. "The question I have, Prometheus, is did she defy the Fates or do the Fates orchestrate all this? You know more about them than anyone. Do they want her to exist?"

Prometheus shrugged. "There is no way we can ever know, but they have not tried to stop me."

I don't want Lucien to die.

Without trying to mind read, Prometheus's voice was inside my head. *You do understand more than just you and Archer will die if Lucien doesn't make this sacrifice?*

So, we have to let him die? How can you be so calm about that? Don't you care?

When you live as long as I have, things like death no longer have an impact. When you have watched most of your family be slain and cast into Tartarus, what is losing one more? When your own child is taken from you repeatedly—

I get it. I wanted him to stop. *You went against your family, so I don't think you have a right to complain about that part of history.*

"Are you two communicating somehow?" Archer asked.

THE IMMORTAL TRANSCRIPTS: SHUDDER

Because I saw what would happen. Call it self-preservation, but I knew even then we'd lose the Titan war; Zeus would rule, and my descendant would one day usurp him. My life has been one long strategic war, and I'm ready for all the strategizing to end. I want to live in peace and only see mundane future days of contentment. Only I can do this. For all of us. Trust me.

Archer huffed out an annoyed breath, and I apologized.

"I'll leave you to explain what you *can*." Prometheus laughed and was gone in a split second.

Archer gave me a hurt expression. I took up his hand.

"Just like that," —he snapped his fingers— "you're best buddies, conversing in your heads, excluding me?"

"It could not be overheard. I'm trying to figure out how and when I can tell you. I will explain it. I promise. No other immortal ears can hear."

His brow wrinkled. "So, it's not some little secret between the two of you?"

He was jealous. "He's my relative, Archer. I lost my father, and he...he reminds me of him in a way, a mentor. He could teach me a lot. Please don't get weird about this."

He pulled me closer, his eyes dancing across my face, scrutinizing me as if he were Lucien reading for truth. Then Archer kissed me, folding me in his arms. All was well, his kiss told me, although his unsettled mind was dying to know what the conversation was about. He knew he could never hear them with our family all around.

CHAPTER 22

Lucien

The Norse and the Celts were a good laugh. We super pranked Chase by attacking him on his morning run, and he almost removed Thor's arm before he realized it was a joke. The Norse gods' antics and liveliness lifted my spirits after Callie's doomsday news about my limited future. After a few talks, the Norse were itching for a fight, completely on our side, and ready to do anything for the new "tribreed," as Odin had called Callie. After thousands of years and disputes over land and mortals, they were embracing a unification of cultures. Titan, Norse, and Greek, Callie was more than unity and freedom. She was a new beginning.

The Celts, however, were wary. They decided they would sit on the sidelines for now. There was some concern about the Asian sector and a mysterious illness after a mortal supposedly ate a raw bat. They implored me to research it, to talk to the gods there. However, I was not on good terms with the Wen Shen, Chinese gods of pestilence, to dissuade them from some epidemic they might have created. These "commissioners of pestilence" punished their people for misdeeds, but in such heavily populated areas, diseases and viruses took on a lifeforce of their own. Humans often made catastrophic mistakes. It was probably mortals' fault, turning it into something uncontrollable as they often tended to from time to time. The Celts' concern irked me, by lowkey insinuating I wasn't on top of this as much as I should be. I might be powerless to stop it, though. How bad of a virus were we talking about? Would I live long enough to even help?

The cabin was an oppressive place for me. Everyone seemed to be one happy family, but I could feel Callie and Archer pulling away from me. Chase and Aroha as well were being cooler and distant or maybe merely preoccupied. The only being helping me stay sane was my son, Aios, who idolized me and was loyal to me foremost. Sadly, it was time to inform my faithful child of my impending demise. I could no longer hide what Callie had told me, and he deserved to know ahead of time. There was no way my last days would be spent ignoring my calling. I had to do something, and Aios would want to go with me.

THE IMMORTAL TRANSCRIPTS: SHUDDER

"A word, Son?" I pulled him from his snowball fight with Archer's brothers. They were adorable in their carelessness, like kids, having fun in the middle of the drama and urgency heading our way. At some point, Zeus would strike. At some point, we would leave this protective land.

He beamed upon hearing me address him as such. We walked on a winding path, leading us toward the inlet. The snow had drifted farther down the mountains, almost twice as thick, enough for the ski season to commence.

Hymenaios sighed. "What's wrong?"

"I have to leave soon."

"*We*, Dad. We leave together."

I ruffled his hair as I had when he was little. I saw him that way still: innocent, impressionable, vulnerable. "Okay. Together."

"What is it? This Callie thing, or more? It's like you know something and are shutting me out." His tone exposed how he hated not being able to truly know me.

"This virus. I have a bad feeling about it. I want to go to your brother and talk to him about it. Do you know where he is?"

"Uh, yeah." Hymenaios looked away and then back at me. He was relaying bad news. "He's with my Mom, like *with* with. She emailed me. I didn't want to tell you. Frankly, I didn't trust her and her nonsense about leaving Fiji after she heard I almost died. I haven't responded."

Perhaps because I was facing death soon, I was kinder to my ex because my son would need her. I had to steer him back toward her for when I was gone. "She's your mother."

"Don't you lecture me!" His melodic voice was, for once, full of anger. How much had he suffered over this without telling me? "She. Abandoned. Me." He paced the rocky bank of the inlet.

I let him collect his thoughts, remaining silent. What could I say? I had abandoned him before.

"Dad, back when all this started, she said many things that made me—and Anteros and Himerus—believe we were the ones in the wrong when it came to protecting Callie. Those two were easily persuaded to this side because, you know, love triumphs with them. It also didn't hurt that Archer was kind to them. I mean, he has never been bad, just—absent."

I felt like he was talking about me as a father when he described Archer and his siblings. The guilt always ate at me. I was an inept father, not knowing how to even speak to my children, let alone raise them. I wish

I had time to start again, raise a child properly from an infant to adulthood, and not run away when things got tough.

"Basically, I could see *Mána* was blind, and I knew Zeus's camp was ill-informed and irrational. My mother let Zeus attack me. For doing my job. I immortally married a couple who asked for my service. My mother didn't bat an eye when Zeus decided it was a crime worthy of death."

"I...I don't know if that is fair until you talk to her. Your mother has always been...naïve. Did she even know what Zeus had planned?"

Hymenaisos's fists clenched tightly, and he glared at me. "You're defending her now?"

"No, sorry. The truth thing forces me to be objective about both sides. I can't imagine your mother would ever put your life on the line on purpose. She had to be misled. She was stupidly trusting. Your mother loves you more than any other being on this planet. If she finally sees Zeus for what he is and has left Olympus, then maybe give her a chance to explain. That's all I'm saying."

We were silent for a moment. I think he finally digested what I said. Euterpe—with all her faults and blindness—would never put our son on Zeus's altar. I could only imagine what she thought of what Zeus had done.

My mind shifted to something else my son had mentioned. She had fled Olympus and was with my healer son. Why? He was not related to her. She had hated his existence and ignored him. Euterpe always fantasized about slaughtering my mortal children out of jealousy, but in my son Asclepius's case, she sympathized with me because my sister so violently killed his mother. Now, Euterpe was *with* him, as lovers? What in Hades was going on in our Olympian world?

"Dad, I want to see her. I do, but if she's gone—if she's one of them, I need you to take me away. I trust *you*. No one else."

If a god's heart could shatter, it did with that confession. I pulled his forehead against mine. "I can't promise you anything. I'm sorry. Callie's prophetic vision has told us that I will betray our friends, and as a rightful consequence, I'll die for it."

"No." He said it a few times, pushing me away as I tried to hug him, until he realized I needed him to face it. "I won't let you."

"If anyone can stop me, it is you." I was giving him false confidence, empty hope. No one could stop Truth, and I was sure the truth was how I'd betray my friends. Something would happen where the truth could be forced from my lips; I never consciously would hurt my best friends.

THE IMMORTAL TRANSCRIPTS: SHUDDER

Someone should kill me to stop the transition of information, to be honest. At that moment, I hated my nature more than ever, talking to my son, while realizing every one of my faults. Only half of them were godly things. How had I become so mortal?

I took a deep breath. "It is hard to say this to you. If I do die, you are the eldest, which unfortunately means you'll be burdened with all my gifts: the sun, truth, arts, healing, the damn prophecies...all of it. It may seem overwhelming, but if I prepare you, it may not come as such a cumbersome shock." The words flowed out of my mouth evenly; I had to stay calm so he would too.

"Dad," Aios said grimly. "I am honored you want to spend your last days with me, but I'm going to do everything I can to prevent it."

I wanted my son to figure out some miracle plan, but I could never rely on it. I knew it was pointless, but seeing what my other kid was up to, what Euterpe knew from Olympus... Maybe I could do something for my friends, my family. I felt useless here and under Callie's foresight radar. Perhaps I could do something to help them abroad, and maybe I could distract myself and help the mortals with this illness, spend my last days healing others.

Obviously, I couldn't sleep that night, so I crept downstairs. I was eager to get away from this Icelandic prison. I was bound by my desire to be with my friend and the little serpent who stole my heart and would not give it back. I hated Callie so much. I wanted to inflict pain upon her, hurt her as she had me over and over again. As the god of truth, I wasn't blind. It wasn't her fault. Callie did not urge me to fall in love with her.

When it came to Archer and me, the girls always chose me. Not that I was bitter he won for once, don't get me wrong. It was the prize. Now I understood why I had been so drawn in by Callie from the start. She *was* immortal freedom. I had needed this severance from always telling the truth. The fever had been the ichor flushing her system, burning off the last remnants of mortal blood, where the powers finally came to pass. She would be powerful. How much? We could only guess. Yet, I loved her ever so much more for giving me the freedom from truth. It was such an inadvertently beautiful gift.

"Can't sleep?" A familiar voice broke me from my reveries.

I turned. "No, you?"

Athena stood, clad in a nightgown, her broad feet bare on the cold floor. I had never found her very attractive. Pretty but plain, with mousy blonde hair and pale gray eyes, but you knew from beholding her gaze, there was a powerful brilliance behind them. Smarts could be sexy, but Athena and I never clicked that way.

"Me neither." She switched on the electric kettle and rummaged around the cabinets. "Chamomile tea?"

"Can't hurt, thanks."

"So, what plagues you?"

"Plagues?" Ironic choice of words, considering what I had heard.

Athena shot me a knowing look. "Gods sleep well, unless something plagues us."

"Yeah, well..." I trailed off, hoping she'd let it all go and not press me.

"I know how you feel."

I didn't like being so easy to read. "Do you?" I shot out more bitter than I meant to be.

"Lucien." She sighed. "I've seen you century after century, never ever happy in the love department."

I deflected the subject onto her. "What about you? Are you happy?"

"Of course not. Why do you think I'm awake?" Smirking, she brought the teacups and bags over. After she had poured the steaming water, she plopped down next to me.

"He's here. He wants to be with you. What's the problem?" I pressed.

Obviously, this secretive history between Prometheus and her was immense. Before I would lay my concerns down, I'd make her tell me about her relationship with Prometheus. Athena was not chatty about anything personal, emotional, or anything social. When it involved her emotions, you were done with the conversation, so I was surprised she actually answered me.

"History," she said simply, with such finality.

I didn't dare urge her to continue. One word spoke volumes. I understood her more after that comment. I should not judge her antisocial behavior; she had always been a tad unconventional, but adding the trauma that must've given her PTSD, I had to be way more understanding. Her children murdered. Even as a terrible father, the thought of my boys being hurt or gone would destroy me.

"Why can't you move on?" she asked me.

"I can't because I don't know why I've stopped in the first place. I have no clue how she transfixes me."

"Prometheus says you will find happiness one day."

THE IMMORTAL TRANSCRIPTS: SHUDDER

"You guys talk about me?" I asked uncomfortably, sipping tea. It scalded my mouth with second-degree burns. I healed it and tried to keep myself busy by blowing it cool.

"I worry about you. I worry so much about all of you. Lucien, you seemed upset about everything we learned when it should be a good thing."

"It doesn't matter. I'm leaving, and Callie's dreamed that I die, so..."

"Prometheus says her visions can be people's thoughts. She can be mistaken," Athena tried to rationalize. She was staring off, thinking.

I pathetically hoped she would see something logical that involved me living. It was pointless. She was lying. No one would be thinking of me betraying them and Callie dying, so she wasn't reading thoughts. Athena would assume I would observe her lie, but her effort was the thought that counted.

"Yeah, what does he know?" I asked sardonically. Then I realized of whom I spoke.

Athena bit her lip, and we both laughed heartily. If anyone knew everything, it was Prometheus.

"Oh, Lucien." She tried to catch her breath. Of all gods, I could not deal with her expressing emotion over my possible death.

"Aios and I are off in the morning, for Vietnam. Don't worry, I'll stay clear of most Greeks. I would like it if you... I'd appreciate it if I could remain ignorant of Callie's whereabouts after I leave."

"Oh, Lo." She patted my cheek. "This is forever, isn't it? An actual goodbye." Athena's rationality slipped away as her sentiments crept forward, threatening to make her cry.

Her admittance told me I was on a path I could not alter. It rankled me. My true happiness would be righting a wrong, not love. "Not forever, I hope, but yes a long time. You see, I will not place myself in a position to betray or harm a hair on that girl's head. I will fight the destiny given to me."

"Everything happens for a reason." A voice made us both jump. It was Callie who stepped into the kitchen from the shadows of the living room. She sure had her immortal stealth skill down already.

"I came to say goodbye, Lucien," Callie said meekly. Was it the light shining in her dazzling eyes, or were they glistening with tears too?

I impulsively grabbed her hand in mine, not in a romantic way but in a desperate need of comfort, as if she could somehow tether me to this world.

"Lucien, it all happens for a reason."

What a crappy mortal saying to use against me. "How can you say that?" I stood up, throwing her hand away from me. "We're going to die, and from your expression and tone, it's soon. Yet you stand here calm as can be!"

"Lucien," Athena said my name in a calming tone. "It is best not to know at all. It can ruin everything. This Prometheus annoyingly tells me way too often."

"She's right," Callie said. Tears filled her eyes, splitting my heart in two. "I cannot even share any of this grief with Archer yet. He knows he might lose me, lose half of himself, maybe all of himself. He doesn't know about you." The last part was barely above a whisper. Callie uncharacteristically fell into a fit of sobs.

I stood and pulled her to me to hold her in a soothing embrace, but her legs gave way, and I sat her down in a chair. I looked to Athena for help, but she was suddenly gone. She either understood we must say goodbye in private or got the Hades out of there because of the emotions bombarding her—probably both.

"Please, Lucien, please..."

"What is it, Callie? I'll do anything. Just stop crying."

"It all has to happen...to happen...and it's all so horrible, and I cannot see...I cannot see what happens to..." Then she shattered, crying harder.

"Archer?" I supplied.

She nodded.

"Promise me. No matter what, Lucien..." Her eyes were wild, her face streaked with tears. "Promise me you will do whatever it takes to help him...to stop him...to protect him."

"From what, Callie? You're scaring me." I shook her shoulders, trying to jumble some sense back into her, or at least get a coherent thought from her.

Her eyes were unfocused and staring off, her face slack. "Follow me. New York." Her voice was suddenly devoid of emotion.

I was lost in her change of topic and tone. New York? The prophecy: glass raining down, a lifeless Archer and Callie. We could not go to New York again.

"Follow me. *Always.*" She said it again and again in this creepy type of trance, reminiscent of my opium-induced oracles, but it was different, raw, and more ethereal.

This situation felt like Themis speaking directly to me. I had to follow Callie to New York, but she wanted me to fight against fate. It was now more imperative than ever that I leave. "I will follow. I promise," I told her quietly.

Callie snapped out of it. Her eyes met mine, and the intensity in them confirmed my fears: I would die.

"I'll come back to bed in a minute," Callie said over her shoulder.

Archer stepped out of the living room shadows. Being preoccupied by Callie's vision-trance, I had not heard him. His face was set in wounded resentment. How much he overheard, I wasn't sure, but something told me he hadn't caught anything but what she'd said in her trance and now was getting the wrong end of the stick. I instantly removed my hands from her shoulders.

Archer desperately searched her saddened features, asking, "What's the matter?"

"I'm saying goodbye to Lucien. It may be the last time we see him," she said quietly.

Archer's face shifted at this comment, and the resentment instantly gave way to surprise. "But..." Archer couldn't finish.

Callie focused on me with those gorgeous brown eyes. "Goodbye, Lucien. Thank you for everything." She leaned over and kissed my forehead gently. A teardrop fell on my cheek.

Callie turned, walked by the pale-faced Archer, and left the room stoically. I suddenly realized how hard life was for Prometheus and Callie, to know future threads and not be able to change anything, no matter how desperately you wanted to.

From the darkness, I heard a whisper about "iron tears." Callie was quoting a myth. I had no idea why. Archer and I exchanged a quizzical look.

"So, this is it?" Archer's voice was awkward and faint. "She saw you die?"

"Apparently."

"How do I...how *can* I say 'goodbye' to you?" Archer's voice cracked. "Thousands of years of friendship...best friends—"

"Actually, we weren't friends until later. Hated your guts when you were young. Stupid Cupid," I reminded him of a taunt I had used against him during our Rome days.

Archer cracked a smile, even though his eyes shone with sorrow.

"Do me a favor, Archer?"

"Anything."

"Don't say goodbye. I don't think I could handle that."

"'Kay."

I offered him my hand. Archer took it, shook it, and pulled me into a hug. I had to blink back tears. He was my best friend, like my brother. The way I had picked on him, but we became friends, lived many mortal lifetimes together, and preferred each other as buddies over anyone else meant so much to me. Knowing you'll die soon sucked. Only then do you realize how much you actually matter and how much impact you make in others' lives.

And how much more you should've done for your loved ones.

CHAPTER 23
Athena

As soon as Lucien and Aios left, everyone grew somber: Prometheus, Callie, Archer, and I. We knew we'd never see him again. Archer's brothers were upset their buddy was gone, while Chase and Aroha grew suspicious about Lucien's departure. Chase knew enough about deceit to sniff it out early, but Theus thought it best not to involve him. He believed Chase might go as far as to kill Lucien to protect his child. I completely understood the sentiment—not merely because my children had been killed by Zeus, but also because Callie had become this type of surrogate child—emotionally—for me. It was unfair on the girl to place that much affection on her—millennia of grief and unspent love—and wrong to think I could replace my losses with this descendant, but I could not help myself. At least I kept it internal. I doubted anyone but Theus picked up on my regard for the girl and the longing to be a mother to her.

"Callie, no, never. We are staying put." Archer's voice followed an angry Callie as she descended the steps ahead of him.

"I saw we went. You can't tell me what to do."

"You want to go? Even if it kills Lucien, you, and me?"

"If we don't, it'll be much worse!"

The couple was arguing, and my innate justice scale was piqued. When they entered the living room and saw me reading on the couch, they stopped.

"Don't mind me." I muttered, pretending to read while eavesdropping.

Callie groaned in frustration. "There is no such thing as privacy with immortal hearing abilities all around you. No such things as secrets around here. I can't stand being cooped up in this cabin with so many people. I'm going back to New York, and you cannot stop me."

"Athena," Archer pleaded. "Tell her it is too dangerous."

"Don't force her to pick sides! I know it is dangerous. I know we might die, but it is how everything must occur to prevent a worse fate." Callie's arms were crossed, and she glared at Archer. On seeing them at odds like this, one would not peg them as a happily married couple.

"Athena is Justice. Blinded to bias. Asking her would be the sensible thing to do."

Archer was right. Even my maternal love for Callie would not sway me. I was unconditionally fair, which was why Zeus had employed me as an attorney—until playing fair was inconvenient for him.

"You want to go to New York?" I asked, trying to work out her motivation.

"My father's book is being published. I typed some of it up for him. There is a chapter that exposes some of you as existing for real, alive today, of your abilities, with enough description that mortals might be able to trace a couple of you. It has to be stopped or—"

"We'll have another inquisition on our hands," I finished for Callie.

Archer cringed.

"Sorry." I often spoke before I thought. The comment wounded Archer because he lost his daughter and ex during the Inquisition.

Archer was right to protest New York for safety concerns, but since he had been horrifically affected through the witch hunts, how could he risk us being targeted again if Dr. Syches's information came out and was accepted as valid?

"We must stop the book, but New York is not a good idea," I told them. There was no right or wrong in this situation, no clear side to take.

Callie insisted, "We go. I've seen it."

This tenacity I had must've passed down to her. When I believed I was right, I never backed down. "Well, it isn't something we should rush. We'll need to plan. When will the book be released?"

"But Athena—"

"Late February," Callie cut off Archer's protest.

I nodded. "We have time to make sure we do this right."

"Callie, this can be done without us going."

Archer had a valid point.

"I'm tired of hiding. We can't spend eternity never enjoying ourselves. There's no point to life then."

So did Callie.

Archer threw his arms up in exasperation. "I just don't understand why you must eagerly fulfill a vision. What happened to you wanting to fight fate?"

Oh, I didn't want to get involved with that. I'd met Prometheus's half sisters once, and that was enough. To not be able to logically maneuver around them unsettled me; they seemed to enjoy that.

THE IMMORTAL TRANSCRIPTS: SHUDDER

"Archer, I need to do this. We cannot let Zeus find us. We have to have them do so on our terms, best protected, all of us together."

Here we sat safely cooped up, but how long could we stand it? How long until Zeus found us and attacked? With Hermes at his disposal, he could snatch her from under our noses as he had in Belize. My mind was preparing for war. "We must plan. I'll get Chase in the fold."

Archer moaned, frustrated he lost the argument.

And plan we did.

Poseidon returned around the winter holidays. He offered to give us safe passage again, but it would take us longer than we wished to reach America. We Olympians could not use the wind gods, for Zeus might note our presence. Three out of four of them would be busy anyway transferring some of our allies to New York ahead of us. The majority of us Greeks were to be on the boat. Putting most of an army on one vessel was worrisome, but we needed some Norse presence to mask us from Zeus's sight, even if it was waning.

We were poring over plans. Archer kept protesting the whole idea, and Poseidon kept explaining that life was a ticking time bomb; we could wait for Zeus to discover us here and start a massive war with the Norse, ending in many of our deaths, or we picked our battleground. It was a conversation recurring way too often, and today was much the same. Chase and Aroha argued about the upcoming trip. Archer stared at the map of New York, and Callie was sitting on the floor, staring out the sliding door at the snow-covered mountains. Prometheus was next to her in the same relaxed pose. They were doing that annoying telepathic thing Archer and I both loathed. Like him, I hated being left out.

"Gray tiles. Light gray, large ones. There's a circle on the floor with diamond shapes. Other little circles as if something was there but is now gone," Callie said.

"What?" Archer looked up from the map.

"Shh." Prometheus shot him a chastising glare for interrupting. "Keep talking," he whispered to Callie.

Aroha and Chase stopped the bickering in the kitchen and came to join us.

"Paper hearts, decorations. Water. Lightning. A torch." She took a deep breath. "A red sign—no, more a brownish color."

"What does it say?" Prometheus quietly asked.

"To Pedestal and Crown."

"The Statue of Liberty!" Archer blurted out. This time, he was not reprimanded.

"You did it, Callie! I knew you could. Good one, Archer." Prometheus was off the ground, pulling Callie up with him into a hug. "Paper hearts? We must go before Valentine's Day. Can you believe it, Thena? She's better than I am."

The pride in his voice was adorable, but yet again, evidence of his foresight DNA in her, not mine. Prometheus released her. I had to get over this ridiculous jealousy. She was my descendant; she came from my daughters' daughter. She was mine too. "How perfectly Greek," I said, giving Prometheus a wry grin. "Symbolic to its core."

"Huh?" Callie asked, distracted by Archer folding her in his arms and kissing her temple.

"Lady Liberty," Archer teased her.

"Forget symbolism," Chase said. "It is the perfect place for a battle. Surrounded by water, giving Poseidon and his people the biggest advantage. Zeus's lightning will be drawn to the copper and can't reach us inside. The only person to worry about is—"

"Hermes," I cut in. "They'll expect us to go for Zeus, but we must go for Hermes instead."

Then we launched into a slew of plan adaptations. Finally having our battleground, it would be much easier to envision certain maneuvers to take down key players. Prior to Callie's vision, it was all *where?* and *when?* but now it was becoming clearer.

I grew excited about a war. "Poseidon is our secret weapon. Zeus cannot expect him to surface. The shock alone could open an opportunity."

Poseidon grinned.

The front door opened, making us all jump. "Am I interrupting?" Chase had Thor in a headlock before he had finished speaking.

"Careful, or I'll drop the brennivín!" Thor protested, twisting right out of Chase's grasp. He set the massive jug of what was no doubt home-distilled godly strength liquor that would knock Dionysus himself unconscious. "Heard some warfare lingo and had to be nosey. We fightin'?" Thor grinned mischievously.

"You heard us or were spying on us? I thought Odin gave you all explicit instructions not to get involved. You're merely cloaking us," I scolded him.

"His exact words were, 'You will not fight unless to protect yourselves.' So, in Norse, that means if I happen to be in the wrong place at the wrong time, and my protective lightning strikes happen to inadvertently hit others in the vicinity, well..." He grinned at the thought. Like Chase, war to Thor was life.

Chase grinned and shook his hand. "We'll be sure to stick you right between Callie and Zeus."

"Can't wait to exchange bolts with that *drullusokkur*."

Callie appeared confused and looked around at others laughing.

I leaned toward her, whispering, "It's a toilet plunger, but in English, more like 'piece of shit.'"

Callie grinned at me, her gaze meeting mine. I did not recoil straightaway and smiled back until another presence distracted me.

Loki entered next, swaggering in his typical cocksure gait. "What's the plan?"

"Will someone shut the door? You're letting all the Norse in." Aroha scoffed, picking a cuticle.

Loki winked at me, making me uncomfortable, and held his hands out to his side in affirmation of his self-appointed awesomeness.

Chase surveyed outside and, seeing no more gods in the vicinity, closed the door. "Where were we? Oh yes, we'll let Poseidon stretch his fins. I'm sure there are thousands of years of pent-up rage boiling in his blood from Zeus suppressing him. It might even sway Nemesis to our side. I enticed her enough to leave my kid alone," Chase boasted.

"I'm sure your wife doesn't want to hear how you might entice another woman," I retorted.

"The almighty Athena making a joke?" Chase teased.

"Why does everyone keep saying that?" I wanted to punch him but squashed the childish notion.

"No, seriously, I never heard you tease someone before." Loki's face seemed serious, but his eyes twinkled.

"I have too!" Just because I wasn't a comedic genius all the time didn't mean I was inept.

Loki gave me a tight-lipped disbelieving grimace.

"She has." Prometheus came to the rescue. "If I recall correctly, she once called you a serpent-brained scalawag with walrus teeth."

Laughter bubbled out of me before I lost it, and we all started laughing. Loki regaled the tale of our first meeting on the battlefield, where

I botched up peaceful negotiations. Well, not really. Zeus threw the first bolt at Odin to kick it off. In hindsight, I think he always intended to start a massive war with the Norse under the pretense of mortals battling over land.

"Good times!" Thor laughed. "I gotta admit. You lot were fun to fight. Looking forward to fighting by your side and beating the worst parts of your tribe, like cutting the worm out of an apple."

Zeus a worm? How fitting.

We drank, reminisced, and discussed the battle until plans became farfetched and our invented curse words in reference to Zeus became ludicrous. The sun began to rise, announcing it was almost noon. We'd talked all night and morning. The Norse finally left, and a groggy Archer and Callie were the first to go to bed.

I made my excuses and plopped into bed, too exhausted to even change. When the door opened behind me, I rolled over to see Prometheus's silhouette in my doorway. "Are you going to continue this ridiculous routine every night? I told you, with Lucien and Aios gone, there is a perfectly open bedroom at your disposal."

"I will say the same thing I say in return each night. I will never leave your side again, Athena."

I scoffed at him. "You might think it romantic, but I find it creepy. My personal stalker for eternity."

"Actually, you find it utterly charming." He closed the door. "Each night, you can't wait to chastise me because you enjoy it, but each time, you also chastise yourself for weakening. You love me, Thena, and you will admit it when you stop being scared."

"Stop reading my mind." I threw a pillow in his direction but missed.

I heard him settle on the floor, fluffing the pillow. By Poseidon's Trident, I put him in a position to torture me. I had started to enjoy the innocent cuddles, his warmth in my bed, and the late-night conversations until one of us fell asleep. He knew that too.

"I'm not scared."

"Thena, you are. The past won't happen again. Not this time. When you open your heart to me, it will be forever. *That* is why I patiently lie on this floor, innocently lie with you in your bed, content just to be in the same place as you...finally."

Ugh. He needed to shut his mouth. He was kind of romantic. Nonsensical, but it was sweet devotion.

THE IMMORTAL TRANSCRIPTS: SHUDDER

"Thena, with Callie, things will get easier. You'll grow closer. You were never some vessel to carry on my line. I'm sorry my DNA overpowered yours, but she is still yours."

"You guys have your little mind-reading games and power lessons that exclude me." When it came out, it sounded petty and selfish, but I was always sensitive to being left out of things during my mortal life—always that "different" kid.

"I'm sorry, Thena. Time is of the essence right now, but later, you two will have those moments. Who will she go to for guidance, for knowledge, with her problems? She has no parents, so we can fill that role. It'll take time."

The irksome but simultaneously great thing about Prometheus was his concept of time. Everything was solvable to him if we'd simply *wait*. He had the patience and the foresight for it.

I was impatient and wanted things instantly fixed, the way I needed them to be. Still, his words were what I needed to hear. I needed to stop worrying about my relationship with Callie, let it grow organically.

Just as I had to with him. "Get off that cold floor and into this bed. Your days of martyrdom are over."

Prometheus laughed lightly, threw the pillow at me, which bonked me in the face, and got up, his tread coming toward the bed. He slipped under the covers, pulling the back of me to his front, his breath stirring my hair. "This is where I belong, where you belong."

I did not protest that, nor could I find the right words to say for such a moment.

CHAPTER 24

Archer

Callie was writhing in her sleep again—moaning, fretting, tossing, and turning. It was obvious her dreams disturbed her. I knew I slept like Hades; I always had a hard time waking up, but she was now waking me most nights. Her dreams had become that bad.

Tonight wasn't any different. She thrashed, tangled in the sheets, mumbling incoherent phrases. As I rolled over to hold her—because usually, it calmed her down—she clung to me. Unlike any other time, she opened her eyes and stared directly at me. However, her eyes were off, as if they were staring beyond me.

"We're in danger," Callie said. "Hymenaios, the messenger of war."

"What?"

The next statement was incoherent. Her head fell onto her pillow, and she went quiet. I had trouble falling asleep after that, even though Callie didn't have any more episodes.

In the morning, Callie insisted she didn't remember her dream. She was lying. She had a bad habit of omission when it was something bad or dangerous, while I had the bad habit of worrying over her as if she were still a mortal. It would be something we both would outgrow soon, I hoped.

When we went down to breakfast, the place was packed. The Norse representatives were there, Thor and Freya. There was literally a feast going down. Aside from the staple foods of breakfast, there were fish dishes and meat soup, and a few traditional Norse dishes Callie was unabashedly staring at.

She gasped, pointing to a dish. "What's that?"

I bit back my laugh from her likely impending reaction. "Um, sheep's head."

Her face turned green.

"What? We Greeks eat lamb heads. They're quite the delicacy."

Immediately, she quickly said, "Stop talking about it."

"Then stay away from these too." I pointed to a bowl as I grabbed a plate.

"What is it, pâté?"

THE IMMORTAL TRANSCRIPTS: SHUDDER

"Well...more like pickled ram testicles." I waited for her reaction, trying to get a rise out of her. Her innocence was endearing; one day, we would see the world together, and she would see cultural differences as something beautifully varying rather than unappealing.

Instead of telling me I was disgusting or making a face, she covered her mouth and ran from the room. Great. She'd be angry at me. I was trying to joke around—lighten things up since it had been so serious these past months—and I made her sick.

Prometheus greeted me. "Archer, glad you're up. We were discussing returning to New York, particularly the travel plan."

"Everyone is ready, and it is February 1st. The cruise ship will take us a week again. We ought to go soon," Chase added. What he really meant was we had to go soon because of Callie's vision.

Pegging travel plans on Callie's unclear visions unnerved me. This whole plan to be ambushed by Zeus was insane. On top of that, there was the whole Lucien betrayal and death problem. I wasn't sure why we were seeking it out. Callie and Prometheus promised worse results if we stayed here, but I was still unsure about meeting destiny face-to-face.

Freya loaded her plate. "The thing is, we had a suggestion. Could you part from her for a few days? Zeus will go where you are. He thinks you wouldn't sep—"

"Yeah, that went well last time," Ma's sarcastic voice cut off Freya. Two love goddesses under one roof were one too many. They had gotten along for a while, but Ma's claws were drawn.

"Stick to beauty and love. I happen to *also* be a war goddess," Freya snapped.

The way Ma and Freya were butting heads so easily reminded me of her and Psyche's awful relationship. I no longer had to guess where Psyche's nasty streak had come from. Any disbelief left over from finding out Freya had been Psyche's mother was wiped away.

"Cat fight brewing," Thor said.

His comment stopped their arguing as now both women were glaring at him. Freya violently stabbed the testicle dish. Thor flinched, and his hand shot down instinctively as if to protect his male parts.

"Riiiiight, anyway." How was I just now noticing how messed up we gods were? "We're not going to New York separately."

"We're going together. The Norse masking us will work." Callie was back and taking a plate, so she must've pulled herself together.

"Another dream?" Prometheus and Athena asked simultaneously.

"Yes. Last night."

I peered down at her, and she up at me. I was forgiven for the cuisine teasing but only because she lied to me about her dream. "What if we are supposed to go later?" I wanted a way out, a way to stay safe in this cabin and away from Zeus.

She tilted her head adorably. "Valentine's decorations?"

"Next year?" I fired back, unable to refrain from giving her a quick, chaste kiss.

Freya and Prometheus exchanged an eyeroll. I would lose this battle, but I had to try anyway.

Callie's eyes begged me to trust her. "When Prometheus told me prophetic time is hard to gauge, I decided not to cut my hair until we have a child. A vision showed me how long it will be. I'm gauging visions off my hair. It's not exact science, but I'll go to New York with it this length."

Despite the serious topic of New York looming, I couldn't help but grin at the idea of a kid, our child. *Philo*. We would live if she foresaw him? He was the future after this storm.

Himerus scoffed. "Well, the way you two have been—"

"Jealous you don't have a girl?" I cut in before he would say his bawdy opinion in front of everyone.

Callie blushed, and almost everyone found a sudden interest in the food on their plates or on the table.

"Stating a fact," Himerus muttered.

"She's immortal," Ma entered the argument. "Children take time, and Zeus controls that."

"Yeah, but Zeus can't control *her*. With our freedom now and everyone's libidos around here..." Himerus surveyed the room and shook his head. "Stop being all Puritan about sex all of a sudden, and listen to me. He controlled that too. Greek gods could not procreate without his creepy blessing until things slipped up, until the liberty goddesses. From the way you all are? I suspect a baby boom."

The room was silent.

"True," I broke the silence, "a valid point we should all think about."

The way Himerus smiled made me realize I could be supporting him more. My father and him were bonding, but I could do more for both my brothers.

"My point is," —Callie shifted her weight away from me and put a roll on her plate with emphasis— "my hair is not any longer than this." She flipped her wavy curls. "We should leave tomorrow."

THE IMMORTAL TRANSCRIPTS: SHUDDER

I wasn't into this whole basing our lives on Callie's dream visions situation because it was so dangerous, but how could I admit that I didn't trust her newly intensified abilities? It would create strife between us. I wanted to believe her.

"Okay." I caved in.

Her smile was worth it. I had been the tipping point. No one else protested. I was weak when it came to her, damn it. At some point, I would insist *we* called the shots, not just her. I could sense that right now was not the time. I had to trust in her in this.

We ate, and afterward, Athena wanted to play cards. Only a few of us played gin, which was a mistake. Playing with Callie and Prometheus handicapped the rest of us. The two would exchange smirks when they foresaw cards; obviously, one of them kept winning.

Dad asked, "How many Norse volunteered?"

"Half of all Aesir," Thor boasted.

Freya gave Thor a murderous glower. "Excuse me? I, a Vanir, am going with you as well as my brother and father. We are one family since the war, so stop being so divisive."

"Freyr, the peace god? What use is he?" Anteros asked. "I don't think there is a chance of peace."

"My brother is handy with the weather, and he has an amazing superfast ship to take half of them to New York before us."

Damn, Freya was catty when she wanted to be. Glad I never knew her as my mother-in-law when Psyche was alive.

Anteros frowned like a wounded puppy.

Dad referred to Freya's oceanic father, "Njörðr will team up with Poseidon."

"Nine of us, plus the three of them. A nice dozen. All the important ones for this: war, revenge, battle, the trickster, wisdom, and Odin and Frigg," Thor explained.

"A sky goddess? Oh, Zeus will not be ready for Frigg." Ma was a little too excited about war, which I found unnerving coming from her. Was her natural self, untethered by Zeus, as war-hungry as my dad?

"And Odin and Loki together—" Dad began, cracking a smile.

Athena interrupted as she was sometimes apt to do, "Will concoct some sweet deceit and trickery."

"Who do you have? Aside from who is here, of course," Thor asked.

"Poseidon, nymphs, and oceanids," Dad said between shoveling food in his mouth.

Like it was nothing, Athena added, "Persephone and Hades."

The room went quiet. Someone dropped a fork. We all stared at her. Athena was confused. "I thought I told you?"

"No!" a bunch of us said at the same time.

"Well, I uh...went to Persephone, and she assured me. Only, she is in the underworld right now. I need to inform her when. Hades has a way to communicate with her when she is above ground."

"How?" Freya asked.

"Is that important right now?" Athena huffed. She didn't want to give the Underworld leak away.

"Gin." Callie placed her cards down with a smile.

Everyone moaned, applauded, or tossed their cards down, annoyed.

"It's not winning if you're cheating." I chided.

"I didn't cheat!" Her smile belied her words.

"I felt a few immortals entering my mind." I tipped her chin to behold her mahogany eyes. "It could be an extremely useful tool."

"Yeah, I keep forgetting to ask, how can Poseidon enter my mind and Zeus couldn't?" Callie shifted uncomfortably, ruining our moment.

"The most powerful of gods can do it." Athena dealt the cards again. "No mind penetration, or you two are disqualified," she warned the telepathic Titan-blooded beings in the room. Then she shifted to her logical teacher mode. "Poseidon, Hades, and Zeus are all equally omniscient in different ways."

"Which is why Zeus had banished his brothers into submissive realms," Prometheus said.

"How exactly did he do that?" Callie picked up her cards and arranged them. "How does a god force another under his power?"

"You mean, how'd you break his 'spell'—for lack of a better word—the one that freed Poseidon?" Athena's poker face did not slip as she took in her cards.

"No," Callie said simply. "Although that would be useful. No, I want to know how he did it to others. More importantly, how we can do it to him."

Everyone gaped at Callie. I was shocked too, but kept on my blank card-playing expression. I wrapped my arm around Callie's shoulder, trying to protect her from their judgmental stares. Then it dawned on me exactly what Callie had said.

She cocked her head to meet my gaze, and I beheld a sinister and eerie vibe in her. Nemesis twinkled in her eye; she was thirsty for revenge, and I couldn't blame her. "He killed my mother. He killed my father. He killed my grandmother. He tried to kill me. He tried to part Archer and me. I'd wish him dead, but my father taught me better than that. I simply want to take all the power away from the god who destroyed my life."

"Well, when you word it that way..." Anteros sighed. "I want him powerless too. Anything for my new sister."

I put my cards down to opt out, and pulled Callie close, placing her head on the crook of my neck. She handed her cards back, not wanting to play any longer either.

Everyone was silent as the game progressed without Callie and me. We swept from the room at immortal speed, but Callie tugged me to a standstill at the foot of the stairs.

"What?" I asked, cupping her beautiful face in my palms. How was I so lucky to find her?

"I want to be alone for a moment."

It was a dagger to my heart. "Callie, don't shut me out."

"I'm just...I'm unwell."

I felt her head out of habit, but the fevers were gone.

"Not a fever, but I can't explain. I feel...odd," she mused. "I am utterly happy one moment and then bitter and angry the next. In there, admitting what I thought about stripping Zeus of power..." She shook her head as if to remonstrate herself.

"No, Callie, you have every right to feel this way. It was the more humane suggestion. I want him dead, and he is my grandfather. Plus, grief can still pang us even when we are as happy as we can be. It penetrates through, even if you're not consciously thinking about it."

"Distract me then," she whispered.

I wanted to sweep her in my arms and continue distracting her upstairs, but she was so vulnerable. I shut my lust down. There was always later, forever—I hoped. Another idea sprang into my head. "Okay. Go get bundled up in warm clothes. We're going for a walk."

"Bundle up? I don't get cold anymore."

"Mortals could see us." I pulled her back in, kissing her gently. "Get dressed. It's a surprise."

Five minutes later, we snuck out the window, and I floated us down carefully. Once our feet touched the ground, we ran for it, immortal speed, through the forest into the clearing by the base of the mountains. I pulled her close.

She giggled. "Why the secrecy?"

"They'd never let us go alone. My parents are overprotective."

"You don't say!" She smiled, taking my breath away. "All four of them are watching over us."

Great. Chase was going to give me a safety lecture tomorrow.

"He will," she said.

"Stop that, my love. Reading our minds. I'm going to miss the spontaneity we had together if you keep it up. Unexpected events are the most romantic."

"Like this one?"

"Bet you didn't foresee this, did you?" I peered up to the sky.

When she followed my gaze, she gasped.

Above us, the green curtains of light undulated gracefully in the dark sky. We watched and didn't speak. I held her in my arms, enjoying the peace and quiet. I watched her joyous face, cast in pale green light, drinking in the wonderment when one saw something for the first time. Damn, watching her awe was an addictive sensation. Not much was new to me.

After a moment, she said, "Aurora borealis. It's beautiful."

"Not as beautiful as you are." I kissed her soundly under the northern lights, not knowing a more romantic way to spend my evening.

All too soon, Callie pulled away. "Thank you. I am thoroughly distracted." She stared up at the sky again.

"Oh, I'm not done yet. I'm sure I can thoroughly occupy your thoughts elsewhere."

Callie turned and looked at me, shocked. Then my wife, like a warrior Grecian, tackled me in the snow, not waiting for "elsewhere."

CHAPTER 25

Lucien

As soon as Aios and I left Iceland, we made the trip to see my son Aristaeus, the beekeeper, who currently resided with Demeter in Appalachia. She was normally in cahoots with Zeus, so I wasn't very trusting, but I had to see my son one last time. I had only been there a minute when she bombarded me with questions about Archer. Lucky for me, I was still able to withhold the truth. Aios saved me from her disdain and kept her busy by complimenting her. The old Ice Queen, as I privately referred to her, due to her frigid heart, had a soft spot for my sunshine kids. Nature loved the sun, only she hated me for my exploits in my youth—or rather most of my life—and my rejection of her. Her regard transferred from me onto my kids after I embarrassed and insulted her long ago. Euterpe told me it was her obsession with the sun and wanting to be with the "elusive sun gods." Biologically, she was my aunt, so I wouldn't go there. Unlike Aunt Demeter, I did have scruples, even though Aroha often teased me about having relations with anyone.

I found Aristaeus collecting honey, bees buzzing around and all over him, a walking hive. They never stung him, which amazed me. On seeing me, he smiled widely and waved. My sweet son. He had hardly lived through the transition of demigod to god. He was eternally innocent, honest, and loving, the best Olympian there was, being spared our conceit, selfishness, and flaws. As the god of truth, having a son who exuded it in every way, who refused to be false or lie, made me immensely proud.

"Dad." He came to me, brushing the bees off before he shook my offered hand. He yanked me into him and hugged me. I squeezed him back hard, trying to show him my pride and love for him.

We spoke for quite some time, but I couldn't tell him I might never see him again. He was too unaffected, and the smile on his face was my sunshine—I didn't want to see it set. He would be told of my death later and remember this last great day we had together. It was all I could hope for.

I let Demeter chastise my poor parenting skills but didn't let her know my real reason for coming. She did not seem to be on Zeus's side, but it wasn't clear if she would bother joining in either. Good. I wanted Aristaeus as removed as possible from the situation, to remain safe.

The next day, we traveled to Hanoi, Vietnam, to say my goodbyes to Asclepius. Aios and I staked out Euterpe and him. He was working as a doctor, while she was a nurse, both on the front lines battling this coronavirus. I would not be surprised if next month it was declared a full-on pandemic. We traced Asclepius online to find his apartment just north of the city, and I picked the lock to get in. Aios was enjoying this type of espionage way too much, but I was merely trying not to surprise his brother at work. I didn't want to be seen and remembered by the staff who worked with him. We made ourselves at home.

He entered alone around five and threw his keys onto the table by the door before switching on the light. Aios stood by me, but I remained reclined on the sofa. I was trying to appear the least intimidating as possible, non-confrontational, but when Asclepius turned the light on and beheld us, he was beyond startled by our intrusion. In immortal speed, he had Aios pinned against the wall, but being more powerful, I had Asclepius restrained on the floor without too much bodily harm to him or his half brother, while also sparing his walls and floors.

I flipped him over, still restraining him, so he could see who we were.

His eyes narrowed at me in hateful recognition.

"Calm down."

"Getoffme!" He shouted as one word.

"Stop attacking your brother." I let go of my vice-like grip on him.

"Half brother." Asclepius stood and dusted himself off as if he were tainted by me, bitterness in his features and every jerky movement he made. "You have thirty seconds to tell me why you broke into my apartment before I chuck you out."

I smiled, thinking of how in Hades he'd budge me one inch.

"Just listen to him, Ass," Aios teased him.

"Don't call me that."

"It's part of your name and defines how you're acting right now." Aios shrugged with a grin.

These kids. I found their brotherly quarrel cute and was proud I had rubbed off on Aios. He was much bolder and more self-confident than he had been before he came to live with me.

"Well, you're a little kiss up. Still dangling over every shred of affection this loser gives you?" Asclepius said.

THE IMMORTAL TRANSCRIPTS: SHUDDER

The two of them at each other's throats would get us nowhere if I let it continue. I sent Aios to wait outside to stop his mother from entering until I had talked to Asclepius first. Aios was annoyed, while Asclepius's telltale blush told me my ex was definitely in a relationship with my kid. Gods, this Olympian life was grossly complex.

There was no point in risking an argument, so I had to be direct. "I've had a prophecy. I will die soon."

"And I should care?" Asclepius shot out to wound me, but his eyes were full of torn emotion and surprise.

I had been prepared for such a reception as this, so his hateful glower and words bounced right off me. I deserved it, but *he* deserved a better type of closure. "I don't expect you to care. I just wanted to be sure to see you one last time, to say goodbye, to try one last time," I rambled, not knowing exactly what to say. I never knew what to say to my kids.

"Try what?"

"Reconciliation. I loved your mother. The last thing I ever wanted was for Coronis to die, for you to be left without a mother."

"Loved her? Didn't you love his mother too?" He pointed to the door in reference to Aios. "Aristaeus's mother? There's a long list of those you supposedly 'loved,' and none of them benefited from it." He crossed his arms. "Dead, abandoned by you, or both."

It was true. Denying how bad of a partner or parent I had always been would ring false. There was little defense I had, but I would try to explain myself in a way he could understand. "I've been alive for almost four thousand years. You tend to fall in and out of love many times. Tell me, Asclepius, you've had your share of lovers over the years, haven't you? Yes, I'll admit I was naïve, fickle, and perhaps not steadfast, particularly in my youth. But I did love your mother. I had nothing to do with her death. That was all your aunt's doing. Artemis has been nothing to me since that day and even more so my enemy recently when she chose to let Zeus try to kill Aios."

"Come on! You had nothing at all to do with it? You didn't get Artemis to kill my mother so you wouldn't have to deal with her? You know, get rid of the baggage?" He wasn't buying into my innocence, but he knew such a forward question directed at me would usually result in an honest answer.

"I had nothing to do with it, and your theory is preposterous. If I was 'ridding' of my mistakes, as you suggest, why would I have kept you? Artemis killed your mother. I performed the first Caesarian to save your life. Do you know how hard that was to do? When I couldn't revive her, I had to get you out and get you breathing. Why would I have taken you to Zeus and begged for the only semblance of Coronis left on the earth to become immortal? Your mother was mortal, so no offense, she would've died. That's normally how our 'baggage,' as you insist on calling her, goes away."

"But you never...wanted me." Asclepius's voice was one of defeat, one without a desire to continue fighting, one that desperately wanted to give in.

"Of course, I did. I would've left you mortal if I hadn't." It would be too much if I dared to touch him or hug him, so I stood there awkwardly as his eyes scanned me at a rapid speed, thinking millions of simultaneous thoughts which eluded me. I did not know my flesh and blood. My greatest regret leaving the world forever would be not raising my boys, not truly knowing them or being there for them. Gods knew I'd had the time to do it, but the inclination hadn't been there. If only I had more time. If only I could do it all over again the right way.

"You barely ever came to see me. You left me to be raised by Athena..."

"I am no good at being a father. I am hardly close to my own half siblings. I hate my sister and father, and my mother rarely had time for me. I didn't have a caring father. These are excuses, I know. I should've done the opposite of my parents, but I didn't know where to begin. I had thought I was leaving you in the best hands. Was Athena not a good guardian and mentor? Look how smart you are, all that she has taught you, what you have become. If I raised you, you would've received a selfish and womanizing education and ended up like me."

"Kind of doesn't sound so bad. I could've—well, still could—use that type of advice." A small smile crept onto his face. When he smiled, which was rare, I saw a shred of myself in him.

"Oh, not you too? How are my sons inept lovers?" I moaned, which made him laugh dryly. "I still have some time left, I think. I had really wanted to talk about this epidemic, though."

"I admit, you did teach me a lot about medicine."

"I have many regrets, and I can't undo the past, but I don't want you to have them. I intend to spend my last days with you two. I've seen Aristaeus already but could not tell him...could not put him through this. I want a chance for you and I to bond, for you to be at peace with me dying."

THE IMMORTAL TRANSCRIPTS: SHUDDER

Asclepius's brows creased as if to tell me he could not handle any more of this talk. What had I done to these boys? Would it have been better to die letting them hate me?

"Why do this?" Asclepius demanded. His mood shifted his emotions, needing a way out through his temper. "I hate you. I want to hate you."

"I know, but how would you feel if I never said goodbye? If I never told you I cared. You had to know that I love you."

Asclepius's hands tightened on my shirt, and I half thought he was about to choke me by my collar. I'd let him, but instead, his head fell onto my shoulder, and he sobbed wildly, all while words of hatred and curses came out.

Unsure of what to do, I simply held him. It was bitter anger and grief wrapped into one, raw and extreme—all his conflicting emotions about me on the surface. I blinked back my tears, trying to be the strong one, but then Euterpe burst in, Aios trailing after her, trying to stop her. Tears were in her eyes. Aios had told her. I was thankful not to have to do it again.

Aios joined us, making a group hug and trying to calm his brother. Euterpe, my first love, stared at me in shock and pain, but her gaze did not falter. She stayed strong. I saw the truth in her eyes. She was over me, finally. My death would wound what had been but not what could've been.

Euterpe surprised me by pulling Asclepius away and soothing him—not as one would a child but as a lover. Aios eyes were wide, his cheeks pink from embarrassment. The penny dropped finally on how it would be when your half brother is your mother's lover. I laughed, and I could not stop. This made Aios's tears turn to bubbling giggles.

The couple gaped at us, completely lost.

"I'm sorry..." I could hardly speak through my laughter. "His face...we assumed you were...you know, together...but my gods... His face when he saw it in person."

We laughed deeply, but Euterpe let Asclepius go and glowered at me, crossing her arms. Asclepius stared at the floor, the walls—anywhere but at me.

"Stop it!"

Aios stopped at Euterpe's command, and I pulled myself together, trying to pinch my smile between my lips to not offend her.

"You were the one who said all those years ago I was destined to love one of the sun line. You prophesied it."

"Did you have to make it happen by going after my son?"

"She didn't go after me." Asclepius's eyes were red-rimmed, but he was wiping the evidence away. "She was searching for Hymenaios and *you*, trying to get away from Olympus. I brought her and my grandmother here. I knew they'd be safer away from Zeus, so I got permission from the others here, the Jade Emperor, to help save the mortals. Then things just..."

"Happened," Euterpe finished. She took up his hand in hers.

It was strange, and yet he was not much like me in looks or personality. It wasn't a weird type of replacement, and she had apparently gotten over the fact his birth had shown my unfaithfulness to her. Things were awkward, so I homed in on one of his comments to change the subject. "My mother is here?"

The two of them stared at each other, oddly communicating in an annoying lovers' gaze I never understood. It was clear they didn't want to tell me something.

"What?"

"We no longer trust her," Asclepius admitted. It didn't seem as if he would expound and speak against his grandmother, one who had doted on him when he was a child.

Euterpe gave me those sympathetic puppy-dog eyes, putting me on alert for bad news. "I think she duped me. She knew I wanted to leave after Zeus and Artemis tried to kill Hymenaios. She tried to convince me to contact you or Hymenaios to free us, but I knew I could not. Zeus would kill you both. She did act increasingly more scared of Zeus and Hera, constantly wanting away from Fiji, so I tried to contact you circuitously through Asclepius."

"And I divulged nothing—not that I knew exact details, but—"

"You saw us last, yes." I cut him off in case he accidentally explained the cruise ship to Iceland and gave away their location to Euterpe and put both of them in danger.

"I will say my goodbyes tomorrow and see where the land lies with her. Today is for you three. Just you." As hard as it was to focus on them, the happy times, what they had been up to over the years I hadn't seen them, I put my friends in Iceland out of my mind.

CHAPTER 26

Athena

Our transatlantic journey went on uneventfully, and between preparations, we actually enjoyed ourselves. The Norse must have been cloaking us well, for Zeus would attack on water rather than near a busy metropolis. There was no way he could know about Poseidon unless his sight somehow returned. If it had, he would've attacked Poseidon the moment he surfaced. No surprises or a peep from Olympus followed us as we cut our path through the icy Atlantic.

The captain's dinner was held on the last night, which was not exactly my thing. I hated formal affairs, particularly the makeup-and-dresses part. All the noise of people's chatter. Aphrodite, of course, became overwhelmingly excited about it and, to my dismay, had brought extra dresses that she must've ordered or bought in Iceland. Trust the god of beauty to bring dresses to a war. Instead of ordering room service and taking a bubble bath—which had been my escape plan—I was in Aphrodite's room with Callie, getting ready for the black-tie event.

Callie slipped into a clingy black dress, and Aphrodite forced me into a loose flapper-style gray number "to make my eyes pop." It was more of my style if I must wear a dress, so it was apparent she had packed for the three of us in mind. I suppose a distraction prior to a war with an unknown outcome could be a good thing. Maybe. There were only so many scenarios I could plot out, and when you're in the moment, all schemes go out the window except the immediacy of keeping your head attached to your body.

A dress was not enough for the goddess of beauty. Aphrodite insisted on the works—hair, makeup, manicures, and pedicures. I was worried about the makeup, for Aphrodite always did too much, but Callie offered to do mine to save time, and I was relieved. She did a wonderful job, accenting my eyes in a down-to-earth tone as if she knew me. I tried to small talk, but our conversation never took flight. She squeezed my shoulder and nodded. I took that as code for her understanding me.

Once ready, we went to meet the men on the main stairs. I saw Chase first, all strapping and gallant. His standard one-day stubble was traded for a clean-shaven look, his wild mane of hair slicked back in a tidy ponytail. It made him more boyish and not the untamed warrior who always came to my mind. Archer was adorably manly in his suit, his eyes glowing when he beheld Callie next to me. She lit up when she met his gaze. They only had eyes for each other. Then, there was Prometheus. He stood with his back to us, and on realizing we were descending the steps, he turned.

My breath caught in my throat, and my step faltered. I grabbed onto the railing for support, collected myself, and continued down, avoiding eye contact as my face burned. What had taken me by surprise, I should have been prepared for. I hadn't seen Prometheus in a tux since...our last mortal marriage in the 1950s. Seeing him dressed as he was, brought the memories flooding back. Our wedding night came to mind, the last time I had been intimate with another being. It was a bittersweet night. I had conceived, and he instantly knew we had, and we knew we had less than nine months together before we had to separate to protect the baby, my poor Eleutheria.

Prometheus was clean-shaven as well and had cropped off all his sun-bleached locks. It was a short disarray of dark hair clustering toward the center of his head. He seemed even tanner dressed in black, his eyes a richer shade of brown. In short, he looked so amazing that I was scared I'd surrender to him tonight if I let myself go. I was tired of being lonely, and unlike some of the others, I didn't have the constitution to toy with mortals' hearts. Sleeping in the same quarters with Prometheus had been creating a tension between us that increased daily.

He clasped my hand with a smile. I noticed the clash of skin, my ivory against his burnt sienna. He never lost the tan after all those years on the rocks, as if the sun tattooed his flesh forever.

"You look amazing." His hand was clammy.

He was as nervous as I was. Why? I didn't know. Being with him should be tantamount to coming home—relieving, welcoming, comforting. Instead, I was anxious, still feeling that having my arm in his, being with him, was wrong. Was it the years of knowing "us" was against Zeus's rules making me so awkward and full of guilt—like a teen sneaking out to meet the "bad boy"—or was it the fear of losing him yet again?

I somehow made it through dinner, hardly talking or eating. After that, there was dancing, yet another thing I hadn't done in decades.

"Thena?" Prometheus raised his eyebrows and offered his hand.

I took it immediately, and he led me to the floor as a slow song began. I placed a hand on his shoulder and the other in his. Prometheus cocked his head at our hands, perplexed, dropped my hand, and pulled me against him. He wanted to be close. My mind battled in protest and assent simultaneously as I tried to process my feelings. I was forced to drape my arms around his neck.

"I'm not some stranger," he said, his eyes wounded by my formal behavior.

"Sorry." I rested my head on his shoulder. He smelled divine as well. I closed my eyes, allowing him to lead me. I indulged in thinking of happy times long ago before trauma ripped us to shreds. I was that young woman again, back when the mighty Titan of foresight saw me coming. He had an entire family of mortals famed in mythology, but waited patiently until he swept me off my feet with promises of love and knowledge entwined. He told me of things I could hardly have fathomed back then, such as cars and airplanes, of wars and weapons and bombs. He didn't know the names for them then, but as inventions unfolded over time, I was constantly reminded of him.

His warm cheek pressed against mine. It was all too much. It felt as if there was a raging river of emotion, love, and passion ramming into a dam of rigid reason. Little holes were bursting through, and it was only a matter of time for the foundation of reason to become so weak it would buckle, crumble, and the river would be free to flow.

"Don't tell me. You're inventing a complex metaphor of your emotions to justify them?" There was a smile in his voice.

"Don't read my mind, then." I extracted my face out of its hiding spot. He was gorgeous, and his omniscient eyes were smitten. I wondered if mine were the same.

"You look painstakingly reserved, but your heart is racing."

"Stop that." I couldn't help but smile.

He smirked. "I'm waiting for you to ask the right question."

"I won't be asking if I'm only thinking it. Asking implies verbally—"

"You stop *that*. Always logical. Just let go for once."

"How? We're headed into a war zone."

"We will be fine." His hands tightened on my hips. "You and I will be more than fine." He smiled mischievously, and I knew he was planting a seed of wonder in my mind. Now I was dying to know what the subtext of "more than fine" would be.

But I was afraid to ask him anything.

"When you're ready. You'll ask." His insufferable overconfidence was apparent in his features.

"I won't ask. I don't want to know. Don't you ever miss surprises?"

He gave me a chiding look, and I laughed at him. Prometheus was rarely ever surprised. The first time we had been intimate was the result of me experimenting, surprising him, trying to find a hole in his abilities. I resorted to the underhand tactic of kissing him. I had done it impulsively. He had not foreseen—and I had not expected—how much I'd enjoyed kissing him and how far I'd taken it. We secretly married the next day.

His mind must've been ruminating upon the same part of history, or he was breaking into my mind, because he leaned down to kiss me. I turned from him, and he leaned his forehead against the side of mine, defeated. "Thena, don't punish me."

"We can't just start where we left off." I broke away from him and walked away.

His hand grabbed my wrist, trying to slow me. "Where're you going?"

"The song's over."

He let me go but followed me to the table. He did not sit with me.

"Want to dance?" Prometheus asked Callie.

"Sure." Callie stood, whispering something to Archer. She turned to leave, but he caught her arm, pulled her in, and kissed her. She beamed at Archer before being led off by Prometheus.

I sighed, relieved at the space Prometheus gave me. I needed to calm down. I was agitated and trying not to run from the room. When panic overtook me, sometimes I fled, foolishly believing the anxiety would be left behind. Every time. It was one of my flaws in logic I never outgrew.

Alone with Archer, we watched the others dance.

"So, what's with all the secret meetings with my dad lately?" Archer asked. He had wanted to get me alone to ask. His eagerness proved as much.

"Preparing for the battle, every situation, assigning roles and strategies."

"I'm left out?" He frowned. "Along with Callie and Ma?"

"You and your mother are too much of a liability out there. They will gang up on you to kill Callie and do anything to take out our best fighter, your father."

He groaned. "Because of our immortal marriages."

"Your mother and father were insane to do that, with him always at war, but for you, it was noble. It was an incredible protection strategy had she been mortal, so don't be so hard on yourself. It doesn't matter. We would make the same battle plan for you, even if you hadn't married her in that way. Who would be better to protect her with his own life if the worst should happen, and we all fail? You three are best grouped together. Archer, you've killed to protect Callie, and she would do the same for you. Your mother would kill to protect you while still playing it safe to protect your father."

He nodded. I knew he wanted to be out there getting his revenge, but he'd see my rationalism.

There was a larger way for him to help in the war. "Have you prayed to her yet?"

"Who?"

"Nemesis." She would be irked by Zeus's attack, and if Archer prayed to her for revenge, she might join our cause.

"You sure you can't read minds too?" He laughed lightly and said, "I will." He watched Callie dancing and talking to Prometheus. "He loves you, you know." Archer suddenly switched tactics. Was this the real reason he wanted to get me alone: Prometheus?

I gave Archer a this-is-none-of-your-business glower.

"Everyone deserves to be happy, Athena, including you."

"Shoot me with an arrow, and I'll cut your heart out," I told him in a serious tone, but I couldn't help but smile.

"It'll grow back."

I poked him in the ribs. "Still the same spoiled brat."

"You know it." He laughed, and his gaze shifted to Callie. "I am spoiled, having her."

I wanted to tell him this would be a horrible war, and some of us could die. I wanted to warn him that all this happiness was on a precipice, and he would soon fall off cloud nine. We all would, because happiness was this evanescent feeling that flitted through your fingers and evaded your grasp. Always. Still, he deserved to be happy. If this was it, our last hour or day of happiness left, shouldn't I live all these moments to the fullest? Should I give in to what I subconsciously wanted? What exactly was that?

Theus. I needed him, wanted him, yet allowing all reason go and giving in to the turmoil of unstable emotions was difficult for me. He had hurt me—inadvertently, yes—several times. The promises ended up being lies for centuries. What if Zeus won and demanded a separation again? Could I bear it? Would Prometheus ever fulfill the promises he broke by failing to tell me it would take thousands of years to come to pass?

These questions—unanswerable ones—plagued me the entire evening. I danced with Prometheus again, but he didn't attempt to make a move, to my relief. The night wound down. Callie and Archer retired early, and

Chase and Aroha said their goodnights to us. Who knows where the rest of the love entourage was, but my guess was hanging out with the Norse.

Left alone, Prometheus shuffled his feet awkwardly, expecting reproof, and asked, "Are you going to kick me out of our room tonight?"

"Not yet. I should check in with the Norse."

"They're patrolling. We are fine. Tonight is our night for fun. The Norse get tomorrow." At this, he smiled and took up my arm.

We walked, talking only about trivial things. We were there in minutes. I did not want the night to end. I wanted to keep him with me, bask in his presence, but I was afraid of where my breaking point was.

We entered my cabin. The tension was palpable. I fidgeted awkwardly.

"Well, goodnight, Thena. I'll sleep on the couch." He sounded quite impersonal.

After sleeping by my side for ages, he was giving me space because of my reaction to his advance earlier, but I longed for him to try to kiss me again. I was past denying him now. If only he'd try. "Goodnight, Theus." I used the nickname, hoping it would give him the confidence to make a move.

His eyes nervously flickered over my face. Oddly, he gave me a grim smile and turned toward the bathroom, undoing his bowtie and slipping out of his jacket. I had denied him too many times. He was giving up on me. I panicked at the thought. I needed him, loved him. Being hurt by him would not be as bad as this, not having him at all. What if the worst did happen, and I lost him for good in this upcoming battle?

He walked away, hands in his pockets, head down, dejected. I felt powerless. I needed to act.

I raced at immortal speed and cut him off in the doorway. Unprepared, he walked into me. He was over the shock quickly and pulled me into a hug.

"Oh, Thena." He was so vulnerable.

I kissed him then and there. Not just any old kiss, but a kiss filled with sixty plus years of longing. He kissed me back, and the sensation was home to me.

He broke away for a moment to gasp, "Marry me, Pallas Athena...again."

I nodded quickly, kissing him again.

"This time, it will be forever," he said with conviction as he led me toward the bed.

"Promise?"

THE IMMORTAL TRANSCRIPTS: SHUDDER

"I'll swear on the Styx if you need that much assurance."

I gasped. "No. No, I believe you."

The thought of forever with him made all my fears and anxieties slip away. The only thing that mattered was the moment here with him, surrendering to the good feelings and banishing the fear, anxiety, and dread.

He was home.

CHAPTER 27

Lucien

I didn't make a mad rush to see my mother. First, I was busy instructing Aios how to work the sun, the rise and set, how to deal with the nagging impulse to expose truth, and how the prophecies came about in dreams. I shared secrets with him I had never told anyone before, god or mortal. I bared my soul to him. He accepted it, so eager for my trust.

I also spent time with Asclepius discussing the epidemic, how countries were trying to contain it, how bleak it could be for mortals, and guessing how long it would last. It had spread and hit the US. Even though cases were not reported in New York, where my friends were headed at some point—much to my dismay—Asclepius hypothesized it had spread already. A lack of tests and knowledge would make mortals miss cases for a while. We discussed the gods of pestilence, but neither of us was eager to speak with them. All too late, I was busy and finding myself wanting to live, to help the mortals, to get back into medicine, figure out how to stop this illness, which was clearly immune to godly healing powers.

After about five days of ignoring my mother, she showed up. "Leto," escaped my mouth instead of a more endearing name she would've preferred.

"'Leto' is the name you dare call the woman who was in labor for nine days straight to birth you?"

"Sorry, Mother, but you know that was all Hera's fault, not mine. Maybe you shouldn't have slept with her husband."

"If I hadn't, you and your sister wouldn't be here."

"I wish she weren't," I muttered.

She cocked her head in confusion. "What?"

"You heard me. She tried to kill my son, two out of three of them, technically."

Aios waved awkwardly. "Hi, Grandma."

"Yes, that was unfortunate. C'mere you two, both of you." She pushed past me into the house, embracing my sons as if they were the best beings on the planet, and I was the biggest disappointment.

THE IMMORTAL TRANSCRIPTS: SHUDDER

At least my mother had always ignored Euterpe. I'd take disinterest over Mother's willful disappointment no matter how many great feats I had accomplished. I let her blasé "unfortunate" comment go for now. It was not worth the fight.

After Euterpe put the tea kettle on, my mother seated herself at the kitchen table and told me to sit down. I sat across from her, not in the mood for her guilt trips or lectures. Somehow, she'd turn my sister's crime into my fault.

"So, what is going on, and where are they?" It was a direct interrogation. Apparently, she was not onto the I-can-lie gossip.

I played along. "Be more specific."

She glared at me.

"What? There's a worldwide epidemic and a prophecy claiming I'll die really soon, so yeah, be specific."

She threw her hand, dismissing the notion. "Die? You can't die."

"I'm going to die, Mother. I came here to say my goodbyes to my children."

"Did you forget one's not present?"

"I already saw him."

She gave me that maternal threatening look. "Anyway. Your best buddy Eros, where is he hiding?"

Aios crossed his arms. "Why would you ask that?"

The kid did not know whom he was dealing with. My mother is sweet and loving when she wants to be, but she'll stab you in the back the moment she realizes she's not the most important being in your life—over your kids, your spouses, friends. It was always about her. I don't remember a part of my long life which did not hinge on her neediness and manipulation.

"Well, because we should hide there too, then. Zeus was losing it. Searching day and night, but never finding them. When Asclepius came for us, I thought Asia was an ingenious place to ride out Zeus's fit. I honestly thought you would be here and they would too."

She was definitely on Zeus's side. The lies and omissions were coming off her like pulsing waves, unnerving me. I didn't call her out. Not yet. It was a careful game we were playing.

The tea kettle whistled, creating more tension.

Euterpe poured the tea, three cups, the boys not wanting any.

"Where is Zeus? Fiji?" I asked casually.

"Oh, he is always on the move these days." She shrugged it off. "Why did you leave your friends?"

I wondered what schemes she had planned, what info she was trying to get from me. "I didn't." I paused to enjoy how lost she was. "I have no idea where they went after their wedding. We weren't exactly on speaking terms. Aios and I traveled. Then the prophecy I had about my death—in case you truly didn't comprehend that part yet—hastened me to see my children. You do realize, Mother, I will die very soon. Are you grasping that?"

"My poor boy." Her halfhearted emotion was definitely in line with her personality. "How will I bear it?"

Yep, there was her classic self-centeredness I was accused of inheriting. I was not nearly as bad as my mother. If I lived to see Archer again, I was going to tell him that.

My boys looked at each other and then at me, also finding her prying behavior unnerving. I winked at them so they knew to tread carefully with her and that I had this in hand.

Euterpe simply picked at a cuticle and blew on her tea to cool it. It spoke volumes. My mother hadn't changed and was treating her like dirt.

Leto leaned over the table to hug me and knocked over my tea cup in the process. Scorching liquid poured onto the table and into my lap, making me leap up. The burned flesh of my leg healed quickly, and her apologies for once were forthcoming. Euterpe mopped up the mess, and my mother quickly poured me another cup. She placed it down and took my face in her hands, her eyes searching mine. "Will you really die, my dear boy?" The pain in her eyes was genuine.

I had to look away. I simply nodded.

"No. I can't accept it. Sit down. Have some tea. We'll figure this out and stop it."

"Prophecies cannot be stopped," Asclepius told her. He understood my wink to stay out of this. Having him suddenly try to defend me might mean that he cared.

"Can't you all leave us be? I want to talk to my son. I've seen firsthand how much you love to scoop up your father's discarded leftovers. Can't she keep you busy?"

"Mother!" I scolded.

"She wants us gone. Fine. She always got her way. Still does." Euterpe left the room in a huff, stomping out onto the balcony. Asclepius groaned and followed after her. Aios gave me a questioning glance. I nodded for him to join them outside. I could handle my mother better than they could, and maybe I could glean some info out of her.

"I'm sorry. I love the boys, but that woman...could you have picked a worse one to marry?" Mother's disinterest didn't last long.

"She's a great girl. No woman ever pleased you, Mother."

"No. No one was ever good enough for you in my eyes. I wanted you to remain innocent as your sister did, but you sowed those wild oats like your father. Anyone, they used to say, was game for Apollo."

"I've calmed down over my life. And innocent, Mother? You are turning a blind eye. You do know Artemis's girls are her own personal harem, right?"

"Do you have to be so crude?" Again. Somehow *my* fault.

"It's the truth. You never wanted to hear it."

She laughed and sipped her tea. "No, I didn't, did I?" She smiled indulgently. "My honest-to-a-fault boy. Do you remember the first time? When you candidly told me you stole my hair comb?"

"I was five? I was trying to lie and say it was Artemis, but I got tongue-tied, and the truth came flying out."

She laughed and patted my hand. "Strange how that power came early and the rest not until you were in your teens. I thought you only had the one power, and when you hit puberty, it was like a new power every day."

She never believed I had any powers until I proved it. Then shook most off as useless, but I kept those thoughts to myself.

"I wouldn't call truth a power; it's more like a curse." I took a sip of tea, forgetting it had just been poured. I sped up the healing process on my burned mouth.

"It had its uses, like detecting others." She launched into stories about all my childhood antics, all the situations where I had tattled on myself. Some I hardly remembered, whispers of memories rendering themselves anew when she retold the tales.

At some point, the others came inside, and Euterpe took her teacup into her room, the boys following. The door closed, and the TV went on. They were giving us privacy, and for the first time in eons, maybe my mother and I could get along. Maybe I could get a wonderful farewell I hadn't expected from her.

"I need you to know, Son, that I do love you." She gripped my hand in hers tightly.

"I love you too, Mother."

Her smile twitched, and her grip became crushing. She yanked me so hard across the table, my head slammed into the wood. Something pierced my neck. I yanked away from her and ripped a syringe out of my neck. It was already empty.

"That is why I'm doing this. I'm saving you from yourself. You will die because you're too loyal to your stupid friends. They're the ones who will get you killed."

I backed away from her, confused and appalled. "What have you done to me?"

"Keep your voice down, or I will call the transporting god and take your little family away. All I have to do is say his name."

"What did you inject me with?"

"Call it poetic justice against my poet-child who defied his family. I know that usurping slut lets you lie. Well, sit down, Lucien. You're about to tell me the truth. Just like you always did before."

I sat down, woozy. My heart rate slowed to a mortal's speed, and then I hiccupped. They were symptoms of my greatest creation. "Thiopental sodium," I slurred out. Truth serum, my revenge for wanting to force the rest of the world to be like me, a way to incapacitate someone, even a god, so far as they'd babbled out the truth. My own weapon against me, and now I was powerless to stop it.

"Where are they?" She asked.

"Why are you doing this to me?" It was so hard and painful to focus, to not say the words bashing around in my mind. The ichor could burn the serum off, but it would take a while; how long depended on how concentrated it was.

She growled at me. "Because you never obeyed me, never respected me or your father, and now you choose others over me. You've always been such a selfish boy."

"Shut up!" I stood up, the room growing dim. I had to keep my mouth shut. If I could make it inside Euterpe's room, they could help. I stumbled and fell onto the floor.

My mother was upon me shaking me. "Tell me!"

I pinched my lips closed as the words came into my mind and demanded to come out.

"Phoebus Apollo, I command you as your elder to tell me where they are!"

The door opened. "What is—" Euterpe almost tripped over us.

THE IMMORTAL TRANSCRIPTS: SHUDDER

"Dad, don't!" Aios tried to cover my mouth as the words burst out. My mother slammed him aside.

"New York," came out, punctuated by a growl of failed suppression.

"Was that so hard?" My mother smacked my cheek hard.

"Hermes!" My mother called.

"Run." I mouthed to the stunned Aios on the ground by my side.

Asclepius was holding up the syringe in realization.

"Run!" I shouted at my boys and ex as Hermes appeared in a flash. I leaped up with the little energy I had and tackled the teleporting god to the ground. "IRIS!" I screamed, hoping she would come to take my family to safety and they could warn Archer.

My eyes and body grew heavy, and Hermes shoved me off. I blinked rapidly to focus my blurred vision and saw Euterpe and the boys were already gone, the door left ajar.

"They're getting away!" My mother was by the door, watching out, not bothering to lift a finger to capture them. "No, take Apollo. We can question him more. He's more important than them."

Hermes pinned me down. "But they'll warn the others we're onto them."

My limbs failed to listen to my mind, which screamed a desire to fight back. If I had full use of my faculties, I might've ripped my mother to shreds for this deceit. I laughed as I blinked and hiccupped erratically. "They'll already know." I laughed, but they turned into sobs.

My own mother forced the truth out of me, forced me to betray those I loved and who cared way more for me than my own parents. The fact my betrayal wasn't done willingly made me feel powerless.

Hermes and my mother squabbled and then bombarded me with questions. I had stayed out of the detailed plans my friends had made, so I could give my horrible mother nothing. Thankfully, they weren't asking the right questions about Callie either. I stayed in my drug-induced listlessness and closed my eyes. Through the stupor, one thought came through: I had betrayed them. Somehow, I would have to undo it. I was ready to lay my life on the line. I would make the great sacrifice for my unwilling crime. At least I'd have power in that. I would embrace my death as a true friend to those I loved.

CHAPTER 28
Callie

As soon as we docked in New York, I called Raphael. I was more than relieved he was okay. Chase had told me Zeus's weakness was forgetting about the worth of mortals. Ergo, in Zeus's head, killing Raphael wouldn't wound me, or kidnapping him wouldn't get my compliance. (Sociopath much?) I was sorry about not bringing Raphael with us, so I would ask him to come with us wherever we headed next (if we lived).

I knew we were headed into a war, but I oddly felt well protected: Archer, Chase, Aroha, Prometheus, Athena, Himerus, Anteros, Poseidon, and Proteus (hadn't seen him since what he coined was the Battle of Belize City). The Norse paired up to cloak each of us, and the unpaired patrolled the city. Archer and I got the "lovely" Freya and Thor combo. After she stabbed me, I was wary of her. It had been an overproduction to prove what she could've simply said. I should've told them the truth sooner (I know, I know), but she didn't have to be so dramatic about it all. And the drama continued. The way those two bickered, you'd think Thor and Freya were romantically involved, but nothing seemed further from the truth.

We checked into a hotel on the waterfront, right by Battery Park for Poseidon and its prime location near Liberty Island. Raphael met us in the lobby, pure joy on his face.

He hugged me. "You're glowing."

"You know why," I teased.

"Any other reasons yet?" Raphael glanced down to my stomach.

"No!" I hit him in the shoulder.

Although I was beginning to wonder about it. I measured visions by my hair length, but it was hard to tell how fast my hair would grow. In the conversation in Iceland, when Aroha pointed out immortal women were not able to get pregnant with Zeus's influence, one would think, with my freeing power, they could now like Himerus said. As soon as this ridiculous war was over, I would check. The last thing Archer and I needed on our plate was knowledge of a third life entwined with ours and on the line. One Zeus might try to kill. I pushed the thought out of my mind. I was only three days late. That was common, or maybe not. I was a "tribreed" who progressively got my powers. Maybe goddesses had longer spans of time between periods, and I was phasing into their pattern. (Who knows?)

Archer and I led Raphael to our room. Raphael had my father's book with him. Archer paced nervously. He wanted to prevent the exposure, but I had promised Dad we'd publish it and Raphael had to fulfill Dad's wishes. I leafed through the proof copy of the book. I read my father's biography and saw his smiling face in the picture. I'd never see his face again. This on-the-run and hiding business had delayed my grief, but it hit me hard, being in the city that had become my home, where Dad should be. I took a deep breath, trying to loosen the tight feeling in my throat, and read the table of contents. The last chapter was entitled "The Gods Today." I flipped to the chapter to assess the damage. How much would he expose? Would we need to go into hiding for decades, centuries? (My potential lifetime was mind-boggling.)

It was only five pages long. I had seen many handwritten pages that I could kick myself now for not reading; it should've been longer.

I read in immortal speed, loving the fact I had trained my eyes and brain to take in things as fast as the others. It took me months, but I was almost as fast as them. Dad recapped his evidence throughout the book: his theory of a berry from which all immortality began, the Gods in Greece, migrated to Rome, slipped into obscurity among mortals, and spread out after the rise of monotheism. Next, he followed a few "clans" through evidence in the middle ages through the Renaissance, Enlightenment, and so on until the early 1800s. He abruptly stopped, concluding they became "better at hiding evidence of their existence after new developments and technology allowed archaeologists to unearth more." The concluding statement asserted the gods might live among us today. That was it. There was no more.

"Raphael, is this it?"

Raphael sighed.

Archer inquiringly perused the book after me.

"He doesn't expose anything post-1800s," I explained.

"In his will, which was unfortunately legally binding, I was to place the last fifteen pages in his casket with him to be cremated. His foremost concern was your safety," Raphael told me. I could see the struggle he had with the decision to follow through.

"That's a relief, but I would have liked to have read it," Archer mused.

"I figured that." Raphael placed a locked briefcase in front of me. "I took the liberty of making a copy of what I had to burn. His handwriting is difficult to read in some places, but Callie, you're used to it. I suggest destroying it afterward. This is the only copy. The code is your birthday."

Tears filled my eyes. "Oh, Raphael." I was up and hugging him. From his flinch, I had moved too fast, scaring him. "Sorry."

"Also, inside are your ancestor's journal and the infamous letter. In short, all evidence. Again, I suggest destroying them. I shall leave you."

"Raphael. Stay safe, and I'll let you know when we decide to settle somewhere. I want to keep you close." It was hard to admit that, but Raphael had to know I saw him as family too and wanted him around. It was just too dangerous for him to be by my side at the moment.

He gave me a warm smile and a bear hug before he left.

"Let's read through this and burn it," I told Archer.

That's exactly what we did.

I was proud of how objectively Archer read over Psyche's letter. He cursed her once for the breach of secrecy relating to her child but otherwise spoke of his ex without hostility or admiration, which was good, considering I still felt bleh (jealous as all hell) about her and the past she had with (MY) Archer. When we finished, Archer flew us to the roof. We burned everything and watched the sunset as the ashes cooled, and then Archer dumped them out.

They blew away in the gusty wind, giving me the similar, somber vibe I would've felt had I spread my father's ashes. We both were saying goodbye to our pasts.

Later, Chase ordered pizza, and we all congregated in Archer and my room for dinner. Prometheus gave me an intense look when he entered, and I knew something was up. He was telling me it was going to happen very soon (crap). We had both thought we'd have more time. I nodded.

I willed myself into Prometheus's mind as the food was set down on the counter and doled out.

This is all too familiar, Callie. We should go. I know it is inevitable, but let's leave New York. Protect you. He was having cold feet, which made me shudder with chills all over my flesh. He was afraid to lose me, another of his liberty descendants, which meant one thing: he had not seen how this would pan out. I was going to die as I had foreseen right before my nineteenth birthday. Lucien was not here yet for some noble sacrifice. It was off and wrong.

"I don't feel right," I said suddenly. My stomach was sour, and my head spun. This was it. We'd be attacked, but how would Zeus find me?

"What's wrong?" Archer asked quietly.

THE IMMORTAL TRANSCRIPTS: SHUDDER

Everyone stared at me, frozen. "Something, I dunno."

There was a pounding on the door. Eyes darted around the room, all of us questioning who was there. Everyone was here, jammed into our suite, some of the Norse included.

Chase automatically grabbed a knife from the kitchenette area and opened the door, so fluidly, it was an instinct for the war god.

I held my breath.

Yanking someone inside and checking outside to assert he was alone, Chase demanded, "What in Hades are you doing here?" He shut the door.

We all turned our attention to Aios, who was panting for breath. He leaned on the table for support and uttered one foreboding word: "Zeus."

"What?" Aroha barked at him.

"Behind me, two minutes, maybe three."

Archer gave me a pointed look. "Hymenaios, the harbinger of war." He repeated a phrase I'd said in my sleep, when I had lied and said I couldn't remember the dream.

"How on Mother Gaia did he find us?" Athena asked.

"Does it matter? Get out of here!" Aios shouted.

They all rushed at human speed to the door, but Archer pulled me out onto the balcony and grabbed me tightly in his arms. He jumped, and we were on top of the hotel's roof, six stories above the street and overlooking the park and the harbor. It was kind of hot (focus, Callie).

"Archer—"

"We've got to get you to Liberty Island, in the statue, where his lightning can't touch you."

"Archer, listen to me." I didn't have his full attention, so I took his face in my hands and forced him to meet my gaze. "No matter what happens to me, promise you won't be reckless."

"Nothing will happen to you." His jaw clenched.

"If it does, I want you to stay by my side, do *nothing*. Promise me."

"No," he said, his eyes probing into mine. "I would get revenge before I'd join you."

"Archer, no," I pleaded.

Anteros suddenly was next to us, bumping into Archer due to his magnetic gravity power. "Let's move to the Statue of Liberty. Those without wings are making their own way."

"Quickest way is Anteros," Himerus said as he climbed onto the roof.

Archer rose in the air, pulling Anteros with him. I grabbed onto Anteros's arm, Himerus his other. Anteros gazed across the bay at Liberty

Island, and I clung on immortally tight as we were yanked across the sky. Archer did some maneuver much like putting brakes on, and Anteros was the only one who smacked into the side of Lady Liberty's face. Himerus laughed at him, but I was too frightened to join in. Archer gently landed us all safely on the ground.

We headed around the back of the statue to the entrance, and the boys broke into the lobby. I wasn't keen on the whole breaking and entering, but this was a life-and-death situation—not just for us but every mortal in the city if we hadn't moved the fight away from them. Cupid and heart decorations mockingly hung in the lobby when Love's life was one of many on the line.

Ear-splitting alarms went off. Over them, Anteros shouted, "What are we doing about security?"

Archer covered his ears. "Dad said do not kill mortals, incapacitate if necessary! Doubt they'll even..." The alarms stopped. Archer lowered his voice, "...make it here. Dad and Athena had Zeph land them in the guard shack."

Himerus smirked. "Guess they knocked them out already."

Aroha and Poseidon entered next, who swam. He had a massive trident in his hand, and I could sense the hum of its power. The others arrived within a couple of minutes.

Chase and Athena arrived next. "Security was asleep, the superintendent and his wife too." He smiled widely. "You know what that means?"

"Hypnos?" Archer asked. "Why would he help me?" True, Archer had killed his brother, Death, to save me.

Athena was strapping weapons to her body. "It means Hades and his people are our allies."

Thunder rumbled out above, announcing our impending doom. I shuddered. I was terrified my visions could be off, and I would truly die. I was afraid of the pain I might endure and what would happen to Archer.

Wind gods came and went, dropping off allies, and it soon became crowded, making me wonder how many gods were out there if this was just the Norse and half the Greeks. Every time they appeared, I jumped, thinking of Zeus and Hermes when they had snatched me in Belize. In between people, weapons came. Gods ran about, stashing them and strapping them on like Athena. Archer grabbed up a bow, a quiver, and a few sheathed knives. He fixed one knife to his right side belt, then proceeded to strap each of my thighs with the other two (stupid body betrayed me under his touch). I needed to focus on the gravity of the moment and prepare to fight for my life. (I felt like a badass–focus!)

Aios was talking to a god who held an old-school doctor's bag in his hand. "There. The mezzanine wraps around. It has good cover for the wounded. I'll set up my infirmary there. Dionysus? Hand out a mini-bottle to everyone and then bring the rest to me." He rushed up the steps, followed by Aios and a goddess. (Mini-bottles? Really?)

Dionysus, the bartender I barely recalled—my memory having been tampered with—rolled his eyes, not a fan of being ordered around. Regardless, he handed the bottles out. "If you are wounded and cannot get back, down this sucker, and you'll be right back up fighting." He stopped and handed me one. "Welcome to the family in more ways than one. No mortal could take a swig of my stock and function."

"You knew?" Archer accused. "Why didn't you tell me?"

"I didn't *know* know. It's not the time or place, Turtle Dove," he taunted, before moving on and handing out the rest.

There was so much going on, I had trouble keeping up. Chase and Athena were ordering people to guard certain areas; the Norse were dividing, spreading out their forces. There were three groups: the offense led by Chase and Poseidon, the defense led by Hephaestus (Beast came to my defense), and the final line consisting of my husband and mother-in-law.

I felt the multitude of things, but what won out, what burned the fear out of my veins, was how much my new family and our Norse allies cared about me enough to risk their lives protecting me.

"You brought me home, Dad," I whispered as I kissed the book charm on my necklace for luck.

"Where's Lucien?" Archer asked Aios as he passed by to join a defense team.

He shrugged, but his eyes were sad. "I think Zeus has him."

Thunder peeled louder as if to confirm Lucien was not coming. It was all wrong, but maybe that was a good thing. Maybe Lucien fought fate and won, and Archer and I would survive.

Prometheus said stoically, "It has begun." He turned to me. "I think up is the safest place for you—"

"But—"

"For now," he said firmly, pointing at the floor.

I peered down. The floor was the very one from my vision: a circle with four diamonds in it. It seemed like something had been there before but had been removed. This spot was where I saw myself dying, reminding me of an altar (cringe). Prometheus hinted for me to fight the vision; if I stayed away from the circle, I might just survive.

"C'mon." Aroha tugged my arm as we followed the sign to the pedestal and crown, the brownish-red sign from my visions, Archer right behind us.

Thunder peeled outside, and a loud echoing boom rattled the doors. I heard a strange noise like rushing water. Looking over my shoulder, I saw water trickling in under the doors in the lobby. Poseidon and his people were attacking. That meant that Zeus and his minions were here.

"Let's head up," Aroha said, running up the steps at an immortal speed, and me tripping a few times, trying to keep up.

Aroha turned on her walkie-talkie, which instantly buzzed with life.

Chase's voice spoke, "Wise Owl, this is Dog Spear. Zeus and Hermes are on the island. Scratch that. Hermes is gone. Bringing reinforcements, my guess. Over."

We hurried along, the sound of shoe to metal stairs echoing through the levels of the pedestal.

"Dog Spear. Eight Muses westbound, over."

"Tango. Four northbound, over."

I couldn't keep track of the voices or their handles.

"Tango. Three south, over."

I felt helpless letting them face the battle and sick at the thought of anyone dying for me. "I can't take this. Can't we help?" I pleaded.

Archer's arms instinctively held me prisoner.

"They will be fine. We have the two best war gods on our side. Plus, the muses hardly count in war, not really vicious creatures," Aroha told me.

How was she so calm? She must be nervous about Chase fighting his father.

"And the Norse war gods have done this thousands of times," Archer added. He didn't sound as sure as his words, though. I could see the anxiety etched upon his perfect face.

There was a loud crash downstairs, making me jump.

"Lobby breached," the radio blared.

Sounds of footsteps headed toward our stairs over the sound of fighting down in the lobby. Archer grabbed my hand in his, and the three of us ran up the double helix steps. We paused on the "lower" platform (a ridiculous name for something so many stories high).

THE IMMORTAL TRANSCRIPTS: SHUDDER

Aroha put her finger to her lips, commanding silence. She turned the walkie-talkie off, then pointed above us and made some flapping wings with her hands. Archer nodded (right? So...what were we supposed to do?).

Archer scooped me up and flew us soundlessly through the spiraling steps to the upper landing. He landed noiselessly. I carefully slipped down onto my own two feet.

"Hermes, so good to see you," Aroha's voice mocked from below.

I heard a growl of frustration from Hermes.

She must have blocked him. "Where do you think you're going?"

Suddenly, a popping noise made me jump, and Hermes was next to me. Aroha was on his back, trying to strangle him and cling on at the same time. She must've grabbed him before he teleported.

When he lunged for me, I kicked him in the place it hurts a man most, and he instantly dropped. Archer followed up with a good punch to his face.

Another pop made me jump, but he was a stranger to me—older, with gray hair and pointy beard, with pale eyes. "I'm on it, Eros!" The wind whipped around, pushed Aroha away, and he vanished along with Hermes.

Another wind god, but on our side. I wondered why they didn't whisk me away to a safe locale, but if they suggested it, I would refuse. This threat looming over us would end tonight, one way or another. We were done running and hiding. We'd fight Fate head-on.

Archer urged, "C'mon."

We ran all the way past Liberty's head, into her crown.

I caught my breath. "What if we get trapped up here?"

"Windows." He unstrapped his bow from his back. I was a bit envious of his weaponry, but limited time only had given Chase enough time to teach me tactical knife attacks and self-protection moves.

I was distracted by a tidal wave smashing into the dock to my left, knocking several gods down. The water was angry, waves crashing everywhere. Arrows were flying. Swords and other old-fashioned weaponry clashed. It was surreal. The next thing I knew, my husband was awkwardly pushing the top of a bow out the window, an arrow in his other hand, and he turned the bow sideways. He cocked the arrow and aimed downward, squinting.

Could he really accurately hit them that far away? Yep. Gods by the water and up to the base were going down.

A resounding crack hit above us, the sky lighting up. The entire head of the structure shuddered. Lightning (Zeus). I wanted to help, to do something, but my powers were mostly of the mind. I heard a thump above. I yanked Archer back in, which snapped his bow, but right where his head had been, a battle axe blade swung down.

Archer met my gaze, wide-eyed. I *could* help. I simply had to keep using my instincts, which seemed to have a tad of foresight in them.

"Down!" I screeched. We ducked a second before the widows shattered and buckled.

Archer grabbed me and entwined our bodies, pressing my face into his neck and wrapping his legs around mine. As we plummeted, I relaxed in his arms as he bent and snaked us through the double helix stairs with perfect finesse and ample speed. I was dizzy, and my stomach dropped with every story until I was abruptly put on my own feet.

My head spun as I took in where we were. The first landing. Aroha was rushing up to us, with a slight limp. "He broke my leg. Sorry for the delay."

"We're breached above," Archer told her.

Her eyes said it all. "And below."

We were losing. Prometheus had said he had seen triumph. I foresaw death and sacrifice. Why would he mislead me?

"That's it." I said with finality. I slipped a knife out of its sheath to be ready at a moment's notice.

Archer's brow wrinkled. "What?"

Footsteps were coming closer from above. We were trapped.

They followed as I raced down the pedestal levels of stairs while shouting my thoughts back to them, "I'm not going to hide. We will face Zeus head-on."

"Have you lost your mind!" Archer slammed down in front of me, and I collided with him. (Ouch! Missed foreseeing that). He braced me. "Callie. He will kill you. You die, I do too."

When he put it that way, it was a foolish plan. "Fine. What I mean is we go out there. Fight our way if we must. Link our three teams together into a retreat back in here if need be. This spreading out of us cannot be good."

"Let's see what is below and go from there." Aroha pushed me forward into Archer.

The thundering of feet above us made him realize there was no other way. Down we went until we came into the lobby, to chaos. The ground was wet, and gods battled gods. I could hardly tell who was who in the rapid movements.

THE IMMORTAL TRANSCRIPTS: SHUDDER

Before we could even enter the fray, someone grabbed me from behind. Archer cursed and latched onto me while fighting someone off. There was the sensation of someone squeezing my entire body, and we reappeared outside by the dock. Zeus stood there, obviously elated at our sudden appearance.

"Good boy, Hermes. You've done well. Too bad you didn't the first time," Zeus said. His cold eyes glowered at me with pure hatred, but his soaking wet appearance proved he was not as strong as he looked. Poseidon's team had given him hell.

Archer instantly had me protectively behind his back. "I was under the impression we had a year or more." Archer feigned nonchalance. "It's only been six months."

"Six months and no child in her womb? I thought even a sappy love god could impregnate a mortal." He chuckled. He didn't know I was immortal. Zeus had no clue.

Lucien could not have fully betrayed us. Archer squeezed my hand as if to say don't tell him the truth (yeah, I'm not that dumb, Love).

"Archer, give her up. Her existence is unnatural. I cannot let it continue."

Talking about me as if I weren't there was utterly rude, but I didn't have the guts to draw attention to myself. While Archer squeezed my hand, I slipped my knife's handle between our palms. His knife was too conspicuously placed on his other side.

Archer had the guts.

"We're all unnatural," Archer growled. "You ingested the ambrosia first. You made us what we are. Only you found out the Titans already existed, and that didn't fly with you. Once you were in with them, you devised a way to destroy them. You're the same. Always. There is nothing wrong with change. You can't control everything."

"Let's get this straight, Archer. Not only will I kill her today, but never would I have ever made her immortal for you. I never wanted to hurt you, Grandson, but you must give her up. I will kill you to get to her. That's your fault. Immortally marrying a weak little mortal." Zeus's speech was devoid of empathy. His gray-blue eyes flickered on me with such hatred, it made my blood boil.

We had an advantage: Zeus would try to kill me in a mortal way. How long, though, until he realized I was immortal and would light me on fire as he had Aios, his own grandson?

Archer's hand grasped the handle, and I withdrew my hand. He tackled Zeus to the ground, burying the knife up to the handle in the heart area. He growled in Zeus's face like some feral beast. Zeus's face went slack. Archer had once said it was hard for gods to die. A knife in the heart didn't do the job; it was merely an insult from the god of love, insinuating Zeus didn't have one.

Lightning struck the ground only a foot from me, making it crack and smoke from the heat. I wanted to attack, to get revenge, to protect Archer, but I had to feign helpless mortality as long as I could.

I unsheathed my other knife. Then ran for it in mortal speed, slashing Hermes's hand as he swiped to grab me. I headed toward the building. Suddenly, eight gorgeous women were in front of me, blocking off the entrance—the nine muses minus one (was my guess). Hermes was still on my tail. I was trapped.

Suddenly, an arch of fire encircled me, and I thought it was the end. This was all wrong. I was to die on the stone floor in the building. Suddenly, two hot hands were on my shoulders.

"Are you okay?" a gruff voice asked. The fire circle was one of protection. Heph (oh, sweet Beast) had come to my rescue.

I assured him I was, stealing a glance at Archer, who was with Thor. Both were ganging up on Zeus, the latter's hammer doing some damage to Zeus's face. I wanted Archer away from the dangerous and chaotic lightning. Let lightning conquer lightning.

Belle and her sisters started fighting the muses, but they were outnumbered. I grabbed a knife from Heph's weapon-clad belt and tried to help out. I stabbed one and then recoiled. I had never hurt anyone before, but I had to remind myself that they were immortal. I could go completely homicidal on them, and they would heal. A muse leaped upon me, and I fell to the ground under her weight. She twisted my arm, so the knife headed to my throat. I shoved her off me, but my knife clattered to the ground. I switched Heph's knife to my dominant right hand.

A beautiful girl stepped slowly out of the shadows with dark eyes, pale skin, and gorgeous dark curls. She picked up the discarded knife and slipped it in the back of her waistband. She winked at me before she rounded on the now shocked and frozen muses. She raised her hands into the air, and the ground shuddered under us. In front of her, the stone slabs cracked, and the sound of something crawling across the pavement unnerved me. Roots, vines, and grass wound around from the grassy areas and holes in the

THE IMMORTAL TRANSCRIPTS: SHUDDER

ground and bound the muses against the walls. The vines covered their mouths, cutting off their screams. They looked like vine statues after they could no longer move.

Persephone shouted to Heph, "Get her back inside!" I was making a lot of guesses about who was who, but plants had to be a Persephone thing.

Suddenly, a tidal wave swept all of us down, and I steadied myself before the others were up. The doorways were now clear, and it was only a hundred feet. I ran for it, not caring whether they saw me move too fast. Before I could make it, two arms snaked behind my own. I was knocked down hard against the pavement under the attacker's weight. My jaw crunched, and blood poured from my mouth. The pain was excruciating.

A woman screamed, "Don't touch her!" Athena went streaking by, swinging her sword like a war-crazed Spartan.

Seriously though, the way she swung her two swords to make the psycho who attacked me back off and gutted another god behind her back, without turning around or looking over her shoulder—total and utter awe. I needed *her* lessons.

I was pulled to my feet by Prometheus, who gave me a wink. His mental voice chided, *Pull yourself together. Don't think. React.* Then he chased after Athena, covering her back from an attack.

I needed to be more aware of my surroundings, but I had never been a fighter. I felt out of my depth. These immortals had thousands of years of trained warfare. Why had we wasted more time on my foresight than battle tactics? Chase had been right to press me for more, but Archer let me get away with shirking it off. I missed my dad. He would've directed me down the right path for this moment. I needed those Socratic moments to make me realize *my* path—not the Fates' or my new family's, but mine. (Pull it together, Callie.)

I made it to the doors but paused, scanning for my husband. He was by the dock, fighting. Lightning flew about everywhere. Waves knocked the gods to and fro. A few beings were zipping around in the sky like hawks. (Were they actually hawks or women with wings?)

Ares was in the fray, having Archer's back. (Wow). I couldn't process a thought. I couldn't think of him as Chase. He annihilated everyone in his path (if they had been mortal), pulled Archer out of the mix, and pushed him behind to safety (effortlessly). Archer searched wildly for me. His eyes met mine and went wide.

I wanted to run to him and pull him into the safety of the building, but another pair of hands were upon me. I recognized the man's scar across his face. It was a faded memory. He was ice cold, and my body went rigid, freezing as if my blood was becoming slush. I stabbed behind me, but my knife got stuck, and I had to remove my hand. Its handle was ice cold. I clawed at the creature with all my might trying to get away.

He growled as he tried futilely to restrain me. "Aren't we a little too strong?" Suddenly, he let me go.

It was hard to see what was going on. I struggled to breathe, to move, my body heavy as lead and just as immovable—and cold. I saw Archer, his hand around the man's head.

"Not again," the man groaned. Archer swung him like a rag doll over his shoulder, and he collided with the ground, breaking the pavement.

Archer pulled me into his arms. "It'll wear off with some nectar." Something slammed us down, knocking the wind out of me.

My body ached utterly. Archer moved next to me. I saw bright lights. Lightning. I looked over to Archer, who gazed at me in pain. Then another bolt rippled over him.

The agony transferred over to me, only delayed by a second. I screamed out in pain. It wasn't supposed to happen here, my death.

I heard a growl of frustration from Zeus. "Why isn't she dead yet?" He had escaped Ares's defense via Hermes.

Archer laughed mockingly on the ground next to me. "Because she's immortal."

"The Norse," Hermes accused. "As you said, Father, a demigod of the others."

I saw his snobby face looming above me. I was losing it, my link to reality. My eyes growing heavy, I was slipping from my body.

"No," Archer grinned. "The product of gods who eluded your waning sight."

Why was Archer telling Zeus all this? I didn't understand why he'd give it all away now. Surely, Zeus would light me on fire, and it would be the end of Archer and me.

"How is that possible?" Zeus sounded frightened.

The sounds of battle coming closer drew my attention, the noise giving me focus. Was Archer stalling for help?

"Psyche," Archer said. He stood suddenly and, with great strength, snapped Hermes's neck. "Athena." He tackled Zeus to the ground in a split second, bones crunching. He had been stalling to heal from the bolt damage. Archer was fine and on his feet again. Neither god moved. "And Prometheus." Archer scooped me up in his arms.

THE IMMORTAL TRANSCRIPTS: SHUDDER

As hard as I clung to my thread of reality, the icy sludge in my chest and the electricity in my body was too much. Archer's soul responded to mine, sensing my suffering and wanting to pull the agony and death into himself. I focused my last thoughts on pushing that addictive assistance away. Immortal marriage be damned. I would give him all the strength I had left to fight just a moment longer. I slipped into unconsciousness with one last regret: my baby, the one I suspected was with me now. I wanted Philo, my little god of friendship-love, to make it. The gods help me if we died and Archer ever learned of the double sacrifice I made without telling him. That would make afterlife in the Underworld hell.

CHAPTER 29

Archer

Once inside the lobby, I placed Callie on the cool marble floor. Inadvertently, I had placed her in the circle where the statue's old flame used to be on display, feeling very much as if I were offering her to the gods as a sacrifice.

"Help!" came tearing out of my mouth, my voice reverberating with love, rage, and the essence of my anguished soul.

Asclepius was to the left side of the room with Himerus, who had a gaping wound in his stomach. Euterpe went to help Himerus, who should heal momentarily, but someone had to push in his protruding intestines as he healed. Asclepius came to my side instantly.

"Help her," I pleaded to Lucien's son.

"What happened?" he asked, examining her pupils, her pulse. "She's freezing."

"Zelus," I explained.

Asclepius growled under his breath. He began to pour nectar whiskey in Callie's mouth, but she wasn't able to swallow.

"Come on. Callie, can you hear me?" I begged her, trying to shake her awake, but it was no use. She looked like a corpse: cold, rigid, and turning blue. She was immortal, we believed, but Zeus's lightning or Zeus's power alone could kill one of us. Together, they were a death sentence.

Asclepius put an IV of nectar into her arm, which she'd get upset about if—no, *when*—she woke up. Callie despised needles, and her immortal flesh would grow over the IV and make it harder to remove. There wasn't another option; she needed nectar immediately.

I waited the longest minutes of my life, hoping she'd improve, but she remained pale and lifeless. Asclepius measured her pulse. He instantly met my gaze, afraid to tell me the news. "I think she's dying."

Ma, who'd overheard, came over. "What?"

"No, do something. You're the best at this. You have to know how to save her," I pleaded with him. "I'm not dying yet, so help me help her or however it works. Aios!" I screamed for Lucien's other son.

THE IMMORTAL TRANSCRIPTS: SHUDDER

I had thought—probably because of Callie and her visions—Lucien would be here with us. Where was he? Was he dead already, and Callie and I were next? Callie had insisted his death had been here, though, and her visions were accurate so far. No. Chaos had not shown up yet. No Olympians were dead, so where was my best friend?

"She needs ambrosia." Ma shook her head. "Himerus, you're useless in battle right now." She handed him her walkie-talkie. "Get a Norse god on here and see if they have any access to their version of ambrosia. Beg Odin if you have to," Ma ordered.

He winced in pain as he reached for the device and started asking for help.

Aios rushed over, his bruised and cut face healing. "Sorry, heard your call but had to extract myself from a muse or two." He scowled, but I knew it bothered him. His mother being a muse, he had been raised by these women. His aunts were willing to kill him, much like Artemis had tried to.

"My soul," I focused on the point. "How am I fine and she isn't?"

He blanched at that and stared at Callie, then me. He snapped out of it. Aios mentally scanned her, his brows contracted in confusion, but next he stared at me in the same way. It was clinical, measuring us up. I didn't want to interrupt his process, but I needed him to tell me she would live.

A few immortals burst into the lobby. Instinctively, I pulled Callie protectively into my arms. It was Prometheus carrying Athena, who was covered in blood. Ma ran to take Athena from him, and Asclepius started mixing a concoction he said could buy Callie some time. He spliced it into the IV.

"Let me back out there. I almost had her!" Athena growled.

"No. Stay and heal. You're useless with your arm mangled like that," Prometheus said gently.

"I'm not useless!"

He ignored her outburst. "I need you safe here to heal, then we are back out there."

Prometheus noticed us. He was shocked. Why was the foreseeing god surprised to see Callie in such a state when she had warned him about this? He came forward, took Callie's pulse, and then sighed, relieved. He had thought she was dead. His head hanging down, he asked, "What has been done so far?"

Asclepius filled him in, and Aios looked at me, his eyes wary. He was not going to tell me good news.

"What is it?" I asked Aios, exasperated.

232

He sighed. "She's somehow pushing her power, her soul, all into you, even while she's unconscious. I've never seen it before."

"Make her stop." She would die if she didn't.

Aios met my gaze, his eyes solemn. You'll never forgive me if I don't do this, but I wish you wouldn't. Take up her hand."

I took Callie's limp ice-cold hand in mine and eagerly awaited more. If there was something that could be done, why had he waited?

"Repeat after me. And, Archer, this will make you weak, both of you. You'll likely both die."

"Get on with it." I growled at the precious moments we were wasting as my wife's life was ebbing away. She would not save me, even if her multicultural power could make it somehow happen. No. Callie and I would stay together, whether it be in life or death.

In ancient Greek, he recited, and I repeated a type of mantra: "This soul of mine bound to yours is one and the same. I renew our bonds."

Nothing happened. "Did it work?" I demanded, my patience wearing thin.

Aios's gaze darted between Callie, Prometheus, and me alternately. Suddenly, as beautiful as the sun rays rising over the horizon, a faint blush arose on Callie's cheek.

I sighed happily, kissing her cheek, pulling her closer to me.

"Archer, you're paling," Prometheus warned me, but I could hardly care. A sign of life overshadowed any injury of mine.

"I don't care."

Asclepius commanded. "Drink this. Do it, Archer."

I downed two elixirs, which I wished were full of some miracle cure. I felt only minutely better. A chill and a deep dull ache resounded throughout me, and I was exhausted. Mentally, this made me stronger; I knew I was relieving Callie of some of the pain.

"He won't stop until he kills her. It's exactly like every time before," Athena's hushed voice told my mother.

After attending to Athena, Ma came over and took Callie's head in her lap. She combed Callie's hair out of her face tenderly.

I crouched over Callie, trying to observe any changes, any signs of life. Nothing seemed to happen. "It's not working."

"Give it a minute," Aios said. "Don't overthink it. We need both of you balancing what shreds of souls are left." He sighed, and I knew what he had done was only a bandaid, a way to make us live longer. We would die.

THE IMMORTAL TRANSCRIPTS: SHUDDER

"Zeus has broken through the front line!" The walkie-talkie on the floor buzzed to life.

Prometheus and Athena, who was now healed, ran toward the doors to intercept him. Hearing his name snapped something in me, something so opposite of my nature: indomitable hatred.

"I'm going after him." I growled.

"No, you're too weak," Ma told me, but it fell on deaf ears.

I had to do it—kill Zeus or die trying. I wanted revenge. I wanted to free my family from him. This freedom to be our true selves without his control, because of my wife, would be gone after we died. He would control and punish. They would die—or worse, end up in Tartarus.

Ma placed her hand on my shoulder. "He'll destroy you."

I had to word it to her right, explain it in a way she would understand. I began with the same sentiment she had used to explain to me why she kept going back to my father. "Ma, I'm dead without her. We are dead already. I can risk myself to free you, Dad—everyone. Zeus must be stopped." My voice cracked at the end, which made tears form in my mother's eyes. She never could see me suffer; it pained her too much. What would she do without me? We had been best friends in my long adulthood. Guilt washed over me, but, damn it, I had to do this. What was done was done.

"Archer..." She began to cry but stopped.

"They are sentenced to death at this point. We need ambrosia," Aios told Ma. "We're keeping her alive via Archer, but..."

Himerus piped in, "The Norse can't get it here in time." He was on his feet and healthy again.

My mother's face froze in realization. I ignored her accusatory gaze. I smoothed a curl off Callie's beautiful face and kissed her forehead. She had become my reason for existence, like the ichor in my blood. How had I let myself, god of love, fall so hard for another being? I knew the power of love, its consequences, and now I was my own victim.

Ma pleaded, "Archer, immortal marriage. You can't risk yourself out there. You'll hasten her death."

"Yes, it's more of a reason for you to *stay* so both of you don't die," Aios said. "Maybe we can think of something to save you."

Wasted words to try to placate me. He meant well, but I was done. I was pissed off as all Hades that my happiness with my wife would end. The rage was boiling inside me. "I want his head." I wanted to lop off Zeus's head as Perseus had done to Medusa.

"If you get killed, she'll die instantly." Himerus put an arm on my shoulder, stopping me.

I gave Callie's cold lips one last kiss, lamenting I might never see her beautiful eyes ever again. "It doesn't matter anymore. I'll meet her in Hades."

My confession stunned him so much that his grip lessened enough for me to elude him. I stood and rushed to the doors, trying to go before my mother could protest. I heard her call my name but ignored it. Suddenly, she was in front of me, preventing my escape. I could hear arguing and stone crumbling outside.

I must've hurt my own mother to get by her, but it hadn't been a conscious action. I needed Zeus's blood. He had done this to Callie and me. I would not give up easily. If I killed him, my family would be free. With fury and a shred of hope in my heart, I ran for the doors.

CHAPTER 30

Lucien

The first thing I was conscious of was a terrible headache. I was on a cot. A little crone with a wart on her nose was gazing at me. The stature and the ridiculous appearance of her persona made me instantly realize it was Iris playing one of her many roles.

"Couldn't you just pity me and let me wake up to a superbly hot visage?"

"Ew, and have you drooling over me? Tree hugger."

"Ha ha," I retorted. Damn Archer for making me love a nymph who became a tree. I had quite a few issues from obsessing over her for a decade, so much so, a shrink today wouldn't begin to unravel that one.

"Maybe you should focus on the war and not your libido," the crone version of Iris scolded.

Her voice was like a spike to my brain. "Oh gods," I moaned as I sat up. "I have to go there."

"You're in no state."

"Take me. I know what I have to do. Trust me. I'm better off half-awake for this." When I fished out my wallet and handed her the entire thing, her eager eyes fixated on it.

"Do I have to fight? Or are you paying me for a drop-off?"

"That's all on you. Iris, I've been told I'm going to die. This is my choice. I'm not asking you to. You are free from Zeus, but imagine if we all could be."

"This little war might take a cut to my business plans if gods die."

I rolled my eyes. "Obviously, you care about money more than your brethren. Take me there, and then piss off."

She gave me a confused and bitter look. "Fine."

I felt as if I were squeezed into a horrid tube where I couldn't breathe until I was released. I was on the dock of Liberty Island. Lightning kept striking Lady Liberty; waves crashed above the breaker.

"Good luck," Iris told me and vanished, but I saw a rainbow streak across the sky above and return to the top of Liberty's crown.

Someone stood watching on one of Liberty's rays. The rainbow goddess on the statue's—my sun's—ray on Callie's liberty. Things seemed so symbolic that it was almost cliché. I dismissed my thoughts. This was war, no time for poetic musings.

From the sights around me, the battle had ensued for a while. There were gods running about, but the main melee was by the front of the statue. I had no idea where to go or what to do. Was I too late? Were Callie and Archer dead? No, Chaos hadn't reigned. My heart was beating hard in my chest, frantic because these were my last moments. I knew this deep down. I wasn't sad about it either. Thousands of years of life had culminated to this day, these last moments. I wasn't scared. I was determined.

I raced around the side of the building and almost smashed into Chase. "Archer?"

"In front of liberty after Zeus's blood." He nodded and pressed my shoulder back, his eyes full of fire and anguish. "You told Zeus where we were?" He framed it as a question, but it was an accusation full of knowledge.

"Leto. Truth Serum. I tried to resist."

He grabbed my hand and pulled me into a half hug. "Good, Brother." He had never accepted me as a brother before. "You won't mind if I took off one of her arms, then."

I wanted to puke after picturing his description, but I shook my head. I didn't have time to process my mother's betrayal and yet could not think badly of Chase for disabling her in battle.

He was gone in a flash, likely attempting a sneak attack. I raced into the skirmish, dodging weapons left and right. Why hadn't I thought to bring a weapon?

Then I saw *her*. The bitch was aiming one of her poisoned arrows at Archer's back, who was holding his own fighting Hermes and trying to get to Zeus. I legged it and launched myself at my sister, Artemis, the woman who would kill her own nephew for spite. We fell hard. She glowered at me.

"You tried to kill my son!" My anger was more potent than I expected, and her cold blue eyes flinched. She tried to move. We fumbled, but I managed to rip the quiver off her back.

Aglaea fell to the ground next to me, her eyes vacant, and blood poured out of her jugular. Archer stumbled back, falling next to her with a sword above him. An impaled Hermes was on it, his eyes wide with shock. Hermes vanished to heal in safety.

THE IMMORTAL TRANSCRIPTS: SHUDDER

With his sword hissing and smoking from ichor, Archer looked at me, then Artemis. She had already stood and hesitated on retreat or attacking us without a weapon. Wordlessly, Archer and I acted simultaneously, sandwiching her between us. Artemis fell to the ground, her body limp. We literally crushed her. I snatched up her bow and quiver.

"We make a good team," Archer said.

"Yeah." I gave him a half grin despite my inadvertent duplicity. He would understand what had happened and not blame me.

Archer stepped toward the skirmish that included Zeus. He'd get himself killed if I didn't stop him.

I placed my hand on his shoulder. "Archer, Callie?"

He froze, his body going tense with indecision.

"Where is she?"

Archer glared at Zeus and then peered over his shoulder at me. "I'll take you to her." It was a hard decision for him, but he was superior to most of us gods when it came to morality.

On the way into the building, I used up half of the stolen arrows on the enemy. We rushed inside, and when I reached the mezzanine where the infirmary was set up, I was accosted by a furious hug: my son, Aios.

"You got away?" He touched my shoulder, not believing I was standing before him. "When we left, we sent Iris back for you. I thought...I thought you had sacrificed yourself, like the prophecy."

He was so hopeful. How could I squash that? I knew my sacrifice would still happen. I could feel it in my limited heartbeats.

"Nothing's working on her, Dad," my other son Asclepius mumbled to me, ignoring my gaze. He was all business but finally called me his dad. Closure. He would be okay. Aios too. Callie and Archer. I felt warm as my *sun* thinking about it.

I knelt across from a pale and weary Archer. He was exhausted from battle and anxiety. I wanted to tell him how much I loved him, as his uncle and best friend. I could not. The words were in my throat, but if I said them, he would never let me do what I needed to do. Archer loved me too much.

I placed my hands on Callie's temples and tried with all my might to heal her, hoping I could somehow impart my energy to her. I'd let her take it all if she could latch on. At once, I realized it wasn't working, but I kept on going while I tried to rack my brain for an idea. I knew I had to save her—no, I *would* save her. This was my sacrifice. I thought of what Callie had said, what she tried to make me promise in Norway: "Promise me you won't do something stupid, Lucien, or you'll be the one who dies."

I needed to do something reckless, my life for hers—this was how I'd die. How could I die in place of her, though? Then Archer's conversation with me about immortal marriage versus soul-sharing came to mind, where my mind wandered into impossible territories: *philia, agape.*

"Nothing?" I asked Asclepius. "What would happen if there was a Castor-Pollux move made by another god? Death will only need one soul."

Asclepius stared at me, confused, until recognition filled his features. He shook his head, eyes wide with fear and pleading with me not to, which proved he thought it could possibly work and save her.

I gripped Archer's shoulder and took a deep breath. "I want to do this."

Archer was stunned, lost, his eyes darting between his dying wife and me, desperately unable to agree. His mind grappled with the ethics of my death. Could I give up my life for them both to live?

"Asking someone to give part of their soul so we can maybe live? That's insane, Lucien. You said so yourself. I'd rather die with her than resign anyone to that fate." He meant it too. The truth was there. I had been such a horrible friend, jealous and selfish. I was going to make up for it now.

It would work. I was strong, and I could give my soul to them, like Pollux did for Castor, and agree to live in the Underworld forever to let them live together above it. If Hades needed one soul to make this possible, he could take mine.

"Aios. Soul-share me to Callie."

"What? But..." He looked at me, flabbergasted. He was terrified to lose me. Prophecies were a bitch. They prepared you to no end, but when the time came, and the details surfaced, the warning made it so much worse.

These were my last breaths, my last heartbeats, the last time I would gaze proudly upon my sons. We were wasting time watching the life slipping from Archer's wife, his soulmate. I had always known she'd never be mine, and she deserved a future with Archer. I had thousands of years and Callie a measly eighteen. This was how I would love her, as a true friend, as a soul given in friendship, giving her my life in a charitable sacrifice. "Stop wasting time. This is the way it was foretold, the way to right everything."

"Dad. This has never been done before," Aios stalled. "You don't know for sure this is the path."

THE IMMORTAL TRANSCRIPTS: SHUDDER

"She is dying. This is my choice. You must do this, or both Callie and Archer die. She is dying, and Archer bound his soul in an immortal marriage. I can save two people. I will give it. All you do is set up the connection."

Although he was acting strong, Archer was paling. He was exhausted.

Aroha came over to me, astonished, and met my gaze. My expression told her all. Her bitter gaze gave way to surprise until it rested in gentle pity. Then her mouth drew in that quintessential displeased expression she often gave Archer and I when flashing her mom-card over him and me by proxy. "You betrayed us. That's how Zeus found us so fast. What? Are you now going to become a noble sacrifice? That's not how you gain forgiveness." She gazed at me with a turmoil of emotions in her eyes—enraged at what I did and terrified to lose me, her best friend.

"He didn't betray us. My grand—Leto gave him truth serum. He fought it hard, but it won," Asclepius told her, but he stared at me as he said it. "He struggled to deny his nature and the drugs to tell us to flee so that we could warn you. He is forgiven. By me, at least. For everything."

"Then, stop this madness," Aroha demanded. She struggled. She wanted Archer to survive. What mother wouldn't choose her child over anyone else?

"This is how I die." I pulled her into a quick hug and smoothed the loose strands that had come out of her braid. "You are more of a sister to me over this long life than my own flesh and blood. I love you, Dite. This is not some choice you need to think over. I'm doing it. I'm saving your son, my nephew, my best friend, and his wife, who happens to be the most important immortal to all of you. My life is one blip in the legacy of freedom for all gods. A small price to pay. Hell, I'll die a hero. What Greek can ask for more than that?"

She gave me a teary smile and squeezed my hand.

"No," Aios roared. "I won't do it!"

"You will, Son." I regretted what I might need to do, worried it might not work with Callie around, but she was so close to death, I didn't think her "freedom" abilities would work so well at the moment. More than that, I worried about the permanent guilt I would place on Aios's shoulders. I had to trust my friends—family—would help him cope. I knew they would.

"There's got to be another way," Asclepius said quietly.

I didn't deserve their pity. I had been a lousy father, a lousy friend. This sacrifice was not just for Callie but also for me too.

I knelt and took Callie's hand in my own. "Aios." I took a deep breath. "I order you to perform the rite: share my soul with Callie's, *philia* and *agape*." The words came out like cement. I tried desperately to hold myself together.

I didn't fear dying or giving over my soul to save them, but I couldn't handle seeing the pain I was inflicting upon my sons. Hurting them was more painful than their hatred and disappointment in me. I knew, because it has always been said, that gaining redemptions and getting them to love me would be better for them in the long run, but part of me worried it might've been better to let myself die with them resenting me.

With Callie almost dead, Aios was unable to deny a direct order from his elder, or perhaps he knew it was the right thing to do—I was not sure—and said the words. After I was finished reciting my end, Callie's eyes opened. She took a deep breath as if she was sleeping Psyche awaking, and regarded Archer with a grin. Her eyes darted around the others until they rested upon me.

"Repeat after Aios." My voice vibrated with emotion.

Confused at her whereabouts, she asked, "Archer?"

"Callie," I took her face in my palms gently. "You and Archer will die if you don't repeat Aios's words—quickly."

She obeyed and repeated the rite. Her brow wrinkled as she saw Aios sob in between words. It was done. I sighed, sat back, instantly feeling a connection to Callie, like an invisible cord was between us. As soon as that recognition crossed my mind, the cord between Callie and I went taut. This was it. Her soul was feeding off mine, and so I envision it leaving my body, going to her. By the second, I grew weaker, the same sensation as ichor leaching out of me, but I wasn't healing. I suppressed the urge to hold onto that power, refusing to attempt to heal myself.

Callie sat up, stronger, her color coming back. Archer embraced her, kissed her head, and then he looked at me, his eyes full of regret and brimming tears.

I was dying. This was what I needed to do, and it was working. They were getting better, and I was fading.

"Oh, no!" Callie realized what I'd done. She'd never forgive me for duping her into my death. "No, Lucien. Why? I told you not to!" She pulled away from Archer and cradled my head in her lap. I hadn't realized my head had been falling, but things were dizzying and confusing.

"I had to." I reached up and touched her cheek.

THE IMMORTAL TRANSCRIPTS: SHUDDER

Callie leaned over, her hair cascading over me. She kissed my forehead and whispered for my immortal ears only, "I think you saved three lives, Lucien."

I smiled at the thought. I felt even better, mentally. I saved my best friend, Callie, and their baby.

"You've created quite a pickle here, sun god," Persephone said from the doorway.

I couldn't even lift my head anymore. I wasn't breathing; my heart thumped slower than a mortal's.

"Poor Death is confused as all Hades on who to take. Soul sharing to save two others, Apollo? Ingenious, but complicated," she commented.

I espied the new Death; she was maternal and loving, a much better choice than Thanatos. Any fright or regret I had lingering about this decision left me upon seeing her warm, caring face.

"Take me." I used all my energy to request it.

"Lucien," Callie cried. Tear-drops landed on my forehead.

Archer grasped my hand in his.

"No, don't. Take me instead." Aios cried out.

I could not hear his pain, and I wanted to leave. "I go willingly. Take me," I repeated as Persephone stared at my son with sadness. Aios couldn't undo what he had already done, nor could he simply take my place. I would never recite whatever soul bonding he'd try with me if he made an attempt.

"One being died here today, so it is beyond my or Hades's skills to stop it." Persephone peered down at me. "So eager to die?"

"No, eager to save his friends," Death said sadly, stepping closer. She sat next to me. She took up my hand in hers. I only felt it because my eyes would not stay open.

A set of lips kissed my forehead again and a whisper in my ear, "Remember, *follow me*." I envisioned Callie's face one last time, but her face transformed into another one—a beautiful dark-skinned goddess with piercing blue eyes. One of my exes, one I had not made peace with. If only I had more time.

I drifted away as if afloat on a sea of listlessness. Noises became muffled. There was no pain.

Then a warm hand touched the base of my head where it met my neck, and—

CHAPTER 31
Athena

I took it all in, surveying where I was needed. I saw Nemesis. She had an arrow pointed at Chase's back but hesitated. I threw a prayer up to her of revenge for the deaths of my daughters at Zeus's hand. We needed more leverage if Archer's prayers were unanswered. Her fingers twitched, and her gaze scanned the battlefield until it locked on me. I nodded in affirmation.

Then there was a spiking pain, and my stomach lurched as I knew what was coming next. As if the world had held its breath, we Olympians faltered and stopped while Chaos now ensued. Dealing with it when it had been my daughters, and seeing it in wars, I let it wash over me and gave reverence to all those who passed away in the name of justice. All the images of all time flew by on a nauseating train. I leaned on the wall and opened my eyes to confusion.

Nemesis's face was hard and full of anger. She aimed her arrow at Chase again, but I noted the angle had shifted ever-so-slightly. Chase and Thor still battled Hera and Zeus, but Hera still was merely a warrior-shield who was on her last leg. She was only still standing because Chase was trying not to maim his own mother.

Nemesis fired. Zeus roared like a lion as the arrow pierced his shoulder. Nemesis nodded at me. She had turned sides, seduced by righting the amount of vengeance and injustice on ours. She was definitely a good addition. The only thing that worried me was why she switched. Had it been the reminder of my children? Or the Olympian who just died? From our side?

I fought my way back inside, fear lacing through me that it could be Archer or Callie. When I fought my way through muses to get to my people, I saw the two safely in each other's arms by Persephone, Aroha, and Lucien's sobbing sons over his motionless body.

Lucien was dead. I pressed all emotions connecting to him down, lest it consume me. I had to rationalize, help us win this war. I pulled Aios off his father's body. There was no way we could fight staring at his corpse. I had to push everyone forward.

"Iris!"

THE IMMORTAL TRANSCRIPTS: SHUDDER

She appeared as an innocent teen of indistinguishable gender, her mouth dropping. "Seriously? You pull me away from fighting to... Oh, no! No. No. No." She stared at Lucien's lifeless body.

"Take his body to my cabin in Iceland. The basement. You know what to do."

"I thought you were over that creepy phase." Iris cringed after referring to my studies of cryonics. I had thought only to preserve his body until we could give him a proper sendoff, but maybe— Now was not the time to think about that.

Iris took Lucien's hand in hers, and with a somber face, she vanished, leaving a rainbow streak in the air, which dissipated when two angry sons stood and glared at me for severing their bereavement short.

"Look, sorry. Grieve over the fallen later. Survival first, mourn second. Do not let his loss be in vain."

"Thena!" Prometheus shouted from the entrance I had just busted through. He was trying to single-handedly fight back about six gods.

I gave the two boys a told-you-so look and raced into the fray. Others joined me as if they snapped out of it and transferred their sadness to a rage fueled by revenge. I clung onto the feeling, knowing Nemesis would enhance my abilities. Once we pushed our way outside, I saw absolute carnage, way worse than I had left it. There was no doubt the Norse took advantage of Chaos's interruption since they weren't affected. Blood and limbs were everywhere, not turning yet to ash as the ichor died off, meaning they were fresh.

Focus. Who needed the most help? Persephone was touching the ground, staring at it, oblivious to danger. Muse arrows whizzed by her head, inches from their target. I rushed over just in time to bat an arrow away from Persephone's face with the blade of one of my broadswords. What was she doing? She had tried using the limited nature of the park at the front of the statue to imprison others, but they broke through her vines. Why was she getting so close to Zeus? I sliced both my swords around deflected arrows from Artemis's annoyingly accurate harem to protect Persephone in the Shaolin Kung Fu techniques I slipped into when I needed to move at an immortal pace.

The muses—not being warriors and terrified of me and my eclectic fighting styles—started to back off, some of them supporting each other due to numerous gruesome injuries. Definitely, it was some of their limbs on the ground.

Before I could celebrate my victory, it dawned on me that they were frightened off by more than just me. Darkness was forming around Persephone and me, black smokey air pervading everything. It had turned to night as we toiled, but this was an artificial darkness. Shadows grew on the stone platform of the statue, the old fort, and expanded around us.

Two dark lines came out from the wall behind Zeus and wrapped around him, pinning his arms to his body and pulling him in against the fort wall. He was petrified. We all were. How had shadows literally pulled Zeus ten feet and pinned him to a building?

A voice spoke that many had not heard in ages. Everyone froze in recognition. Even the Norse were distracted. "I can smell the fear of death on you, *Brother*." It was Hades's voice—deep, rumbling, full of anger and power, echoing oddly as if he was in all the darkness around us, in the night sky, the air.

Persephone had come through, but now she delivered Hades in the only way he could participate. Could he do more than shadow-link? Or should we be attacking?

Hades made an eerie sniffing sound. Maybe he could actually scare Zeus to death.

Zeus gasped, "What in Hades?"

"I'm not quite in Hades, not all of me, *Brother*." He laughed, the eeriness of it a powerful weapon. "You destroyed my helm of darkness, foolishly believing it was my only way to escape the Underworld. What you never thought of, since you only think of yourself, was how I was even able to court my wife in the first place. The helm of darkness, psssh. I AM DARKNESS!"

I covered my ears as Hades's voice ricocheted off the statue, rippled the water, smashed windows, and set off alarms of the museum behind the statue and, from the sound of it, Ellis Island as well—maybe even half of Manhattan.

Zeus screamed almost as loud, thunder echoing Hades's voice. Lightning struck Lady Liberty, the electricity running down her as Zeus struggled to get free. Bolts struck repeatedly, which brought Thor out of his shocked stupor. He met Zeus's lightning with his own, the statue attracting the brunt of it. His hammer whipped around out of his hand and smashed Zeus so hard into the stone wall, it cracked.

Through the darkness and flashes of lightning, a figure stumbled toward me, hand over his heart, hunched over.

THE IMMORTAL TRANSCRIPTS: SHUDDER

Archer! He fell to his knees in pain. Callie! It meant she...

I searched around frantically for Prometheus. Another child—no, I meant great-grandchild—dying. I could not bear it.

Zeus laughed. His teeth were stained with blood, his body trapped by the shadow arms of Hades's, vines twisting around him from Persephone's help, yet he was laughing. "Eros, Eros. Look at you. It means I got her. I'll live through this, but you two won't. I can't regret it because it was your fault for immortally binding yourself to a weak abomination. Gods aren't supposed to mix to make a *thing* like her!"

Two arrows shot into Zeus's shoulders, making him scream.

"I regret your comment." Freya stood next to me, yanking me back to the moment. Freya lowered her bow and spat on the ground by Zeus's feet.

What was I doing staring off blindly, being a bystander?

I yanked Archer to his feet. So much was happening. I hardly noticed a shout from above. A blurred form shot past, colliding with an object that landed softly in front of us. A ray of Liberty's, Lucien's light—often misunderstood by mortals as spokes of a crown.

A weakened Archer shrugged off my assistance, somehow lifted the massive copper spike, and ran it through Zeus, embedding him into the fort wall. Archer backed away, trembling.

I rushed to help him. Himerus ran to us, as well as Anteros. The spike move was the love entourage boys' work combined—strength and speed, magnetism, and flight.

Zeus tried to pull the nine-foot-long spike out of his abdomen, but it made more blood spill, and he could barely withhold his screams of agony. Archer had almost cut him in half and was now backing away, no longer staggering or weary.

He straightened up, a smirk spreading across his face. "I'm fine, *Grandpa*." He glowered at him. "And so is my wife."

His feint was so well performed that even I, who saw Callie alive minutes ago, had worried the lightning had struck her. Then, not twenty feet away, Aroha and Callie rushed out of the building.

Zeus's gaze locked onto Callie. Pure hatred filled his chilly sky-blue eyes.

Hera had broken through the Norse line, and we dumbfounded Greeks, and put herself between Zeus and us, awkwardly ignoring the 150-pound patina-covered copper spike that impaled him.

We hadn't won yet. All we had managed to do was hold off Zeus's allies. He was still trapped, but the darkness was ebbing away. Hades only had so much power on the surface. The water sprayed us and sucked the muses into the sea, which gave us some breathing room, but we still needed a final push.

Prometheus kissed me hard, then yanked my arm, leading me back into battle. He always broke my inattentive spells where I became lost in myself. Euterpe stood spinning on her toes, shooting arrows to stave off Zeus's demigod army. Two lines of our side broke to make a tunnel toward Zeus for her, their backs toward the emotional Euterpe. They were fighting off anyone who tried to stop her or break their lines. Behind her, Aios and Asclepius marched in solidarity, their heads bowed low, swords in hand. I rushed to bring up the rear, protecting them, and I saw the horizon.

The rising sun stood frozen, and the rainclouds consumed it as if to tell all a message: The Sun was dead.

Archer shot the last few arrows out of a gaudy, bejeweled quiver at Zeus—Artemis's arrows that Lucien had a hold of last. Being hit by one of her arrows earlier, I knew they were dipped in poison, not a deadly one for us, but an incapacitating one, a poison that worsened if the arrow was left in the wound.

Zeus was now hardly standing, the spike holding him up. Hera, with a couple of arrows in her, was still shielding him.

Leto broke through a line behind Euterpe, wrapping her remaining arm under Euterpe's, who had her bow nocked at the ready. Euterpe's bow-wielding arm was forced upward. Leto held a knife to Euterpe's jugular. She froze, dropping her bow, unable to make a move without being incapacitated.

A sword came flying at me, and I retaliated, disarming a lesser Roman god whose name escaped me. I turned to help Euterpe, but Aios and Asclepius were already freeing her. We should be winning this, but Zeus had more numbers than we had anticipated. Our Roman and Greek lesser gods were still on his side, and some new ones it seemed—demigods of his many conquests, some in the forties, from the look of them, down to teens. Our lines started to fall.

I swept through, attacking whom I could, defending whom I could, in a rhythm of adrenaline only a true warrior found comfort in. *Swing. Duck. Swing. Feint. Stab.*

Something distracted me. The sun was rising, and the rain clouds were swept away. In the night sky, with a sun rising earlier than it should, I saw a silhouette.

THE IMMORTAL TRANSCRIPTS: SHUDDER

Lucien? How? When my eyes adjusted, I saw... Helios, and with him Phoebe, Theia, and Epimetheus. Prometheus was right about his brethren. They came through and escaped in the end.

They fought alongside us. Prometheus gave me a wink as he momentarily slayed a now-returned and soaking wet muse. With Helios came fire. His intensity was much more than Lucien's or Hephaestus, which was part of why Zeus had imprisoned him. The intense heat made me sweat, my ichor not enough to cool me against his power, and I tried to dodge areas that burned my flesh. He was concentrating it on Zeus, but some demigods foolish enough to come near him were burned to cinders by his raw power.

I checked on our prisoner. Zeus and Hera were turning a good pink, like mortal sunburn, and waves of heat rippled in the air.

Chaos kept erupting, making me stumble and become careless. Most of us were. I hoped none of the occurrences were on our side. As soon as we were all on our feet—the Norse not being affected by Olympian deaths—another demigod-turned-immortal was killed. As I knew firsthand, Zeus cared little for his offspring, but it was now clear why Zeus had not attacked for so long: he'd built this army by seeking his spawn and giving them ambrosia.

That's when I saw Prometheus rush toward Zeus and leap into the air with his blade aloft. He swung with all his might. Metal clanged against rock. The sheer force propelled Theus back onto the ground, proving Newton's third law yet again.

Zeus's head teetered before it fell off and hit the ground. My stomach dropped. I had seen gore in war many times, but to see your father decapitated eclipsed any warfare I had ever witnessed—even if he was the sick bastard who murdered your children in front of you and was willing to kill you too.

Prometheus stood; his stoic face and flexed muscles made the action even hotter. He was our hero of the day, breaking me free from Zeus's abuse and tyranny, the control and trauma. Prometheus would wash it away. I loved him, and in this moment, he showed me how much he loved me. To the goddess of war, it was the most romantic gesture possible, even if a bit twisted.

Hephaestus limped up, slower than usual, wounded. We all started to defend him from the dwindling Zeus army—most of them fleeing. A few steadfast—Artemis and her girls, a couple remaining muses, Hera, and some minor gods—were getting mangled and full of arrows for him.

Hephaestus shoved the wounded Hera away. "Really, Mother?" he scoffed. "He disfigured me and tried to kill me, yet you want to protect him over me? What kind of mother are you? They call you the mother goddess? What a laugh." Then he grabbed ahold of Zeus's head. If he burned the head, Zeus would be dead, his soul destroyed.

In a blur of movement, Hera vanished into thin air. Zeus's head was gone.

How had we forgotten? Hermes. He wasn't in this latest skirmish, and he would never abandon his master and father or, more importantly, Zeus's bank account.

We went silent in defeat. The last of Zeus's army fled, the Norse chasing them down. Zeus's impaled body was still pegged to the building, still moving, its arms reaching out as if we could help it somehow. Heph, with Helios, incinerated the body until it was nothing but ash.

Death said the soul was in the brainstem, and I had seen Thanatos remove it from the back of the base of the head many times, but they weren't taking chances. Ares told me tales of the bodies still able to fight and move, like headless zombies until they were incinerated or the ichor cooled, but I had never seen it until now. If the body would have regrown a head, would we have dealt with two Zeuses?

Theories were for another time. Zeus had eluded Death, but none of us knew what that meant. What could he do without a body?

"Right. The show is over. All immortals leave at once. I've got a lot of work to do!" Mnemosyne shouted. "Mortals all over the mainland are on this. Lightning struck forty-four times here tonight, and they think there was a sonic boom. Lots of minds and cameras to erase."

Sirens were heard, and police boats were already headed this way. How would she have the mortals explain away the damage we caused? We'd find out on the news the next day. Poor Lady Liberty; she was bruised but still standing.

CHAPTER 32

Callie

I was alive. The prophetic visions had come true—all of them. I was still here, in the hotel suite, war-weary, on a sofa, with my Archer. I clung to him, and he held onto me tightly, afraid someone would tear us apart forever at any minute. It was too hard to come down off that high, knowing you had escaped death's clutches. It was a feeling I knew would last days, months, maybe even years. I'd look back centuries from now and think nothing in life was as difficult, raw, or harshly terrifying as you and your loved one being in the clutches of death. I had faced Death once and eluded him, but when Archer and I together were on the precipice? Nothing would ever be as horrifying ever again.

Lucien. I tried not to ponder his sacrifice or think of him, but as the sun rose, I couldn't help but miss him. The somber gods who had congregated in our room—some without rooms yet—talked out their experiences and what had unfolded with pride, sadness, awe, horror (you name it). I had a hard time processing it all. War had too many emotions wrapped into it. Ones I never wanted to experience again (Living forever? I'm sure I would).

Chase and Aroha discussed how everything unfolded, filling me in on the events I had missed during our own private battles and when I was unconscious. Apparently, Chase single-handedly incapacitated half of the enemy, a couple of times. Overall, we were the stronger side, but gods did not die easily.

"A muse or two died, I think. Not sure which ones," Aroha said blankly.

"Ma." Archer gave her a stern look, and his gaze darted over to Euterpe, who sat on the couch with a son of Lucien's on either side of her.

Asclepius seemed numb, but Aios was a wreck. They didn't have a room, but they should have peace to grieve alone. I felt so guilty for being alive when I witnessed their anguish.

Chase spoke up next. "Zeus's not dead, you know. We were so close. He'll be back for us, but I think we bought ourselves some good time. If we spend our time forming more alliances...it'll be him against the world."

Archer asked exactly what I was thinking, "How, Dad? He has no body."

"Hera and Hermes took his head. Remember when you asked me about war and growing body parts back?"

Archer cringed.

I wanted to vomit. I was so confused how exactly it would grow back. Like a baby's body that would grow up or some freaky man-sized torso that would sprout limbs?

Chase continued, "He can grow his body back. It'll take time and a ton of ambrosia—I'm guessing. Athena could do some amazing mathematical equation to tell us how long, and maybe our seer gods can guestimate too, but I know from all my experiences of losing pieces of myself in war, we have time."

"We should attack now, then." Aios stood up, his fists clenched and his frame shaking. "While they are down, we should strike."

Chase gave him a sympathetic sigh and shook his head. "We need rest, regrouping, and plans. They will relocate and hide out. Or fortify Fiji to our disadvantage. They lost more people than us, so recruiting is paramount on both sides."

More people than our side? We lost Lucien. That was enough.

"My dad is dead!" Aios's heart-wrenching cry made me shudder from the agonizing pain in his voice.

I wanted to soothe him, tell them all about my vision, but I couldn't. If it didn't happen, and I failed...

"Sit down," Asclepius urged quietly. "Dad's powers will come to you soon, and you truly need to lie down. I've never seen the transfer happen, but heard it's intense."

I looked to Archer for an explanation. "When a prime god dies, his or her powers transfer to the eldest. Aios will gain everything Lucien could do." (Whoa, definitely intense.)

"I'm sorry." Chase touched Aios's shoulder and pressed him back onto the couch again. "War god, thinking of numbers, sides, and viewing sacrifice as the best way to leave this Earth has made me overlook things. 'Come back with your shield or on it' mentality."

"What he's saying is he was insensitive, Aios. We all feel the pain of his loss, but you three most acutely," Aroha translated Chase's sentiments for them.

"Thank you," Euterpe said quietly when no one else had spoken for a moment. "I think I'll see about us getting some rooms."

THE IMMORTAL TRANSCRIPTS: SHUDDER

"No," I said quickly. "Stay here. It's fine. I'm exhausted and want to go to bed." (Because almost dying calls for *days* of rest.)

"I know a hint when I hear it." Chase took Aroha's hand. "We are next door if needed."

They left. The boys started getting the sofa bed in order, and I gave Euterpe all the spare blankets and pillows. Then Archer and I retreated into our en suite.

Guilt wracked me. I should've shared everything, but these visions weren't trustworthy. Or were they, and I couldn't quite decode them properly? Would it be better for them to never know what I hoped I could do? Or for them to know and not have it work out at all?

Archer turned my thoughts away from my worries by kissing me with shaky lips. "We're alive." He marveled over it by running his finger along my lips, his eyes boring into mine with such love and devotion.

Our union was so intense and so potent because he was Love and I was Freedom. We were both so necessary to the mortal and immortal word alike, and linking those two godly powers was prominent: freedom to love whoever you wanted. No one, not even the gods of gods, could stop that.

We slept most the day away ("we" as in everyone). Not a peep was heard in our living room until well past noon. Archer had other ideas rather than joining them, such as celebrating the fact we lived, and my nineteenth birthday, through acts of love, followed by a shared shower. A perfect start for Valentine's Day.

When we finally joined the others, we were informed an early dinner feast would ensue. Most likely, it was some Greek (morbid) postwar custom. At dinner, the table seemed to be a spectrum. From the already merry Norse on one end to the grieving three on the other, with us in the middle, it was a strange mixture of a celebration and a wake. The table exuded impressions of giddiness, confidence, grief, and hope. That last emotion, I held onto.

Then a server wheeled in a cart of glasses of what appeared to be champagne, but it didn't bubble. "Nectar," Archer said quietly, anticipating my question as if he were the mind reader of our relationship. "The pick-me-up we all physically need right now." The poor man waiting on us had no idea what he was serving, I was sure.

I wrinkled my nose.

"No alcohol in it. Just pure liquid healing and sustenance." He laughed at my dislike of alcohol, particularly Heph's stock.

A clinking of a knife on a glass stole our attention to Odin at the end of the table. "To a night well spent," Odin said cryptically since mortals were at tables all around us, and he was one of the gods with a booming voice for all occasions.

"And," Prometheus cut in before everyone could cheers to Odin's tribute to a war won. He lifted Athena's hand to flash a ring on her left hand. "Congratulations are in order."

Athena blushed and blurted out, "Only *he* would bring a ring to war."

We laughed, but Chase cut in. "No, wisdom goddess. Every warrior in love should, to use when he lives to see the next day." He held Aroha's hand aloft, which had a hugely outlandish rock on it, which sparkled so much, you could not stop staring at it (so Aroha).

"We weren't copying." Aroha touched her lower abdomen. "We always do these things in the wrong order." She laughed. "A new baby Olympian is on its way." She gazed at me lovingly as if I had done that for her.

Maybe I was the reason. I was okay with that, more than okay. If I could stop Zeus's control over gods and goddesses' bodies, good. What a horrible and wacko thing for him to do anyway.

Archer clinked his glass, and my stomach dropped. He could not know I might be pregnant too, could he? "Not copying over here—that I know of—" (oh, the guilt) "but today is Callie's nineteenth birthday, so I think she should get in on the celebratory cheers as well."

There were cheers and congratulations all around. Drinks were clinked together and then consumed. The zing of the nectar restored me, taking away my fatigue. It was sweet, much like those tonics Lucien had made me. How it felt so incomplete without him.

"Archer, when is your birthday?" We had never celebrated it or talked about it, despite knowing each other for more than a year.

The Greeks at the table laughed. Aroha blushed.

Archer gave a wry laugh of amusement and embarrassment. "Ask Ma that question." His devilish eyes darted to her. Some inside joke of theirs was afoot.

She huffed, crossing her arms, not amused, and yet all eyes were trained upon her. "Fine. It was during *Hekatobaion* when Archer was conceived. He was born in early April." No one said anything. "I got really lost when they gave us those new Gregorian calendars, okay? So, I said the 8th and another time he asked, I said the 10th."

"It doesn't matter, Ma," Archer offered. "It's not like we celebrate birthdays anymore. Most of us are estimating our age anyway."

I gasped. "Seriously?" They laughed at me, but I didn't mind. They were all happy after so much strife.

Archer's beautiful blues met mine, and I was whole again—almost. There was this niggling itch of something missing: Lucien.

Archer's eyes crinkled in sadness, which made me feel worse. He nodded ever so slightly, then kissed me hard. He felt the same as me about us, the future, and the missing part of our family.

Despite trying to indulge in family members' happiness, I had to speak up. "I can't celebrate. Lucien." The whole table went awkwardly quiet. I had stolen their happiness by saying his name. We could not pretend this was a full victory with him gone.

"Callie is right. This is a day to celebrate, but we should raise a glass to Lucien and the future he has given all of us." Archer smoothed over my outburst quite craftily, giving me time to collect my real thoughts. His hand squeezed mine as if to say he understood, but we'd deal with this later. He believed they deserved their joy right now. Yes, they did, particularly the grieving trio at the end of the table. I was resolved to speak.

"To Lucien," the table cheered and drank.

At the end of the table Euterpe, Aios, and Asclepius were rightfully deeply depressed. I had to do it, and I would do it here and now in public. My husband would lose it because I had wanted to explain this to him before I told the others.

"To Lucien, yes, but not to mourn him. He is gone to us, but not forever if I can help it." They all went quiet, all eyes on me. (Right, maybe this whole public outburst was not the best idea.) I lowered my voice so no mortal could hear me. "I'm getting him back."

Archer goggled at me as if I were a hydra sprouting new heads. He was exasperated, too tired to fight my stubbornness and terrified of my foresight.

"What?" Athena's gaze was intimidating.

Oh, she was furious enough to rip my head off. I knew she would be; most of them would. They risked their lives to protect me, and now I was seeking a dangerous mission that could end badly. But I held onto hope.

Lucien was a part of this family, and it wasn't the same without him. He'd sacrificed himself to keep Archer and me alive. The guilt was overwhelming as well as the regret. I shouldn't have told Lucien the future. I had thought he would reject it and fight fate. Gods were supposed to be selfish beings, not embrace self-sacrifice as he had. I had undervalued the power of all forms of love. He sacrificed himself for friends, family, and unrequited love. It was only fitting that those Lucien had died for would do the same for him.

If there was a way to get him back, I would, and I knew it directly tied to me. I could do it. I had my unabashed hope that had never let me down yet, and a solid vision, but I had more than that: I had *power*.

There was no hesitation in my voice or conviction: "I'm going to the Underworld. I'm bringing Lucien back."

COMING FEBRUARY 2024

THE IMMORTAL TRANSCRIPTS IV

GLIMMER

A MESSAGE FROM THE GODS

Anyone suffering from suicidal thoughts, such as ones portrayed in this novel, please seek help. Talk to someone.

If no one is available,
call the National Suicide Prevention Lifeline at

9-8-8

or

text the Crisis Text Line at

BRAVE (741741).

Never give up hope.

OLYMPIAN FAMILY TREE
(from the journal of Dr. David N. Syches)

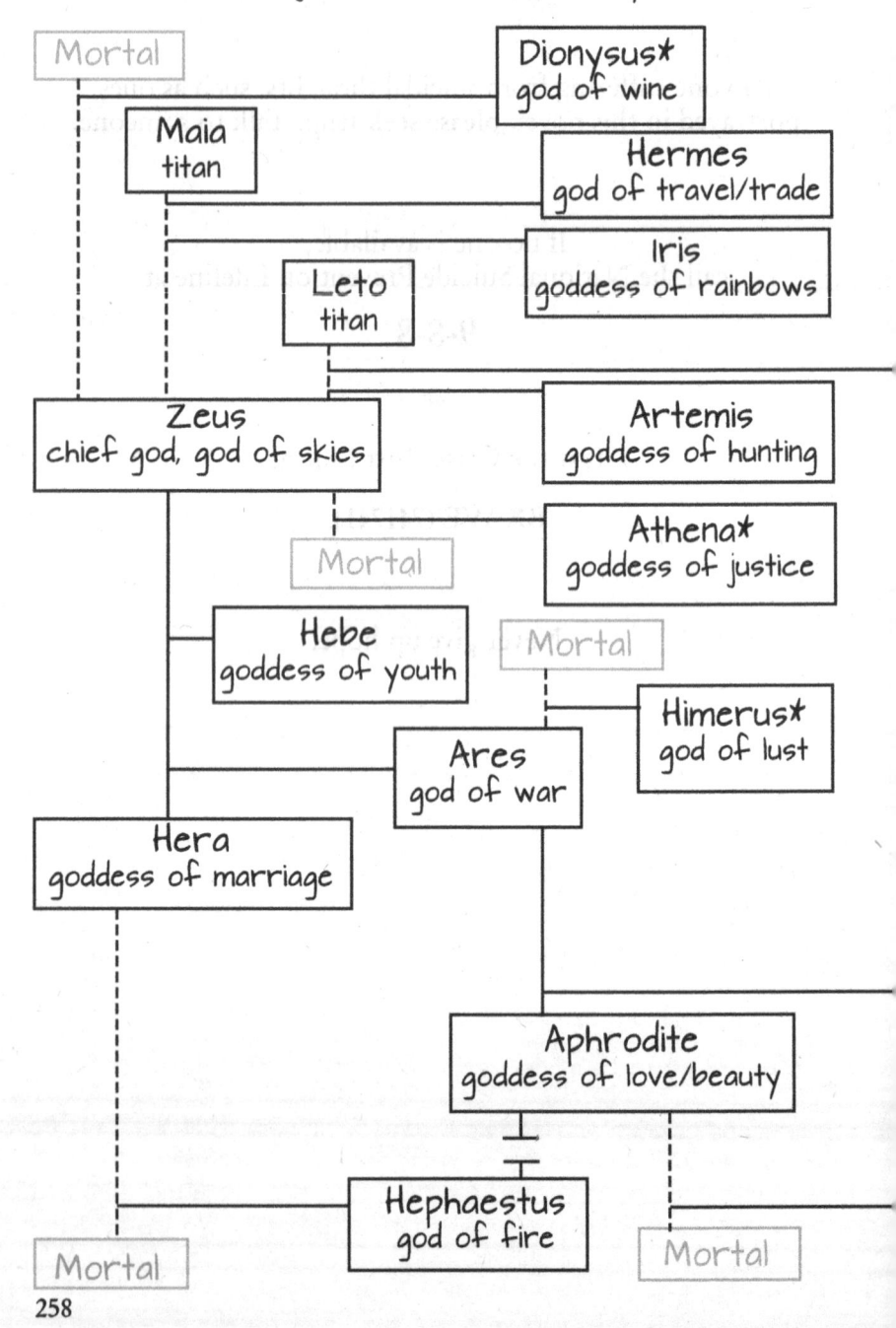

```
Mortal ---- Dionysus*
             god of wine

Maia
titan ------ Hermes
             god of travel/trade

             Iris
             goddess of rainbows

Leto
titan

Zeus ------- Artemis
chief god, god of skies    goddess of hunting

Mortal ---- Athena*
            goddess of justice

Hebe
goddess of youth    Mortal

                    Himerus*
                    god of lust

Ares
god of war

Hera
goddess of marriage

Aphrodite
goddess of love/beauty

Hephaestus
god of fire

Mortal                      Mortal
```

258

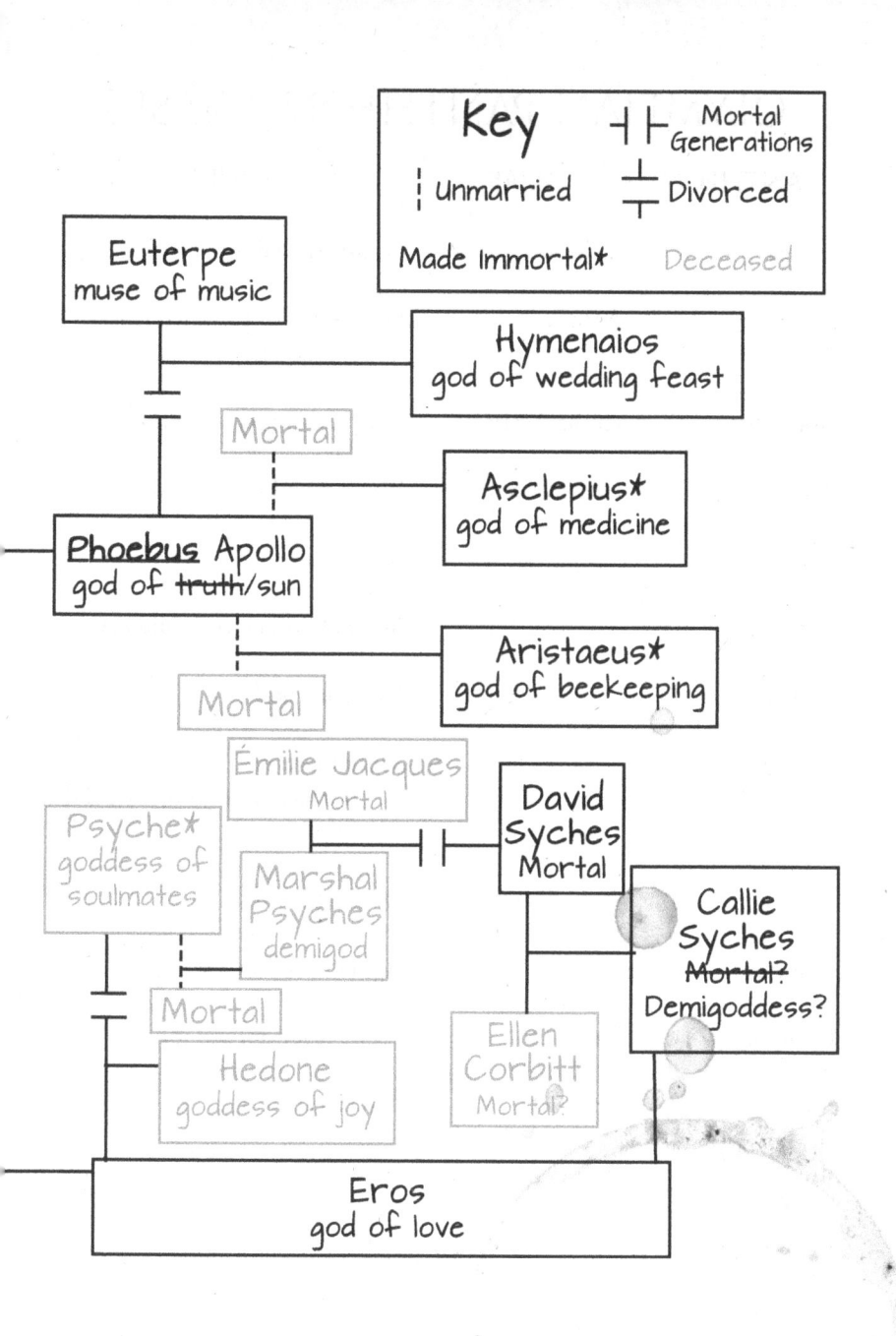

Key
- ┤├ Mortal Generations
- ┊ Unmarried
- ┬/┴ Divorced
- Made Immortal ★
- Deceased

Euterpe — muse of music
┬ **Hymenaios** — god of wedding feast

Mortal ┊ **Asclepius★** — god of medicine

Phoebus Apollo — god of ~~truth~~/sun

Mortal ┊ **Aristaeus★** — god of beekeeping

Émilie Jacques — Mortal
David Syches — Mortal

Psyche★ — goddess of soulmates

Marshal Psyches — demigod

Callie Syches — ~~Mortal?~~ Demigoddess?

Mortal ┊ **Hedone** — goddess of joy

Ellen Corbitt — Mortal?

Eros — god of love

Anteros★ — god of counterlove

OLYMPIAN PANTHEON ALIASES

PANTHEON	ALIAS	POWERS
Aglaea	Belle	Beauty, splendor
Anteros	Antony	Unrequited or thwarted love, "magnetism"
Aphrodite	Aroha Ambrose	Love and beauty, swimming
Ares	Chase Gideon	War, strength, and speed
Aristaeus		Beekeeping
Artemis		Moon, hunting, and childbirth
Asclepius		Medicine, healing
Athena		Wisdom, justice, warfare, courage, inventions, arts, and crafts
Atlas		Holding the sky
Demeter		Agriculture, harvest
Dionysus	Uncle D	Wine, madness, and theater
Epimetheus		Afterthought
Eros	Archer Ambrose	Love, "flying"
Euphrosyne	Ada	Mirth, bliss
Euterpe		Music, lyric poetry
Hades		Underworld, scotopia, and invisibility

PANTHEON	ALIAS	POWERS
Hebe		Youth
Hedone		Joy, pleasure, and "flying"
Hephaestus	Heph(ie)	Fire, forging
Hera		Marriage, family, pregnancy
Hermes		Messenger, teleporting, theft
Himerus	Russ	Lust, strength, and speed
Hymenaios	Aios	Marriage ceremony, soul fusing
Hypnos		Sleep
Iris		Rainbow, teleporting
Janus		Duality, passages
Leto		Motherhood
Mnemosyne		Memory
Moirae	The Fates	Birth, destiny, and death
Muses		9 sisters of the arts
Persephone		Spring, plant life, and death
Phoebus Apollo	Lucien Veras	Sun, light, truth, prophecy, music, poetry, medicine, and healing
Poseidon		Sea, earthquakes

PANTHEON	ALIAS	POWERS
Prometheus		Foresight, prophecies
Proteus		Shapeshifting, foresight
Psyche		Soulmates, mindreading, and "flying"
Thalia	Thalia	Delight, charisma
Thanatos		Death, soul bearer
Themis		Justice, law, prophecy
Zelus		Zeal, ice, and "flying"
Zeus		God of gods, lightning, thunder, sky, and omniscience

ACKNOWLEDGMENTS

I'd like to thank everyone who contributed to this book to make it possible. In order of the book's creation, thanks Mom. You're the best alpha reader and typo finder who took on typing up the (awfully) handwritten version of the book to save me time. Thanks to the Lewis family for the lockdown video chats that kept us going with the socialization we needed in a pandemic world. Next, much appreciation to the National Park Service of the US government for posting virtual tours to make my battle at Liberty Island accurate and realistic. Thanks to the Carolina Forest Author's Club for critiquing the book and our online meetings; both were instrumental in revising this manuscript. I want to particularly thank author Ann Jefferies, who gave me great, quick edits of the final draft.

Thanks to author Caleb Wygal for his marketing assistance. Of course, huge thanks to Authors 4 Authors Publishing for taking on this novel and working hard to get it completed in time—Becky and Brandi on edits, Renee with the marketing and publicity.

The most appreciation goes to my husband who, during the writing of this book and beyond, has done more than his fair share of everything in a household to allow me to juggle two careers—while making me laugh every day despite life's hardships. To my son, the warrior child, who is the strongest human I ever met since the day he fought to survive and thrive: If you can overcome what you must, I can do anything.

Last, to my dedicated readers everywhere. Thank you for following my characters' journey. I'm particularly thankful for my recent influx of local readers and support. Meeting and talking to you in person has been by far one of the greatest experiences of my life. If you got this far in this series, I'd like to assure you that the next book is coming your way in 2024. Be ready for *Glimmer*, the final installment of The Immortal Transcripts.

Love and hope to all.

ABOUT THE AUTHOR

LISA BORNE GRAVES

Lisa Borne Graves is a YA author, English Lecturer, wife, and supermom of one wild child. Originally from the Philadelphia area, she relocated to the Deep South and found her true place of inspiration. Her love for all literature led her to branch out from the academic arena to spin her own tales. Lisa has a voracious appetite for books, British television, and pizza. Her inability to sit still makes her enjoy life to its fullest, and she can be found at the beach, pool, or on some crazy adventure.

Follow her online:

lisabornegraves.com
Twitter: @lisabornegraves
Facebook: @lisabornegravesauthor
Instagram: @lisabornegraves

Also by Lisa Borne Graves
CELESTIAL SPHERES
FYR

At seventeen, Toury arrives in Fyr, where magic is power, a prince's love is deadly, and female autonomy is a dream. Formerly a loner and burden to her adoptive parents, she ruins her chances of a fresh start by offending an ogler who just happens to be the prince.

Alex, the Prince of Fyr, is no novice when it comes to pressure. He has to face his father's ailing health, the expectation to marry soon, and the hidden necromancers trying to take over the realm by exploiting his dark curse. At least there's hope in a cheeky savior, but Earth girls aren't so easy.

Toury and Alex learn that the strongest magic cannot be conjured but must be earned. They must risk their lives, hearts, and futures to save the land from a darkness of apocalyptic proportions. But can they trust each other enough to save Fyr? Or will everything they hold dear turn to ash?

books2read.com/fyr

Authors 4 Authors Publishing Cooperative

A publishing company for authors, run by authors, blending the best of traditional and independent publishing

We specialize in speculative fiction: science fiction, fantasy, paranormal, and romance. Get lost in another world!

Check out our collection at https://books2read.com/rl/a4a or visit Authors4AuthorsPublishing.com/books

For updates, scan the QR code or visit our website to join our semi-monthly newsletter!

Want more romantic fantasy? We recommend:

Kiss of Treason
by Brandi Spencer

Two forbidden lovers share the rare gift to heal others with a kiss—but at a cost. Odelia's life has been a lie. When the queen tries to remove her from the palace, Odelia uncovers the truth. Now she must decide whether to forsake her people or embrace a destiny that would pit her against the current heir to the throne...her best friend. Though her only hope of avoiding a civil war lies in winning his heart, revealing her secrets too soon could cost both their lives. And a kiss might not be strong enough to save them...

books2read.com/kisstreason

CPSIA information can be obtained
at www.ICGtesting.com
Printed in the USA
BVHW040833300123
657433BV00020B/741